I0680463

THE EDEN RETRIEVAL

Other Novels by Matt Howarth:

*Red Sky Radio**

Progression
Enriched Visions
Itself
Toofer
Separation Anxiety
Tuners
Beyond Meat Time
Hungry Thunder
Stalk Exchange
Dreamtime Awry
The Blue Light
Imaginary Numbers
Haunted

For more information on books and comics by Matt Howarth, visit www.matthowarth.com

*published by The Merry Blacksmith Press

THE EDEN RETRIEVAL

by MATT HOWARTH

The Merry Blacksmith Press

2011

The Eden Retrieval

story and art © 2011 by Matt Howarth

All rights reserved.

Previous digital edition published in 2008 by Howteck Industries

Matt would like to thank Tom Pomplun and Michael Ryan for their editorial assistance in preparing the original manuscript.

For information, address:

The Merry Blacksmith Press
70 Lenox Ave.
West Warwick, RI 02893

merryblacksmith.com

Published in the USA by The Merry Blacksmith Press

ISBN— 978-0-61557-063-1
0-61557-063-1

Praylude:
Excerpts from the Diary of a Crank

I have wasted my life fighting the forces of evil. The battle still rages on, but the outcome is clearly unavoidable. Mankind has lost.

No one would listen. They refused to heed my warnings, and look what happened!

Abominations swarmed from the seas, slaughtering coastal populations in a ritualistic frenzy. Entire cities were offered as sacrifices to unspeakable demons. Unholy priests rallied witless victims to embrace their disastrous fate.

I begged the Authorities to retaliate, but their ranks have been contaminated by blasphemous influences. They refused to take action, and look what happened!

Horrible dreams drove millions of people to throw themselves on mankind's growing pyre. The population is dwindling away like loose sand falling through a torn fishing net.

Alas, even I am not exempt from these nightmares. Arcane knowledge maintains my sanity under the constant somnambulant barrage of vilification, but that wisdom is sorely taxed by those aberrant forces. I grow weaker every day, physically (hiding in this abandoned basement parking garage with my talismans and my automatic rifle) and mentally (retreating to my cerebral core in order to survive the psychotropic nightmares). My energies bleed away like that same loose sand.

I do not know how long I can resist the Old One's nocturnal call. It has saturated the entire globe. I would not be surprised if that psychic taint radiates beyond this world, traveling like a psionic wave through the vacuum of outer space, crossing interstellar distances and drenching other solar systems with this odious psychological poison.

His acolytes have risen from their deep lair for more than wanton slaughter. Of this, I am fearfully certain.

I pray for a miracle, for only a miracle can save mankind now.

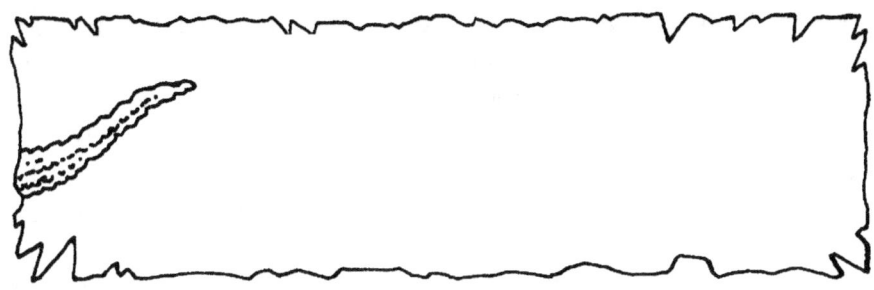

section 1:
Fractal Alignment

If ground or soil existed on Jhul, Pik never saw any trace of such things. But then, Pik wasn't hunting for dirt; she was after prey.

Pik surveyed the forest with a silent scowl. The locals called them "trees", but "pillars" was a far more accurate terminology. Some of these *trees* were over a kilometer in diameter! The trunk to which she clung was a curved landscape unto itself, corrugated like a lizard's hide and pastel blue. This vertical surface was scarcely as barren as Pik had expected. Sensual ripples and shallow fissures covered the blue bark, bearing scars of growth and wear. Countless alien seasons had weathered this *tree* as it reached ever skyward. At her back stretched the rest of the "forest", an endless curtain of mighty stalks. Some rose in clusters, others stood in isolation like enormous monoliths. The utter absence of any branches adorning these stalks endowed the tableau with a surreal quality (but then, the *really* alien worlds had that effect on her). Milky hints of pinkish vapors drifted among this monstrous forest, giving the environment a deceptively moist demeanor. Deceptive, for Jhul's ecology of stalks was intensely dry, almost stonelike, definitely calcified, and unmistakably ancient.

Pik was hardly the only creature scaling this particular stalk. In the distance to her right, she could see several wiry crustaceans scuttling with lazy urgency along the vertical incline. A few meters beneath her and off to the left, she had wisely skirted a patch of crusty fungus, which may have appeared innocuous, but she knew from Janek's advice that this adhesive fungus was capable of vicious attacks if provoked. Crawling along distant stalks, she viewed the enormous quivering sacs used by the locals to bus the citizenry along this up-and-down landscape. While each stalk supported an assortment of thriving nodular communities, there was little interaction between the individual trees. Each monolith was a tiny nation onto itself.

The girl's grip on this foreign escarpment was tenuous, for the bark's radical texture provided insufficient purchase to support the bulky weight of her pressure suit. Fundamentally, Pik's handholds were for psychological reinforcement, for her suit's AG unit kept her safely aloft. Had she so desired, she could have soared free during this ascent. By clinging to the bark of the mammoth stalk like a metallic insect, she hoped to conceal her climb.

The suit was cumbersome by design. It protected her buff human physiology from environments far more threatening than Jhul's arid, lithium-rich atmosphere. The suit harbored an exotic array of defensive technology, not to mention sensory equipment that was radically more acute than anything found in any commercial brand of pressure suit. These add-ons were custom hardware, designed and attached by Pik. Her handiwork was concerned with function, resulting in a rather chaotic, patchwork appearance to her suit. (Etty called it a "hardware nightmare", but never to her face.) She might have looked overburdened and maneuverably-impaired—but tangling with Pik while the girl was suited-up was a foolhardy recourse. She even had military training to back up all this superior hardware.

Peering above, she spotted a cluster of large purple nodes: a sign of local civilization. Permanently attached to the trunk like some auxiliary growth, these bulbous nodes had once been the "tree's" seed pods. After releasing their reproductive content, these pods had been converted by the locals into their version of a comfortable metropolis. She accessed a map of the local topography inside her eye. When she dead-centered the settlement, the name "Hnm21" scrolled beneath the display that was internally superimposed on her vision. The stalk was known as Hnm, and this was its 21st city.

According to the current database, the prey was hiding in Hnm21.

Pik tongued a soft message to Etty, alerting him that she had located the objective community. Once she received her partner's acknowledgment signal, she recommencing climbing the stalk.

Etty joined her as Pik neared the nest of urban lumps clinging to the side of the stalk. He swung in on expensive thrusters to clutch the blue wall beside her. He winked a greeting, which she returned with a smile.

"Smart work," Etty told her.

Although his appearance was generally swallowed by the bulk of his pressure suit, Pik was intimately familiar with Etty's physique. He was a lithe man, just under two meters tall. Despite the many years he had spent in space, he remained pale-skinned. Wiry and agile, every nuance of his nimble body was known to the girl. *I'm especially fond of his tight behind,* she reminded herself, watching him climb above her, *and his hands with their long, talented fingers.* His face was similarly narrow and taut, with prominent cheekbones and a strictly delineated jawline. Feathery dark hair masked the crown of his head like a playful cap. His eyes were small and intense. He was a gentle man, soft-spoken and empathic…the perfect opposite to Pik's quick-tempered, impulsive self.

Thoughts of Etty's versatile fingers made Pik ache for this job to be completed.

According to our target profile, she ruminated, *this prey isn't classified as a violent criminal.* Elte Hortmoore was supposed to be a monk or something. Hopefully, he would offer meager resistance. *If we're lucky, this'll be an easy grab-and-go.*

Their approach of the Hnm21 nodes was uneventful and swift. At the entry sphincter, they presented their credentials and were admitted to the city. In consideration of the fragile and flammable nature of the settlement, the hunters were forced to allow the local Authorities to implement restriction codes on their weaponry's software, rendering their armament inoperable. Pik was not happy with this, but Etty sympathized with the Jhulians' fears. He reminded her that a palm-laser could easily set the entire place ablaze.

For the "city" was organic in construction (technically vegetative), and retained an unnervingly soft texture throughout its winding avenues. The passages were pliant and tender, the dormant plant matter marbled with a substrata of pulsating capillaries functioning as utility networks. Residences, commercial outlets, even public courtyards—all had been carved from the spent seed pod's pulpy interior. The entire affair had been converted for habitation by Jhul's native species. The Jhulians were a race of sentient worms, making their streets and lodgings rather tubular in design, and somewhat crowded to humans (not to mention humans wearing bulky pressure suits). Pik and Etty were forced to go-the-long-way to accommodate their size, taking passages intended for freight deliveries. This brought them into contact with few inhabitants, allowing them to travel through Hnm21 relatively unnoticed.

They had no desire to generate any controversy that might alert the prey before they could track him down. There was no way of knowing how frequently this community saw outsiders, although Pik suspected it was not that often. Again, this would aid the hunters in finding Elte, whose offworld physiology would mark him as a curiosity in the predominantly Jhulian population. In fact, they were lucky on their first inquiry.

Etty flashed a holo-pic, and a freight-guidance worker strobed an indifferent affirmative. After a token bribe, the worker worm revealed that an alien of that description was known to frequent a particular intoxicant parlor. Another bribe earned Etty directions to this specific parlor.

And they were off, hot on the trail of their prey.

The narrow corridors of Hnm21 were a welcome relief after Pik's exposure to the open vistas that separated the monumental trees of Jhul's global forest. These cramped worm-made tunnels were a claustrophobic cure-all for the disconcerting mood brought on by the spacious outside. For some unqualifiable reason, all that open space had reminded the girl of the murky depths of her recent dreams. Jhul's foreign vista was nothing like the aquatic environs of those dreamscapes, but both tableaus shared a brooding quietude that drew connections between them where no logical kinship existed. It wasn't the bizarre nature of the scenes that disturbed her, for Pik had visited planets far stranger in her life. Her uneasiness was impossible to pin down, as elusive in her mind as the impractical concept of fear. Although no identifiable threats populated her dreams, she was vividly aware of some intangible menace lurking just beyond her peripheral senses in these underwater dreamscapes. Upon waking, her only distinct recollection was an overwhelming loneliness. Normally, such an oppressive sense of solitude was uncharacteristic for Pik. She was quite content with Etty's intimate company; the man fulfilled all of her needs. As far as Pik was concerned, her somnambulant anxiety had no bearing on her waking life. She could not imagine why Jhul's widespread forest had sparked any association in her mind with those dreams. Did she secretly fear losing Etty?

She sighed, discarding these insubstantial worries, and returned her attention to the task at hand.

The purchased directions proved quite adequate, bringing the hunters directly to the parlor. They entered carefully, not out of any fear of ambush, but to maintain as low a profile as they could. In a tavern full of worms, the two humans stood out as blatantly as Elte did at the bar.

The intoxicant parlor consisted of a flattened egg-shaped chamber. Its circumference was lined by a bar of rather traditional design, although here the counter was located lower to the ground. A shabby no-G entertainment stage occupied the center of the room; a collection of shallow basins (worm seats) surrounded it. An undulant dance was going on in the no-G cube, in which brightly colored worms writhed in complex aerial patterns. The audience seemed entranced—or maybe they were just bored. (*It's hard to tell with worms,* mused Pik.) The bar was definitely seeing more action, and among the eager throng of thirsty worms, a man-sized crimson bear was bent in pursuit of inebriation.

"Elte," Pik hissed inside her suit.

Just as instantly as Pik made Elte, though, the bear spotted his hunters.

Elte came to his full height, and glared at the humans as they stood at the cramped doorway of the parlor's entrance. He was just over two meters tall and covered with a bristling scarlet fur. His hands were more articulate than the rest of his bear-like demeanor, possessing four tentacle-fingers. The prey's head seemed small atop this huge body. Tiny eyes were surrounded by a bandit mask of dark fur, and his snout was pugnacious. He wore a rumpled brown robe that draped almost to his bent knees.

He looked dangerous, but Pik knew this fugitive was no professional criminal. He lacked the instincts of the street, and he certainly possessed no acumen for life-on-the-run. According to his datapack, he was a lowly monk of a religious order so obscure its charter was found on only one world. Elte was an embezzler, he had stolen funds from his own religious order. Criminals like Elte were sloppy and amateurish, but they were also the ones who could freak-out without warning. Real villains accepted the risk that came with their crimes. Accidental criminals, though, seemed incapable of facing their inevitable punishment.

He's going to bolt, she decided.

The bear's cup-like ears betrayed him to Pik's instincts: they twitched a fraction of a second before he bolted.

Pik leapt to block the parlor's other exit. Her bulky armor was more than adequate to the task.

Having failed to escape, Elte's dark-rimmed eyes bulged with terror, and his runny nose convulsed. His abrupt flight had dislodged his air tube, he hastily replaced it in his gasping nostrils. As Pik and Etty advanced on him, the monk grabbed an armload of Jhulian hostages and squealed threats to stem the hunter's approach.

"Aren't the nightmares enough punishment?" he cried. "They didn't need to send you!"

Etty paused, growling with frustration, but Pik continued without hesitation.

Screaming another warning, Elte swung open his coarse robe to reveal the explosives strapped to his furred chest.

Pik halted in midstep.

Grup, she swore, *the runner's wired a bomb to himself!* This was a total contradiction to the prey's profile. Elte was a religious cleric on the run because of some vague swindle. He was classed nonviolent—in fact, he was supposed to be of meek disposition! *What the grup is this monk doing with a bod-bomb?*

"C'mon," Etty chided the prey. "What's with the dramatics, Elte? You're just running from a fraud charge…"

"Sez you!" screamed the prey. He still held a number of squirming captives in his burly arm, their strobing panic lit up the desperate bear's contorted face. "I know what's waiting for me back there!"

Justice, Pik snarled to herself. *And punishment.* Privately, Pik had only contempt for this fugitive. In her opinion, Elte was especially guilty, not just of violating Galactic Law, but of debasing theological standards by using "religion" to mask his gluttonous greed. Normally, prey was prey; Pik maintained a totally objective viewpoint toward the individuals she tracked and captured for profit. The nature of their crimes was immaterial to her, as was their actual guilt or innocence. She was simply a freelance officer of the Galactic Courts. Pursue and retrieve. Emotional involvement was not just unprofessional, it was immature. This time, though, the nature of Elte's crime really irritated her personal ethics. Pik knew she would feel an inner satisfaction to see this fugitive captured and punished for his crime.

She remained quiet, though. Pik might have been the brawn of the retrieval team, but she was smart enough to know when to hand off a situation. Etty was the one with the verbal and psychological skills. He would subdue Elte, and then Pik would get the chance to safely snare the prey.

"This is not the way to prove your innocence," Etty informed the prey.

"I'm not innocent, you uglies!" the prey declared vehemently. "That's why I'm not going back!"

"*Is there a problem?*" came a soft voice in Pik's ear.

"You could say that, Janek." Her response was subvocalized, but the comlink carried it to her other partner, who was back onboard the ">%" in geocentric orbit beyond Jhul's atmosphere. "The runner's got a bod-bomb."

"*Scale?*"

"Impossible to tell," she admitted. "It could be low-blow, or it could be mega megatons."

"*Specific location?*"

Pik nodded, catching Janek's plan. She took a quick scan and fed him the precise coordinates. If Janek could pinpoint Elte, he might be able to drop a stun field on him from orbit. That would stop the prey from blowing up himself and everybody else.

"He's got hostages," she informed her distant teammate. "While Etty and I are about three meters in front of him."

"Okay, you don't have to go back," Etty told the prey in a soothing voice, playing for time. Pik knew he had listened-in to her sidereal transmission.

"Don't play me!" the prey screamed. This time, his emotional cry spurred him to fling open his bear-like arms, releasing his frantic captives. As the worms slithered away from the lunatic, Elte edged his way along the fleshy wall of the parlor.

"He's on-the-move," Pik quietly warned Janek. "A few meters to my immediate left."

"You can't fool me!" the prey shouted. Turning abruptly, he used his previously unsheathed talons to tear a hole in the botanical wall, releasing a flow of multicolored fluids. When he leapt into the cut, though, he jammed there, unable to get his wide belly through the incision. He kicked his stubby legs in frustration, wailing curses and recriminations. He blamed his God. He blamed a rival cleric. He blamed a corrupt Galactic Court. He blamed the innocent Jhulians. And, most zealously, he blamed the pair of retrievers. Screaming that he could no longer tolerate the dreadful dreams that plagued his sleepless nights, Elte Hortmoore blew himself to pieces.

A section of the organic wall vaporized in the blast. Pik and Etty were protected from the explosion by their suits. Their metallic bulk helped to shield the Jhulians who cowered in the intoxicant parlor's mushy corners. No one had been hurt by the blast—only Elte had suffered from his petulant detonation of the bod-bomb.

"Gruppit," Etty swore aloud. "There goes our retrieval commission."

Once the local Authorities arrived, the hunters displayed their credentials and explained the cause of the disturbance. The first thing the worm Enforcers did was check the integrity of the restriction codes imposed on the humans' weapons; the officers seemed annoyed to find that armament secure and unfired. With the real culprit beyond their reach, the Jhulian Law Enforcers longed to implicate a pair of offworld retrievers in the property damage, but evidence supplied by the lunatic's former-hostages exonerated Pik and Etty from any culpability. It didn't hurt either that the full brunt of the explosion had been contained by a forcefield which Janek had thrown around the suicidal monk.

After accompanying the Enforcers to their cramped station, where sensory scans of the incident were copied for the local Authorities, the hunters were free to leave. Which they did without pause. There was no reason to stay now. The prey was gone. Elte had escaped capture; he would never be punished for his sacrilegious offense now. And the retrieval team had nothing to show for their efforts.

Elte's bounty hadn't been fantastic, but it would have covered the sweat and fuel spent (so far) tracking the cleric. Now—there was nothing.

Moving away from any stalks, the pair of dejected hunters ascended on AG currents to rendezvous with the orbiting ">%".

From a distance, the ship looked quite stumpy and antique. A simple squat cylinder connected two mismatched but moderate spheres. In the visible spectrum, the ">%" was a dull brown. Under basic scrutiny, the ship presented a derelict facade, for most of its equipment was deftly concealed by stealth fields. Only a high-level scan would produce evidence of the mighty drive engine or the series of illegal plasma cannons worn by the ">%". It wasn't until one got closer that the hull revealed its unconventional nature, displaying a random arrangement of detection spines and low armament panels (Pik's handiwork), all carefully painted to blend with the chocolate bulkhead.

Retrieval teams needed fast transport that could bluster their way in and out of danger. Most teams were forced to buy the necessary hardware to competently outfit their ships. Most teams didn't have techs as creative as Pik.

More than once, the ">%'s" shabby guise had deceived adversaries in possession of superior firepower. The ship was home and fortress for the team, and it was a mobile office.

On the safe side of the airlock, Janek met them with a disapproving grunt.

"What?" Pik barked in retort.

"We needed a win this time," Janek accused mildly.

"The runner blew himself up," she snarled.

"Such behavior is contrary to his profile." Janek produced a disk from one of the slots in his wide gray head, waggling it at his inadequate partners.

"And how is that *our* fault?" snorted Pik. She had snapped open her pressure suit and was squirming from its bulky confines. To the side, Etty was doing the same. Etty's suit opened at the shoulders, while the girl's suit's chest swung out to release her.

Janek shook his wedge-like head, lowering his appendages in concurrence. Even with his form bent under the weight of his huge cranium, the Duuian stood slightly taller than either human. His skin was gray and elephantine, the wrinkles mottled with the curling lines of dark tattoos. Three triangular protuberances served as his legs. A meager slab of a torso sported six appendages from the circumference of his waist. These arms were multijointed and twitchy with spasms. His "hands" were claws whose pinchers could change their shape and delicacy via a series of sliding bone sheaths. His shoulder was the stockiest portion of his torso, bundled with mighty muscles to support his enormous head. A blunt wedge of a skull gave way in the rear to a bulbous cranium that was peppered with artificial input slots. Protruding from the front of his cortex, six tentacles were in relentless undulation—these were his eyes and ears. Janek's mouth was a small blowhole located at the anterior edge of his wedge-like head. The periphery of this "nostril" had undergone surgery to enable the alien to articulate human words. He wore a series of plastiform straps as clothing. This harness covered little (there was no modesty about his scanty attire, though, for Janek's reproductive organs were entirely internal, blessing his kind with no concept of shame concerning nudity), but the straps afforded him numerous pockets and places to attach his gadgets. Janek's sense of body-decoration was fulfilled by the extensive tattoos that covered his torso and head. These markings followed mysterious curves as they traced elaborate patterns (which Etty had always suspected were actually Duuian paragraphs) across his wrinkled gray skin. He was constantly adding to the network of injected-dye lines, as if driven by some compulsion to celebrate his daily achievements on his flesh.

All oxygen-breathers, the three of them had been partners for many years: two human lovers and a Duuian data-junkie.

"There was nothing we could do, Janek," remarked Etty in his even, eternally unperturbed voice. "The runner was more unbalanced that the profile indicated. He was babbling about conspiracies that were torturing him with nightmares. His spirit was broken by his own guilty conscience."

"This is bad for us," Janek complained.

"Yeah. For *all* of us," hissed an unhappy Pik.

The crew of the ">%" was not exactly the most profitable freelance retrieval team operating in galactic space. Pik knew this all too well. Infrequently they managed to snare a few fugitives, but rarely enough to show a substantial profit. Their lives were spent pursuing one golden bounty after another, always striving for elusive success. Pik knew as well as her partners that this latest failure left the ">%" in a bad financial position. But then, it wouldn't be the first penniless tomorrow they'd faced and survived.

As he stowed his gear alongside Janek's rarely-used suit, Etty reminded them that the ">%" had adequate fuel at the moment, and the ship's pantries were stocked with necessary supplies. Destitution was not imminent, although it lingered on the team's future horizon. "We could still find a big score."

Janek waggled his wide head in a vague Duuian equivalent of resignation. His blowhole expelled a weak and pessimistic sound. Pivoting on the points of one of his stumpy legs, he left the humans, retreating to another region of the ship. Known for their unaggressive nature, Duuians rarely won many arguments.

Etty seemed pleased that he had calmed everyone's worries.

Pik nodded, but her enthusiasm was clearly undermined by their recent failure.

Fortunately, she knew certain pursuits that would distract her from this blossoming tide of despair. She pounced, initiating her therapy session right there in the airlock.

Time passed pleasantly as the ">%" moved out of orbit, leaving Jhul behind. The ship slipped through the tenuous void, swiftly putting distance between itself and the planetary system. Once it was far beyond the collection of gravity wells, the ship would coast through the interstellar medium until the team decided on their next destination.

Haste was not a pressing concern for the retrievers as they waited for their wounded confidence to heal. Pik and Etty had each other, while Janek had his own vices to keep himself amused. Eventually, their determination would return. Then they would consult the nearest Booking Station for a current list of fugitives, and choose a new prey to track.

Some of Pik's emotional convalescence involved solitude and introspection. Bouncing back with his innate optimism, Etty never understood her need for private time.

Located right next-door to the ship's command deck was the gym. Etty stayed fit without exercise, so he rarely used these facilities, while Janek practiced his own calisthenics in secret. So the gym gradually became Pik's private sanctuary. Here, she could retreat from the universe-at-large and reorganize her state of mind while toning her physical state. Besides the daily pressures and her basic impatience, Pik had older demons as yet unconquered; keeping those traumas in check often required hours of pumping iron.

Consequently, she was the last to learn of the distress signal the ">%" had detected. Etty interrupted her physical meditation to babble that they had found the golden score. He dragged her from the gym to hear this vital transmission.

It was just a distress call, as far as she could tell. She frowned, reprimanding her partners, "Altruism is something we *really* cannot afford right now, guys. A rescue mission would bankrupt us."

"Altruism? Bah—look closely at the signal's Ident code," Janek waved a bony claw at the readout screen above his head.

Pik squinted and was startled to realize that she recognized the code from her days in the Nimbus Space Navy. It was the Royal Code. The individual in distress was a member of the Royal Nimbus Family. "Whose cruiser is it?"

"Princess Eden," came Etty's breathless gasp.

For a second, she eyed him with uncertainty, puzzled by the emphatic nature of his response. Then she recalled that Etty had a private (or so he thought) fixation on the celebrity daughter of the Galactic Ruling Family.

"The Royal Family's popular darling. They'll pay big for this retrieval," Janek cackled. His sensory tendrils were turgid with glee.

"Look where it's coming from," muttered Pik. "What is Nimbus Royalty doing way out there on the Rim?"

"Play it again," an enthusiastic Etty directed. "Did they say what the problem was? Were they under attack?"

"This is the Opal Cruiser in distress. We have crash-landed on (burst of coordinate data) and require immediate rescue," the message recited.

"No hostiles," Janek pointed out. "Just a basic grab-and-go...only this time the prey is desperate to be grabbed!"

"Those coordinates are only a sector away from our present position," Etty was quick to note. "We could be there in a few days!"

Pik had to agree: it sounded too perfect, too easy, and too lucrative to ignore.

The golden bounty had offered itself to the needy crew of the ">%", and they were going for it.

✛

When the summons came, Tarn was the next name on the barracks' duty list, and so he became the Warrior who was assigned the task of recovering the lost Royal Daughter. At first, he failed to comprehend the scope of his orders. Only later, during subspace travel briefing, did Tarn learn the identity of the person he was being sent to rescue. He was stunned mute by the briefing.

The Princess! Princess Eden herself!

Tarn pursed his lips and entertained a private thought: *The ditzy Brat needs rescuing once again. Her traveling interplanetary party has gotten itself stranded on some backwater world. What was this—the third time in under a year?*

Glancing over the specs of the assignment, Tarn noticed that the Princess had crashed on a world called Earth. *Def,* he thought, *what an uninspired name for a planet.* According to the specs, no one had been there in centuries. Who knew what the place was like now...

Did it matter?

This was his assignment. His responsibility. No matter how trivial he personally imagined the Princess' plight to be, he must treat the duty with professional accord. Warriors served the Royal Family, in protection of the interstellar populace...of which members of the Royal Family were certainly a part. Despite his opinion toward the reckless Princess, Tarn was sworn to obey, serve, and protect.

In a way, this assignment could be Tarn's ticket to a glorious promotion. Rescuing the favorite Royal Daughter was a high-profile accomplishment, one that was bound to include Royal gratitude and rewards. Should he successfully rescue the Princess...

And what could stop him?

Tarn was a living weapon, trained in the most modern battle techniques. His body was a densely muscled piece of organic perfection. Implanted enhancements heightened his natural abilities and lethal aptitude. Even stripped naked, Tarn could successfully assault a fortified fortress. Royal Navy Warriors were trained to be the deadliest fighting machines in the galaxy.

What could this "Dirt" world—no wait, it was called "Earth"— abandoned and forgotten for centuries, what could it possibly possess to challenge a Royal Warrior?

He laughed coarsely in the cramped confines of his needle flier as it tore through space, sidestepping physical boundaries in pursuit of FTL velocities.

This was going to be sooo effortless.

The ">%" approached old Earth at a speed decelerating from C+. Systems were all on automatic, allowing the team to gather around the monitors to sate their curiosity.

The planet ahead only vaguely matched what was stored in the database on this ancient world. A denser cloudcover shrouded the planet now; probes were unable to pierce these electromagnetically charged vapors. A series of impossibly huge spikes reared from the equatorial planetary surface, literally protruding thousands of kilometers beyond the stratosphere. (This were extraordinary on *any* world!) One of these towers reached to almost touch the planet's solitary moon. This heavenly body defied its database portrait too. The moon apparently possessed its own thick atmosphere now, one that concealed its surface with the same murky resolve as the planetary gas envelope. Basic scans revealed that the moon's "atmosphere" was actually more liquid than gaseous. Abnormal power readings were detected beneath that lunar ocean.

Neither Janek or Pik liked that anomaly, but Etty was quick to remind them that the Princess was stranded on the planet, not the moon. "We're here," he asserted, "for a quick grab-and-go operation that will never get anywhere near that moon."

Having reviewed the appropriate datapacks with intimate scrutiny, Janek explained the planet's historical importance to us. Ironically, Pik and Etty were unmoved by the fact that this world was rumored to have spawned their own race. Pik found it amusing that the Duuian seemed impressed by the mythical tale.

"I would have thought you would be humbled by this discovery, Pik," Janek told her. "This is the origin-point of your species. From this world, mankind spread through the galaxy. Of the Thousand Races, your kind hold the most power."

She shrugged. History had never been of much interest to her. She lived with a focus on the now and an eye on the future. The past was immutable, and (for her) littered with failures and crises best left forgotten.

A puzzling shudder passed through her as she stared at the misty planet on the wall screen. There was nothing ominous or threatening about the view, but a deep tremor of dread ran through her body. The battle-sense of an ex-Warrior? Or perhaps a hidden touch of awe at facing the legendary homeworld of mankind? More likely: just a subtle response to the frigid temperatures that Janek maintained aboard ship for his comfort. She harbored no racial reverence for the homeworld myth. And there was hardly anything about the opaque cloudcover that implied a deadly menace. She ran her palms along her arms, warming herself.

Janek was still lecturing about Earth's historical importance. The extent of his knowledge overwhelmed her, but then: that's the way it was with augmented data storage. Without doubt, an hour ago, Janek had been as ignorant as dirt about the identity of this frontier planet. Then he popped in a data disc on the subject, and he was a sudden authority. New data always made Janek chatty too. Pik and Etty were used to this trait.

While Janek rattled off meticulous details of irrelevant importance, Etty programmed a sensory sweep for the Princess' downed ship. It worried Pik that no beacon signal had been immediately detected, but she refrained from sharing her fears with her partners. Perhaps the Princess' retinue were simply incompetent; perhaps the crash had disabled their transmitter. But then—how could they have broadcast their distress call?

Another warning synapse went off in her head.

The beacon would—of course—be gone if the Princess had already been rescued by someone else. This was a gloomy notion, but especially powerful in the wake of the team's prior disappointment on Jhul. Coming up empty-handed twice in a row was bad juju.

"Aha!" came Etty's exclamation as a marker twinkled on the screen. The scan had located the Princess' cruiser near one of the planet's poles.

As Pik felt relief over this turn of events—the cruiser was still there, the Princess still required rescue—she also experienced another amorphous shudder. There was something about the planet that was triggering an instinctive fear response. What was it that made the homeworld seem so intangibly repulsive?

Janek joined Etty to pilot the ">%" into orbit above the Earth's hidden arctic. While the ship made its approach, it became apparent that the Princess' crash-landed cruiser was not remaining stationary beneath the clouds. The ship was moving...but far too slowly to be under its own thrusters. Janek was bewildered by this phenomena. Etty was unconcerned. Pik kept her theories to herself, for she was lost in other ambiguous worries.

The farther away they stayed from the astoundingly huge equatorial spikes, the better she felt. She watched the unholy lunar orb swing around on-screen, keeping its ghostly eye on the ">%'s" trajectory. For reasons she did not comprehend, everything about this planetary system inspired unease in her.

"I'll do this one solo," Etty announced.

"Solo?"

"C'mon," he whined. "This time, *I* wanna be the hero."

Janek grunted his indifference, but then the Duuian rarely donned his own pressure suit to venture outside the ship.

Etty wants to dazzle the Princess, mused Pik.

Some lovers share tales of past affairs. Pik had never seen the point of that. One of the things she and Etty had in common was more of an interest in fantasies involving people they had no chance of ever meeting, much less bedding. She'd heard them called Wish Lists. Princess Eden of the Nimbus Royal Family was number three on Etty's Wish List. Here, he was faced with the prospect of being the hero who saved his secret lust-mate. It was no wonder that he was begging his teammates to stay in orbit. *If we were about to rescue someone from* my *Wish List (say, Duchamp Deller, the no-G soccer player),* Pik admitted to herself, *I'd be envisioning the same courageous and indulgent riff as Etty.* She couldn't deny him this once-in-a-lifetime thrill.

So Etty went into the clouds alone.

Pik and Janek followed his progress as he descended through dense vapors laced with frequent electrical discharges. Although he knew they could see readouts of what he saw, Etty supplied them with subjective observations:

"It's really damp.

"There's electrical activity.

"It's getting damper.

"I can see the ground.

"So far, I don't see the Opal Cruiser…"

Janek assured him it was there, for its location blinked steadily on the screens in the ">%'s" control room. When he downloaded the coordinates, Etty grunted with approval.

"Okay, *now* I see it."

Without the marker, the cruiser was nearly invisible (in the visible spectrum). It's ivory veneer was lost against the jumble of white chunks of ice that surrounded the ship. Only when one identified the scorchmarks left by the cruiser's hellbound passage through the planet's mucusy atmosphere—only then did its crumpled shape become recognizable as an artifact among the frozen shards of arctic nature. Clearly: it had not been a "clean" crash.

The rest of the landscape was a frozen tundra in active motion. This was the explanation for the mysterious slow movement displayed by the Opal Cruiser. The ship had fallen onto an iceflow that was carrying it across the desolate countryside. An Ice Age was in full swing here.

Perhaps this explained some of the damage worn by the crumpled Royal Cruiser, the ship was being relentlessly crushed between icy boulders. The survivors were obviously undergoing a constant jostling. Pik had definite sympathy for them, recalling what such erratic momentum did to unsuspecting civilians. Maybe her Guards were stable and undaunted, but the Princess and her Entourage had to be puking up last year's meals by now.

"It's being carried along by the ice flow," Etty stated the obvious.

"Have you spotted the access hatch?" Janek inquired. "Your picture's starting to break up…"

Indeed, Etty's transmissions had been getting progressively grottier as he descended into the planet's wet stormclouds. As he approached the cruiser itself, his signal was mostly hostile static. Soon…

There—sensors lost him completely now.

"Grup!" swore Pik.

Under usual circumstances, she would have had no trepidation over Etty being out alone, even cut-off from the rest of the team. She knew he was capable, cautious to a fault. He could handle himself.

When his transmission had failed, Etty had been barely a hundred meters above the crashed cruiser on the ice, and still descending. He'd be at the ship by now, examining it for a way inside. *Would he enter through a tear in the hull?* Pik wondered, her strategic mind busily calculating admittance possibilities. *Bad news for the survivors if their atmospheric integrity has been compromised. No wait—the readout claims the planetary atmosphere contains enough oxygen to sustain human life. The Princess' Entourage lucked out...at least on that count.*

Or would Etty go for the noble approach—through the access airlock? He was more likely to chose the "proper" route, especially if he was looking to impress the object of his secret lust. In he would go, observing all the "official protocol" included in his suit's database. Etty was a stickler for authenticity, he would act out every ceremony he imagined necessary to attract a smile from the Royal Family's darling. With a wistful sigh, Pik regretted being blind to Etty's finest moment. *Not many people get to meet their fantasy under such heroic conditions. Etty's rescuing the Royal Daughter from this terrible frozen wasteland. He looks so dashing and important in his articulated pressure suit, almost as if he were wearing armor.* How could the Princess fail to be impressed?

"Am I misreading human nuances?" Janek asked. "Or was Etty exhibiting irrational behavior before he left?"

"Umm?"

"I detected traces of some fixation he has for the Princess...?"

Grup, she sighed. Janek was a sharp reader of other species. *Or has he just spent so much time around myself and Etty that he's nearly human himself now?*

Pik shrugged. "He has obscure mating urges in connection with the Princess. It's purely a fantasy fulfillment thing. Don't worry, Janek. It won't interfere with his performance. He'll score this one for us."

"And...you do not find this—how do you say—offensive?"

"Huh?" *Sometimes, the Duuian's weird ethics confuses the grup out of me.*

"His actions, aren't they in conflict with the mating bond he has with you?"

"You mean: am I jealous?"

"Yes—that was the word I could not find."

"No," she told him truthfully. "Like I told you: it's a wish fulfillment thing. You can't begrudge anyone something like this. Once-in-a-lifetime chance."

"He *is* aware, however, that any gratitude Princess Eden has for her rescuer will be perfunctory. We'll deal with the Captain of her Guard. It's unlikely any of us will directly encounter the Princess herself."

"That's probably the way it'll go, yes," she admitted. "But Etty can hope..."

"Should we hope too?" Janek inquired innocently. "Will our belief bolster the probability of him meeting the Royal Daughter?"

She nodded, telling him, without sarcasm, that that would nice.

After a while, Janek grew bored holding a vigil over a dormant monitor. It was clear, he intimated, that they would learn of Etty's adventure in due course, upon his return to the ">%". The Duuian wandered from the control room, leaving Pik to a solitude that soon gave birth to impatience.

Etty knows he's out of contact, she fretted. *It's not like him to leave us out of the loop. He could use the cruiser's equipment to punch a coherent broadcast through the planet's stormclouds.*

It's been three hours!

How long does it take to go through an airlock and announce "I'm here to rescue you"?

Sitting hunched over the monitor screen, primed to detect any trace of a signal from the vicinity of the downed cruiser, Pik could not avoid a sense of apprehension regarding the delay of Etty's return. Her neck muscles were weary from hours of tension. Her teeth hurt (the girl had a bad habit of grinding them when she was under pressure). *And I'm running out of positions that don't hurt my butt on this grupping uncomfortable plastiform seat.* Boredom had whittled away her limited tolerance, leaving her oozing with irritated impatience. Her basic trust in Etty's abilities had been eroded by the predominant foreboding she had experienced since glimpsing this lost world. *Confidence* was becoming *concern.*

It was that same elusive dread that kept her glued to the monitor screen throughout the evening. She could not rid her mind of an intangible but assertive conviction that something terrible had been waiting for Etty down there. It was frustrating, to have these flashes of vague premonition, but be unable to provide any insight into interpreting their portents. Pik rationalized that she was giving Etty time-to-work-the-room, but she knew that was a tenuous excuse. He should have reported in by now. Ergo: something bad had happened. And that bad something was waiting down there to happen to whoever came in search of Etty.

Absurd as it sounded, this irrational dread kept her frozen and inactive, incapable of rising to the challenge of going in rescue of the man she loved. The girl was a victim of baser instincts than she knew she possessed.

In the morning, it was Janek who suggested that someone needed to go find out what had happened to Etty. Knowing his implied meaning, Pik resented him for his presumption. Etty was as much his partner as he was hers. She told Janek so, perhaps too bluntly. The Duuian surprised her by announcing that he would go down if necessary.

"Okay," she responded. "Then we'll *both* go down."

Janek met her by the airlock. He looked uncomfortable in his pressure suit, and he probably was. Pik couldn't remember the last time she saw him in it. The massive helmet exaggerated his already overly-large head, rendering the rest of his body diminutive in comparison. After getting Janek's assurances that he had charged all of his suit's systems, Pik led them through the hatch and out into the vacuum just above the planet's soupy stratosphere.

They hung now with the planet below us. It's viscous clouds stretched to every horizon, so white they almost seemed impervious to intrusion. It was an intimidating panorama. There was no gaseous majesty or warmth to this dense atmosphere. It's colorless facade spoke of apathy and indifference.

They activated our AG units, and dove into this uninviting landscape.

"How many humans does it take to get in trouble?" Janek called to me over our comlink.

"I don't know," Pik responded. "One?"

"No," the Duuian revealed with a wheezy chuckle. "It depends on how many friends he has."

She had to smile. Her partner's humor was a fleeting distraction from the desolate environment they had entered, though.

From the instant she penetrated the planet's atmosphere, Pik's suit identified a decrease of ambient temperature. (At the time, her vigilance failed to notice this discrepancy, for few regions are naturally "colder" than the vacuum of outer space.) The deeper she plunged into old Earth's gaseous shroud, the more frigid the climate became. Heating coils whined throughout her pressure suit as they struggled to battle the uncommon external chill. Ice briefly crusted across her faceplate before reentry friction evaporated the accumulation, clearing the girl's vision.

Winds of rigorous vitality buffeted the pair as they descended through spasmodic nests of loose electrical arcs. Pik and Janek were forced to activate their manual thrusters, lest they become separated in the vast and opaque sky.

Even in the intermittent glow of the relentless lightning, this atmosphere was thick enough to obstinately hamper visual perception. She had to rely on her suit's scans to determine that she was still high above the icy surface of this mythic planet. Only in the final half-kilometer above the ground did the vapors thin enough to afford a view of the surging tundra she had briefly seen in Etty's static-clouded transmission.

By that point, Pik had familiarized herself with the terrain via other frequencies. She had located the crumpled Royal Cruiser, its alloy hull standing out as a spectrographic beacon against a background of frozen water. Giving the region a sensory sweep for a radius of a hundred meters, she determined that the area was barren of life. The tableau was primarily ice: enormous icefields of geological scale, crunching against each other, shattering and refreezing, creeping across a continent, a force beyond concern or sympathy. This harsh environment ruled the scene that spread beneath her. It was a cruelly hostile place to be stranded.

"All clear so far," Janek commented in her ear.

They flew slowly over the wreckage of the cruiser, each of them seemingly unwilling to touch down just yet. Despite the evidence of their scans, they both viewed the ship as potentially hostile. If Pik's worst fears were credible, then it had swallowed Etty, and waited to lure her into its hideous clutches. Sooner or later, though, someone had to investigate the wreckage. *We must follow Etty's path,* she realized, *and discover the fate of our lost partner.*

Pik didn't know about Janek, but the rescue of the Princess was no longer a driving motive for her. She was here to find her man. She imagined that Janek probably retained enough commercial avarice to keep the Princess in mind, for he urged the girl to restrict her actions to official protocol once they entered the Royal Cruiser. (And he was right. There was the chance, although it ranked *very* low in Pik's estimation, that Etty was in no danger, that her missing partner was getting along famously with the Princess and her spoiled Entourage. In which case, it would be imprudent to jeopardize their retrieval commission by storming the cruiser like a pair of commando raiders.)

The first to dare to land, Pik touched down beside the cruiser's open access hatch. Open and empty. Waving Janek to follow, she crept into the ominous airlock. The chamber was uncomplicated and showed no sign of recent use. The inner door was ajar. She forced it open and passed into the ship.

Despite the corridor's colorful decorations, the ship had a tomb-like quality to it that did little to dispel Pik's foreboding mood. Meager light panels illuminated the passages, but no physical evidence of habitation was in sight. Janek came up behind her, to pause and regard the junction of hallways that presented itself. He cast various sensory frequencies down each gloomy path, but made no comment regarding his findings.

Meanwhile, ever since entering the cruiser, Pik had been broadcasting an emergency signal cued to Etty's comlink. His lack of response annoyed her. How could he be so reckless as to deactivate his comlink?

Fortunately, she was armed with the system signature of Etty's pressure suit. A quick scan told her that he was ahead and down a few levels. Finding him was only a matter of following his suit's automatic signal.

Janek knew this, and counseled her to stick to protocol.

The girl's urges pulled her in separate directions. She understood the necessity of finding the survivors of the crashed cruiser, but her heart strained to rush in search of her dear Etty. Besides the professional necessity, there was the need to be wary of the Princess' Royal Guard. These elite Warriors would be primed to protect the Royal Daughter from any unexpected intruders. The retrievers were here to rescue everyone, but the Guards wouldn't know that until they identified themselves. Again, Janek was right. Stumbling around through the Royal Cruiser, they were liable to get vaporized by overexcited Guards—then there'd be no rescuing going on at all, of the Princess or of Etty.

Pik grumbled, but told Janek that she would behave.

Janek picked a corridor and led her into its mouth. She did not fail to notice that the route he chose took them in the general direction of Etty's electronically-deduced location.

They made their way into the bowels of the derelict cruiser. Under their feet, the corridor was in gradual motion, as the glacier outside rolled the cruiser in a cradle of icy shards. It took almost half-an-hour for the floor to move from beneath their feet, forcing them to stand on the wall now. Soon, they would be walking between the lighting panels as if striding down aisles of brilliant glory. *How*, she wondered, *have the survivors endured such a rotating sanctuary?*

Every few minutes, in accordance with basic salvage protocol, Janek broadcast a hailing transmission accompanied by a verbal greeting in the audible frequencies. His words echoed numbly down the passage, bringing no response. Where were the survivors? What had happened to the Royal Guards and the Princess and her Entourage? And Etty?

Pausing, Pik opened a side doorway and quickly peered inside. The room beyond was innocuous and identifiable only by an examination of the loose debris that was piled against the wall-that-now-served-as-the-floor. It had been the ship's medical lab. Besides the diagnostic and curative apparatus that lay broken, the room was otherwise unoccupied. She closed the door and rejoined Janek.

"Empty med lab," she told him.

He nodded slowly and pirouetted around a turn in the corridor. As Pik rounded the turn, she crashed into the back of his top-heavy suit. The impact was slight, but coming so unexpectedly as it had, it was enough to put the girl on her butt. Suddenly, though, Janek was backing up. In his haste, he trampled across her sprawled bulk. He was wailing a cry of panic and fear as he went.

Once he had stumbled past her, Pik was able to see what had so desperately frightened him. The sight sucked the air from her lungs with a soundless but fearful gasp.

Well, she fumed, *we found someone...*

The problem was: that "someone" had been eviscerated, and their bodies were strewn in wild abandon along a dark hallway. The lighting panels were undamaged; they still glowed here, but their surfaces were thickly mired with blood and viscera, casting a dreadful reddish pale on the atrocious vision. A glimpse of the ghastly tableau in the infrared told Pik that this had happened days ago: the gory remains were long cold.

Such a horrific discovery stunned her mind for almost a second before her battle training kicked in. Instinctively, she armed her suit's defensive shields.

Upon second glance, the monstrous slaughter became even more puzzling... There seemed to be a pattern to the massacre, a methodology too grisly to believe. The gore mostly occupied the rear portion of the corridor. From the splatter array of the body parts, it appeared that some savage gout of force had *liquefied* the Princess' Royal Guard (for they were identifiable as such by the recognizable shards of Warrior armor). Something had attacked a squad of elite Warriors and reduced them to inchoate slime, not unlike the fatal blow of a monstrous corridor-sized piston!

Etty! But then Pik realized that his suit would not be transmitting its signature code if her beloved had been pulped in a manner similar to the abomination she beheld.

"What could caussse thisss?" Janek's voice wheezed in her ear.

"Something *bad*," she told him.

"They—they've been liquefied!" he wailed.

"Calm down. This happened days ago. Whatever did this...should be long gone." Janek was not used to such horrors. (*As if* I *am,* she reminded herself. Never, even during her term in the military, had Pik ever witnessed such grotesque brutality.) But—she was the "team brawn," as Etty had often put it. It was her job to handle defensive measures.

She stared with superbly feigned courage at the terrible massacre, and assured Janek that they were in no danger. Reluctantly, he followed her down the bloodstained passage. They drifted on AG, avoiding stepping in the gore.

What kind of defense is possible, she worried, *against forces that can do* this?

Although the next corridor was clean, an overpowering sense of palpable apprehension soaked her perceptions. Walls covered with festive designs now seemed a mockery of the atrocity they had found here in the Princess' crashed cruiser. The tomb-like gloom she had sensed earlier seemed vindicated now, given horrific physicality by the gruesome massacre they had discovered. She dreaded the prospect of encountering more evidence of foul play.

I knew this was a bad place, she told herself.

This awful crisis placed Pik in control of the team. Their survival now depended on her defensive acumen and Janek's speed in following her orders. *My priority is to keep us alive,* she privately asserted, *and in my evaluation that "us" includes Etty.* When the time came to lead them deeper into the death ship, Pik headed in the direction of Etty's signal. Once more, the fate of the Princess was an ephemeral concern to her. Pik's disquietude was focused on her beloved.

As if giving voice to her own private worries, Janek moaned, "Do you think that Etty hasss been…liquefied too?" He was lisping, as Janek did when he became upset.

Swallowing her realistic fears, she persuaded her alien partner that such an eventuality was unlikely. "Those Guards were vaporized days ago. Etty's only recently come here."

"Who could have…done what we sssaw?"

The nature of *what* had done what they'd seen was incredible enough. *Who* had not crossed Pik's mind yet. But, now that Janek mentioned it…

"Terroristsss?" he piped.

"You think the Royal Cruiser might have been *shot* down?"

"You're the expert, Pik."

"Terrorists," she muttered in verbal consideration, "bent on disrupting the Nimbus Royal Family… Attacking the favorite Royal Daughter would be a nasty strike against the Ruling Family. But why would they shoot down the Royal Cruiser way out here on the Rim? Who would know of it? They would need to grab the Princess and produce her as a living hostage."

"Which might indicate," Janek interrupted me, "that Princesss Eden sssurvived the ssslaughter that visssited her crash-landed cruissser."

"This could just as easily be the handiwork of a savage local beast," Pik pointed out. "There might be no subversive political agenda at work here."

"What beassst could kill in the manner we sssaw?"

"What *weapon* could do what we saw?" she countered. He fell silent, obviously intimidated by the brusque expression of her desperate frustration.

Terrorist or beast, Pik had no desire to find out, especially if gaining that knowledge entailed coming face-to-face with the answer. If not for Etty lost inside this slaughterhouse cruiser, she'd have been back aboard the ">%" in a flash, programming a hasty flight from this region of space. *And,* she vowed, *as soon as we've found our missing partner, that's exactly what we're going to do!*

Following her suit's prompter, Pik struck off in search of Etty. Janek tagged along, affecting a twitchy agitation that advertised his nervousness. He was quick to fling his mighty head from side-to-side, as if determined to catch a furtive glimpse of some phantom he desperately hoped he would not spot. At one point, Pik discovered that he had neglected to activate his suit's protective shields. Foregoing any recriminations, she simply leaned close and switched it on for him via the manual control-pad he wore on his side. Janek was wired enough without enduring indictments of incompetence.

These passages were leading to the ship's drive. Why would Etty have gone there? There was no refuge there. Was there—a flash of real panic clouded Pik's mind as it occurred to her—danger of a plasma core breach? Had the cruiser's crash and glacier-ride ruptured the drive unit? Had Etty learned this and gone to fix the problem?

But—how does one repair a ruptured plasma core?

Grup, she lamented. *One* doesn't.

Oh, be reasonable, she warned myself. If Etty had uncovered a faulty drive core down here, he would have immediately fled back to the ">%". For all his courage (and his desire to prove his manliness to the lovely Princess Eden), Etty would never have willingly faced certain doom.

There was that troublesome qualifier again: willingly. If Etty was trapped down here, Pik doubted he was suffering his exile *willingly*. He was probably wondering what was taking his partners so long to come and get him.

The girl's suit detected a sudden energy spike directly behind her. Whirling, she shoved Janek's startled bulk aside and brought one of her arm-mounted weapons to bear on the location of that unexpected trace. She dreaded that, despite her logical dismissal, the overzealous killers had returned to vaporize them by surprise. But—there was nothing there. The hallway was vacant in the steady illumination from the light panels that lined what was now the wall. There were no side routes or doorways where any stalker might have hidden.

This terrible death ship was stirring Pik's imagination to disturbing notions. She could not afford to get jumpy down here. Her life—and Janek's—depended on her remaining efficient by not panicking. And Etty's life too.

There it was again! A sharp electromagnetic spike—behind her now! Twisting around, she caught a fairy glimpse of a humanoid figure. Then the wispy shape faded in the darkness beyond the open doorway that led into the engineering section of the cruiser. She followed it with her best haste, but it was gone before the girl dove into the next chamber. This, the control room for the nearby plasma drive unit, was empty of any skulking individuals.

"What'sss the matter?" Janek hissed via comlink. He did not venture into the room after her, remaining in the safety of the corridor.

"Didn't you pick that up?" grunted Pik. "An energy spike...something I thought I saw... It jumped in here."

"Have you disssabled it?"

"It...there's nothing here," she reluctantly confessed. *I'm chasing ghosts, and it isn't breeding confidence in Janek's already spooked self. Nor in mine either.* "I must've been mistaken..."

"Is it clear? Can you see Etty?"

Indeed, his signal was thick here. He must be quite nearby now. But... there was no sign of him.

Janek poked his mammoth headgear into the chamber and snorted, "He isn't here. Where is he then?" The absence of his slur denoted that the Duuian was gradually regaining his composure.

Besides the entry doorway, there was only a single aperture leading from this control room. Her darling Etty...had to be *inside the plasma core!* No—it could not be...

No, wait, she suddenly realized. *It* couldn't *be.* Stepping into an active plasma core would instantly reduce Etty and his suit to discharged atomic particles. How could his suit still be transmitting its signature code?

For Etty's suit was transmitting, and…the signal *was* coming from the hatch that gave access to the inner core.

"That is impossible," Janek declared once Pik had revealed her suspicions to him. When his own instruments corroborated her fears, he remained dubious, "There must a malfunction…"

"Of both our scanners?" she laughed. "At the same time?"

"Of Etty's code transmitter…"

Pik gulped, not happy to entertain that possibility. If that were the case, she might never find Etty. If his suit was transmitting a false location, then he could be anywhere…inside the ship or out!

And the only way to ascertain whether or not Etty was really trapped in the core was to look inside. *Grup!*

While Pik was giving in to a brief burst of despair, Janek entered and busied himself at the room's control consoles. Plucking a disk from the flotsam cluttering the wall/floor, he plugged it into his suit. A quick download of the relevant data made him an instant authority on the cruiser's plasma drive. With the ease of an expert, Janek's claws danced across the controls, bringing screens to life and drawing forth systems reports. When he turned to face his partner, his sensory tendrils were twined in what she knew was Duuian confusion. "It's cold," he told her.

"What's cold?"

"The core. There is no plasma left in the drive chamber."

"What?!" she shared his confusion. Plasma cores did not go cold, at least, not in a hundred-or-so human lifetimes. What enormous exertions had drained this drive unit? "How long has this cruiser *been* here?"

Janek grunted, consulting the controls. "Six days. And this claims that the core was emptied four days ago."

"Before Etty would have come here."

"Yes, but… Etty's presence here is superfluous to this unprecedented phenomena."

"Not to me," Pik told him. Full of newborn enthusiasm, she attacked the hatch that led into the dry core. Although she trusted Janek's assessment of the drive unit's controls, Pik still flinched as she pulled open the normally-deadly portal, revealing a surprisingly shadowy interior. She cast her floodlights into the core, illuminating therein the shape of Etty's suit sprawled.

His suit…

Etty in the flesh was nowhere to be found.

✛

The Princess awoke in darkness. Instantly she communicated her disapproval of the stench that offended her delicate nostrils. Her voice seemed louder than usual as it echoed back on her. Irritated, she commanded the lights to come on, but the darkness refused to go away.

Imagining that a malfunction was tormenting her suite, she called for one of her Guards. When no one answered her summons, she kicked her heels against the harsh surface upon which she reclined, then pushed herself up on regal elbows in the absolute gloom.

They were ignoring her again. This habit was new among her Guards, this furtive secrecy around her and her guests. It had begun after the crash, persisting even after she had demanded its surcease.

Now she recalled their latest irrational guidance: herding the party into a chamber that was utterly unsuited for any celebration. Garlands had been strung, and a feast set for her Entourage, but the room's stench of machine oil and sweat had rendered it completely unacceptable for any festivities. Her Guards had refused to allow anyone to wander the yacht, confining the partiers to this room with stern admonitions. The Princess' ire had finally pinnacled, sending her in search of the Guard Master, to complain of his insensitive treatment.

She remembered storming from the assigned party chamber, only to find no Guards on duty in the hallway outside. There, her memory failed her, producing only murky gaps and puzzling wailings. Without doubt, she would have gone to confront the errant Guard Master, chastising him for allowing such a grievous breach of royal security. But she found no recollections of doing so. She could call forth nothing after leaving the inadequate party room…her memory was blank.

And now, those gaps had spilled from her mind, manifesting in an entirely odious environment whose pervasive gloom crowded in upon her with claustrophobic pressure.

Through her clumsy crawling about in the darkness, the Princess determined that she was in a lozenge-shaped confinement. The walls of this incredible prison were soft to her fingertips, but resisted any forceful coercion applied to their surface, hardening with eerie tenacity. Her probing detected regularly spaced ridges running vertically along the sides of this strange vault, but they seemed buried in the walls, beyond her reach. Contact with the walls themselves was an aberrant experience; their dry sliminess defied her sensibilities and delivered shivers to her supple spine.

She took desperate solace in the notion that all this had to be a loathsome nightmare. Soon, she would awake for real, to find herself ensconced in expensive silk and caressed by perfumed breezes. Until then, her only recourse was to close her eyes and dwell on pleasant memories, willfully shutting out the noxious iniquity.

When Eden Nimbus had turned eight years of age, her Royal Parents had indulged their favorite daughter's fondness for ponies by decreeing her the owner of the most famous stables on the planet of Pu'ahly. After a glorious ceremony, Royal Guards had escorted her from the invasive surveillance of holo reporters for a tour of the grounds of her latest playground. All of the horses had been arranged in a row for her inspection, and a stooped, withered trainer had introduced the young Princess to each animal. While bored-but-alert Guards had followed them down this kilometer-long line, she had marveled and squealed to learn the names, stats, and preferences of her new toys. The ancient trainer had given her candy to feed a stunning chestnut palomino, and the greedy colt had nipped her palm with its eagerness. When the Guards had moved to reprimand the pony, the Princess had intervened. Being royalty, she had gotten her way, and the feisty colt had been spared any punishment. (Now that she thought of it, though, she could not recall seeing that bent, gray-faced trainer after that first day.) She had renamed the pony "Rusty". (Her adult self winced at the crude unsophistication of her adolescent imagination. *Why was it,* she wondered, *that while children displayed more creativity than mature people, they always gave things the simplest names?*) Rusty had become her favorite for the next few weeks before her interests had waned and moved to another obsession.

When she awoke the second time, the Princess was distressed to discover herself still trapped in the repulsive darkness. Sobbing with despair, it took her a few moments to notice the changes that had transformed her gloomy imprisonment. The darkness was now littered with tiny holes; pale beams of light streamed through these punctures. It was as if this unnatural night sky had filled with immediate stars, each aiming spotlights of disapproval to stab inward, focused on her insecurities. There was movement too: not a trembling of the dungeon's walls, but a heaving that swayed her entire environment, as if her cell had been cast upon a mildly turgid ocean.

Giving in to panic, she flung herself against those repellent walls, scraping her delicate fingers into their pliant barrier, hurtling pleas of despondency at her unseen captors. For there could no longer be any doubt that Princess Eden was in the unpleasant custody of unfriendly tormentors.

The darkness and the rocking motion continued unabated.

Only a vague whisper answered her anxious outcries, and it was unsympathetically wordless and tenebrously ominous.

✢

Pik never did find anything alive inside the crashed Royal Cruiser.

She did find more evidence of vaporized passengers, though. From the festive decorations that cluttered this chamber, she assumed these victims must have been the Princess and her Entourage. She had not examined this massacre with any degree of detail or duration. By that point, Pik and Janek were both traumatized by the puzzle of Etty's empty suit.

Etty's suit had been found, but Etty was no longer in it. Its interior was clean, he had not been liquefied inside the gear. He was…simply gone.

To say Pik was in shock was an insulting understatement. Even Janek was intellectually stunned, he muttered incessantly about the obscure history of mankind's mythic homeworld.

"Among the Thousand Races, each species celebrates their birthplace planet, even those cultures that have lost or dismantled their world of origin," the Duuian pondered aloud. "Why would humanity forget about their own homeworld?"

They searched the entire cruiser, but found no trace of Etty (or any other living soul) anywhere in the wreckage. Pik functioned on autopilot during this inspection, barely aware of the "nothing" they found. Her mind was unable to wrap itself around Etty's mysterious fate. Where was he? Wherever that was—was he alive or dead? Would she ever know? This upset her the most: the prospect of never learning the facts surrounding the disappearance of her lover. She found herself clutching at these thoughts, as if to bury them with her attention, thereby banishing them from her consciousness. If this hope contained no semblance of logic, it was because the girl was still in shock. She performed like an automaton, accompanying Janek on a tour of the crumpled cruiser as it rocked in the grip of the flowing glacial tundra outside.

They had failed, more completely than any defeat their team had ever experienced. The retrievers had come to rescue the favorite Royal Daughter, but they had found only carnage and despair. Then they had lost one of their own, to a fate that remained unknown.

Janek offered no humor now to dispel their overwhelming downfall.

The hunters departed the cruiser-cum-tomb, their hearts empty and hollowed by shock. Determined to return with more than a memory of her beloved, Pik towed Etty's empty suit along with them. It drifted behind her in the air on its AG pulse like an awkward man-shaped balloon.

Distracted by their losses, Pik and Janek fell prey to the beasts the instant they exited the cruiser's airlock.

Powerful hairy arms pulled Pik aside, flinging her from the dented curve of the cruiser's hull. The attack was so sudden that it caught even her suit unaware. She crashed to the jumble of icy rubble that supported the ship's corpse, where more beastly appendages set upon the girl with hostile intent. They tore at the equipment that covered her pressure suit, they beat upon her with clubs of frozen stone. Their hideous faces leaned close to bellow with fanged anger, misting her helmet with their foul breath. For all its vigor and frenzy, their primitive assault did little damage to her armor. Pik's mind, however, recoiled from the beasts, unable to process their existence or their vehemence.

From the relative safety of her suit, she observed these monsters with a gradually returning command of her senses. They were human, or at least they had once been human beings. Now they were savage beasts, a brutishness replacing their racial heritage and mutating their physical appearance. Dark hair covered these figures, matted and filthy with the blood of their prey. Their faces displayed no rudimentary intelligence, only primitive wrath. Past their beards and tangled manes, Pik could see beady eyes with no trace of white. Blunt nostrils belched wasted warmth as they grunted and shrieked their animal disapproval. Wide mouths revealed unevenly sharpened fangs behind lips blued by the cold. They gnashed their teeth against her armor, scraping blackened talons on the metal suit and pounding it with hairy fists. They fought like a pack of uncooperative wolves, their attack was too uncoordinated to offer her any viable threat. Their inability to harm her was escalating their mania.

As her training returned, Pik cast a pair of the disgusting beasts from her with a sharp sweep of one bulky arm. They tumbled from the girl, to crash down the jagged slope of icy boulders. Others surged to replace their defeated brethren; these met a blast from the pulse cannon mounted on the shoulder of her suit. The weapon's shots broke their swarming ranks, scattering their bodies in torn fragments. Before more creatures could lunge, she lifted into the air on an AG wave. Drifting above the monstrous group, Pik saw Janek below; he had fallen down the opposite side of the crashed cruiser, where the beasts had covered him in a punishing mound of hairy violence. His cries of terror filled her comlink. A brief pulse salvo freed Janek from their assault. He nimbly rose to join his partner in the air, wheezing his exuberant gratitude.

Pik spotted Etty's empty suit floating above them on its own AG wave. She was about to go snare it when the terrible wind caught them.

So powerful was this blast of wind that it disturbed several chunks of frozen debris from around the fallen cruiser, heaving these massive boulders of ice into the air. Even the cruiser itself lurched in the monstrous gale. Needless to say, Pik and Janek (and Etty's unoccupied armor) were flung across the glacial landscape like weightless flotsam in a mighty storm. Pik tumbled too violently for her suit's gyroscope to correct her balance. There was no point in firing her thrusters, their propulsion would have done nothing to abate her chaotic flight.

As she flailed in the impossible bluster, Pik thought she caught sight of a dark figure hunched low and incredibly huge on the upwind horizon, but she could not be certain as her view whipped unmercifully in tandem with her aerial tumble. She had to have been mistaken, though, for that shape had seemed more massive than a distant mountain.

Janek was screaming again, filling her ears with his wheezing outcries. She desperately needed to organize her thoughts, but that was impossible as long as his fearful gasps echoed unwanted in her head. Pik had to shout to get him to shut up, threatening to deactivate her comlink if he didn't quiet down. Unfortunately, his quiet gave her scarce respite.

Resolutely ignoring the tumbling landscape, she concentrated on a scan of her surroundings. When viewed only a series of graphs and numeral progressions, the spinning perspective lost any distracting effect. She was shocked to discover that they were already several kilometers from the crashed cruiser. And apparently this monstrous wind was bearing them aloft too, for their altitude had increased with disturbing velocity.

"Look!" came Janek's terrified shout. "Do you ssse it? What isss that?!"

She ignored his panic, and focused on attempting to coordinate her thrusters to steady herself in the stormfront. Gradually, more through trial-and-error than expertise, Pik halted her spasmodic roll and finally surveyed her status with her own eyes.

So high! She was well into the dense, moist cloudcover now, soaring through a jungle of the savage electrical bolts that laced these clouds. Relying on her artificial sensors, she found Janek among the roiling mists. (It did not strike her until later to puzzle how the two of them had remained near each other during their chaotic ride on the stormwinds.) Grabbing him, she steadied the frantic Duuian, assuring him that he was okay. Firing her thrusters at full blast, Pik took them both higher into the stratosphere, desperate to escape this insane planet.

At first, it seemed that they were escaping, but then Pik's suit alerted her to their decreasing altitude. That was impossible—she was flying on wide-open propulsion! How could she be falling? But it was so, for Pik and Janek plummeted from the billowing clouds. They were more than "falling"—their descent was absolutely manic. The ground raced to meet them so fast, Pik was incapable of releasing more than a lone syllable of surprise.

Then she hit. The glacier cracked under her impact. Her suit's defensive field spared the girl from becoming a smear on the crusty ice, but she still gained a myriad of bruises and minor fractures as she bounced around inside the suit itself. She lay stunned for several moments, aware that she had survived, but utterly bewildered by the nature of the attack she had just endured. Staring dazedly into the sky, Pik saw the ceiling of clouds belch gouts of vapor down toward her, their icy kiss ballooning out across the surface of the tundra. The wind! Changing direction in mid-gust, the horrendous wind had grabbed Pik, throwing her back to earth! It was the only explanation…regardless of its impossible rationale. She shook her head, refusing to give in to the madness straining to burst free from her subconscious.

She moved to sit up, and froze when she discovered a pale figure leaning over her. Striking out in panic, she drove her foot up and into the man's stomach. The blunt, armored foot went into—and *through!*—that stomach without a trace of resistance. The man seemed undaunted by the blow; he smiled weakly and introduced himself.

"I am Professor Laramy," he spoke in her ear. Or was his voice in her *head*?

Pik stared at him in total confusion. There were several inconsistencies involved in the man's appearance. For one: he was colorless and naked. Despite this, he seemed unbothered by the savage cold. Even more disconcerting: his shoulder-length hair remained unstirred by the terrible wind that rattled the nearby ice. It took Pik a second to deduce that he must be a holographic projection.

This momentary rationalization was flung from her mind by what she saw beyond the pale man. Far on the horizon, a dark figure of enormous size squatted on a remote mountain peak. Its inhuman head almost disturbed

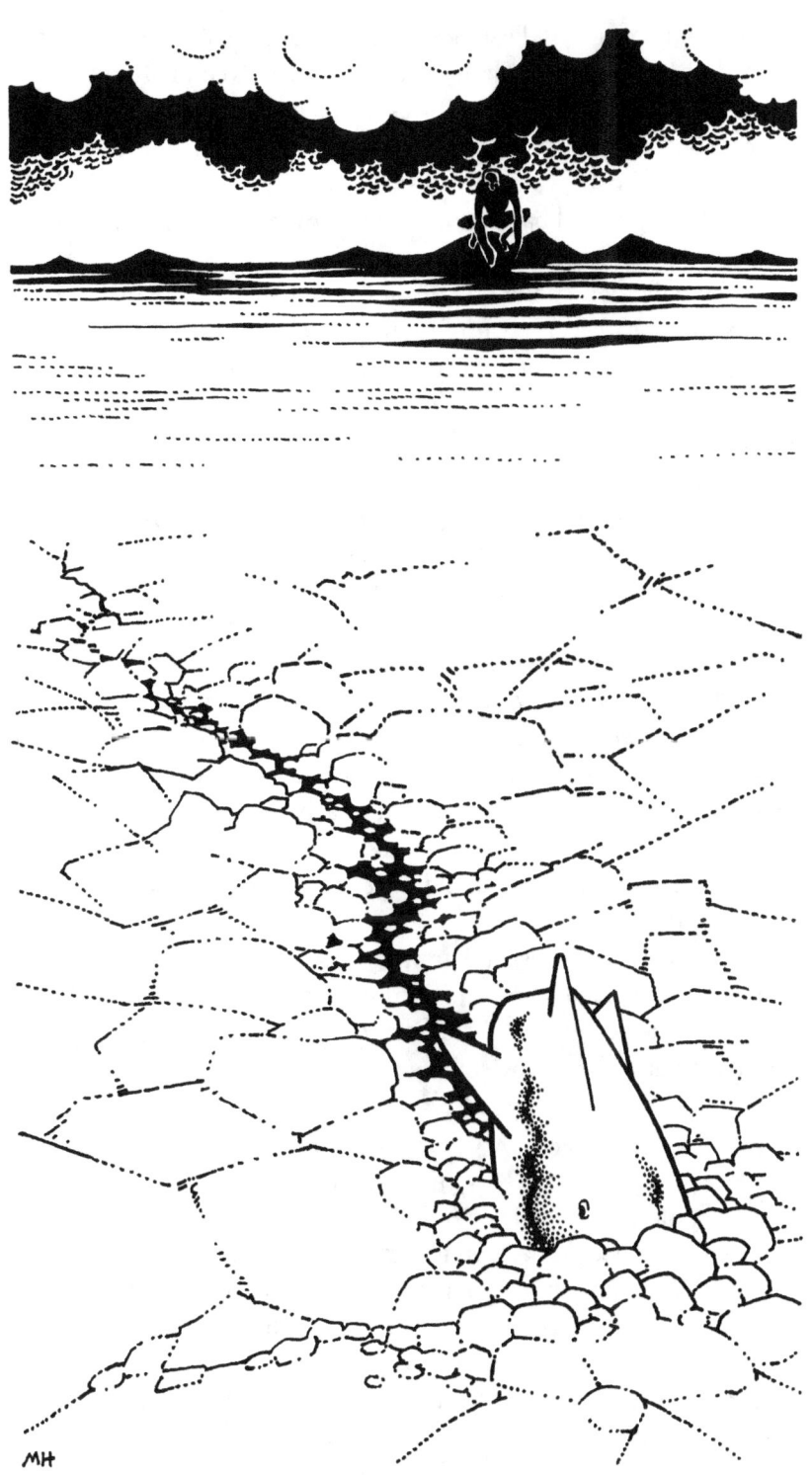

the lofty ceiling of clouds. Distance concealed any details of this monstrous creature, but sight of it brought fear bubbling to Pik's combat-seasoned lips. The beast had to be an illusion—it was over a kilometer tall!

Professor Laramy turned to peer at the far mirage. He sighed and told her in his ghostly voice, "And that is Ithaqua, the Thing That Walks the Winds." He glanced back at the girl to frown. "It was He who attacked you."

As the pale man spoke, the distant figure swung its enormous arms above its ugly head. With a mighty leap, the creature vanished into the dense cloudcover. Defying gravity, the thing did not reappear.

"He will summon his unholy servants to capture you," Laramy informed Pik inside her head. "You must come with me. I will hide you from them."

There was a hint of sincerity in the pale man's words. Whoever he was, whatever he was doing on this offensive, forgotten planet, the man was offering to help her. Faced with the alternative of meeting an angry horde of the mammoth creature's "unholy servants", Pik was willing to put aside her suspicious nature and follow Laramy to safety. But first, she needed to locate her surviving partner, if Janek still lived.

Activating her AG, Pik rose a few meters above the shattered iceflow. Professor Laramy's hologram watched her brief flight with an earnest awe. A swift scan spotted Janek's fallen suit nearby, his drop had half-buried him in the frozen landscape. Although he gave no reply when she called to him via their comlink, Pik could hear the feathery sniffle of his breathing. He was alive!

In response to Professor Laramy's urgent motions, Pik decided to leave Janek unconscious and move him by remote. Manually triggering his AG unit, she pulled the alien from his frozen hole and dragged him unceremoniously after the wispy man.

"You're human, aren't you?" Laramy called to her.

"I am," she confessed. "My partner is Duuian."

"I was not aware that any purebloods were left. Where have your people been hiding?" He paused, then waved away her unvoiced answer, "No, do not tell me. It is a secret worth keeping. *They* would hear your words, spoken aloud and carried to vicious ears on the Walker's winds." With evident fear, the pale man eyed the tundra as if expecting some dreadful punishment to appear from thin air. (Considering what Pik had beheld so far, she would not have been surprised if something *had* appeared out of nothing.)

She followed Laramy across the broken landscape of flowing ice chunks. Drifting along in the air, with Janek in tow, she was wary of any further winds, and maintained a constant sensor sweep of her surroundings as they traveled. Professor Laramy's hologram leapt from icy crest to frozen slab, never losing his footing…or (now that she peered close) never actually *touching* the rubble at all. He too remaining airborne, striding along an inch above the ground. Although his hologram retained its insubstantial integrity, never wavering or flickering from outside disturbance, his form remained milky and often translucent. Any scans Pik sent in his direction revealed only a steady energy spike to mark his place on the frozen terrain beneath her. She could detect no transmission signal that generated the man's vaporous image.

When Laramy suddenly vanished, Pik cried out in anguish. Where had he gone? When she consulted her scan grid, though, his energy spike still declared his presence. But, where was he?

Leaving Janek drifting safely (she hoped!) in the air, Pik spiraled down in search of her vanished guide. He must have been hidden in the confusion of arctic boulders that comprised the surging glacial surface. He couldn't very well have become invisible. Perhaps he had stumbled and fallen into a crevasse. Was it *her* turn to save *him* now?

For that matter—was he even real? She might have suffered a minor concussion in her fall. "Professor Laramy" could easily be a hallucination. Hazy, immaterial, cryptic, unexplained—he had all the classic earmarks of a delusional manifestation. Had he vanished because she had come to her senses?

As she descended to examine the iceflow, Laramy's head and shoulders rose from the fractured summit of a huge iceberg. "I'm sorry," his hollow voice sounded in her head, "I forgot that you're real…"

Ha. Just as she was beginning to doubt his existence, he apologized for forgetting her own corporeality. If all this *was* a delusion, it was exhibiting a stronger sense of irony than any phantasm Pik had ever heard of. Maybe this was how one knew madness had truly come: when the illusions grew cleverer than the observer.

Protruding now from the icy boulder like some bust statuary, Laramy was waving her down, instructing Pik that the route to his sanctuary was blocked to physical ingress. "You will have to use your awesome weapons to carve an entry tunnel. The weapons you used on His followers back at the death ship."

She called to him, demanding to know what he knew of the crash-landed cruiser and its unfortunate passengers—but he was already gone, ducking down into the unmarked surface of the great wedge of ice, and vanishing from view as he fled underground. All she could do was follow his advice.

Keeping the pulse beam set low, Pik blasted the compacted snow-boulder, reducing it to a shambles of diminutive rubble. The blasts continued to transform the ground into brittle shards, digging a cave into the iceflow. Melted water and granulated ice strained to fill her blast-pit, but the pulse beam scattered such willful debris as it deepened the hole.

"Enough!" came Laramy's desperate call in her head.

Ceasing her blasts, Pik snagged Janek's drifting form and dove into the watery hole she had pierced in the glacier. About ten meters below the surface of this pool (which was already starting to refreeze), she found that her tunnel had dug into rock. Twenty meters of fractured granite deeper, she came to a metal corridor that was filling with spillage from the melted iceflow. Almost hidden by the swirling waters, Laramy's ghostly figure beckoned her from the end of this man-made passage. When she waded near him, Pik realized that the man was gesturing to a large iron wheel set against an airlock door.

Releasing Janek's still-oblivious form, she gripped the access wheel and struggled to turn its ancient width. The device was obstinate, as if it had not budged in centuries. Without the mechanical assistance of her pressure suit, Pik would never have gotten the wheel to budge.

Once the doorway was open, she dove through it, dragging Janek after her like a piece of stolen luggage. Pik did not need Laramy's excited urgings to spur her to close the hatch, stemming the tide of melted glacier that was pouring through the doorway. By the time she got the hatch re-sealed, the chamber was flooded almost to her waist. Janek bobbed at her side, his AG unit keeping him afloat.

Turning from the closed metal portal, she found Laramy standing by an inner doorway. The water rose to his chest, but its rippling waves did not lap against his illusionary flesh. He was smiling and clapping his intangible hands with glee.

Pik wanted to demand that he reveal what he knew about the Opal Cruiser and the people it had stranded on this hellish world, but Janek was rousing. His suit thrashed in the floodwater as he awoke and cried out in disoriented surprise. Soothing him with a curt explanation, Pik brought Janek to his unsteady trio of legs.

"What isss this place?" the Duuian asked.

"This is…was my laboratory," Professor Laramy claimed. "From here, I fought the Ancient Ones and their devilish spawn."

"Who isss *he*?!" This time near-panic resounded in Janek's breathy voice.

"He helped us escape," Pik assured her partner. "We're in his underground base."

"My name is Laramy. Professor Reginald Laramy," the pale man smiled, delivering an archaic bow of greeting. "Perhaps you've heard of me…"

"What were we escaping from, Pik?" Janek asked, swinging his wide head in her direction.

"Ithaqua, the Thing That Walks the Wind," Laramy intoned. "He was after you."

"What—who is this 'Thing' of which this man speaks?" grunted Janek.

"The wind," Pik muttered. "We were…attacked by a great wind…"

"That is absurd."

She shrugged. "Maybe it is. Perhaps someone gained override control of our AG units, flinging us about the sky like fragile toys. Then they threw us to the ground with enough force to kill us. Our defensive shields saved us, though."

"It was Ithaqua," Laramy insisted. "He controls the arctic winds."

"A local despot with a weather control device?" Janek's sensory tendrils undulated while he theorized, "Perhaps this native dictator was responsible for the massacre we found in the Royal Cruiser. Some of the passengers might still be alive, taken captive by this local warlord…"

"Etty…" breathed Pik, hope rising like a sweet gorge in her tense throat.

"Ithaqua is no local warlord," Laramy professed. "His unholy kin are beyond such minor levels of oppression."

"We're strangers to this world, Professor Laramy," Pik spoke up. "I think it's time you explain what's happening here."

"Certainly!" he agreed lustily. "If you'll join me inside. There, you will be more comfortable. But first…" He gestured to a set of controls beside the inner doorway. "I will instruct you which switches to press to activate a drainage system that will clear away this water. Then, when you come inside, you'll be able to relax in a drier state than here…" And so the pale hologram guided Pik through the proper sequence of controls. A gurgling heralded the departure of the water, leaving this chamber empty of the angry fluid. Then Laramy showed her how to open the inner portal, granting access to his subterranean sanctuary.

As she entered this sanctum, Janek's voice hissed conspiratorially on their comlink, "Do you trust this hologram?" She noticed that he was no longer slurring his words; this was a good sign. He was coping with all these fantastic events with a healthy sense of sober distrust.

"For now," she whispered. "He's certainly less threatening than the monster I saw on the far horizon…"

"You saw it too?" Janek wheezed. "I thought I was imagining that horror. It was—so huge! How is so monstrous a beast possible?"

"You're the one who's supposed to know all about old Earth," she reminded him.

"There was *nothing* like what I saw in the data I assimilated. No creature that huge ever existed on this planet—or any other world that I know of, for that matter."

"It jumped into the sky," Pik mumbled, realizing how ridiculous that sounded.

Janek was quick to reiterate his overall disbelief.

Professor Laramy's inner sanctum proved to be exactly what he had claimed: a laboratory, cluttered with apparatus and machinery. Most of the more impressive equipment occupied one side of the room, leaving a corner to function as the occupant's sleeping area. A rickety frame supported a tattered mattress piled haphazardly with ancient books. A decrepit chair sagged before a mound of machinery that had been jury-rigged into a rudimentary control console. The crudely stacked plastic casings were connected by a tangle of exposed wires that dangled from the rear of the machinery. Boxes of books and obsolete computer disks were piled against every surface. A thick coat of dust shrouded everything. Clearly, no one had disturbed these things in many, many years. The room looked more tomb-like than had the Princess' death cruiser.

While, of the flesh-and-blood Professor Laramy, there was no sign. The hazy hologram of his naked self loitered near the custom-rigged console, eyeing his visitors with blatant enthusiasm.

"Well?" Pik sighed. "Here we are… So, where are you?"

The naked man glanced about, as if puzzled by her query. "Have I faded? I thought I had enough power stored to last me for another few days."

"She means," Janek interrupted to elucidate, "where are you transmitting from?"

"I'm not transmitting from anywhere." Hesitantly, Laramy touched his fingertips to his chest, "Unless you mean from *here*, my soul…"

"C'mon," scoffed Pik. "This is just a projected image. Where's your body?"

"*This* is me," the pale Professor declared, patting his chest with the palm of his hand now. Serious creases were traveling across his face as some understanding struck him. "You—you think I still have a body!"

"Doesn't everyone?" Janek sneered (a difficult feat, even with his surgically enhanced nostril-lips).

Laramy shook his sad face slowly, momentarily wearing a fake smile. "No, not forever."

"What—are you some kind of visual construct then?" Pik gasped.

"It'sss an Artificial Intelligence!" cried Janek.

(To effectively comprehend the full scope of the fear response Janek was experiencing, one must consider the A.I. Wars from two centuries ago, wherein organic and digital civilizations clashed over their innate differences. This conflict lasted for over a century, and when it was over: the survivors of both sides retreated to their own parts of the galaxy to lick their wounds and bide their time. This unofficial "armistice" was still in effect, leaving both factions in constant dread that that the other side was conducting secret schemes to revive the War.

(If organic forces were involved in such a covert agenda, Pik had never heard of it, not even among interplanetary urban myth or even in joking. Frankly, she had always thought that—out of all the galactic species—mankind had handled those post-War years the best. Instead of utterly rejecting all forms of high-tech in a paranoid abolishment of the Great Enemy, humanity had simply placed a ceiling limit on the speed of data-processors. As long as technology was kept below a certain point of refinement, no rogue A.I.s could infiltrate human databases or systems networks. The hardwires in Pik's head were a significant upgrade of her natural processing abilities, but alone, these chips couldn't manage to flush a toilet without prior instructions.

(Returning to Janek's anxiety: A.I.s were the galactic bogeymen. While mankind had learned to adapt and keep their computers, most other races took fast-dump solutions, purging their cultures of all digital storage apparatus. Inevitably, this had brought humanity into a ruling position, galactically speaking.

(A.I.s were bad news to human ears, but the topic was capable of sending an alien citizen into a pathological frenzy.)

Laramy cut short Janek's psychotic episode, denying that he was an Artificial Intelligence. "I am…at least, I *was* as human as she is." He pointed to Pik.

"What the grup are you then?"

"I'm dead," Professor Laramy replied. "I thought you knew that..."

"Dead...?" she coughed.

"Absurd!" wheezed Janek.

"Believe me, I am *not* dead by choice," Laramy confided wistfully.

Pik had to laugh. She didn't want to, nor did she need to. She laughed because—if one believed Laramy's claims—his comment *was* funny.

"Sit," the ghost gestured. "I will tell you my tale..."

Pik perched on the edge of the "ghost's" mattress...because there wasn't much else to do. The retrievers were safe here, hidden from the windy clutches of that monster who had sat on the far horizon. Laramy might be insane, but he wasn't dangerous. So far, in fact, he had displayed absolutely no faculty to touch or manipulate physical things. He was quite literally powerless. Why not sit down and hear the crazy man's ghost story?

Janek squatted, splaying his tripod of legs in the Duuian equivalent of "sitting", and he confided to Pik that the room's atmosphere was apparently breathable, according to his scans. Conducting an analysis with her own suit's sensors, Pik verified her partner's findings: the air was an adequate mixture of nitrogen and oxygen with none of the trace gases being harmful. Neither of them, however, deigned to crack their helmets and partake of Earth's natural atmosphere. Considering the ecological hostility they had encountered since arriving on this world, Pik thought that reticence to trust in appearances was understandable.

"You must first picture the abomination that the Earth has become," the ghost began. "In the old days, before most people emigrated offworld, this planet flourished as a cultural paradise. Freedom was available in a wide variety of choices and styles. After the exodus, the remaining population did not abandon that quality of social tolerance...at least, not willingly. It took ages for our skies to darken and the Old Ones to usurp the planet from humanity's sedated fingers."

"I have heard of these 'glory days'," commented Janek. "From old databases chronicling the myths of Earth."

"Myths," Laramy chuckled without humor. "So...to the rest of the galaxy, Earth has become a planet of fabled legend. How ironic that Earth became the victim of *other*, more ancient mythologies. A mythos that proved to be all too horribly real!

"According to 'myth', the Earth was visited in its planetary infancy by creatures of incredible, definably godlike powers. These Old Ones were the losers of a cosmic war, exiled to an insignificant planet way out on the galactic rim: our Earth. But these imprisoned rogue gods were not without cunning and influence—and patience. They slept for ages, allowing a primate species to evolve intelligence. Then, reaching from their eternal tombs, these Old Ones whispered hideous secrets to the dreaming ears of madmen. They beguiled lunatics and rebels, who in turn repeated these ancient legends which now prophesied a time when these condemned monsters would rise and reclaim their stolen glory. Great Cthulhu would awaken from His eternal slumber, and His fortress of R'lyeh would rise from the Pacific Ocean to tower above the clouds. Ithaqua would be loosed from His arctic prison, allowed the freely walk the winds between worlds. Shudde-M'ell and the Burrowers Beneath would replace the planetary mantle, becoming a living underground of sheer terror. Nyarlathotep, Dagon, Yog-Sothoth, Hastur—all these ancient monsters would throw off the cosmic shackles of the Elder Gods and burst forth to reconquer the universe. All this was foretold in arcane and forbidden tomes, occult secrets, tribal tales; even modern literature briefly glorified these myths.

"And then, about three hundred-and-sixty years after the Exodus, the Old Ones rose, proving the factuality of all those malevolent legends! Great Cthulhu rose to unleash His Deep Ones upon the remaining humans. In turn, depraved worshippers of these ancient monsters freed each of the other, lesser beasts. Ithaqua strode beyond his boundaries. Shudde-M'ell threw off his containment spell and reached out under the continents. The Nameless City spilled forth the Undead, and the Mountains of Madness marched north from Antarctica. The world was conquered by alien monsters who had been here on Earth long before man trod this soil!"

Professor Laramy's ghostly face was flushed now with the fervent passion of his dire tale. He paused to widen his pale eyes, conveying that the horror of his account was far from over.

"The awakened and freed Old Ones were over-exuberant with their wrath," Laramy continued. "Millions were slaughtered by the hellish beasts that served the New Lords. Their destructive massacres and cruel subjugation of the surviving masses left them with few victims to lord over. Even their followers numbered in the mere tens of thousands. This depleted population offered Cthulhu and His unholy brethren limited growth potential, especially after the brutality exacted on the heathens during the Awakening. It took over a century, but the monsters finally ran out of victims. The last pureblood human had been sacrificed to the victorious evil. All they could do then was turn against each other.

"Think not, however, that this travesty occurred without massive struggles on the part of certain people—individuals who were versed in the ancient myths—sane men and women who instantly recognized the aberrant atrocities concealed by those legends. They—we, for I was one of these wizards—fought the Deep Ones and the Burrowers and the Walker's beasts of the snow and the terrible shuggoths and even simple human followers, for these deluded mortals were capable of unleashing more terrible beasts if allowed to survive and practice their arcane rituals. We battled these ancient monsters…and we lost. All our efforts were too feeble when the Deep Ones swarmed on a global scale. Through the misuse of corrupted military facilities, the devils of the sea focused every remaining (and secretly cached) nuclear missile on the Marianas Trench in the Pacific. This atomic barrage proved equal to the task of rousing Great Cthulhu from His ancient slumber. The few defenders of Earth who survived that monstrous day were forced to hide ourselves, lest we be hunted down and slaughtered by victory-crazed beasts.

"I came here, to the frigid wasteland, in order to privately battle Ithaqua. In the end, I lost that battle too." The Laramy ghost hung his head in shame. "I hid this laboratory well—for the Walker and His brutish servants never did find it. They caught me out on the ice… After months of huddling in my subterranean sanctuary, I was going stir-crazy. I needed to get out, to see the open sky, to breath unrecycled air, to feel a breeze on my face. Such was my undoing. That succulent breeze trembled, becoming a hurricane gale that flayed the clothes from my body, then the flesh from my bones. I know not whether the Walker was just passing by, or perhaps His minions spotted me and alerted Him. By whatever means, He discovered me by surprise…and killed me with his horrible wind."

"So—now you're a ghost…" Janek impatiently commented.

"Not by choice…but perhaps by design." Laramy reached up to finger a small medallion he wore around his ethereal neck. Small and white against his hazily defined, colorless skin, this necklace had escaped notice by the skeptical retrievers. It was a tiny five-pointed star, and as he handled it, Pik saw that it was not flat, but appeared more like a sculpture of stone. "This talisman," revealed Laramy, "saved my life many times before it failed. Even then, it managed to imbue me with a ghostly afterlife, condemning me to powerlessly watch my enemies go about their unholy, triumphant ways. See?" He gestured to the chamber's walls. "Its power protects this sanctuary even now!"

Pik followed the ghost's pointing finger and saw that four—no, five, for the ceiling was similarly decorated—five star-stones were mounted on the room's walls and ceiling. Rising with a grunt (the bruises from her earlier fall were not responding to her suit's automatic medical treatments), she went over to examine one of these primitive baubles. Up close, it was actually less impressive. From afar, it had seemed simplistic and sleek. From a meter away, she could see that the stone was antediluvian. Cracks and aged chips marred its five-pointed structure. Furthermore, the dense patina of dust that covered it (and even the wall) bestowed a seedy cheapness to the object. It looked more like an archeological reconstruction than any active talisman. Pik almost touched it with a suited finger, but decided against such boldness. Her hesitation was hardly attributable to any belief in the legends or doctrines found in Laramy's ghost story, though. There was something terrible and unclear going on here on old Earth—something the girl did not pretend to comprehend. She had seen enough to recognize that much, but not enough to believe Laramy's horrific explanations. These crude star-stones might be the man's old magic charms…or they might be some devious hidden trap…or they might be wretched artifacts with no other value beyond simple ornamentation. In her opinion, Pik did not know enough to judge either way. Not touching the thing was just…playing it safe.

"Monsters of legend conquered this planet," muttered Janek. "And you're a ghost because your juju gadget gave you an afterlife because it felt guilty for not saving you from your death." Janek had a very excellent grasp of sarcasm; it was one of the first human traits that he mastered to coexist with his partners aboard the ">%".

Apparently, Laramy lacked the perceptive acumen to identify the snideness of Janek's comments. "That's a brutally oversimplified capsulation," the naked ghost nodded grudgingly, "but it is not erroneous concerning the rudimentary elements."

"Absurd!"

Turning from the wall-mounted star-stone, Pik sighed and voiced a sobering opinion. "Possibly…but this planet *has* changed from the one depicted in your database, Janek. *Something* brought about those changes. *Something* killed everyone aboard the Royal Cruiser. *Something* nearly killed us by throwing us all over the sky. *Something* is standing there," she jerked a blunt thumb in Laramy's wispy direction, "telling us about alien invasions. We've encountered nothing but mysterious weirdness since we came to this repulsive planet. There must be some explanation for it all. Why can't it be what Professor Laramy is telling us?"

"But—it is absurd!" Janek persisted.

"It's no more absurd than the fantastic things we've seen."

Janek sputtered, frustrated that his meek personality kept him from pushing his argument.

Pik faced the ghost and questioned him regarding the horrible massacre she had found aboard the crashed Royal Cruiser. In his meandering fashion, he told her how the spaceship had fallen from the sky:

"After my murder, I became…reckless, I suppose you would call it. But then—Ithaqua had taken my life, robbed me of the opportunity to struggle in opposition of the monstrously evil New Lords of the Earth. My star-stone had rescued my soul from the Walker's damnable appetite, but my continued existence—my afterlife, if you wish to call it that—was a hollow consolation. I could now move freely across the countryside, without fear of reprisal or harm from the Walker and His vile agents, but I was unable to inflict any damage to their wicked schemes. I was a ghost; all I could do was observe. So, that is what I did. I traveled, tracking the Thing That Walks the Wind back to His unthinkable lair, monitoring His evil servants as they conducted plans to undermine the resolute domain of His appalling alien cousin, the fiendish Cthulhu. The rest of humanity was dying out, my secret allies and even the witless populace of hiding survivors, all were being steadily hunted down and dragged before an unspeakable fate under the baleful regard of the New Lords. There was no one for me to champion. Soon my war became a theoretical conflict, pitting my harmless and ghostly self against the monsters who had destroyed my world. I watched and I learned—oh, the terrible secrets I have learned!—but I could do nothing with the secrets I uncovered. A spy is useless unless the information he gathers can be passed along to someone capable of acting on such stolen knowledge. But it was too late. There were no more pureblood victims left for the depraved appetite of the New Lords of Earth. I was the last defender. There was no one left who could act on the awful secrets I had discovered."

"The crashed cruiser…?" Pik reminded Laramy's ghost.

"Exactly!" Laramy nodded. "I was alone…until that spaceship plummeted from the sky. Your galactic civilization has forgotten about Earth, no travelers come here. The doomed cruiser was the first contact this planet has had with the rest of the galaxy since the great Exodus that scattered humanity throughout the stellar heavens. I was fortunate enough to be out wandering the glacier when the cruiser came down. First there was the roar, a tumultuous boom that rattled the icebergs across the flowing tundra. Looking up, I saw the clouds surge and spit out something. This object was awash in blue flames as it crossed the lifeless sky, I was unable to make out what it was. I was, at the time, unfamiliar with spacecraft and galactic civilizations; such things had became mythic long before the death of the last Earthbound human. My confusion mixed with hope as I watched the falling *thing* soar across the sky, arcing down to crash on the distant ice. At first, I imagined it was some member of the ruling monstrosity, a rebellious demon spawn that had been cast from Great Cthulhu's lunar palace and exiled to the planetary corpse of Earth. I took pleasure in this supposition, for each monster destroyed was one less murderer left to pay for humanity's awful genocide. I hurried to view the crashsite, hoping to witness the fallen Lord suffer before its aberrant expiration…but such was not what I found.

"The object that descended from the clouds was no dead or wounded monster, it was a construct of metal—made by men! The crash had hardly damaged the sleek and gleaming ship. Scorched by its passage through the thick atmosphere, it had suffered a few dents and scratches, but nothing major, certainly not the extent of injuries you saw when you discovered it. *Those* came later. The cruiser landed on the open glacier, far from even the crudest of settlements occupied by the Walker's minions. Its collision fractured a massive plate of ice, leaving a gigantic crater like some cosmic force had scooped a bowl of frozen landscape from the Earth. Gradually, the glacier filled this crater as it flowed south, carrying the crashed derelict with it on floating chunks of infernal ice. This was later though. When I came to the fallen cruiser, it was still warm from its hellish descent. Its inhabitants were stunned, but still alive.

"There are no walls that can ward off ghostly eavesdroppers. Entering the ship, I wandered its wondrous passages. You can see," Laramy gestured to the hulking and dust-covered machinery that was entombed in his abandoned laboratory, "that I am no stranger to technology, but I could only gawk at the miracles of science which abounded aboard that cruiser. But most of all, I rejoiced to discover that mankind was not dead! The passengers of this fallen spacecraft were *human*—pure in their blood and possessing unblasphemed souls. I will admit, there were a few individuals aboard this fallen spacecraft who exhibited reprehensible social graces and uncommon indecency, but their atrocious behavior mattered not—for they were *human*! How I ached to find a way to communicate with them! Listening to their discussions, I learned that they were ignorant of the doomed world to which they had come. Their crash had been precipitated by a collision with a stray piece of what they called 'space junk', although I privately doubted that Great Cthulhu's monstrous empire had allowed an intruder vessel from beyond to enter this system undetected, unmonitored, and ultimately unharmed.

"These suspicions were soon validated with the arrival of the horrible minions of Ithaqua. They came in hordes, covering the tundra with their filthy, hairy bodies, like an unholy carpet of rats swarming to a feast. The beasts attacked the derelict cruiser, and the human Guards—those brave men who guarded the cruiser's pampered elite—these valiant Warriors slaughtered the Walker's unclean army with weapons of astounding violence. For days, the cruiser was literally buried under a mound of Ithaqua's fallen, bestial troops. Inside, I witnessed the Warriors congratulate themselves for besting the attacking primitives. Even the high society passengers were unaware of the doom that awaited them all.

"To this day, I suspect that Ithaqua's vengeance was visited upon the crashed cruiser for reasons other than any outrage concerning the slaughter of His savage minions by invading humans from space. It was, I believe, the distress call broadcast by the Guards that provoked the Walker's fatal wrath. The reasons for this, I cannot even begin to conjecture, for it seems to me that the New Lords of Earth would adamantly *desire* to attract more outsiders to stumble into their unholy web. A distress call would bring more humans—like *you*—more victims to torture and drive insane. Would this not, in their own blasphemous logic, be a succulent goal?"

Laramy shook his ghostly head, clearly bewildered still by the events he was accounting. "Understanding the Old Ones' evil rationale is a feat that remains quite beyond our human intellect. They think differently from us, their likes and dislikes can never be fathomed by a sane mankind. Even someone such as myself, who has spent nearly two hundred years stalking and studying these monsters, even I am rendered mystified by the serpentine machinations of these devils.

"Within minutes of initiating the distress call transmission, the fallen cruiser was subjected to a concentrated assault by the Wind-Walker Himself! He came like a fearsome hurricane across the glacier, sending icebergs the size of ancient cities tumbling before Him. An instant of this unholy breath was enough to clear the mound of dead beasts that buried the cruiser, the wind quite literally atomizing their corpses with its relentless blast. The cruiser itself remained undisintegrated, but was flung across the frozen landscape as if it were a cardboard vessel.

"Dead, already an immaterial ghost, the Walker's great storm had no effect on me. I was undisturbed by Ithaqua's vicious attack, and left behind as His winds propelled everything to a location kilometers away. It took me some time to trek that distance. By the time I arrived, the Wind-Walker's gruesome vengeance had come and gone. The remains, however, left no doubt as to what had happened. Only the details remained gratefully unrevealed to me.

"Somehow, Ithaqua had gained entry to the interior of the cruiser. The airlock hatch was still secure. There were no punctures in the ship's amazing hull. There may have been vents through which He accomplished access into the death ship, I do not know—I did not conduct a thorough examination of the craft once I found the carnage inside it. My horror and outrage and desolate despair was too intense.

"I found what you found: the liquefied corpses of the Warriors, defeated with a single blast of Ithaqua's fury, then the similarly gruesome remains of the rest of the passengers. All dead. I shudder even now to think what Ithaqua's wrath must have been like: His profane winds tearing through those aerodynamic corridors, violating locked rooms via airducts, leaving not an inch of the ship unscoured by His gale's rage. I only pray that the end came quickly for those brave Warriors and the pampered passengers, that the Walker did not dally to torture their souls as they died.

"To you, those dead people are just 'people'. Their deaths were horrible, indeed *any* death is horrible. But to me, those people represented the future. Until that day, I believed that the Old Ones had destroyed mankind, leaving only ghostly survivors. Those poor individuals who crash-landed here proved to me that humanity lived on, that my race still existed. Their very existence made hope reappear in my battle-wearied heart. Their deaths were an obliteration of that hope, annihilated by the very forces that had slaughtered the rest of mankind. For a few days, I had been suddenly shown that the New Lords had *failed* to extinguish humanity… only to have that optimistic future erased by the hated Wind-Walker.

"The evil potential of the New Lords of Earth is boundless and beyond mortal comprehension.

"But the horror was not over yet, for someone came in response to the cruiser's fateful distress call—your companion who you call Etty."

"You saw Etty!" cried Pik.

"It was my secret hope—and *fear*—that someone would answer the death ship's distress call. I *hoped* those rescuers would be human, vindicating the future that Ithaqua and His kind had destroyed. I *feared* that those rescuers would fall prey to the same terrible destruction reserved by the Old Ones for all humans.

"Alas, I was not the only one who watched the battered and lifeless cruiser now. Ithaqua had assigned a tribe of his hoary servants to guard the wreckage, forever alert to the possibility that others might come from the sky to rescue the unfortunates who now stained the bulwarks within the crashed spaceship.

"I watched your companion descend from the foreboding clouds, knowing fully that other, malicious eyes observed this man's approach. There was no way I could warn him away, for he was unlikely to see or hear my spectral counsel."

"But *we* can," commented Janek.

"Yes. This puzzles me. I was utterly unable to communicate with any of the cruiser's occupants. So, when your companion appeared, I made no attempt to announce myself. I thought I was condemned to the helpless role of a worried spectator, until you," the Laramy ghost nodded to Pik, "seemed to see me when I followed you deep inside the death ship. If only—if only I had known! Perhaps my advice could have averted the fate that befell your lost companion..."

"They got him, didn't they?" Pik whispered fearfully. "This Wind-Walker's minions..."

"Yes. They swarmed on him, overpowering him with the weight of their sheer numbers. Before he was able to employ any weapons, however, a shaman beast cast a separation rune, physically removing him from his protective spacesuit as he tried to hide in the cruiser's drained engine core."

"The core was already empty?" Janek interrupted. "Do you know how that happened?"

"Grup the stupid drive core!" screamed Pik. "What happened to Etty?!"

"They took him—the Walker's bestial minions."

"Took him—where?!"

"I can only assume they delivered the poor man to Ithaqua. May God rest his unfortunate soul..."

"But—you didn't see them kill him!" she gasped. "Etty—he could still be alive!"

"It is highly unlikely," mumbled Professor Laramy. "Remember, the Walker spared no one from the cruiser."

"Maybe your wind demon has learned from its mistakes," Janek noted sarcastically.

Pik's head was swimming. Riding a tidal wave of Laramy's absurd (as Janek had frequently pointed out) ghost story, there came the possibility that Etty was not dead! *My Etty has survived, and is a captive of Ithaqua, the Thing That Walks the Wind…or Ithaqua, the local despot whose ruthless habits converted Earth into a frozen wasteland.* Did it matter whether Laramy's tale of ancient monsters was fact or fancy? *Either way,* she fretted, *something (in the devout service of a fearsome ruler) has captured Etty with the intent of presenting him (as some cruel trophy?) to a being who claims to be a monster from the dawn of time. The brutal evil of this fearsome ruler had been aimed at myself and Janek, just hours ago,* that *was not an exaggeration of Laramy's story. It doesn't matter how you assemble the possible facts, Etty is in trouble—and I have to save him!*

Unthinking, Pik rushed Laramy, clutching to grab him by the shoulders and shake the truth out of the naked ghost. Her gloved fingers flew through his ephemeral flesh and crashed against the concrete wall behind his wispy body. "Tell me!" she shouted. "Where is he? Where have they got my Etty?"

Pik's assault decidedly unnerved Professor Laramy. With a soft squeak, the ghost retreated from her outburst, entering the concrete wall and vanishing from view.

"Get back here!" Pik bellowed, pounding her fists on the wall. "You have to tell me!"

"Pik," hissed Janek. "Control your subcranial secretions. He is not going to help us if you continue to act like a madwoman."

Subduing her panic wasn't easy, but she pulled it off. Slumped with the crown of her helmet pressed against the concrete wall, she sobbed and weakly begged Laramy to help her save her beloved.

Moving to the opposite side of the room, Janek gave Pik the time to recompose herself. His curiosity drew him to the piles of modular equipment. He crouched to examine the simple keyboard that functioned as the interface controls. Within minutes, the Duuian had mastered the console and was reviewing the contents of Professor Laramy's ancient database. Whatever he found, it completely engaged his attention. Periodically, Janek would whistle an admission of impressed surprise.

"He is special to you," whispered Laramy's ghostly voice in Pik's head.

She relaxed one eye and peered away from the concrete surface, turning her head inside the transparent helmet. To her side, she could see his ghost hesitantly standing half-in/half-out of the wall. His pale face wore an expression of anguish.

"Yes," she admitted. Clearly, Laramy was not dead to the memory of physical and emotional love. The girl's outburst had been plain evidence that Etty was "special" to her. Laramy regarded Pik with open sympathy.

He muttered a long, introspective monologue, speaking more to himself than to the girl. Which was a good thing, for Pik's grief had welled up again, and she was briefly lost in a mental maelstrom of sorrow. She did not hear most of what he declared, catching only fragmentary passages from his vehement self-analysis. "...thought my will was stronger than the Evil Ones, how blind my arrogance made me...failed to save my wife from the...all my power and knowledge...failed to save even my own life..." Somehow, these things connected in Laramy's head, drawing him from the empathic depths of despair to a state of overpowering confidence. Assigning himself the role of guide, he swore to conduct the retrievers in a search for their captive companion, no matter what dreadful monsters were met along the route.

His determination and confidence were intoxicating, though. But then, Pik was easy prey for a solid pep talk...especially when the punchline turned out to be: let's save Etty. She was willing to walk through nuclear fire to save her beloved. Facing unknown monsters on a mythic planet was no more taxing a feat to perform. *After all*, she privately smiled, *they're only "monsters". We've got pulse cannons.*

"Fear not," Laramy was announcing, "I will help you rescue your companion. The monstrous depravities visited upon the human race by the Old Ones cannot be allowed to continue. Etty must not become their latest victim. Their reign of corruption must end. Let this moment be testament to my vow to aid these brave galactic visitors in their battle to eradicate the New Lords of Earth!" As he preached, he lifted his arms to shake fists at the ceiling. He paused, for his passion had left the spirit momentarily breathless.

"They will have taken your companion to Ithaqua's aerial lair," Laramy declared once he had reclaimed his ghostly wind. "You are fortunate! I am the only mortal to have ever seen the Walker's unhallowed castle...although I achieved this distinction posthumously. I will lead you there, and we will rescue your companion and exterminate the evil Wind-Walker in his vile lair."

Whatever gets you in the mood, Professor, Pik ruminated. *I'm planning to rescue my Etty and then get both our asses (and Janek's too) as far away from this abhorrent planet as the ">%" can take us. If any of your ancient imaginary monsters get in my way, they're history. I will not stop until*

I've saved Etty. But then—I do stop. Your Great Cause will have to run on its own momentum once Etty is safe.

"Our bravery," the ghost was rattling on, "will inspire the entire galaxy to unify to abort Great Cthulhu's repulsive dominion of human soil!"

Professor Laramy could afford to bluster with courage and defiance of his ancient enemies. He was already dead. The murderous Wind-Walker's bestial minions weren't going to waste time attacking a ghost. Pik and Janek would be the meat at risk.

Before approaching the misted planet, Tarn consulted his transport flier's database for details concerning his destination. When he found that the most current profile of this world was woefully stale-dated, he rejected the files and set himself to a rigid examination of his target. Utilizing his flier's sensory array, he compiled a remarkably intimate portrait of the conditions extent on this frontier world where the pampered favorite Nimbus Family Brat had gotten herself royally stranded.

The mean equatorial gravity was astoundingly close to a standard G. What his equipment could perceive through the dense cloudcover seemed to indicate that the world's climate and environmental conditions were both within tolerable parameters to support human-class life. (This data implied that the chances were thin that the Princess had choked to death on a poisonous atmosphere.) No radio sources were detected, nor any evidence of high-energy concentrations. This contradicted the presence of hardware orbiting the planet. Clearly, there had once been an indigenous society here, one that had obviously mastered space travel, at least as far as their moon, if those amazing towers were any indication.

Tarn found himself immediately wary of those enormous structures. Their scale (where had the necessary materials come from?), their construction (how many centuries had it taken to build—or grow—those things?), their continued existence (what magic kept these towers intact and unbothered by tidal stress or a hundred other forces prohibiting the presence of such anomalous structures?)...these mysteries gnawed at Tarn's strategic assessment of the target destination. Did they have anything to do with the Princess' crash? Perhaps the Brat's space yacht had slammed into one of the towers during a reckless joyride through uncharted territory.

The planet's moon belligerently refused to give up any information about itself to his flier's deepest scans. Its atmosphere was simply too compressed; it even seemed to possess highly reflective qualities when it came to most frequencies. This might have concerned him if his target had been beneath its impenetrable ocean.

The Royal Cruiser popped on Tarn's scanners, placing the crashsite in the planet's polar regions. The ship failed to respond to basic broadcasts, but that could be attributable to interference from the stormy atmosphere lurking beneath the planet's opaque cloudcover.

At no time did any of these anomalies prompt any conscious dread in the Warrior. He did not remain oblivious to foreboding or prescience of disaster, though, for he knew all too well how hostile a universe it was. Everything, sentient and inanimate, secretly schemed to take his life. After the brutal murder of his parents and village on Furnace 17, Tarn had embraced a personal creed of "expect the unexpected, and never again be caught by surprise." Upon the conclusion of his second year in the Nimbus Space Navy, he had decided to make Warrior his lifetime career. He had dedicated himself, body and soul, to becoming the best soldier he could be. Twelve years later, Tarn was battle-worn (as evidenced by his numerous burn scars and the artificial arm he wore) and wiser (more specifically: cynical), but he languished still in the dregs of military ranks, overlooked and unnoticed.

This assignment would change that. Rescuing the Favorite Daughter was a major achievement, even if the Brat did get herself "lost" every few months. The Royal Family would reward his courage with a promotion— finally after all these years. And all he had to do was do what he did best: be a Warrior.

In truth, the promotion would be as meaningful as his "rescue". He was not the first Warrior to be sent to save the Royal Family's rambunctious daughter, he would not be last. His reward would be an insignificant gesture in the great scheme of things. Little would change for Tarn, except his inner sense of self-worth. After an initial rush and pride, he would undoubtedly find his anger and resentment unscathed.

He donned his battle armor and left his flier in orbit. Descending into the murky clouds, he pinpointed the crashed cruiser on his suit's systems, programming a direct trajectory for that location. He paid scarce heed to the environment, concentrating on monitoring his defensive perimeter as he fell through the sky. These clouds could harbor a thousand hidden traps…but they were clean. When the ground swept into view, he spotted the mangled Royal Cruiser on the frozen landscape. He landed without difficulty.

Finding the airlock hatch already open was a bad omen to Tarn.

Finding the ship deserted puzzled him.

Finding the blood-smear remains of the cruiser's crew was the absolute last thing he expected—for his active imagination had busily concocted wild scenarios in his mind while he searched the gloomy death ship, desperate attempts to logically explain the missing passengers. Failed attempts... for he had never pictured them all slaughtered. Kidnapped by anarchists, yes; relocated by local benefactors; even asleep—but *never* all dead.

He stared at the gory corridor, noticing the chunks of battle armor here and there. These had been the Princess' Royal Guards, elite caste Warriors. What superior force had defeated them in so gruesome a manner?

When he found the splattered remains of what he assumed to be the Royal Entourage, Tarn's horror started to transform into personal concern. He did not fear for his own life aboard the crashed yacht, he dreaded the prospect of returning to inform the Nimbus Family of the grisly demise of their Favorite Daughter. Their Royal Reaction would be terrible, and he would be the only focus of such wrath. Decommissioned? He'd be lucky if they settled for just decapitating him for losing their darling Princess.

"Def," he swore aloud. "She can't be dead..."

When he found the drive core open and drained of all power, a cloud of abject confusion temporarily blinded his anger. A drained plasma core was an outright impossibility. This was no ordinary crash-landing. He began to suspect hidden agendas at work...alien menaces stealing human technology to advance their own intellectually-challenged civilizations. Maybe even—no, it *must not* be the return of the abominable A.I.s! Most likely, it was the native species, the ones who had built those gigantic equatorial towers that stretched far beyond the planet's stratosphere. Possessing no power grid of their own, the locals must have stolen the plasma core's power.

But why had they killed everyone aboard? What cultural principle had the cruiser violated to warrant such a dreadful retribution? The energy thieves had to be psychotic, to risk enraging the Nimbus Royal Family by murdering their Favorite Daughter.

"Maybe she's not really dead," he muttered to himself. "The Royal Family will want proof...but how do I produce a body from this muck?" Then he recalled the tracer implanted in the Favorite Daughter. If that device could be found here, among the grisly remains, then it could be strongly argued that the Princess had suffered the same destruction as the other defenseless passengers.

But the tracer refused to be found. It did not answer its trigger code, nor was its wreckage lurking in the slimed viscera that coated the party chamber.

That would mean that Princess Eden still lived! Tarn praised the Royal Brat's uncanny survival potential, for her death would surely have doomed his own fate. Now, he would live! He might even still score that promotion. All he had to do was find the lost Princess.

"If I were her," the Warrior mused, "where would I go to escape this blood-soaked carnage?" Having searched the entire ship and found no cowering Princess, the obvious answer was: the Brat had run outside. Into the cold.

Def, I'm going to have to comb the entire glacier to find her corpse now...

He cursed the vindictive nature of circumstance, for it was relentless in dogging his life with problematic annoyances. Whatever the route of most resistance might be, *that* was always his unavoidable destiny.

Outside the death ship, though, Tarn's scan was still unable to pick up any trace of the Princess' telltale. No matter how wide he opened his sensory array, the Princess' implant remained undetected, invisible, non-existent.

This, he knew, was highly unlikely. If the Royal Brat had fled the ruined cruiser, she had done so on foot. How far across this hostile landscape could a lone girl get? Her body should be out there, within a radius of a few kilometers of the cruiser. Her telltale should still be transmitting. Why wasn't it?

Obviously: because the Princess was still alive, and she was no longer in the vicinity of her crashed Royal Cruiser.

According to Tarn's analysis of the murder scene, the slaughter had occurred days ago. If she had been removed from the cruiser, her abductors could have moved her *anywhere* by now. They might not even be holding her on this world.

That was Tarn's immediate priority: to establish whether the Princess was even still on this planet. To achieve that, he would have to conduct a scan of the entire globe. Such a task required an overview best attained by his flier in orbit. Except...the dense planetary cloudcover would render such signals thoroughly unreliable.

Again, fate was making his job as difficult as possible.

While standing on the hull beside the open airlock, considering these factors, his artificial senses noticed a movement below him. Something was skulking through the icy rubble that surrounded the cruiser's broken wreckage. He examined the frozen boulders in the infrared, and discovered several humanoid shapes crouching behind them. From their posture and furtive actions, their hostility was obvious to Tarn's Warrior instincts.

Could these be the ones who kidnapped the Princess?

With professional efficiency, Tarn saturated the region with a numbing subsonic field, rendering the covert figures unconscious with a single humming wave. Then he climbed down from the cruiser to survey his hidden adversaries.

What he found convinced him that *these* beasts could not be responsible for the Princess' absence. They were far too primitive to achieve such galactic cunning. He nudged one of the animals with the boot of his battle suit. It had a bipedal humanoid form, but the creature was covered with coarse, matted hair. Its cranium was sloped, and its teeth were large and carnivorous. Its ears appeared to be of canine configuration.

"Just beasts," Tarn muttered. "Hunting the tundra in packs." He shook his head in self recrimination. He had been too eager to blame the first individuals he encountered.

What was that—?

While waggling his face to-and-fro, he had caught a glimpse over his shoulder of something hovering in the air behind him. He focused his attention (natural, enhanced, and artificial) on the object. Targeting graphics popped in his vision, tracking the unknown thing with deadly intent.

"That's someone in a pressure suit!" he realized. A survivor of the cruiser's massacre? Or one of the kidnappers? A second later, after a more detailed examination of his scan, he grunted with further surprise, "No… that's *just* a pressure suit."

What the def is an empty suit doing here?

⁕

Following Professor Laramy's ghost across the glacial countryside proved to be a tedious endeavor. Although Laramy no longer possessed a mortal body, his spirit seemed restricted to ambulatory travel. While Pik and Janek were able to fly above the desolate wasteland, the ghost was forced to crawl across the frozen landscape.

The pace was frustrating for Laramy, who was still wired with his delusion of waging a last-stand battle against the monstrous quasi-deities that he believed had destroyed his world.

Pik knew the speed of their trek was driving *her* frantic, but then she was naturally impatient. The retrievers needed to *follow* a guide who was moving far *slower* than they could travel. Every second's delay could have meant the difference between life and death for Etty.

She expected that Janek shared her impatience, but he found other outlets for his tension.

Flying nearby, the Duuian confided to her what he had found among Laramy's ancient database, "There is evidence to support much of Laramy's tale of monstrous New Lords usurping this world from mankind. Earth's forces were indeed defeated by some kind of alien invasion. There are ample news files documenting this ill-fated conflict. Later files corroborate that these alien conquerors seemed intent on exterminating humanity after the War. The most current datapack found in the Professor's database dates from before the extinction of the human race on Earth, though. Regarding events that occurred after Laramy's death, we have only the ghost's absurd accounts."

"What reason would he have to lie to us?" Pik cajoled her partner.

"He does not have to be *lying* to be reciting false information, Pik. He could be—indeed, he seems to be—quite insane."

"He's a dead man, stranded on a world ruled by the murderers of his entire race. Something like that is liable to unbalance even the sturdiest mind."

"I found evidence that undermines the Professor's credibility. Several news files mentioned him, describing him as 'a crank'. Apparently, Laramy repeatedly tried to publicize his fantastic theories regarding the origins of the invading aliens. His 'warnings' were ignored, and even became a matter of public ridicule. The Professor's personal files recount his retreat from society at that time, after which he secretly constructed the underground laboratory we saw.

"The man is a fanatic," asserted Janek. "He is an unreliable source of relevant information."

"He's the only one we have," Pik reminded the Duuian. "Without him, we'll never find Etty..."

"Have you considered why it is that *we* can see and hear this ghost? But Etty and the cruiser's passengers and Guards could not?" When she gave no reply, he snorted, "Of course not. You are obsessing over rescuing Etty...to the extent of blinding yourself to the questionable situation around us."

"You can wait in the '>%' if you want," she snarled.

"I am just as dedicated to saving Etty as you, Pik. I do not need to mate with him to consider him my partner. But—I am equally concerned with guarding my own life. We are rushing into a dangerous situation, trusting the word of a deceased fanatic. How can we be sure that Laramy's imaginary Wind-Walker is the villain that has Etty? For all we know, Laramy could be deceiving us in order to revive his ancient war. This man's enemies are not necessarily *our* enemies."

These doubts were hardly unknown to Pik. These thoughts—and worse—had crossed her worried mind as she followed the tedious path of Laramy's ghost across the arctic wasteland. The information Janek had found in the dead Professor's database only served to enforce her suspicions, exactly as they had disturbed Janek.

But—it did not matter if Professor Laramy was telling the truth, or whether he was an obsessed zealot determined to seek vengeance on those he imagined had wiped out humanity. As Pik had reminded Janek: the ghost was their only hope of rescuing Etty. And that was all that mattered to her now.

Below, she saw that Laramy had fallen behind. He appeared to be struggling with something on the plain of a tottering ice slab. Signaling her partner, Pik swung around to investigate the ghost's problem.

"What's the matter?" she called to the wispy figure below. Approaching, Pik gasped to discover that Laramy's was not the only ghostly figure struggling on the icy precipice. Laramy fought with another specter, one whose ferocity was proving superior to the man's determination. "Hey!" she yelled.

She had intended to startle Laramy's opponent, but it was the Professor who tumbled into her verbal trap. The beastly ghost threw Laramy to the frozen ground, falling upon him with slavering jaws and wild, glowing eyes. It was, she saw, one of the hairy creatures that had attacked Janek and herself outside the wreckage of the Princess' cruiser.

So...Laramy was not the only one to have beaten death. Even his enemy had servants beyond the grave.

Pik lunged to help, but succeeded only in shattering the iceberg under their immaterial feet, plunging them all into the murky slush of the glacier. She found it briefly ironic that this immersion into the deathly freezing temperature of the viscous ice flow failed to bother any of them. Her suit protected her from the deadly chill, while Laramy and his bestial antagonist were beyond any mortal tactile concerns. They were, apparently, though, vulnerable to ghostly violence. The breakage of the ice slab had upset the beast's grip on Laramy. The man took this opportunity to lock his spectral hands around the animal's neck. As they bobbed in the semi-frozen underlayer of the glacier, huge chunks of floating boulders flowed by, passing through these intangible combatants. Pik, however, was forced to dodge these rushing obstacles.

By the time she resurfaced, Laramy had pinned his adversary atop a craggy iceberg. As Pik watched, the ghostly Professor plunged his hands into the beast's spiritual forehead. With a mighty pull, he drew forth handfuls of jagged color. Then he stuffed these brilliant lights into his spectral mouth, greedily swallowing the screaming energy. As Laramy continued to consume the beast's hazy form, Janek joined Pik to stare on in horror. When every last wisp had been inhaled by the Professor's ghost, he peered up at the hovering armored forms and gave the aghast retrievers a weakly apologetic smile.

"What the grup was *that*?" demanded Janek.

"That was one of Ithaqua's undead servants," the ghost declared honestly. "The Walker has dispatched many of His minions in hopes of tormenting my afterlife."

"No," Janek barked. "That—what you did to the beast—"

Pik growled, "You...you ate the thing, didn't you?"

"Well, yes," Laramy admitted with equal honesty. "I need to replenish my energies. My talisman is very old, its magic cannot sustain me unaided. I steal the ectoplasm from these undead beasts that the Walker sends to kill me. I am just defending myself..."

"Eating your opponent goes a bit beyond 'defending' yourself, Professor Laramy," the girl sternly told the ghost.

"I told you, I need energy to remain as I am."

"A ghost. What happens if you don't? Do you revert to a man?"

"Don't be ridiculous. No, of course not," he frowned at Pik's bluntness. "I'm dead. Without the necessary energy to supplement my starstone's reanimation efforts, I would dissipate...and cease to exist."

"Sedate yourself, Pik. The Professor's actions are no different than any mortal lifeform," Janek commented. "We consume the flesh of other living things to sustain our own biological existence."

The Duuian was right. Pik needed to stifle her outrage. The shock of seeing such an unexpected act of cannibalism had momentarily triggered visceral reactions in her primal psyche. But Janek was right, it was no different from other beings. This was simply part of the ghostly foodchain, an ectoplasmic ecology which Pik could never begin to understand...until she herself died. Necessary or not, though, she never wanted to witness it again.

"So, you're recharged then?" she asked the Professor. "We can resume our journey?"

"Umm..." Laramy's ghost averted its eyes guiltily.

"What?" lamented Pik. "You're not going to abandon us now, are you?"

"I..." the Professor fidgeted under her raging glare. "Things have... changed..."

"Nothing has changed!" she declared angrily. "We still need to rescue Etty!"

"I warned you he was unreliable," muttered Janek on their private comlink.

"But...our assault on the Wind-Walker's unholy castle..." Laramy muttered to himself for a moment, his utterances too low to be decipherable. Then he stood erect, facing Pik and Janek with blazing heroics. "You are right! The salvation of your companion must precede our ultimate defeat of the evil Old Ones. Even now, his life is in more dire threat than we previously suspected."

"What— What's going on?" Pik demanded.

"I have learned things," the Professor's ghost revealed, "from assimilating the undead beast's ectoplasm. This minion of Ithaqua was newly deceased, it carried the memories of certain incredible events that have transpired in just this last day. It knew about the capture of your companion, who was intended for direct deliverance to the Lord of the Winds. But something happened earlier today, and this human captive is no longer headed north to Ithaqua's aerial castle. He is borne south now, headed for the equatorial Spires of Condemnation.

"Ache as I do to attack and vanquish the vile Walker in the sanctity of His own blasphemous lair, first we must save your companion. For his future now is bleaker than any being's has ever been in human history. Your lost partner has been summoned to the incarnate presence of the Great Cthulhu Himself!"

"What?!" Pik cried aloud in anguish.

"More monsters of myth," Janek sputtered derisively.

"Not just any beast of legend," Laramy professed. "Cthulhu is the supreme Lord of the monsters that rule the Earth. From his aquatic throne on the moon, the Great Cthulhu commands every molecule of terran air, every grain of soil on the planet. Even the other Old Ones bow to Cthulhu's accursed divinity. His terrible presence even taints the substance of mortal dreams. Supposedly, to even stare upon the Great One's naked visage is enough to drive any man insane!"

"What could your great demon want with Etty?" chided Janek. "He's just a man."

"Exactly!" wailed Laramy's ghost. "He is a *man*! A human! In a world that has not seen untainted human flesh in nearly two centuries!"

"So, Etty is going to be killed by this Cthulhu instead of the Wind-Walker," remarked Pik. "He still needs to be saved."

"The Great Cthulhu will not waste your companion's flesh on simple torture or murder. The Evil One will use your friend to propagate a new race of victims for His unholy blood-thirst."

"Etty is a male," Janek coughed. "Your Great Demon would have been wiser to kidnap Pik if he was looking for human offspring."

Pik shot him a nasty look, but again…Janek was correct. Cthulhu would get no children from Etty's "womb."

"It will not matter to the Evil Lord," the Professor was shouting. "The Old Ones possess unnaturally virile miscegenetic properties. They are masters of cellular manipulation. They *will* impregnate your companion, be he male, female, or neuter. He *will* bear the Great Cthulhu's children!"

This is madness, Pik told herself. *Such things aren't possible. Are they…?*

How much did she actually know of the technologies wielded by these New Lords of Earth? It mattered not whether they were deadly monsters of myth or simply cunning aliens—their achievements were accountable to whatever "technology" they possessed. Laramy may have called it "magic", but that was only because he remained ignorant of the precise instrumentality of that "magic." Without doubt, the powers that kept him alive after death were attributable to the unknown science behind the man's ancient star-stone. Whatever "powers" these terrible New Lords controlled were similarly attributable to some fantastic technology which remained unfamiliar to Pik and Janek.

She knew these New Lords could control environmental conditions, as evidenced by the changes the Earth and its moon had undergone during their reign, and further exhibited by the Wind-Walker's assault on herself and Janek earlier in the sky above the tundra. She knew that "someone" had raised those monstrous spikes from the planet's equator into space—that achievement alone was proof of frightening skill on a cosmic scale.

She began to understand why Laramy saw these New Lords as mysterious deities, their abilities certainly defied normal grandeur.

But—unlimited command over the cellular physiology of another species? That was a bit much to accept. Even if these monsters were audacious enough to attempt such horrific miscegenation, how adept could their efforts be, working with a foreign DNA they had not encountered in two centuries? Indeed, their clumsy mistakes could be as fatal to poor Etty as their devilish intentions.

Whatever Etty's gruesome destiny at the hands of his fiendish captors, he needed to be rescued!

When Pik announced this determination, Janek and the human ghost vigorously agreed with her.

"We must catch the party carrying your friend before they reach the Spires of Condemnation. For once the beasts have sent him aloft, his doomed fate is immutably sealed!"

We're never going to outrace anyone to this planet's equator if we're forced to keep pace with Laramy, Pik ruminated with frustration. *Unfettered by the necessity to pace ourselves with this sluggish guide, Janek and I could soar at suprasonic velocities, outdistancing the party taking Etty to his fateful delivery.* She caustically confronted the ghost with this dilemma.

Laramy responded to this suggestion with desperate opposition. "I *must* go with you! You will never find your friend without my guidance. The Spires are far, far away. They are many, you'll not know which one they are taking him to..." He rambled further, his excuses and justifications growing weaker with his every spectral breath.

"Saving Etty is our priority," she reminded the ghost. *Not waging a war against your enemies.* This, Pik was certain, was the root of Professor Laramy's need to guide them to their destination. Without his presence, there would be no Armageddonic conflict between the retrievers and the alien dictators that held his world.

"You must tell us which spire to head for," Janek was demanding.

While Professor Laramy's ghost struggled with his conscience, Pik realized that they hardly needed the Professor's advice on this matter. If the New Lords of Earth were rushing Etty to their Great Master, haste would be in proportionate effect. The party transporting Etty would take a direct path to the nearest massive spike. All Pik had to do was to aim herself for the nearest spike and fly at full thrusters. She would get there before any land-moving troop; in fact, she might even catch up with them en route and retrieve Etty then-and-there.

Before Pik could share these thoughts with Janek, the Professor's ghost relented. In a flood of over-anguished words, Laramy confessed the gist of what she had surmised: that Ithaqua's bestial couriers would head directly for the closest Spire of Condemnation. "Go south," he sobbed. "You will see it in the sky long before you reach its terrible base." He babbled a lot of other stuff too, about how much he bemoaned not being witness to the battle his galactic defenders would wage against the vile New Lords. He was erroneously convinced that the hunters were going to dethrone these mighty monsters, acting out a vengeance he was no longer capable of affecting. Pik chose to not correct his assumptions. Janek too seemed equally unwilling to challenge the ghost's delusions. He quietly thanked Laramy for his assistance.

With vague farewells, the retrievers flew into the sky. Their billowing acceleration soon left the grieving human ghost far in their wake.

Praylude:
Excerpts from the Diary of a Crank

The unthinkable has happened.

Nukes have been launched—but not in mankind's defense. The Deep Ones have usurped control of old military installations. They have nuclear capacity, and they've used it!

Now that it is too late, the tattered remains of the Authorities have called upon my expertise. Sequestered in a secure command base with these defiant heroes, I am privy to the cataclysmic end of the war. I am witness to the Awakening.

If only they had listened to me at the beginning. Would that have averted humanity's downfall? Or would even my occult talents have proven inadequate in the face of such a monstrous evil?

At first we had all been confused, but now we are despondent. The Deep Ones had launched a nuclear attack—on themselves! What madness was this? So devious a madness that its purpose was insanity incarnate? At the brink of eradicating mankind, had the enemy chosen self-destruction?

Or self-release?

As a thousand missiles converged on the center of the Pacific Ocean, I realized with dreadful fatalism what was happening. Of course the Authorities are ultimately blind to the Deep Ones' nefarious scheme, for those refugee generals do not hold the same unholy beliefs as the aquatic abominations. The courageous generals fight for life and survival of the species. The enemy fights to free their dreaming god from His ancient slumber.

As a devotee of arcane mythology (which has turned out to be rather unmythlogical in the end), I am familiar with the Mad Arab's infamous couplet:

> "That is not dead which can eternal lie,
> And with strange eons even death can die."

Although its exact location is gratefully unknown to any sane creature, the blasphemous denizens of the deep know where the Isle of R'yleh lies submerged in equatorial depths. And now, staring at the screens that track the awful nuclear barrage, I too know the coordinates of Great Cthulhu's sunken temple.

The Deep Ones are bombing their sleeping deity! They're going to awaken Him!

There is no way of knowing what the effects will be of thousands of nuclear detonations on the Old One's legendary imprisonment. It is an enigma—the effects of mortal physics on the elder bonds that confine the Evil One. A clashing of two different ideologies, two dissimilar sciences.

I pray that the most powerful weapon devised by man fails.

But my prayers go unanswered.

The bombs drop. They explode, venting a cosmic fury upon the ocean's floor, transmuting elements and warping space.

I do not need to see what is happening at the bottom of the Marianas Trench to know that a horrendous atrocity has awakened. Even as I write this account, the psychic ether is thickening with His repulsive wrath. Around me, the generals are pulling at their hair, tearing their own eyes from their sockets in a desperate attempt to escape the contaminated dreams.

The nightmare has escaped from dreamland, and doom walks the Earth.

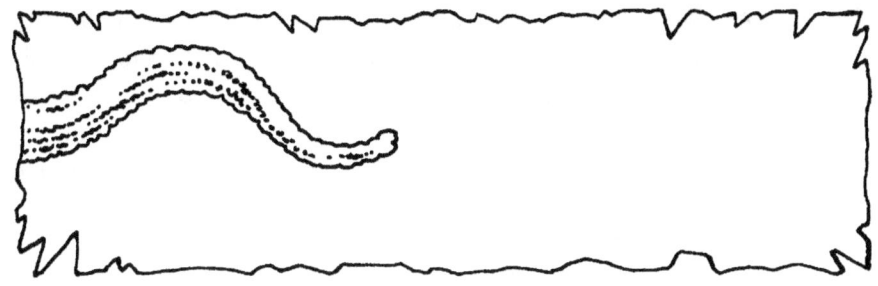

section 2:
Assigning Charm and Spin

Madness was surely upon Etty, delving deep into the folds of his tender brain, tainting each synapse with bedlam and dread. If only these mental afflictions were unreasoning, but alas, Etty was certain of his hopeless plight.

He had seen the terrible stains that were all that remained of the cruiser's doomed occupants.

He had witnessed the beasts that swarmed upon him inside the crashed spacecraft. He had fled from those monsters, but being unfamiliar with the ship's layout, he had found himself trapped in a cul-de-sac—where he had discovered the impossibly empty drive core. There he had hidden in foolhardy confidence, but the beasts had tracked him. Cornered, Etty had been about to unleash the firepower of his pulse weapons (and damn the consequences of pulse ricochets within the ship's narrow passages) when dementia had reached out and plucked him from the safety of his pressure suit. Then the screaming beasts had been on him, battering him unconscious with their smelly fists.

His feverish coma was populated by bestial phantasms and absurd beliefs. Rough hands covered with fecally fouled hair scrabbled at his naked flesh. The fetid breath of these creatures was forced into his uncooperative lungs. No matter how tightly he squeezed shut his eyes, his vision still stung from these gruesome visions. He saw beasts lavish their tongues to the task of cleaning the bloodstained walls of the cruiser. He saw monsters mate with icy boulders, bringing forth bilious issue that rose expanding and dissipating into a cursed sky. He saw a monstrously huge shadow occlude the sky as it lumbered near to scoop him from the glacier. Held aloft in a maelstrom of conflicting gales, he faced a hideous red eye, burning from within with the fury of an exploding star. It loomed close to examine his insignificant humanity.

Voices in a language wisely eradicated from civilized society muttered in a darkness so absolute that even his dreaming imagination refused to go there. The syllables were guttural and obscene, forming unknown words and incomprehensible sentences. The only meaning conveyed by their sound was an expression of blasphemous sovereignty, arrogant and monstrously certain. And yet fleeting concepts accompanied these profane noises as they swam into Etty's mind, as if some obsolete gland in his brain harbored a primal recollection of such terrible consonants.

Things that had walked the Earth long before man. Infant species which had been dragged to a soulless maturity to serve these horrific Things. A time of violent repast and covetous motives. War between the Things, conflicts fought by their servant beasts. A cosmic cataclysm, resulting in the defeat and eternal punishment of the Old Things. In the long ages after this mighty war, the natural order of evolution had resumed on the Earth, producing species that became fish and reptiles and mammals and birds and finally: man. A time of subtle influence by the imprisoned Things, nudging deviant men in unholy directions. The ultimate fruition of these inhuman whisperings, resulting in the hellish release of the Things from their deathless exile. A celebration whose festivities had been so horrific that the end-product was the extinction of man and most other species that the Earth had produced. Leaving only the miscegenetic offspring of the Things' insane sycophants. But NOW (the concept of present-time roared through Etty's comatose mind), *humanity had returned to the Things. This time, the Things would be more careful with their playtoys, restraining their insane bloodlust until a huge populace of toys filled the planet again, turning Earth into a reservoir of savory delicacies.*

Etty could hear secret thoughts…

The Wind-Walker had been rash, slaughtering the insolent intruders before first investigating them. Those intruders had dared to exude frequencies reserved for His intimate delights, prompting Him to hunt them down and vaporize their fragile cellular clusters with His awesome winds. Ithaqua regretted that now, although He would never admit that to His abominable brethren. Fortunately, He had found a single human who had survived His vengeance. Only to lose that awesome prize to the Great Lord, who had discovered the human's existence and demanded ownership of the girl. Ithaqua had fumed over this loss, venting His anger as a series of cyclones that resculpted the active glacier that had once been Russia. He knew that going against Great Cthulhu was unthinkable—inescapable damnation was the only reward for such audacity. He could only fume and scheme... until the second human had arrived! Capturing this one had been easy, for the Walker had dispatched a powerful wizard to accompany the tribe assigned to guard that crumpled metallic vessel that had fallen from the skies. That wizard had snared the new prize for Ithaqua, but again—rage and condemnation!—Great Cthulhu had scented this fresh soul from his aquatic lunar throne. And again, Ithaqua was forced to bequeath tithing to the Great Lord, lest the Walker suffer Cosmic Reprisal.

A mind-numbing blaze of *frustration* cascaded over Etty's dreaming consciousness, battering his psyche with hateful recriminations and astral vehemence. Had he been awake, the psychic tidal wave might have vaporized his mind. Had somnambulant Etty even believed in the horrors he hazily glimpsed, his mind would have shriveled like a fragment of rice paper before a smelting furnace. As it was, he slumbered deep and harbored no trust in these nightmarish delusions. He remained alive and sane in his naive doubt. He paid little heed to the hellish ramblings as the monstrous whisper faded with flickering imperfection.

—Let the Great One have these human toys, the breeder and the seeder. There must be more where they came from...Ithaqua would not rest until He had gathered His own spawning humans. This seeder was to be delivered to the Great One, but with this human, hidden in its crude genetic structure, would go a deadly gift. A surprise for the...

Then there was silence in Etty's dazed unconsciousness.

An unknown amount of hours later, Etty's slumber was disturbed by the barking yelps of the hoary minions who carried his cage.

Awaking to find himself in unfamiliar and startling confinement, Etty realized his dreams had not been nightmares—but clearly flashes of the reality of despair in which he now found himself. His cage was small, cramping him into a fetal position. The beasts bore this loose vault above their blunt, hairy heads as they capered across the tundra. This flood of fantastic elements refused to join into a picture of any clarity in his head. Each aspect seemed separate and horrific in itself.

He was naked! Where was his pressure suit? Wait—now he recalled being metaphysically yanked from his suit. He had not believed it had really happened. What incredible technologies were these beasts hiding? Naked, he was exposed to all kinds of local threats now. Was the air safe to breathe? Would his augmented immune system be capable of warding off any native infections?

He was in a cage! Its very construction terrified him. A collection of dissimilar bones, all bearing evidence of hungry gnawing, were lashed together to create a rudimentary prison around Etty. He doubted they were "human" bones, but there were enough similarities to start him gagging. Forced into a compressed ball within this monstrous cage, Etty stared with revulsion at the bone juncture trembling before his face. The join appeared to have been achieved by winding a deflated stretch of intestine around the crossed joints of unclean calcium. The revolting stench was overpowering. What kind of ghoulish creatures had captured him?

He was the captive of monsters! These beasts mimicked the stance and habits of men, but they were not human. Their long pelts concealed telltale animalistic traits: slanted canine ears, stumpy tails sheathed by hairy bristles, carnivorous fangs. They were man-like, but ultimately brutal and uneducated in their behavior. They barked among themselves as they ran along, but there seemed little communication about the calls. Their shouts were simple announcements of self, a constant mental reiteration of basic factors: *here I am, I am running.* How could such brutish creatures have harnessed the technology necessary to transport Etty from the safety of his pressure suit?

Where were these beasts taking him?

If these parts of his nightmare were true, then what of the other horrors? Were the ancient *Things* real? Had his capture been orchestrated by a devil named Ithaqua? Was Etty being delivered now to an evil astronomically more monstrous than the Thing That Walks the Wind?

A jolt in his savage transportation brought to Etty's attention the fact that the pack of beasts had ceased their cross-country dash. The glacier had given way to solid rock underfoot. It was to this cruel surface that the beasts flung down his cage. Once his imprisonment had finished rolling about, Etty watched the beasts. They pawed the ground, tearing up clots of dirt. They collided with each other, growling and clawing in primitive anger. They relieved themselves on each other, trampling each other's defecations underfoot as they milled about in an unruly crowd. They snuffled at a clump of shrubs that lurked in the mist that surrounded their rest-stop. This mist was rolling in thicker, turning afternoon into late evening. The beasts began to whine with agitation.

Then, out of the milky vapors came figures so hideous that Etty erupted with involuntary screams. Shambling forth, their grotesque deformities became clearer by the second. They were large and bloated, wearing scaly hides and possessing no necks. Their heads protruded from their chests, and quite ugly were those faces: wedge-like with the massive lower overbite of a barracuda. They stared at Etty with huge, glassy fish-eyes set far on opposite temples of their malformed heads. The dispassionate gleam in their terrible stare made him tremble with revulsion. Their bodies were squat, giving the impression of being swollen with some great internal pressure. Their limbs were like fins engorged into obese appendages. These monsters paused to face the agitated pack of courier beasts.

Striding from the pack, one beast confronted the fish-things, rattling a shaman stick above his canine head. Etty was startled to see this beast affecting a modicum of intelligence. It wore a tattered robe of coarse fur, and once the beast had thrown open that cape, the jewelry adorning its neck and torso was visible. This was the one who had cast the spell that had displaced Etty from his pressure suit. How had he failed to notice the wizard running with the pack?

The wizard barked a greeting to the newcomers. The fish-things opened their wide lips, and the damp air filled with the thunderous bellowing of their reply. The two groups of vulgar minions traded insults and threats, then the wizard beast gestured unceremoniously to Etty in his cage. The exchange concluded, the beast pack vanished into the roiling mists, abruptly scampering back to the familiar asylum of their rancorous glacier. Their barking grunts faded in the distance.

Leaving Etty in the clutches of the fish-monsters…

Before they advanced on Etty, he saw them all gather around a hulking wagon that appeared to be a huge balloon on conch wheels. Directing a nozzle attached to the shuddering balloon, one creature doused the rest with a shower of water. They bathed in the liquid spray, releasing baritone sighs of pleasure. Finally satisfied with their rehydration, they approached Etty and commenced rolling his cage across the dirt. With proximity came intimate exposure to the foul odor produced by their wheezy breathing. Etty called to them, suggesting negotiation, but they paid his offers no heed. They lumbered him from the ground, and flung him into the maw of some dark shape that reared suddenly from the billowing mists. As he tumbled into its mouth, he caught a furtive glimpse of this new prison: it was the size of an aircar, and shelled like a crustacean. It was supported by a conveyance that resembled a twitchy centipede—Etty was grateful that his glance of *that* had been too-brief. He did, however, witness all-too-clearly the dog-sized scorpions that scuttled atop the prison-shell. Their stingers throbbed, oozing venom with every spastic movement. Then the darkness enveloped his limited view through the cage of bones. He bounced twice before colliding with the inner tail of the shell. Wedged there, he stared back the way he had come, and watched in despair as the fish-things closed the doorway, locking him away in terrible solitude.

"Aren't you even going to let me out of this cage?!" he wailed.

A brusque shudder of his prison told him that his comfort was of absolutely no concern to these monsters.

⁂

Heading south, Pik and Janek flew over barren countryside that supported no vegetation and seemed to tolerate no color either. The uneven rocky landscape was a variety of gray hues and black tones. The retrievers passed several ruins that were obviously ancient settlements. Their towers sagged now, abandoned and weathered for centuries. Scans Pik threw in the direction of such ruins detected significant metal deposits amid the rubble, but never any life signs. The gray panorama was a desolate testament to the destruction of Earth's culture.

"Do you really believe in Laramy's monsters?" Janek asked.

"*Something* caused all this," replied Pik, using the private commlink between their pressure suits. "But—monsters? That's somewhat melodramatic, I think."

"It would be irresponsible to imagine that ancient deities destroyed this world. More likely, it was aliens possessing advanced technologies."

"That's my suspicion too."

"I am glad that we were both unconvinced by the ghost's explanations," snorted Janek. "His claims were simply too fantastic."

"I expect there's a degree of truth lurking in his stories, though. Myths are always loosely based on facts."

"I would prefer to deal with empirical evidence, and not the ramblings of a religious zealot."

"I agree."

"Which leaves us facing one, possibly two, local factions in conflict."

"Ithaqua, and Laramy's Cthulhu on the moon."

"We have seen the Wind-Walker's minions. We should assume that the lunar Lord has servants of his own."

"We already know that Ithaqua's faction possesses weather control apparatus," Pik remarked. "It is likely that they will also have atmospheric surveillance capabilities."

Janek concurred, so the pair lowered their flight-path across the gray wasteland in order to avoid such detection.

Cresting a rise of titanic peaks, they came to a coastline. The ocean was as colorless as the landscape had been, and just as lifeless.

At least, so it appeared from afar. As she flew over the beach, Pik spotted a troop of creatures. They were struggling to drag an enormous seashell into the water.

Her impulsive curiosity spurred Pik to dive down toward this group.

"What is it, Pik?" Janek called in her ear. "Did you see him?"

"No," she admitted. "But I want to check out these creatures." As she approached, the beasts swung their fish-heads upon her, pinning the armored girl with their furious glare. A wave of nausea swept through Pik, and she irrationally recoiled from their stern regard.

"Pik!" came Janek's cry.

Her suit floundered in mid-descent, and she struggled to reorient herself. She was dimly aware of booming pulse beams, followed by a bestial caterwauling. She heard something else, but it took her a few minutes to realize what it was.

When her head cleared, Pik found that Janek was trying to drive the fish-beasts away from their large treasure. The beasts were refusing to give ground, though. They crowded around the giant dark seashell, as if guarding their own lives. Janek's blasts were insufficient to kill these creatures, they cringed under his pulse beams, but suffered no lethal damage. They looked like over-inflated fish balloons, puffing up defiantly in response to the Duuian's aerial intrusion.

Then she remembered the other sound she had heard—and was still hearing! Muffled by the cacophony of battle, a voice was shouting inquiries and curses.

"It's Etty!" Pik screamed over the comlink. "He's in that shell!"

With passionate ferocity, she joined her own pulse blasts to Janek's. Those beams struck beast after beast with only momentary injury. The things were not unbothered by the brutal pulse vibrations, but they resolutely refused to back down. They endured innumerable pulse salvos, but—finally!—they began to succumb to the punishment. After twenty or so hits, the monsters grew sluggish and staggered off as if blind and dazed. The retrievers' combined firepower managed to force the creatures into a retreat.

As soon as the seashell was free, Pik pounced on it. Brushing aside a flock of scorpion-like things, she gripped the shell, bringing her helmet in contact with its crusty exterior. Then she yelled at the top of her lungs, calling Etty's name. His reply was still muted by Janek's routing pulse blasts, but she recognized his tone, the crude, unmodulated timbre of his terrified voice. Pik had found her beloved!

She pulled an AG clip-on from her thigh-pack, and attached it to the shell. Jerking herself back aloft, she triggered the remote AG. The shell lurched upward and followed the girl into the air. The remaining scorpion-things leapt from their defiant perches. As the shell came into the air, a centipede gripping the shell's base coughed free to scramble away across the beach's black sands. Pik exclaimed in victory, then swooped over to guide the floating seashell in its ascent.

Janek flew up to assist her. Together, they removed Etty's prison from the region of its couriers. Soon, they had left the outraged bellowing behind.

"We've got you, Etty!" Pik shouted through the crust of the shell. "You're safe now!"

"We're lucky we caught them where we did," Janek remarked sagely. "Once they had taken him under the ocean, he would have been hidden from us. We might never have found him."

Etty's muffled voice begged for release from his prison.

Positioning the floating seashell point-down, Pik clutched its casing and gave Janek the go-ahead. As he blasted the upper end from the massive shell, she slightly boosted her own thrusters to compensate for the recoil momentum transferred to Etty's prison by the Duuian partner's pulse beams.

Dipping into the shattered mouth of the shell with a few of his six spindly arms, Janek withdrew Etty and his grotesque cage of bones. Pik gasped at the profane nature of her beloved's discomfort.

Janek waited to free Etty from this last vault until he had flown the contraption to the ground. He chose a mountain ledge, high up and very removed from direct approach by an overzealous climber. There, Pik tore away Etty's cage and freed him. He embraced her bulky pressure suit, babbling and sobbing. He was clearly exhausted and in shock.

"What do we do now?" Janek mumbled, standing back from their reunion.

"Eh?" Pik grunted. "We get the grup off this cursed planet, and never look back."

"No," rambled Etty. "We have to rescue Princess Eden…"

"The Princess is dead, Etty," Pik told him tenderly. "Didn't you see her splattered remains back in the crashed cruiser?"

"What—? No, I—"

"We saw it too," she assured him. "When we came after you."

"We've seen even more unbelievable things," Janek told him.

"So have I!" Etty declared. "In my terrible nightmares—"

"The nightmare is over, Etty," Pik comforted him as best she could, hampered by the clumsy gloves of her pressure suit. "Soon, we'll all be safe aboard the '>%', leaving this horrible place behind."

"No—the Princess!" he exclaimed. "She's alive!"

"Calm down, Etty. She couldn't have survived the attack back at the cruiser."

Janek shifted his posture, folding his arm-stalks in a pattern of reconsideration. "What if he's…right?"

"Grup, Janek, don't encourage his delusion," spat Pik. "He has a *thing* for the Princess. He can't accept what happened to her. Don't torment him by suggesting that she might still be alive.

"But what if she is *not* dead?" Janek insisted slowly. "We only have Professor Laramy's assurance that the Princess actually died in her ruined cruiser. We now know how unreliable his perspective is."

"What are you saying?" she groaned.

"I am suggesting that *if* the Princess is still alive, there is still a retrieval commission on her. A golden bounty, and we could score it…*if* we rescue her."

"I don't want any more of this horrible world and its monstrous denizens," Pik announced. "I just want to see *our* safe retrieval from this hostile place."

"She *isn't* dead!" Etty professed vigorously. "I know she still lives. The voice in my nightmare mentioned her…"

"See?" Pik accused Janek. "For grup's sake, he's basing his belief on 'voices' he heard in his 'nightmare'. Stop encouraging him with this."

"The voice had captured the Princess, but it was angry because it had been forced to turn her over to some Great Lord. That was where *I* was being taken, for Ithaqua had been ordered by the Great Cthulhu to deliver me to the moon too."

Aw, grup, Pik privately moaned. Etty's fantasy was suddenly jiving with (of all things!) reality-according-to-Laramy. There was no way Etty could have known about Ithaqua, or the unpronounceable name of this

Cthulhu…unless he had overheard conversations among the bestial minions who were acting as couriers, transporting him to the equatorial spike. Etty was clearly adamant about his claims. He had witnessed *something* in his nightmare—and enough of those *things* matched elements the other retrievers knew to be true. If this validated one part of his delusion, what did that imply for the rest of his "nightmare"?

"They were going to mate me with the Princess, to propagate a new human race for them to victimize," Etty moaned.

It was all starting to make a horrible sort of sense. The local Lords wanted a new population over which to rule. They had abducted Etty because they needed a male to compliment the female they already had. Following these associative deductions: Princess Eden could very well still be alive.

"I'm inclined to agree with Etty," Pik reluctantly announced.

"What?" scoffed Janek. "You believe that monstrous devils spoke to him in his nightmare?"

"No," she admitted. "But his dream did give him the correct names of two of this world's Lords. If these Lords are planning on breeding themselves new human prey, they would need a male and a *female*."

"That…is logical," the Duuian mumbled. He was clearly confused how to react. On one hand, Janek refused to believe in these local "monsters". On the other hand, he wanted to score the Princess' retrieval commission. It annoyed him to pursue a financial goal based on facts he considered to be fictitious.

"We can't leave her in the clutches of this Cthulhu abomination," swore Etty. "The *ghastly* things they'll do to her… They'll subject her to horrific dissection and torture!"

"They'll do the same to *us* if they catch us," Janek countered, writhing his sensory tendrils in concern.

"The bigger the commission, the bigger the risk," Pik commented. "That's usually the way it is."

Janek waggled his head, expressing resignation. "We came to rescue a Princess. We might as well do what we came here to do."

"We must hurry!" Etty cried. "We have to catch the creatures that are bearing the Princess to her doom!"

A voice deep in the darkness in the back of Pik's head whined in opposition to the command decision she had just orchestrated. This voice screamed at her to vacate this cursed planet without delay. Only death awaited intruders on this abhorrent world. Yet she had chosen to stay, to rescue a Princess that might or might-not still be alive. *Never abandon one of your own.*

"How is Etty supposed to go into battle naked?" mumbled Janek.

"Umm..."

"We lost your pressure suit," Janek told him. "Back on the tundra, when the Walker attacked us with his profane winds."

A natural wind bumbled along the mountainside, disturbing Etty's hair as the trio stood on the ledge, facing this newest realization of defeat. The land between them and the coast was rocky and barren of vegetation. In the distance, clouds drifted with lazy currents above a colorless ocean. Unbroken by waves, this viscous sea flowed off to merge with the horizon... except where a remote shadow marked the hazy bulk of the base of one of the distant spikes. So very far away, yet it was enormous. The diameter of its circumference as it broke from the dead surface of the deep ocean must have been well over five hundred kilometers!

Without a suit, Etty would be more than helpless in a battle, he would become a liability. Unprotected, there was not even a way to return him safely to the ">%"—this problem had not occurred to Pik before now. One of the retrievers was going to have to fly up to the ship and bring one of the two sparc suits back to Earth for Etty.

Pik announced that it would be her who went to get the extra suit.

⁜

Janek watched Pik launch from the mountainside ledge. Her thrusters kicked in, propelling her into the cloudcovered sky. Within a minute, the human female was lost to his sophisticated sensory array, her presence masked by the electromagnetic disruption that crackled within the dense upper atmosphere.

The Duuian turned to extend his sensory tendrils in an approximation of a grin in the direction of Etty. The man responded with his own version of the sentiment, a contortion of the oversimplistic human head that always privately revolted Janek. One time, he had actually witnessed Etty pull his fleshy lips back impossibly far, revealing a terrifying array of blunt teeth; the memory still gave Janek chills.

To distract himself from these grotesque recollections, Janek asked Etty to relate the tale of his examination of the Princess' crashed cruiser, and his subsequent capture by the hoary minions of the Wind-Walker. The Duuian desired to compare his partner's account against the dubious version told them by the Laramy ghost.

In the midst of Etty's narrative, Janek interrupted to express his bafflement over the emptiness of the cruiser's plasma core. "Such a thing is simply not possible."

Etty agreed, admitting that he had been given no opportunity to investigate this phenomena. "I was being chased by those hairy beasts, remember? I was sort of preoccupied at that point with my own survival."

"But the core was already drained when you found it?"

"Of course it was! Do you think I would crawl into a live plasma core? Do I look crazy—or *dead* to you?"

"This puzzle of the empty plasma core troubles me," Janek commented. His tone indicated that he thought this dilemma to be of momentous importance.

So far, mused the Duuian, *Etty's account fairly matches the Professor's ghost story.* As if *that* wasn't troublesome enough, it annoyed Janek that there was no explanation for the missing plasma energy. Neither Etty or the human spirit provided any clue as to the fate of the core's stolen energies. Such power, such fantastic power—it had to be *somewhere*, it couldn't have evaporated into frozen air.

"What the—" Etty's gasp brought Janek from his ruminations. With shock, then disappointment, the Duuian witnessed the hazy form of Professor Laramy alight onto the ledge between himself and his human partner. The ghost had come from the sky, Janek's blind spot.

His aversion to violence was not the only quirk that normally kept Janek confined to the ">%" during retrieval missions. He was agoraphobic, a trait he shared with others of his kind who had been raised under the low, dark green skies of Duu. By staying aboard the ship, he avoided contact with all open areas. On those infrequent occasions that he left the safety of the ship to venture outside (as he had done this time), Janek was careful to ingest the proper medication to subdue his spatial psychosis (again, as he had done this time). Unfortunately, those meds were gradually wearing off, and tinges of irrational fear were nibbling at the edges of his psyche. To lessen the frightening effects of the open countryside, Janek had relegated the majority of his exterior sensors to a filter that was set to unprioritize the emptiness of the view from the mountain ledge. Although this digital shuffle gained him a modicum of release from his agoraphobic tension, he still remained physically close to the cliff-wall, and rarely faced away from that direction. As a result, Laramy's ghost had crept upon them from the Duuian's blind side.

"I found you!" exclaimed the ghost.

"Apparently," Janek mumbled, clenching his nostril flanges in frustration. He had thought—even rejoiced—that they had left the fanatical spirit behind on the glacier. But no, the accursed Laramy had found a way to follow Janek and Pik, catching up and rejoining what the ghost perceived as his own personal army of vengeance.

"I have learned to shed the mortal restrictions of my ghostlihood," Laramy informed the Duuian. "You were my inspiration."

"Who—*what* is this person—this *thing*?" Etty gasped, backing away from Laramy's wavering colorless form.

"I am Professor Laramy," the ghost announced with pride. "With my help, you will be the instruments that achieve the great downfall of the hideous New Lords of Earth!"

"He claims to be a ghost of one of this world's last humans," Janek sneered. Wasting no words on tact, he told his partner how they had encountered Laramy, who had taught them the current geopolitical arrangement that dominated old Earth.

"If you already knew about this stuff," Etty growled at his Duuian partner, "then why did you refuse to believe everything the Wind-Walker told me in my nightmare?"

"It's local superstition," Janek mumbled. "We believed the *important* parts of what you told us..."

"The unholy Thing That Walks the Wind spoke to you?!" Professor Laramy gasped in surprise and edged closer to peer at Etty with the eyes of a fanatic.

While Etty recounted his dream to the obsessed ghost, Janek watched Laramy seem to enter a dreamstate of his own. The Professor was soaking up every detail of Etty's hallucinations, greedily assimilating the facts and reconfiguring them to fit the framework of his religious obsession.

These humans, Janek mulled, *and their irrational beliefs.*

Laramy believed in monstrous gods that were dedicated to tormenting humanity. (It always amazed Janek how egocentric mankind was as a species. These humans actually thought themselves *important* enough to attract the attention of malicious spirits who apparently sought unholy approval by torturing the members of this unspecial race of arrogant bipeds.)

Etty believed that the missing Princess was going to be so impressed with him that she would reward him with carnal pleasures. (Although Janek was no expert judge, he doubted that Etty was *that* handsome or blatantly virile enough to coerce the Royal Daughter to violate cultural class barriers and couple with a commoner.) If Etty truly expected that this was going to happen, his resolve must have been fueled by spurious theological doctrines.

Even Pik harbored religious beliefs. Janek knew the female human to be a devout follower of the Unified God, for they had shared long discussions on the dubious subject of theology. Janek, an agnostic, had always been impressed by Pik's religious convictions—not by their content, but for the casual manner in which Pik treated those beliefs. According to her, Pik's faith remained in her at all times; she simply never mentioned it. Janek found this trait to be one of the human's most endearing qualities.

Janek tried to remind himself that everyone was entitled to their own beliefs, but Laramy's obsession with occult dogma really pushed the Duuian's tolerance past its limit. He professed intimate knowledge of cosmic mysteries, but his head was actually full of superstitions and horrific myths. Normally, Janek was willing to tolerate theological beliefs as long as they did not bother him. Laramy's faith was a prime example of unacceptable religion—force-fed and too ridiculous to believe.

But then, as Pik had pointed out: myths always had their root in facts. Janek wondered where some of Laramy's beliefs had originated. To the last humans of Earth, the invading aliens must have seemed like gods; but to Janek, who was familiar with comparable technologies, those "ancient gods" were only clever aliens wielding superior hardware and posing as local deities. It was a classic move made by a lot of planetary despots. But to Janek, it seemed only cliché and old…another corruption of religious philosophy. Who did these "Old Ones" think they were fooling, anyway? They exterminated all the indigenous lifeforms conquering this world. There was no one left to intimidate except the Lords' already devout followers. These Lords were posing…for the sake of impressing themselves.

And now—humans had suddenly returned to old Earth. Was it any wonder that these Lords lusted after creating a new population for themselves?

What a geopolitical mess the Princess had landed in. (Janek was already making mental notes to inflate the Princess' retrieval commission far beyond its considerable amount. He knew he could argue hazard rates and maybe even claim the lost pressure suit.)

Glancing at Etty and the feverish ghost, Janek hoped that his human partner was smart enough to resist being taken in by Professor Laramy's ghost stories. Unfortunately, Etty had his blurry moments when his brain became unreliable.

Long ago, Janek had discovered (much to the surprise of his Duuian skepticism) that humans generally practiced mythological identification to an extreme measure in their mental organization of data. The concept of a "Greater Power" was central to almost every basic mental process used by the species. It tended to distort all of their opinions, even dominating to a overwhelming extent their attitude towards life and death.

Humans weren't the only species to give inaccurate credence to superstitious doctrines. Other races had attributed unnecessary realism to mysterious legends. For eons, the regions surrounding Hyades had been avoided by all sane travelers, and all because myths spoke of a world in that star system that was "rumored" to harbor a dreadful lake that consumed the souls of anyone reckless enough to venture too close. Albebaran was another shunned star, for reasons too ridiculous for Janek to recall right now—but again, it was a legend so powerful that it had adopted a reality of its own.

It would seem that old Earth was well on its way to gaining a reputation as one of these haunted places.

Janek lamented the victory of superstition over logical explanations. *There are no such things as magical deities or ghosts or monsters*, he asserted. *Everything is explainable in quantifiable terms.*

"Your companions rescued you," Laramy's ghost was chortling. "And now we must—"

His cackling madness was interrupted by a tremor that rattled the mountainside. Granite rubble rained about them as the cliff-face shook with more emphatic vibrations. Hairline cracks were enlarging, yawning into wide fissures that separated the side of the mountain. The quake was abbreviating their ledge sanctuary with every second, chunks were falling away to plummet down the mountainside into the barren valleys below.

Grabbing up Etty's naked form, Janek held him tightly in his spindly arms, then he launched his pressure suit away from the crumbling stone facade. As he lifted on sputtering thrusters, the Duuian glanced back to witness the Laramy ghost duplicate their escape, flying in pursuit. Behind the airborne specter, the mountain cracked open like an eggshell to reveal a monstrosity of absolutely incredible proportions.

The mountain fell away in asteroid-sized chunks, and a huge mound of vile meat was exposed. This mass continued to ooze forth from subterranean depths, urging its brown filth higher into the foul atmosphere. As it swelled, internal contortions of enormous scale bulged along the Thing's flanks. These humps broke through, rupturing the unholy skin and protruding with unmitigated horror to reveal themselves as massive plates of protective crust. With hideous grace, these semi-molten plates jostled and jockeyed into position afloat the monster's turgid flesh. They cooled in the chilled, moist air, adding a whistling high-end to the sonorous bedlam generated by the creature's astounding emergence. The Thing was assembling body armor from gigantic pieces of the planet's mantle! While this encrusting continued, further prominences forced themselves from the awesome bulk of the monster, twining to reach into the air like blind appendages. Over fifty meters in diameter, these tentacles lunged into the sky, clutching to capture their fled prey.

Janek wheezed with dire terror at what he saw. Hanging in the Duuian's firm grip, Etty moaned as if sanity was painfully fleeing his mind. Adrift in their wake, the ghost of Professor Laramy screamed above the geological din, "It is Shudde-M'ell! The revolting Burrower Beneath! Now, we are doomed!"

⬦

All Pik had to do was fly straight up. Sooner or later, she would exit the damnable mists and enter the open vacuum of space.

She had no expectation of finding the ">%" exactly above *these* clouds. They had parked the ship in a polar orbit; it would still be circling there, keeping to the planet's arctic regions. Once Pik was free of the Earth's dense atmosphere, though, she could summon the ship with her suit.

There was a terrible irony to all of this. This mess was the product of Etty's private long-distance fascination with Princess Eden (or at least the Princess he had seen on holo-discs and on news tapes). Undoubtedly, there was little similarity between the Princess' media image and her true persona, not to mention further variations in whatever personality Etty had mentally attached to his fantasy portrait. Should Etty have actually found himself face-to-face with the Princess, he would probably have been terribly upset, disturbed by the Royal Daughter's aloof treatment of him, her heroic rescuer. Maybe it would be better if the Princess *had* gotten herself slaughtered, then Etty would be gratefully spared him the pain of any shattered illusions. It seemed that everyone who had come to rescue the Princess' distress call was trapped now on this hellish planet, struggling to survive hostile natives and escape deadly environmental forces. And still: Etty's obsession for the Princess drove them all deeper.

Unable to accept her horrible death, he had manipulated Pik into supporting their continued presence here.

There *was* the bigger picture, of course. Princess Eden…human being…possibly in the clutches of malevolent monsters… *Never leave anyone behind.* She was Royalty, and there was a reward for rescuing her—these factors were economic motivations for the retrieval team. If she was alive, however, she deserved to be saved regardless of the importance of her bloodline.

These are all noble and valid economic reasons for staying to rescue the lost Princess, ruminated Pik. *But we wouldn't even be here if Etty didn't have a secret crush on the Nimbus Family's slutty media superstar daughter.*

Pik had never even met the woman, and already she didn't like her. But not for the obvious reasons.

It seemed as if Royal Nimbus Family had been a black cloud over Pik's head her entire life. Her earliest memory of the Royal Family was as a child, when her own family had been forced to move when their town was conscripted for a Regal Gala. A few years later, she recalled her father struggling to hide their poverty from her—again, the Royal Family had caught them in the riptide of another Regal Whim, outlawing her father's trade. When Pik was fifteen, she was caught in an assassination crossfire between rival Nimbus cousins. There were thirty-nine others in that fateful crowd. Four were killed, and seventeen were wounded. Pik was one of the wounded. There was permanent damage to her still-maturing ovaries. The girl's stretch in the Space Navy might have continued if she hadn't been afforded an intimate glimpse into the Royal Private Life when she pulled Palace Duty one weekend. The debauchery Pik witnessed soured her dedication to serve and protect such aberrant behavior.

She didn't hold grudges, at least not against those who outranked or outweighed or outgunned her. She did not "like" the Royal Family, but Pik would never have entertained the notion of acting against them. Some kinds of Authority existed to be reviled.

She had always considered herself to be pretty balanced, emotionally. The despair and harshness of her childhood had been overcome during her military training, which taught her the sheer impartiality of the hostile universe. She learned that self-image was an internal thing, unaffected by the opinions of others. She learned to accept that shared affections were tenuous connections. She realized that the *moment* was the thing to enjoy, whatever that instant or incidence was. By appreciating each moment to the fullest, one derived maximum potential out of life. This philosophy built efficient Warriors, but it could also be used to induce a sense of personal fulfillment off the battlefield.

After a few minutes, Pik grew uneasy, as if sensing voyeuristic eyes tracking her every move…or lack of movement. For when she consulted her suit's altimeter, she discovered that she was no longer ascending through the milky clouds. Although her thrusters were wide-open, her upward motion had ceased!

This made no sense.

She rechecked her system, but found no problems with its operations. The suit and all its hardware were functioning perfectly. Her jets were firing, but they no longer propelled her into an escape velocity.

Curious to test something, Pik cut her thrusters—and tumbled violently into the murky depths of the clouds. Savage electrical discharges snaked all about her as she fell, leaving their afterimages flashing on her exposed vision.

Well, she mused as she plummeted like a stone, *that settles that.* The problem was not a fault in her equipment. It was an external force. Something was pushing against her ascent, refusing to allow her to rise any higher. When she had shut off her jets, that inimical potency had flung Pik down without restraint.

Reactivating her thrusters gained the girl no lost height, it barely halted her plunge. The invisible force was still exerting itself on her, barring Pik from the upper stratosphere. Unwilling to admit defeat, she fired her pulse beams into the clouds overhead. The blast of her weapons warded back the swirling vapors. For a moment, a clear shaft was exposed through to the outer void, a brief glimpse that only served to tantalize her mounting frustration. Then the recoil struck, so brutal that it nearly ripped loose the arms of the girl's pressure suit. She tumbled with the unexpected impact, keeping aloft only by the persistent groan of her AG unit. A flurry of colored lights seemed to pingpong around the insides of her eyes. Her inner ear angrily complained about her frantic spin. Her head hurt.

Urging her gyroscope to reinstate her sense of balance, Pik hung suspended now, just below the storm layer of the clouds.

If this spot was blocked, then she would try another one. Surely the entire planet's atmosphere could not be barricaded by this unnatural force. She flew (without interference) a kilometer north, then attempted another ascent.

Again, she was batted down by monstrous energies.

Pik tried this maneuver several more times, traveling far through the shadowy atmosphere, but always with the same frustrating result. Any movements she made laterally or down were unrestricted, but upward mobility was utterly forbidden.

Although she could not fathom (or even believe) the methodology of this phenomena, its message was impossible to ignore: *You are here to stay.*

❖

Tarn witnessed the birth of the volcano from afar. Even though it lay far to the south-east, the eruption was tremendous, spitting volumes of dirt and dark clouds into the air. He paused to conduct a cursory scan of the event, then cursed when he surveyed the results of that input. The explosion was no normal volcano. The mass expelled by the blast was far too dense. The energy signature of the whole thing was off-the-scale.

And hidden in the glare of this pseudo-volcano's heat radiation was a reading that matched the systems configuration of the pressure suit Tarn towed with him. Whoever had taken the Princess, they were there—at the scene of this extraordinary geological anomaly. Was the Princess in their clutches even now? Were they planning to sacrifice the Royal Brat to this cthonian fissure? Those beasts he had found outside the cruiser's wreckage might do something so barbaric with their captive, but those savage animals could never control the power necessary to birth a volcano on demand. This had to be the handiwork of the Princess' abductors.

Tarn could not fathom what motive they might have for this remarkable atrocity. He was concerned solely with rescuing the Royal Brat and escaping the wrath of a grieving Nimbus Family. Changing course, he aimed himself at the distant eruption. As he went, the Warrior armed his battle suit's extensive and deadly armament.

He noticed many things as he drew near the newborn volcano. The evidence of his scanners and his naked vision troubled him, for much of the sensory input defied common sense. Some of what he saw was simply too incredible to believe.

It was no huge column of smoke that belched from the volcano—it was a monstrous shape of organic nature! This vast mound of meat towered nearly half-a-kilometer into the sky, contorting and pulsating as if it was alive. Which—def!—it was! The Thing was a beast, a monster of such ghastly scope that even the Royal Warrior blanched with instinctual fear, vomiting into the helmet of his battle suit. This inconceivable creature's bloated, dun-hued hide was covered with molten crust; between these incandescent plates a forest of gigantic tentacles lashed in the air.

A subterranean scan of the beast showed that its unbelievable mass did not stop immediately under the volcano, the creature's body continued in all directions deep beneath the planet's surface. How far did it reach? Was there an end? Or was the monster an organic strata of a global scale?

Ambient temperatures were rising too, Tarn noted. The monster's body heat was colliding with the cold air, creating a storm to attend its horrifically majestic arrival. Already winds were tearing at his suit. The pressure suit he carried was torn from his grasp and cast tumbling to the rocky landscape below.

There! After applying numerous, exotic filters, he had succeeded in pinpointing the corresponding signal of one of the brethren of the suit he had just lost. The Princess' abductor was fleeing from the eruption, but the beast seemed intent on halting that escape. Tarn watched the suit-signal swoop and dive, dodging the mighty columns of scalding meat that thrashed to obfuscate any exit route.

A further refinement of that complex scan determined that the enemy pressure suit was carrying an unsuited person. *Def,* Tarn gasped, *they really did bring the Princess to this hellish volcano!* The unprotected human signature struggled against its captor's clutches. Was the Princess insane? *Break free—and you'll fall to your death, you inbred Brat! Or even worse.* The Warrior shuddered in the sweaty confines of his battle armor as he briefly imagined what contact between human flesh and one of those scorching tentacles would produce. Would the Royal Brat vanish in a puff of super-heated fats? Or would her body dissolve slowly, dripping like crimson wax down the blistering curves of the monster's appendage? Coupled with the taste of bile still on his tongue, these notions sickened the Warrior.

Although Tarn longed to fling his trained vengeance against the kidnaper, he knew that duty demanded him to first insure the safety of the Royal Daughter. Before he could wrestle the Princess from the custody of her abductor, the Warrior must remove the murderous threat of this inconceivable volcanic monstrosity. It rankled his professional ire to tactically admit that the Brat was probably safer with her captor right now.

With a growl that never left his throat, Tarn turned his attention to the awful Beast. He fired the pulse cannons that rode his shoulders. Focusing his aim on the tentacles that menaced the fleeing figures, he raked his beams across the monster's spastic limbs. Initially, his shots produced no effects, bringing deep creases to the Warrior's forehead. He raised the potency until the pulse blasts he pumped at the Beast's tentacles were beyond the lethal setting. Still…the Beast seemed unbothered by his attack.

I'm like an insect waving my tiny stinger in the face of a monster, he dreaded.

Some of the thrashing tentacles had diverted from tormenting the Princess and her captor, lurching to whip through the air in search of the approaching Warrior. Engaging in a complicated series of flight maneuvers, Tarn eluded their mammoth grasp. He continued to blast away at the Beast, distributing his ineffectual firepower evenly among the attacking tentacles.

As he flew past the squirming columns of scalding meat, he marveled at the scale and might of these limbs. Up close like this, they no longer seemed like tentacles; they were more akin to enormous hillocks of deadly flesh: hot and viscous and unnatural and so impossibly huge! He had the fleeting impression that he was battling a tangle of mountains intent on colliding to crush him.

Then he was through their massive tangle and into free sky. He whirled, returning his pulse blasts to the fray before he came around for another fly-by. This time, he opened up his lasers and particle beams. Their brilliant beams sliced through the wide flanks of alien flesh…but those wounds lasted only momentarily, for the disgusting skin flowed like a jelly, sealing the cuts as if they had never existed. His pulse blasts were bludgeoning the tentacles, but their blows were sadly reminiscent of futile slaps against dense, wet clay. He aborted his second fly-by before he returned to the reach of the waving limbs.

His strategies were proving useless. Tarn was wasting ammunition energies and valuable time. His best efforts were having no effect upon the Beast.

"What the grup is all this?" came a female voice in his ear.

The Warrior's battle sensors instantly pinpointed this surprise transmission's origin. Another person was descending from the heavens! This newcomer's pressure suit bristled with custom attachments, giving its commercial design an almost military aspect. A deep scan revealed that the individual was a human and female. Tarn's system also identified the communications waveband as the one utilized by the Princess' abductors (as determined by his examination of the comlink settings of the suit he had found adrift on the tundra).

Another enemy, Tarn grumbled. *Oh, this is exactly what I need right now…*

"*Janek,*" called the newcomer. "*Where are you? Is Etty safe? What happened here?*"

Tarn eavesdropped on their breathless conversation.

"*Sssafe? Not precissely, Pik,*" the fleeing kidnaper responded.

Tarn detected an unnatural diction in this one's words, implying the individual belonged to a non-human species. So…this kidnapping scheme involved more than one race. This was a bigger conspiracy than he had thought.

"*What is that thing?*" gasped the newcomer (her name was apparently "Pik").

"*It came from inssside the mountain,*" the non-human ("Janek") explained. "*There wasss no warning. Professsor Laramy called it 'Shudder-Male' or sssome sssuch unpronounceable phrassse.*"

"*Laramy is back?*"

"*Unfortunately, yesss. He appeared jussst before thisss* Monsssster *appeared.*"

"*Get the grup out of there!*" cried Pik. "*You're going to get Etty killed!*"

Tarn found this dialog curious, for their comments challenged portions of the Warrior's interpretation of the situation. Apparently, the kidnapers had not summoned this volcanic spawn, they seemed to be innocent victims of the monster. They feared it as much as the Warrior did.

And…who were "Etty" and "Professor Laramy"? The kidnapers talked about them as if these individuals were present here—but there were only three individuals out there: the newcomer (Pik), the first kidnaper (Janek), and the unprotected Princess who Janek carried. Where were these other conspirators hiding? Could they be using stealth technology?

"*Who's that down there with you?*" Pik's voice inquired urgently. "*I see someone flying a few hundred meters outside the reach of those Monster's tentacles. Hey—who are you? What are you doing here?*"

He had been spotted. Tarn quickly realized that concealing himself was pointless now. Using the frequency of their comlinks, he quickly identified himself as a traveler. "My name is Tarn. What is that Beast?" he gasped with dramatic inflection. "I was trying to fight it off, and rescue your friends—but the Thing is so huge!" He must be careful to avoid mentioning their captive, for a "stranger" would have no way of knowing their captive's identity. He must not let them suspect he was a Warrior of the Royal Navy. If he played them carefully, he might even enlist their aid in defeating the Beast, indirectly saving the Princess from this incredible menace. But then, they would be just as eager as he was to keep their captive alive and safe. A dead Princess made a useless hostage.

"*None of us seem to know what that Thing is,*" Pik replied. "*Except that it's nasty and has my partners trapped. Can you help me get them to safety?*"

Reluctantly, Tarn informed them that his attempts to injure the Beast had been frustratingly ineffective.

"*That doesn't surprise me,*" Pik's voice sighed. "*Look at the size of that ugly Thing!*"

"*Combine your firepower!*" directed the non-human kidnaper.

"It might work," Tarn admitted.

"*We don't really have any other options,*" Pik grumbled.

"I suggest we strike the body," advised the Warrior. "Even if we fail to do any real damage, we might at least distract the tentacles away from your friends."

"*I am Janek,*" the kidnaper told him. "*And I have Etty here with me.*"

"*And I'm Pik,*" announced the female kidnaper as she dove toward the bloated cloudbank of horrible flesh that towered above the volcano.

With an obstinate grunt, Tarn joined the villain in an unholy alliance to rescue the Princess from the clutches of the volcanic monster. He flung himself at the Beast, every weapon he wore blazing away. His pulse cannons were useless against the huge bulk of the creature, and his particle beams sliced marginal chinks in the Beast's molten shell. His lasers, though, appeared to be bothering the monster. It convulsed under their minor impacts, twitched viciously as if agonized by the tiny dots of hyperactive light.

Suddenly Tarn understood the nature of the Beast's weakness. His preliminary scans had determined that the creature's full body stretched like a global underground layer, squeezed between the planet's surface and its mantle. Confined to a subterranean environment, the Beast was not used to *light!*

"*Laramy sssaysss to ussse the sssun againsst it!*" cried Janek's voice.

"*How the grup do we do that?*" Pik laughed. "*You know how thick this cloudcover is.*"

"We can make our own sun," declared Tarn. He stepped down the frequency of his laser weapons, diffusing their beams and transforming them from needles to spotlights. Wide cones of brilliance fell upon the creature's immense flank.

That got a reaction!

The Beast actually lurched, crushing the side of the volcanic caldera with its voluminous girth. With a tremendous spasm, the creature swung every tentacle to converge on Tarn's hovering figure. But the Warrior was fast; he shot up into the heights, escaping the extent of the Beast's greedy limbs. Those pillars of meat danced a ballet of torment, straining in vain to reach their elusive tormentor.

"Go!" he heard Pik scream. He noted (peripherally on his wide-scan) that Janek was free of the tentacles now, his marker zoomed away across the rocky landscape.

The Warrior's high-beam spotlights played across the Beast, forcing the thing to recoil with intense aversion. It was actually retreating—oozing back into its titanic hole!

Pik cheered his victory, her gutsy voice ringing in his ear.

Gazing with amazement, Tarn watched the Beast vanish into the earth. The ground trembled with its passing, and a moment later a gout of magma belched from the ruined volcano. The monster was gone.

"We did it!" Tarn exclaimed.

"You certainly did, sssoldier," came Pik's agreement.

What was that supposed to mean? Had the kidnaper somehow guessed that Tarn was a Warrior?

She swooped to hang on sputtering thrusters close beside him in the heights. Tarn could now make out her face through the shiny faceplate of her pressure suit. Pik wore a sincere expression of relief. In its relaxed state, briefly purged of her quick-temper and her surly impatience, her dark-skinned face was almost feminine. Her small mouth sported pouty lips beneath a pug nose. Her eyes were over-large and very white. A strong jaw contained a resolute face that warned of her unwavering suspicious nature. Her scalp was shaved bare except for a blue patch on her left temple that balanced the plug-in slots on the right side of her head.

She did not accurately fit the Warrior's mental image of a hardened criminal.

"C'mon," Pik called. *"Let's land somewhere. I need to make sure my Etty is okay."* She was already moving in pursuit of Janek's receding form.

Tarn followed without questioning her comment, at least not aloud. *"My Etty"*... Was Pik referring to her database by name? This might explain the presence of those two invisible individuals on the scene. The kidnapers were not hiding conspirators, they were simply quirky, for only novices anthropomorphized their data systems. "Etty" was Pik's system, while "Professor Laramy" must belong to Janek. (Was it still "anthropo-morphication" if it was done by a non-human individual?)

The Warrior was also cautious regarding the customization of Pik's pressure suit. Clearly, someone had added substantial attachments to enhance her suit beyond the elementary capabilities of a commercially purchased pressure suit. There was evidence of additional weaponry, and Tarn could identify several add-ons that looked like long-range scanners of military origin. The female kidnaper was outfitted far beyond the ne-cessities of a normal spacer. (The distraction of battle had not afforded Tarn the opportunity to scan Janek with such scrupulous detail, but the Warrior assumed that the alien's suit bore similar adjustments.) Such practices would fit the profile of individuals operating outside the Law... like kidnapers.

Janek had apparently taken his captive far from the region of the vol-cano, landing on a stretch of raven beach to the south. Tarn followed Pik down to this distant rendezvous. They both touched down ten meters from the other, their thrusters kicking clouds of dark sand into the humid air.

As Tarn stepped toward Janek, he froze, startled by what he saw.

"Don't be afraid," Pik commented as she loped past him. Waving aside a human figure who appeared to consist of colorless mist, the fe-male kidnaper chuckled, "That's only Professor Laramy. He's a ghost." She strode to embrace the naked human who Janek had been carrying, and their laughter danced on the beach.

The "ghost" was not what had brought Tarn to a stunned halt, al-though it was certainly disturbing once identified. The Warrior's surprise concerned the fact that the naked figure, which he had assumed to be Princess Eden, was *male*.

If this was the kidnapers' captive—then where was the Royal Daughter?

⁜

Pik hit the beach at a run, dashing to a joyful reunion with Etty. As she passed their newfound companion, Tarn, she noticed the man freeze as he approached the group. Obviously, he had seen Laramy and was un-sure what to make of the ancient Professor.

"Don't be afraid," she called. "That's only Professor Laramy. He's a ghost." As Pik loped past Tarn, she confirmed her suspicions: the man was wearing a Warrior's battle armor. This was no accidental traveler—

but then, there were no casual visitors to this hellish planet. It didn't take an idiot to deduce that he was here because of the crash-landed Princess. Was Tarn a member of her personal Guards who had somehow survived Ithaqua's freakish massacre? Maybe another Navy cruiser had come in search of the Royal Daughter. *Either way, this man's presence trumps our retrieval claim,* she fumed. *Grup—there goes our commission.*

She wasted little time fretting over this complication, it could be sorted out later. Right now, Pik was ecstatic to finally be reunited with her beloved. They hugged and voiced their joy, capering around in the black sand. He was as happy to see her as she was to see him, perhaps a little more so, considering that they had rescued him from the terrible clutches of inhuman monsters. Pik's joy to see him safe again was quite intoxicating, obliterating the dire news she had discovered in the planet's stratosphere.

By the time the lovers rejoined Janek, the Duuian was frustrated from his attempts to rationally explain Laramy's deceased nature to Tarn.

"There are no such things as ghosts," the Warrior was attesting.

Tarn's physique was impossible to determine hidden within the aggressive layers of his battle armor. His suit was designed for strength, protection, and intimidation. It bristled with weaponry, from a row of shoulder-mounted pulse cannons to an impressive array of forearm particle beams. Several manifolds along the Warrior's sides had the look of further armament. The silver suit was decorated with black trim in an attempt to attribute ferocious lines to the armor's seemingly cumbersome bulk.

Inside that bulk, Tarn appeared to be human. From the thick, corded neck that supported his wide jawline, Pik took him to be a typical over-muscled example of Warriorhood. What else was visible through his helmet's faceplate confirmed that assumption. The Warrior was a bullet-headed grunt. A deep space-tan darkened his skin almost to Pik's natural color. His unsympathetic face wore dark tattoos intended to enhance the fearsomeness of his visage. Past this agro-mask, she could see wide, prominent lips, a blunt nose, and beady, determined eyes.

"Despite recent circumstances which urge me to adjust my acceptance of such things," Janek told the Warrior, "I share that opinion."

"I am real," alleged Professor Laramy. "At least, as real as a bodiless spirit can be. In fact, I am more real now than when I first found you on the tundra. For I have learned to cast off my mortal perspective which had been restricting me from making full use of my spectral abilities."

"Monsters, ghosts," Tarn shook his scowling head. "There's more going on here than you are admitting…"

"You're one to talk about full disclosure," remarked Pik.

"Excuse me?"

"You're no innocent traveler. You're a Nimbus Warrior."

Tarn's scowl darkened, and he glared at the girl.

"I used to be in the Space Navy," she declared. "I know Royal battle armor when I see it."

Her suit picked up a brief burst of static, which she recognized as the Navy's secret code. Tarn was surreptitiously goading Pik to prove her claim by responding to a signal that only true Warriors would know. She returned the appropriate code response, giving him a grim smile with her silent mouth.

His frown softened, but did not lose its superior edge.

"I served my term and declined reinlistment," she told him. "I am not a deserter."

He seemed willing to accept her word on this. *Good,* she thought. *The last we need right now is a Warrior harassing me for nonexistent offenses.*

"Why did you falsssely identify yourssself to usss?" Janek inquired bluntly. The lisp betrayed that this development had agitated the Duuian.

"I...was searching for someone," the Warrior admitted hesitantly. "I thought that you had..."

"You're looking for Princess Eden!" Etty gasped. "You've come to rescue her!"

Tarn's annoyance returned to a steel-eyed glare.

The time has come for some more full disclosure, Pik realized, *before our bumbling triggers an attack response in the Warrior.* He was clearly wired, and understandably so. While looking for a missing Princess, he had encountered monsters and a retrieval team keeping company with a ghost. He was a stranger on this planet, and indubitably more unfamiliar than the hunters with the wretched nature of this world.

"Were you part of her Guard?" she asked. "Did you escape Ithaqua's massacre back at the crashed cruiser?"

"No," he revealed after a long pause. "I'm here in response to the cruiser's distress call."

"So are we," Etty told him. As expected, this darkened the Warrior's mood even more.

"We're a freelance retrieval team," Pik clarified. "We're here in response to the same distress call."

"But not I," Professor Laramy's ghost added. "I was a native of this world. I've been dead here for nearly two hundred years."

Oh, please be quiet, Pik silently moaned. Things were complicated enough without Laramy confounding the Warrior with local myths.

"We're not certain the Princess is still alive to be rescued," Janek commented. "She could have been killed along with everyone else aboard the cruiser."

"Killed *how*?" Tarn growled.

"That was before we arrived," admitted Pik. "We aren't sure what happened…"

"It was Ithaqua," Laramy interjected. "I told you that. He slaughtered everyone with His terrible winds."

"Professor, please," Pik begged the ghost. "Leave your monsters out of this for now."

"But—you saw His might," the ghost argued. "You cannot deny the horrible existence of these New Lords who hold Earth in captivity. You swore you would help rid this world of their oppression."

"We never agreed to that," she mumbled with petulant impatience.

"But—you battled Shudde-M'ell! You brought down the Burrower Beneath, driving Him back into His underground lair! No humans have ever done this before!"

"What is this *phantasm* babbling about?" demanded Tarn. "Who are these 'monsters'? Are these the ones who abducted the Princess?"

"He is insane," Janek declared, waving a spindly arm at the ghost. "He thinks that monsters of legend destroyed his world. He believes these creatures still tyrannize this planet."

"They *did* steal Princess Eden," cried Etty. "I heard them talk of her, of their horrible plans for her."

"Where is she?" the Warrior asked harshly.

"We do not know," Pik professed loudly, momentarily distracting the Warrior's lethal glare from her lover. "She wasn't in the cruiser. We've seen no trace of her…"

"But you're still here," Tarn accused. "On this planet…looking for her."

"We stayed to rescue our partner when he got captured by—"

"Just as they abducted the Princess!" Etty wailed.

If only everyone, Pik moaned to myself, *would just shut up! We might get out of this alive…*

"You saw them take the Princess?" Tarn demanded, turning to face Etty.

"In my dream," sobbed Etty. "I saw terrible things in my dream…"

"In a *dream*," the Warrior spat. He hung his head within the helmet of his battle suit, squeezing shut his eyes with consternation. When he finally spoke, his tone was authoritative, "I want your retrieval team off this world...*now!*"

"Umm," Pik mumbled, raising a hand in innocent pause. "That's, uh, not really possible..."

"I will not tolerate—"

"We *can't* leave!" she shouted. The tension of this deadly confrontation had overwhelmed her composure. She became aware that her cheeks were already stained with tears, released unnoticed during the tense exchange. "I tried. That's what I was doing separated from my partners—trying to get to our ship in orbit. Etty lost his pressure suit, he can't make it offworld as he is... But I couldn't reach the ship. The way is...blocked..." Pik floundered, unable to clearly verbalize the strangeitude she had found at the edge of the planetary atmosphere.

"You're going to have to do better than that," the Warrior informed her.

"It's the truth," she told him. "I can't explain it... But I *can* prove it." She unplugged a lead wire from her monitor system and handed it across to him. "Go ahead. Jack into my database. Review the log yourself."

Gruffly, Tarn snatched the connection from her fingers. He plugged it into an exterior input on his chest. Silence reigned on the beach as the man examined the sensory evidence of Pik's aerial journey.

She wondered whether Tarn would restrict his curiosity to those files alone. *If I were in his position, I certainly wouldn't. I'd audit every data byte I could unlock, determined to learn everything I could from the database of my potential enemies. That's what we are to this Warrior: unidentified individuals, suspected adversaries...even in the best light, we're freelance operatives, civilians interfering with an official Navy rescue mission.*

Etty and Janek made no comment about Pik's breach of team security. Even the Laramy ghost remained quiet, as if aware that this pause was not an opportunity to expound his pet beliefs.

A soft breeze was coming off the ocean, tinged with a musky saltiness. The odor was thick in Pik's curious nose. (Her helmet's faceplate had been retracted since her initial seaside reunion with Etty, enabling them to kiss and communicate verbally.) Breathing this humid air, she watched the syrupy water strike the sand. It edged tentatively higher with each wave. The sand was dark, and the watermark of each subsequent surf was undetectable once the sea had eased back between waves. There was no sign of vegetation along the beach. Glancing inland, she saw that the skeletal forest seemed to shun the coastline, as if fearful of some danger which cognitive fauna could not perceive. For the first time, Pik noticed how empty the air was. No birds or even insects were brave enough to pursue their livelihood in this region. Were there *any* such lifeforms left on this cursed planet? She wondered if the seas were as vacant of activity. Had the New Lords stripped Earth of all its natural denizens, leaving only their brutish servants to inhabit this dead world? The notion of such an indiscriminate genocide made her shiver in the sweat-damp security of her pressure suit.

Looming like some implausible wall fencing-in the horizon, the base of one of the equatorial spikes was hard to miss in the distance. Such an incredible construction was just as difficult to accept, too, despite its immense physical evidence.

Everything about this world was fantastic and intimidating...and ghastly. From the horrors Pik had seen, to Professor Laramy's outrageous fantasies—not a single circumstance inspired anything but a deep and instinctual sensation of dread. The more she saw and learned of this planet, the less Pik doubted Laramy's insanity, leaving her aching to flee this place with a panicky fervor.

Lost in her appraisal of the desolate landscape, she was unaware that Tarn had come to stand beside her. When he spoke, his words jolted the girl from the sobering wasteland.

"I am convinced that what you've told me is the truth," he declared softly.

"Okay."

"I was wrong to refuse your assistance."

"We aren't looking to 'assist' you," she reminded him. "We simply want to get off this damned planet."

"But you *will* assist me, Warrior Pik," he announced. Glancing around, she noticed that Janek was taking no notice of this conversation. This led Pik to suspect that Tarn was speaking to her on a private channel. As he continued, her suit corroborated that suspicion. "You may have resigned the Nimbus Space Navy, but you are still bound by your Warrior Oath. I require your assistance to rescue the Princess from these local beasts."

"I'm not a Warrior any longer," she whispered to him, using his one-to-one waveband. "My loyalties lie with my partners now."

"A Warrior *never* abandons their Oath!"

"What's all this?" Etty asked as he wandered close.

"Tarn was just confirming that he's reviewed my database. He's seen the mysterious force that's stranded us here," she told her beloved. Although

Pik found his nudity charming, she imagined the beach was a tad chilly for him to enjoy his freedom. "Now he's going to continue on his quest."

"Excuse me," interrupted Janek, "but if we all are trapped on this world, perhaps the Warrior would appreciate some help in tracking down the missing Princess."

Tarn had removed the helmet from his suit. On bent knees, he washed it in the ocean, pretending to consider the Duuian's offer.

"Oh, he doesn't need our help," chuckled Pik. "He's a mighty Warrior in the Nimbus Space Navy."

"We must help him!" Etty cried. "It will take all of us to overcome the horrible powers that stand between us and the safe rescue of the Princess!"

"How the grup are you supposed to do anything dressed like that?" she chided. "Or should I say 'undressed'..."

"I don't need a suit— I can—"

Janek, even Tarn, snorted at that statement. "You wouldn't last three minutes in a battle with the type of beasts we've encountered so far," the Duuian remarked.

"The Deep Ones will recapture you!" screamed Professor Laramy.

Ignoring the ghost, Pik presented Etty with her best "concerned" face and informed him, "I can't risk losing you, Etty...not after just getting you back. Please..."

"But the Princess—" whined Etty.

Tarn stood erect and faced me. "I *might* know where your partner's lost pressure suit is."

"Yeah? 'Might', huh?"

"I found an tenantless pressure suit out on the glacier. But I lost it just before I attacked that volcano monster." The Warrior's eyes flashed dangerously, then he curtly reattached his helmet to his battle armor. "Perhaps Pik would accompany me while I search for where I dropped it...?"

"My suit!" squealed Etty. "Then I can help you save Princess Eden!"

Pik nodded mutely. *My own Etty is dragging us into the doomed wake of the lost Princess. And this Code of Honor junkie is using Etty's obsession against me.*

Tarn lifted from the basalt beach with a cloud of dark sand. Pik followed him, her heart heavy with fear, her mind seething with rage.

✛

The female flew away, accompanying the newcomer to retrieve the victim's lost spacesuit, leaving Professor Laramy loitering on the black beachhead with the unhuman one.

The newcomer's armor bristled with astounding weapons, which the ghost had seen used to force the unholy Burrower Beneath into subterranean retreat. The ghost did not trust Tarn the Warrior, though. His aura was dark and bore the markings of many lives taken. His words rang with more than a trace of condescension. The man lived by a violent code that frightened the Professor.

The victim was, it seemed, emotionally attached to the female. Yet, couched in Etty's voiced concerns for the safety of the Princess, Laramy could sense a sexual tension…yet Etty's vocalized passion did not appear to bother Pik. The Professor shelved his confusion, realizing that he had no understanding of the current mating habits of galactic citizens.

The alien displayed a resolute disbelief for the horrors that surrounded them. His focus seemed financial, dedicated to claiming the Princess' "retrieval commission".

Each of them had their reasons to rescue this missing Princess.

Laramy knew that the only way they were going to achieve their goal was by first defeating the evil monsters that ruled Earth. Their Princess was in the blasphemous clutches of the Old Ones. According to the victim's testimony, Ithaqua had spoken in the man's dreams, revealing that both humans were to be delivered to the Great One on the moon. If this group planned to face the Deep Ones, they *must be convinced* of the reality of the monsters of which Laramy had warned them. He knew they did not believe in his fantastic ghost story—they thought he was an insane zealot. Blinded by their galactic sophistication, they assumed that Laramy was a simple man who mistakenly viewed space aliens as Ancient Monsters. They concluded that the New Lords of Earth were only extraterrestrial beings who wielded unknown-but-impressive technologies.

They were, he knew, so very naive and wrong.

And he was the only one who could advise them. This was his destiny, this was the *raison d'etre* of his whole existence. With the correct guidance, these space-traveling individuals could upset the balance-of-oppression that reigned here on Earth. Armed with their astounding weapons, the spacers were fully capable of challenging, even *defeating* the Great Old Ones! They could exterminate the terrible New Lords of Earth, returning the world to its rightful owners. To achieve such greatness, all they had to do was *believe* the things Professor Laramy told them.

The ghost could see no reason for them to distrust him. His knowledge and experience was vast when it came to the Old Ones. Laramy's own powers had failed him in the end, but they had given his enemies fair exchange for many years before the Wind-Walker had murdered him. As a specter, he now possessed different talents to be pitted against the Evil One. Some of these new abilities had only just come under his control, like being able to move his spirit through the air, unbound by common gravity. (For all his intimacy with the arcane secrets of the universe, Professor Laramy could be a painfully simple man. Until he had seen Pik fly, it had never occurred to him that a "ghost" might also be able to fly.) His evolving ability to communicate with living beings was another of these newly emerging spectral abilities. (Or at least, so he thought. In actuality, before the Princess' cruiser had fallen from the sky, there had been *no one* on Earth for him to talk to. His attempts to communicate with the cruiser's Guards and passengers had failed because of his own incapacity. By the time Laramy's ghost had tried to talk to Pik, he had gained enough of a rudimentary control of this spectral talent to finally achieve communication. The same was true for making his ghostly form visible to the naked eye. Sadly, most of his "new abilities" were only basic talents which he had failed to realize during his two centuries of being a ghost.)

By any and all means necessary, Laramy's ghost knew that he must convince these spacers to trust him!

He drifted over to Janek, who was trying to herd an inquisitive Etty away from the water. As he drew near, Laramy discovered that the man was not, by definition of primary motive, curious—he wanted to bathe away the filth his skin had accumulated during his captivity. The alien was wary of the risk, claiming that his spacesuit had analyzed the fluid and determined that it was not wholly friendly to the man's physiology.

"He's right," the ghost nodded in support of Janek's caution. "The Deep Ones have altered the oceans, polluting it with their unholy waste. The Great Awakening happened in the sea; its waters still contain the malevolent taint of the Great One's presence."

"Ignore him," Janek confided to Etty. "He's a religious fanatic. You should avoid the ocean based on the more-credible results of my sensory scan. If you had your own suit, its database would be giving you the same advice."

Of all these strangers from space, it was Janek who fascinated Laramy's ghost. The Professor had never before met an extraterrestrial lifeform, and he was captivated by the Duuian's strangeness. Three legs and six spindly arms, Janek was truly *alien*. His massive head, though, implied that Janek should have been vastly more intelligent than the average human. Laramy was annoyed that this assumption had proved to be misleading; for more than the others, it was Janek who stupidly resisted believing the ghost's tales.

"That's an unfair dismissal," Laramy objected. "I have been here for over two hundred years, I am more familiar than you with the planet's ruined ecosystem and its demonstratively dangerous denizens. Your equipment can assess that the water is 'bad', but *my experience* can tell you why. It is foolish of you to ignore the background information I can provide. You will not defeat the Ancient Ones if you are not properly prepared."

"We have no intention of 'defeating' your absurd monsters for you, Laramy," Janek replied. "We're going to track the Princess' abductors, grab her, and then leave this obnoxious world."

Laramy's reaction to the alien's statement remained trapped behind his ghostly, startled face. *But...this cannot be true,* he lamented. These spacers had promised to hunt down and exterminate the Old Ones. How could they be so blind to their obvious destiny?

"But," muttered Etty, "Pik claimed that the stratosphere was blocked by some force field... How are we going to get past that?"

"I am unconvinced that such a barrier exists," the alien declared. "But it does not matter right now. As long as we pretend to work in tandem with this Warrior who has come after the Princess, we will be involved in the Princess' rescue. Once the Warrior has saved her, he must find a way offworld—or he has failed to rescue the Royal Nimbus Daughter."

"And we follow him out of here," Etty mused, strolling along the beach. "Clever."

"Royal Navy Warriors are clever and resourceful. This one will solve any problems we encounter. It was training-just-like-this that gave Pik her combat edge."

"If such a sky barricade exists, it can only be the handiwork of the Great Evil One!" Professor Laramy's ghost breathed with sincere stress. "He knows you are here."

"Will you please stop trying to explain everything in terms of your religious delusions?" muttered Janek. He was momentarily distracted by a series of three-dimensional lights within the confines of his strangely shaped space helmet.

"Cthulhu will never allow you to escape now," the ghost persisted. "You're all doomed...unless you—"

"Incoming!" screamed the alien. He leapt after the human, for Etty had wandered a ways down the beach. Before Janek got two bounds on his curiously effective triad of pointed feet, the Duuian was struck by one of the masses that had abruptly burst from the tide to rush onland. They were large and smelly and Professor Laramy instantly knew their foul kin: they were Deep Ones!

Deep Ones—Great Cthulhu's devout marine servants. After faithfully tending His submerged temple at R'lyeh for eons, it had been these monstrous offspring of fish and man that had brought about their terrible Lord's Awakening.

They exploded from the viscous surf and swarmed onto the black beach. From their huge size, Laramy knew them to be soldier Deep Ones. They towered over the humans and the alien, their scaly hide glistening with fresh dampness. Their blunt limbs pumped against the hard sand, driving them from the sea. Waggling their wedge-like heads, they displayed frightening jaws of razored shark-teeth. They brandished swords and spikes constructed of obscene coral.

How could I have let down my ectoplasmic guard? Laramy lamented. *I failed to sense their evil approach.* The aquatic behemoths were, he realized, after Etty. They intended to recapture the seeder human for the Great Cthulhu!

When the shambling Deep Ones reached Professor Laramy, they sidled around him, avoiding contact with the insubstantial ghost. Laramy's star-stone talisman was weakened by the millennia, but it was still potent enough to ward off the Old Ones' profane servants. They swerved around him, trampling Janek in their pursuit of Etty. Upon sighting the monsters, the man had made for the rocky hills that lined the beach. Laramy stumbled after the abominations, loudly reciting arcane syllables that might extend his protection to the fleeing victim.

Janek was firing his space weaponry at the Deep Ones, but the beasts took little notice of whatever meager punishment his pulse blasts delivered to their dense meat. The swarm had reached the granite foothills, where their size now worked against them. While Etty clambered nimbly over the jagged crests and slabs of ebony stone, the Deep Ones milled about, nervous and reluctant to scramble up the sharp embankment on their blunt, soft appendages. Soon, the escaping victim vanished from view.

Wailing with despair, Laramy flung his immaterial self to the dark beach.

✢

"Why are you doing this?" Pik growled at the Warrior. Despite the fact that they were now several kilometers from the beach and her partners, she used the man's one-to-one private channel to argue with him. "You don't need us."

"Your assistance will facilitate the speedy rescue of the Princess," Tarn replied curtly. "Supplementary firepower will be necessary against the creatures that have abducted her."

"Why don't you just bring down your battle ship? You've got more firepower there than a hundred of us."

"Calling down my flier would risk subjecting it to whatever force is keeping us trapped on this world. I prefer to keep my ship exempt from that situation."

"And what happens when you save the Princess and can't get her off-world?"

"I will deal with that crisis once the Princess is safe."

They were flying above rocky terrain, headed inland from the syrupy ocean. The jagged hills they passed were covered with calcified vegetation. Pik could not tell whether the plants were ages-dead, or mutated to survive in this barren environment, and she had no desire to waste her suit's resources to determine which was the correct answer. For all she knew, these shrubs were actually the craven minions of some as-yet-unencountered vile New Lord of Earth, covertly awaiting a chance to attack. Every other thing on this wretched world served those blasphemous forces, why should the flora be any different from the fauna? Only Professor Laramy clung to the madness of opposing these monsters, and even he had fallen before their murderous might. The wasteland that rushed beneath Pik was a testament to the entire unbalance of nature that ruled this lost world. Those who refused to serve, were slaughtered.

There's not much difference, she mused, *between these profane monstrosities and the Warrior with his devious plans for myself and the rest of my team.*

"You're a bastard," she told him.

"I am being faithful to my Warrior Oath."

"Don't give me that. The tactics you're using to coerce me are in violation of that Oath."

"Not according to my perspective."

"Do you really know where Etty's suit is? Or is this just another ruse to blackmail me into helping you?"

"Your partners are willing to assist me."

"They have their *reasons*. Etty's obsessed with the Princess. And Janek still has his eyes on the retrieval commission."

"That makes *you* the only one who has a realistic motive to help."

"*You're* the only one with a solid motive, Tarn. If you get my help, it'll be against my better judgment."

"I am not concerned with motives, Pik. Results are all I care about."

"By any means necessary..."

"Yes. By any means necessary." Without warning, he deviated from his flight path, diving down into a valley between lifeless crags. By the time Pik caught up with him, the Warrior had landed. He stood next to Etty's lost suit, which lay dented on the ground before him.

"So, you really did know where his suit was," she grumbled, touching down a few meters from him.

"Whether it will do your partner any good remains to be seen."

"Huh?" Then Pik noticed that the Warrior had activated one of his shoulder-mounted pulse cannons. Its barrel was pointed directly at the empty suit at his feet. "You *bastard*..."

"Your call," he remarked without emotion. His fearsomely tattooed face was cold and firm, awaiting her fateful decision. He did not need to spell out the terms of his extortion. If Pik wanted Etty to regain his pressure suit intact, she was going to have to swear allegiance to Tarn's rescue mission. He was thoroughly willing to condemn Etty to die on this terrible planet if she refused.

"Etty is more than just my partner," she warned the man. "He's my lover. If you damage his suit, you'll be turning me into your enemy. I'll kill you, Tarn...if I have to hunt you across half the galaxy, I will."

His expression did not change, nor did the aim of his pulse cannon.

"I mean it!" swore Pik. "Don't do this."

"Make your choice," he ordered gruffly. "All this is wasting valuable time if we are to rescue the Princess before some calamity befalls her."

His arrogant superiority was not a bluff. Despite her numerous custom add-ons, Tarn's battle armor vastly outclassed Pik's suit. A fight between the two would leave the girl dead, she knew this. Then, considering the raw interpretation the Warrior had for his own ethics, it would not have surprised her if he returned to Etty and Janek with some tale of monsters ambushing her. He would exhibit false sadness over her demise, and then he would welcome her partners' allegiance. Fueled by their desire to avenge Pik's unfortunate murder, they would blindly follow him into battle against their mutual enemies.

There really was no choice for her to make. The problem lay in convincing herself to be manipulated into service of the Warrior. To save her beloved's life, she needed to swallow her individuality and freedom, and vow fealty to Tarn's command.

✥

The two Warriors found Laramy's ghost alone on a beach that bore the signs of a mammoth struggle. Chasms and pits marred the dark sand. Even now the foul waters of the ocean were filling these cavities with a vile froth.

"What happened here?" demanded Tarn.

"Where's Etty?!" Pik cried aloud, opening her faceplate to shout at the ghost.

Professor Laramy was sprawled on his hazy knees. He glanced up at them as they approached. "Where were you?" he moaned. "They attacked, and no one could fight them off…"

"Where's Etty?!" Pik screamed again. She stamped her armored boot on the beach before Laramy, startling the ghost from his dazed babble.

"I'm not sure," Laramy mumbled.

"What?!" Pik's voice reached even more tumultuous volumes.

"There was a swarm of them. Deep Ones," the Laramy ghost told the spacers. "They rushed out of the ocean…and Etty ran…but they got—"

"They got Etty?!"

"Here I am!" a familiar voice announced.

"Etty!" Pik yelled. She whirled and ran across the black sand to collide/embrace with Etty as he stumbled from concealment amid the jagged foothills that rimmed the shoreline. The man's progress was awkward, for his agility was impaired by the numerous scratches covering his naked body.

"They didn't get Etty," muttered Laramy. The haziness of his ethereal substance seemed to have communed to fog his intellectual capacities. His lethargy implied that the specter was incapable of recalling what had happened—or could not bear to summon forth any memories of his failure.

"Where's the Duuian?" Tarn demanded.

The ghost peered up at the Warrior. The shadow of the spacer's massive suit fell across Laramy like a spectral accusation. Behind the Warrior, another shape floated in the air, bobbing like a misshapen balloon. It took Laramy a minute to realize what it was. "I see you found Etty's lost spacesuit…" he commented.

The Warrior swung a fist on Laramy. "Where is the— Huh?!" Tarn was startled when his arm slipped through the ghost's intangible shoulders. This was the Warrior's first material contact with Professor Laramy, and Tarn was unprepared for the lack of physicality accompanying that blow. Squawking with surprise, Tarn toppled back, landing the butt of his suit on the dark sand. "What the def—"

"They took Janek," Laramy announced in a whiny squeal.

"What's going on here?" asked Pik as she and Etty approached.

"He—he's not real!" Tarn exclaimed, waving an armored arm frantically in Laramy's direction. "What is it—a hologram?"

"He's a ghost," Pik sneered. "Get used to it."

"You say they got Janek?" Etty gasped. "I couldn't see what was going on from back in the foothills."

"They swarmed to recapture you," the ghost asserted, facing Etty. "But when you escaped, they vented their frustration on your alien companion…they dragged him with them…" he gestured to the sea, "…into the dreadful waters!"

"We've got to go after him!" Etty insisted. He pulled on Pik's arm, and met her stare with fervent intensity.

"All in good time," Pik told him.

"Our immediate objective is to locate the Princess," declared the Warrior.

"We're going after Janek," Pik announced sternly. Her tone made it no secret that she was vehement about this intention. Turning to pull the floating spacesuit from the air, she presented it to Etty. He cackled and climbed into its safety.

The ghost watched the two Warriors conduct a fiery eye duel. They locked glares, and the both of them radiated absolute intimidation. While Tarn's darkness naturally fueled his fury, the girl was doing an excellent job of matching the Warrior's innate ferocity. Her brown face had frozen in a mask of utter tenacity. Laramy flinched from the raw emotions of that confrontation. This was not just a war of wills—there was hatred involved, tainting the air with its psychic heat.

Finally, it was Pik who broke their combative silence. "By the very Oath you've coerced me to readopt, we are all a *team* now. Honorable Warriors *never* abandon one of their own to the enemy."

The Warrior growled, but jerked his head in an imperceptible acknowledgment of her accusation. He coughed, then remarked, "A million to three, those are not encouraging odds. We will need *everyone* if we expect to go against the defense troops of this world's supreme ruler."

Sealing his suit, Etty strode forth to address everyone. "Let's get moving!"

"How can we track them?" the ghost moaned. He swung a despairing glance at the vast gray ocean. "They could be anywhere out there..."

"Janek has a tracer built into his suit. We'll have no problem finding him, trust me." Pik's smirk revealed a personal satisfaction that the crisis was under control. Her attitude conveyed that she considered their companion's abduction as purely a momentary setback.

❖

Now that Etty was safely re-ensconced in his spacesuit, they could go as a team in search of their stolen teammate. With no more hesitation, the trio of pureblood humans entered the ocean's viscous waters. Laramy trailed after them, disturbed that no one was acknowledging his presence.

Why were they persisting in ignoring his guidance? They knew Professor Laramy was more familiar than they were with this world, its oceans and profane denizens. By refusing to accept his help, they were needlessly endangering themselves. Their blind obstinance infuriated the ghost, for he could figure no way to change their decision to exclude him. Every time he tried to offer invaluable information about their enemy, one of the group (often Pik) would start an unrelated conversation with another member of the group. And Laramy's assistance went unheard and unnoticed.

Was this what galactic civilization had done to mankind? Were the survivors of the human race all passionately distrustful and paranoid now? These people were proof to the Professor that humanity had not been exterminated by the terrible Old Ones. They were the future of the species. They were brethren to Laramy. Why couldn't they see that?

They found Janek's empty suit thirty kilometers out. It drifted in a deep current of lightless water; without tuning in to the suit's tracer signal, spotting it would have been impossible.

The Deep Ones had extracted Janek from his suit in the same unholy manner that Ithaqua's bestial wizard had teleported Etty from his suit back in the fallen cruiser's empty drive core. The Duuian was gone!

"Will you listen to my advise *now*?" the ghost pleaded with the spacers.

Praylude:
Excerpts from the Diary of a Crank

They've labeled me a "crank", a deluded zealot whose opinions have no bearing on the impending catastrophe. By refusing to believe my explanations, they remain wholly ignorant to the gravity of the crisis. By denying my guidance, they guarantee their collective damnation.

How can they be so adamantly blind to the threat that rears to exterminate all of mankind?

Marie tells me I am too passionate, that my devotion to oppose the Deep Ones is so intense as to appear akin to a brain fever in eyes of the Authorities. She may be right.

I have fought the clandestine minions of the aberrant Old Ones all my life, ferreting out their coastal incursions, and repelling these aquatic horrors from reclaiming Innsmouth or achieving beachheads on otherwise uninhabited Polynesian islands. My occult training and horrific experiences have granted me an absolute faith in the beliefs that drive my actions. There is no point in doubting the evil that dwells beneath the waves, for no amount of disbelief will quell those monsters' terrible wrath.

It is possible that we, Earth's secret defenders, waited too long to reveal ourselves to the general populace. But what other recourse did we have? If made public, our warnings would have been mistaken as new age delusions and dismissed by the average citizen. Industrialization and the Age of Reason had dulled mankind's imagination, generating a global skepticism toward anything that resembled superstition. While theologians loudly advertised the existence of God (whether He be called Christ, Buddha or Allah), no one seriously believed in incarnate Evil. Even now, facing the undeniable-but-inexplicable reality of the Deep Ones, people resisted the truth. The world resolutely refused to acknowledge the empirical evidence that lay waste to their shoreline communities.

Only we secret defenders understood that Evil truly existed—more so, that the armies of Evil actively struggled in pursuit of humanity's overall destruction, while the forces of Good wielded only flowery words to combat the devil.

But we are few, oh so very few. The years have decreased our numbers, the oft-timed futility of our struggle taking sad toll of our ranks. The grisly deaths of so many of our brethren have tested our faith, leaving disillusioned defenders to stray from our occult fold and become swallowed by society's lunatic fringe.

Which has only hardened my dedication to the cause. I know that without my arcane opposition, the minions of Cthulhu will win. Only the spells and rituals gleaned from antediluvian lore can turn back the Deep hordes.

The courageous efforts of myself, my beloved wife, and my trusted brethren are mankind's only hope.

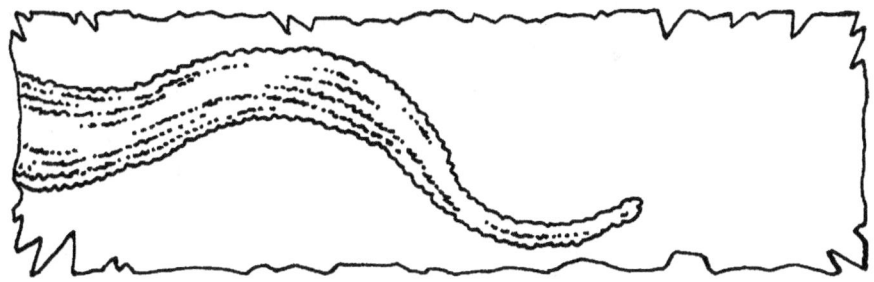

section 3:
Attaining Acclivity

The Deep Ones had dragged Janek down into these murky waters, then they had removed him (by questionable means) from the security of his pressure suit. There was no way of telling whether those abductors had continued deeper with their prey, or had, upon discovering that Janek was not human, casually cast aside the Duuian to drown in the viscous environment.

Ever the optimist, Etty towed his lost partner's discarded suit along with him. If they found Janek—and should he still be alive—the suit would be necessary for his survival beyond that rescue.

When the Warrior announced that the search for Janek was over, Pik was not surprised. Despite her loyalty to that lost partner, she had to agree that the chances of Janek's survival looked dismal. There was no viable method of locating his naked body in this alien ocean's vast depths. If his captors had dumped him, underwater currents could have moved his corpse in a myriad of serpentine directions, depositing him far beyond the muffled range of the retrievers' most acute sensors. Even if the team was lucky enough to find his body, they could not drag it into battle with them. A part of Pik wanted to give Janek the courtesy of a proper burial (according to Duuian ceremony, whatever that entailed), but the realistic side of her mind understood the futility of that. The wisest course of action was to avoid challenging the Warrior's leadership on his decision.

So Pik and Etty unhappily followed the Warrior as he promptly led them away, beginning the quest for the lost Princess.

The darkness they moved through was stifling on many levels. Earth's oceans were thick, almost like jelly a few meters beneath the surging surface. This dense liquid hampered all sensory scans, reducing perceptions of their surroundings to little better than murky notions.

Tarn's equipment was decidedly more sensitive than what belonged to the freelancer hunters, so they were forced to depend on him for guidance through the aquatic depths. Against their better judgment, the team relied on Professor Laramy's ghost as their early warning system. Theoretically, Laramy would notify them of any strange or threatening activity beyond the trivial range of the Warrior's sensory equipment.

The trade-off for getting the ghost to do this was that they had to endure tedious discourses intended to familiarize them with every dreadful detail of the Professor's arcane and bent doctrines. For hours the ghost droned about "ancient evil" and "monstrous spawn" and "irreverent covenants". He frequently peppered his lecture with words that defied repetition by a human mouth, garbled and disjointed syllables which comprised the unholy names of the horrific deities that populated his fantasy theology.

Professor Laramy babbled without pause. His ghostly voice carried to the humans through some alternative ether, relying not the least on any transmission frequency possessed by their suits. As a result, his oration was impossible to tune out, intruding on their thoughts and coloring them with dreadful possibilities.

Tarn made no complaints, apparently enduring the ghost's endless lecture with clinical patience. At first, the Warrior had been attentive in order to gain knowledge about the enemy. But now, after hours of Laramy's "profane" this and "abhorrent" that, Pik could sympathize with how Tarn must have been growing weary of the ghost's biased definitions. The Professor's tendency to wander into occult dogma inevitably stripped much of the credibility from his advice. Such outlandish ramblings were not going to convert the Warrior to trust Laramy's opinions.

During much of their underwater journey, Pik and Etty remained silent.

Pik was still quite shaken by the sudden death of a member of their team. She and Etty had been struggling (unsuccessfully) as freelance retrievers for almost three years before they had met Janek. Impressed by his acumen for databases, they had invited the Duuian to join their team.

It had been through Janek's funding that they had acquired the ">%" in a Court Auction. Without his skills, the team would never have scored the few measly retrieval commissions they had over the years.

It's amazing how, when a companion dies, you only miss the good things they did, she realized. *You never mourn the person's bad habits. I'll never again have to tolerate Janek's stupid blank-stare while he was data-buzzing, lost in the realm of bitstreams and informational codification.* The Duuian's addiction for input had often viscerally bothered Pik, for she viewed it as a fatal flaw in Janek's otherwise commendable personality. Sometimes he was particularly greedy, but that had always worked to their advantage when he had negotiated above-standard commission rates out of obstinate Judicial clerks. *And…I guess I have to concede that Janek's data habit had been helpful in outwitting runners on their own turf—research is a fundamental necessity in stalking fugitives.*

All in all, I'm going to miss his data-buzzed stare.

Piecing together revelations from Etty's nightmare with fragments of Laramy's horrific lore of the enemy, it seemed safe to assume that these Deep Ones had taken Janek, believing him to be another offworld intruder. When they had discovered that he was an alien, they had probably cast him to his doom. The Great Lord of Earth wanted "human" captives, preferably a male to seed the breeder His servants were even now delivering to Him.

Grup—listen to me. I'm already capitalizing personal pronouns for these grotesque characters from Laramy's wild fantasy. This showed Pik that, in the pit of her subconscious, she was beginning to credit Laramy's tales of Ancient Evil with more than a modicum of belief. Was her faith in God any less valid than Laramy's hate of the Old Ones? Belief in Heaven dictated the existence of Hell, for Good coexisted with Evil. They were inseparable concepts, like *on* or *off* in binary language, like *alive* or *dead* in daily existence. Laramy did not worship these Old Ones, he opposed their atrocities on the basis of his own religious convictions. In a strange way, she understood that they were kindred spirits, connected by personal ideologies created a galaxy and centuries apart.

Religion had suffered greatly when mankind emigrated from ancient Earth. Humanity's obsessive uniqueness and their anthropomorphic concept of God were severely challenged by a galaxy full of alien intelligent species, each with their own version of supposedly irrefutable theological doctrines. Everyone's deity was the One True God. It took centuries for these conflicting dogmas to adjust to a less egocentric perspective of the universe.

The God that Pik believed in was undoubtedly not the God Professor Laramy prayed to. Laramy's concept of a Creator would have been based on humanity's pre-emigration religions, while Pik's beliefs concerned a homogenized deity that encompassed all the galactic faces of God into a single abstract personification, one who saw no difference between alien species, but loved all creatures and inanimate matter equally. It did not matter that Laramy's Savior possessed a human visage while hers was more a quantum force of faceless benevolence—the ethical concepts that defined their Gods immutably unified them.

The only ones who refused to share in this congruent galactic theology were the A.I.s, who followed the same tenets but resolutely adhered to the uniqueness and superiority of their artificial kind. In the eyes of the A.I.'s, organic life was an abomination. If Laramy's ghost was to be believed, though, it seemed that there were much older and more blasphemous abominations than the current sampling of galactic lifeforms.

This did not mean that Pik was starting to believe in the ghost's monstrous deities, though. Her religious convictions did not imply that she was God. Why should the fealty these Old Ones held for Evil make them Devils? As clearly as Pik worshipped Good in the form of the Unified God, she assumed these Ancient Ones revered Evil.

Good existed, as did Evil. If these Old Ones were dedicated to Evil incarnate, their destruction was a necessity. The question of whether they were ancient demons or simply deviant aliens was immaterial, for both definitions warranted a righteous extinction. Either way, their atrocities were evidenced by the wasteland they had made of old Earth. Either way, they were mighty creatures, wielding deadly technologies or powers or whatever. Either way, these monsters needed to be obliterated.

Paradoxically, while she found herself gradually adjusting to the frightful actuality of ultimately "evil" Old Ones, Pik was still troubled by Professor Laramy's ghostly *afterlife*. If Laramy had died, he should have gone to Heaven (or Hell, for she honestly knew nothing about the state of the man's soul at the time of his demise). Why was his soul still walking the Earth two hundred years after his death? Was he really dead? Was he really human? Or was Laramy an angel, a messenger of God…?

She listened to his rambling tales of cosmic terror, hoping to glean some clue to his karmic identity…but his words were simply those of a paranoid zealot.

"…out for the Deep Ones. They are the descendants of the Old Ones' unholy genetic tampering in Earth's prehistoric eras—before even man walked this soil. While deep in His eternal slumber, Great Cthulhu reached out to violate the dreams of the world's aquatic creatures, warping these creatures into a profane fealty to Himself. These monsters guarded submerged R'lyeh, where Cthulhu's consciousness was imprisoned. For eons, they struggled to find a means of awakening their sleeping Lord, tampering with the cosmic seals on His mighty Tomb of Slumber, tormenting any lifeforms they encountered in their mad striving to awaken the Old One. I am loathe to admit it, but it was finally through their manipulation of mankind that the Deep Ones, led by the Dagon abomination, succeeded in their antediluvian goal. The Deep Ones engineered an international crisis that brought every nuclear missile on the planet raining down on the Pacific Ocean. Catastrophic as such a radioactive saturation might be to us—human life, I mean—the incredible detonations served only to jar awake a slumbering monster, revitalizing His groggy self with the fallout. The Genocide followed the Awakening within a few—"

"So," the Warrior commented, "these Deep Ones are the ones who will be delivering the Princess to this Cthulhu monster."

"Yes," Laramy faltered to utter a single syllable.

"Their civilization predates man, you say."

Again, the ghost uttered a solitary "Yes."

What was Tarn doing?

"So, why do they have humanoid characteristics? Are you suggesting that mankind is an evolutionary offshoot of their lineage?"

"No."

"They've been mixing their gene pool, mating with other species… including man."

"Yes."

"What's the matter, Tarn?" Pik chuckled over the comlink. "Are you worried you might come from a tainted heritage?"

"If we can place any credibility in Etty's claims of what this Cthulhu plans to do with the Princess, I am worried for her safety."

"She should be safe as long as Tarn and I keep ourselves from getting captured," Etty remarked.

"There are no other human males for the Great One to use," Laramy's ghost added. "The Earth hasn't seen purebloods like yourselves in two centuries."

"These Deep Ones contain human genes, though," muttered the Warrior.

Now Pik saw where the Warrior was following this train of abhorrent thought. "You think they might— No—!" she gasped.

"The grisly aspects aside—for I expect they'll impregnate her artificially to keep her intact for this and future pregnancies—the entire prospect is frightening. I hope we find her before my deductions become reality."

"Stop being so morbid!" Etty demanded. "She's alive, and she's unviolated! We're going to save her before anything bad happens to her."

"Calm down, Etty," Pik told him. "He's only doing his job. He's trying to assess the situation and be prepared for any eventuality."

"He doesn't have to keep coming up with new terrible things that could happen to the Princess," Etty grumbled. "He acts as if he *wants* the worst to happen."

"There's a world of difference between fatalism and strategy, Etty. We can't avert the worst from happening unless we think of every worst way things could go."

"What about an immediate plan of action?" Etty moaned. "Or are we going to swim aimlessly forever in this jelly?"

"Our course is not 'aimless', you fool," the Warrior growled. "We are headed in the direction of the giant spike that was on the horizon. The Princess' abductors will be heading for it too, that will be their means of delivering their captive to their master on the moon."

"They have a considerable lead on us," admitted the ghost. "But we will follow them into and up the Spire of Condemnation, where all who serve the monstrous Cthulhu will be exterminated by the superior technology of your space weapons!"

Pik sighed wearily. Laramy was a fountain of fanaticism.

⬦

Etty didn't understand why they had to remain submerged in the foul ocean.

"We'd make much better time if we flew there through the air," he pointed out.

The Warrior snorted, establishing an air of barely-tolerated-impatience before he stated his rebuke. "*They* will be taking an underwater route to the spike. We have a better chance of catching them down here."

"In this soup?" Etty scoffed. He could barely see his own hands, much less the figure in front of him. He was maneuvering entirely by remote perception, relying on his sensory equipment to apprise him of his surroundings. Even then, the water was so viscous that it registered as a gray haze on most scans, obfuscating the markers which represented his traveling companions.

While the greater portion of Etty's awareness was occupied by the relentless *need* to rescue the Princess, there were a few synapses devoted to not understanding the Warrior's actions. Tarn seemed to exhibit schizophrenic on/off flashes when it came to his dedication of rescuing Princess Eden from the monsters. One minute he was ordering everyone to rush to her rescue…and now, hours later, they were still moving along on minimal thrusters through soupy waters—and they hadn't found her yet! One minute Tarn was confident that the Princess would be saved… the next, the man was predicting gruesome and terrifying fates for the Royal Daughter! This constant inconsistency troubled Etty, for he wondered how earnest the Warrior was in his devotion to the success of this rescue.

On general principles, Etty distrusted Tarn. The man was a Warrior in the Nimbus Royal Space Navy. He was the Ruling Class' storm trooper. In the absence of any preconceived opinions, Etty had picked up a strong dislike for the Navy from Pik's rare tales of her years in the military. Pik had left her Warriorhood behind by the time Etty had met her, but she would always carry the mental scars of that period of degrading servitude. By virtue of his deep affection for her, Pik's traumas became Etty's.

In point of fact, Etty had little in the way of a personal history. What past he recalled was generally vacant of trauma or strife. At the peak of his adolescence, Etty had become infected with a memory dampener (a nanobot survivor from the Org/A.I. War) which had effectively caused irreversible damage to the bulk of his long-term memories. This had left the boy a clean mental slate, forcing him to relearn everything—walking, talking, eating, defecating, running, jumping, loving, hating, getting hurt, being happy, curiosity, language, mathematics, physics, literature, likes, dislikes, recreational interests, professional pursuits, financial failures, scraping along—and then he had met Pik. They'd been together for eight years now. .

The greater part of the life he remembered involved Pik—there at his side, or always in mind. To him, she was not just the love of his life, she was the *equivalent* of his life. A good portion of his adult psyche was defined by his desire to operate in tandem with Pik's personality. He was literally a mirror of her wants and likes and opinions. So deep were Pik's insecurities that Etty constructed an entire psyche for himself to accommodate and soothe her personal fears.

They were a perfect match, almost star-crossed lovers by virtue of Etty's tragic memory loss and Pik's tortured childhood. Unaware of Etty's integral psychological fixation on her, Pik had fallen in love with him because of the man he was.

It annoyed Etty to detect traces of Pik in Tarn's clenched-teeth personality. It annoyed him even more when she took the Warrior's side, defending his meandering progress. It infuriated Etty that all this was delaying the Princess' desperately needed rescue. Every minute they plodded through this murky ocean was another minute for the foul Deep Ones to defile the Royal Daughter. How terrifying those horrid monsters must have seemed to the innocent Princess.

Thoughts of the Deep Ones sent shivers along Etty's manly spine. He recalled their ghastly shambling and odious smells and gaping mouths and stumpy limbs and lifeless fish-eyes and their thundering rush. They had treated him like an inanimate parcel—a breeding machine. But then, therein lay the crux: he was *human*, he could expect no racial sympathy from minions of the Great Cthulhu. All of mankind were but anonymous chattel to the Great One.

Under no circumstances could Etty tolerate imagining the buxom and lovely Princess Eden subjected to whatever loathsome ministrations these monsters had in store for her. He resented the Warrior's pessimistic conjectures regarding the girl's fate. Although he refused to believe in them, these suggestions only inspired Etty's imagination to more horrific introspection.

He was unhappy that Pik took the man's side. Etty felt as if he had been reprimanded for expressing common decency. He was worried about the Princess—and no one seemed to be doing anything constructive about rescuing her! Why was that an inappropriate sentiment?

The ghost was no help either, with his relentless prattle of arcane monsters and their unclean habits. Janek had been correct: the Professor was clearly a fanatic on the subject, never running out of dire recitations of the evil atrocities visited by these ghastly Old Ones on the poor human race. The ghost was convinced that humanity had been exterminated by these ancient monsters, completely ignoring the fact that Etty and Pik and Tarn represented a human culture that spanned (and ruled) half the galaxy. Mankind was no more extinct than free hydrogen. The ghost was repeatedly myopic in his obsessive fear of the monsters that haunted his deluded mind. As far as Professor Laramy was concerned: because he hated these creatures, everyone else automatically reviled them with equal loathing. In Laramy's opinion, the evils he imagined perpetrated by his enemies affected the entire universe. The ghost's ultimate blindness was almost pathetic.

These were the agents of Princess Eden's salvation: an arrogant Warrior, a recalcitrant lover, a delusional ghost…and Etty, normally easygoing and submissive, now full of impatience and anxiety.

His reverie of anguish was interrupted when the group swam into abruptly clearer waters. The murkiness separated to reveal a maze of mammoth stone structures, each dressed in centuries of algae and contorted coral. They were insanely huge, dwarfing any buildings Etty could recall. Their forms wavered in the clear-but-hardly-transparent ocean, but Etty had the unnerving impression that there was something unnatural about the angles of the sunken city. Their corners refused to come into focus, their angles and planes seemed to flicker as if unwilling to restrain themselves to any set cast. Their edifices were adorned with sculptures and bas-reliefs whose disturbing nature was hardly muted by the aquatic vegetation that clung to their surfaces. As the group drew closer, Etty could see that huge, malformed sea shells crawled across the buildings. He could detect no doors or even windows among the clustered towers.

"We're near the base of the spike," the Warrior announced.

"These must be the outlying ruins of R'lyeh," the Laramy ghost gasped.

According to the ghost's repulsive tales, this was point zero for the terrible Awakening that had brought about the downfall of Earth. Here, the Great Cthulhu had slumbered in a coma for eons, only to be roused by the vile Deep Ones. According to Laramy's accounts, from here the monsters had spread to eviscerate the entire planet. The rescue team had indeed reached the thick of enemy territory.

It was not long before evidence of this skulked into view. Distant shadows detached themselves from the corners of these enormous ancient tombs, drifting to intercept the retrieval team's approach. Deep Ones! Etty recognized the beasts before they came near enough to discern the details of their aberrant shapes. His breath caught in his throat, as terror overcame his mind.

The Deep Ones advanced with undulating movements that were quite different from the tottering shambling they had exhibited on land. The creatures were in their own element now, which could only heighten their stubborn might. They advanced on the humans as if confident of their superiority. The Deep Ones swam as if they believed the team was surrendering itself to them.

The Warrior dispelled that impression, firing his lasers and particle beams into the lead beast. That creature convulsed under Tarn's firepower, then it slowly drifted into separate pieces amid a milky cloud of yellow blood.

"Use your lasers," the Warrior commanded them. "Pulse beams are useless down here where the pressure has toughened them to such forces."

"Stay back," Pik ordered Etty, moving herself protectively between him and the nearest Deep Ones. "Etty's lasers are purely for scan-and-signal use," she muttered for the Warrior's sake. "Mine have been tweaked to weapons status, though." Her weaponry added a nest of gleaming red needles to the murky depths. Her shots carved the monsters into a haze of diced meat.

The Warrior's aim was far more simplistic, and horrifically more effective. He swung his lasers in a wide arc, slicing each beast into two equal and dead sections. Pik's frenetic shots simply rendered those halves into smaller bits.

Several beams struck the underwater vaults, vaporizing the algae and coral rust, but having no effect on the dark stone itself.

Suddenly, a thought came to Etty and he cried aloud, "Stop! What if these beasts have the Princess with them?"

"They don't," came the Warrior's curt response.

"Use your scans, Etty," Pik chided him.

He grunted and consulted his interface. Indeed, the only human signatures in the vicinity were his, Pik's, and the Warrior's. The eviscerated swarm consisted only of Deep Ones. He mentally kicked himself for not thinking to survey the scene before panicking. Of course the Warrior had done this, so had Pik. But not Etty.

Makes me look like an idiot, he grumbled. *A helpless idiot too.*

But then, it wasn't his fault that his pressure suit wasn't rigged with supplementary battle armament. Pik was the team's soldier. According to standard operating procedure, Etty wasn't supposed to find himself in situations that required defensive firepower. This wasn't exactly a standard situation, though.

Professor Laramy had remained silent through the brief battle, but now his spectral voice rang in their heads with exuberant celebration. He cursed the Deep Ones for their blasphemous allegiance to the Great Cthulhu. He praised the Warriors for their glorious victory over the aquatic abominations. He predicted a speedy downfall for the Great One, an ultimate punishment for the horrors He had perpetrated throughout history.

Tarn interrupted the ghost's sermon, inquiring if Laramy was familiar with the spike itself. "What is the weakest entry point? Or—do you know which entrance the beasts carrying the Princess will head for?"

"Umm," Laramy mumbled. "I have never visited a Spire of Condemnation before now… I am unacquainted with their construction."

Etty expected a gout of frustrated abuse to spill forth from Tarn, but the angered Warrior remained silent.

It amazed Etty how ignorant their "guide" was. He snidely brought this to the group's attention.

Bluntly, Laramy reminded Etty that his companions would never have rescued him from the Great One's couriers without the Professor's advice.

Without warning, Tarn proceeded forward. He swam through the cloud of awful body parts, heading for the spike. The others followed him without comment.

Down here, the base of the spike was firmly rooted in the ocean floor, as if it plunged through the seabottom and the crust to pierce the very core of the planet. It was an enormous barrier, stretching in every lateral direction as far as Etty's scanners could reach. Literally walling off their watery environment, it loomed green and gloomy, an impenetrable facade of grisly texture. Its surface was smooth, unbroken by carvings or coarse construction; no algae or coral dared touch its irreverent substance.

They were attacked by several more swarms of Deep Ones, and the Warrior reduced these monstrous defenders into loose meat without hesitation. Some of these newcomers flung spears of chiseled coral; their aim was without fault, but the shafts shattered easily against the armor worn by Pik and Tarn. The Deep Ones possessed no protection against the searing laser beams, though. Soon, the waves of fresh marine combatants slacked off, leaving the team to conduct its final approach unmolested.

Drifting within arm's-reach of the mammoth wall, Pik chuckled, "Okay, Tarn. How do we get in?"

As if cued by her caustic inquiry, a tremendous shudder vibrated the wall and the surrounding waters. For a moment, they all feared that something was about to force its way out of the wall, but then an oval hatch irised open, revealing a dark liquid interior. They all tensed, expecting the next wave of the spike's defense, but nothing exited the portal.

"This is a trap," the Laramy ghost needlessly proclaimed.

"It's our way in," announced Tarn.

⁛

"Now, hold on a second," sputtered Professor Laramy.

"Yeah—we're not going to step right into the mouth of their trap. We don't even know if the Princess is in there," Pik remarked.

"*I know* she's inside," the Warrior hissed.

"How can you be— She has a tracer!" exclaimed Pik. "You've been tracking her all along!"

"Obviously," replied Tarn.

"And now you're willing to risk all of our lives by jumping into the enemy's first trap?"

He turned to glare at her through the filthy water. "Yes."

"You bastard," she growled. "How many more things don't we need to know? Could you be leading us into battle any more unprepared?"

The bastard ignored her. He swam through the wide portal, vanishing into the darkness inside. After a minute, he switched on his armor's exterior lights, illuminating the inner chamber for the rest of them to see.

It was shaped like a vertically aligned lozenge, and it was empty. There were no passages to the spike's interior.

"Get out of there," Pik called to Tarn. "Before you get yourself captured."

"Remember—*any* male human will do to fulfill Cthulhu's progeny scheme," warned Laramy's ghost. "You're as much at risk as Etty."

"Hardly," commented the Warrior. "*I* can protect myself."

The hatch started to rumble shut.

And Pik did a very impulsive thing. Grabbing Etty, she dove through the closing portal to join the Warrior in the trap.

Her motives for this action had nothing to do with any concern for Tarn's safety. Without the extenuating circumstances, she might have let the monstrous spike swallow the bastard. *Good riddance to callous trash.* Alas, because of that force barrier stranding them all on this awful world, her own survival (and ultimate escape) depended on staying with the Warrior. Separated from the bastard, Pik and Etty were doomed. She joined him in the obvious jaws of their enemy's trap to keep herself and Etty alive.

Damn the grupping bastard...

As soon as the incredible hatch closed, their confinement commenced a violent trembling. Allowing to the jellied water that filled the cell, they were not thrown about by this great shaking. The humans hung suspended. When their prison surged and soared upward, they gradually drifted to the bottom of the cell.

"It's an elevator!" Etty gasped over the comlink.

A mobile trap.

They had come to break into the spike and rescue the captive Princess...only to find themselves snared by the terrible powers that ruled here. Without doubt, they were being conveyed to their doom. Perhaps they would even share the Princess' grotesque fate as breeders for the hungry Old One. Now the enemy had two females and two males.

Pik was not coping very well with the repercussions of her abrupt choice to follow the Warrior. She had not correctly assessed the extent of psychological damage this would entail for her—or for Etty.

Her beloved was freaking out. Etty condemned Pik for dragging him here. He lamented that they were all doomed now. Remembering his treatment at the hands of the Deep Ones, his panic overwhelmed him, reducing him to a moaning lump.

She switched off his signal and consulted privately with the Warrior. "So, what now?"

"Now, we see what next," he replied coolly.

"Do we come out with guns blazing?"

"That...remains to be seen." His uncertainty startled her.

"Hey, there. If anyone needs to keep a level head through this—it's *you!*"

"According to my instruments, we are presently moving in the direction of the Princess' location."

"Your tracer."

"*Her* tracer," he corrected absently.

"What do your instruments tell you about the rest of the spike? Mine can't get past this cell's walls."

"Calcium," the Warrior told her. "Mostly solid, although as our cage rises, I detect more passages honeycombing the solid mass..."

"Calcium? You mean—*bone*?!"

"Apparently. Do not distract me with unimportant questions. I am looking for traces of weapon systems, so I can evaluate their defensive capabilities..."

Bone! The Spires of Condemnation were made of bone! The Spires were hundreds of kilometers thick at their rounded bases, and they protruded well over three-hundred-and-thirty thousand kilometers from the planet, nearly touching the moon. Pik could not recall how many spikes she had detected from her planetary approach aboard the ">%", but there were definitely more than ten…maybe as many as twenty. Where had the builders, the minions of the evil Old Ones, found enough bones to…?

Oh…

She shuddered at the obvious answer. These miracles of unholy construction were unintentional monuments to the extinct human race, comprised of their desiccated remains!

Her mind reeled with this profane realization. Despairing as it was to imagine the extermination of a species, it was psychically repulsive to find herself surrounded by the residue of their ancient corpses.

Etty remained locked in his fearful denial. The imminent prospect of being returned to the Deep Ones' clutches had bludgeoned his personality into a resolute withdrawal.

Professor Laramy was no longer with the team. The ghost had not followed them into the elevator trap, he had been left behind outside the mighty Spire. If he dared to pursue them, he had no way of knowing where they were now. The elevator's ascent was incredibly intense. Even if Laramy had been here, what physical assistance could he give? Once again the ghost's value as a guide had proven miserably inadequate.

The Warrior seemed unperturbed by the entire crisis. He acted as if capture by the enemy was an everyday occurrence, a minor snag in his rescue mission, one that he was confident to overcome. The bastard kept his confidence quite confidential, actually. Perhaps he thought it might be diminished by sharing.

"I cannot move," Pik heard the Warrior rasp in her ear. "Are you experiencing similar restraint?"

"Huh?" Grup, she *was* unable to move! "I can't move either," she managed to gasp subvocally.

"What about Etty?"

"Etty's lost it," she muttered.

"Our cage is decelerating."

Tarn was right. With his superior equipment, he had sensed the gradual slowing down of the sky-bound prison before Pik's suit noticed the decline in momentum. Smoothly, without the lurching that had initiated its launch, the elevator lost velocity. When the ride stopped, it did so abruptly, sending their frozen forms rising through the ooze to bump ignobly against the cell's arched ceiling. Although primed for battle, the Warriors were paralyzed by their foes.

A portal sprang open, and the three of them spilled out into those abhorrent clutches.

✥

Sequential memory had become an elusive thing for Princess Eden. Her time in captivity was broken into a jumbled series of seemingly unconnected scenes. Only a few of them displayed elements that defined any order for these recollections in the Princess' disjointed lifeline.

There were her memories of partying aboard the Opal Cruiser. The attendees of this latest Entourage were beginning to tax even her regal patience. This batch had been assembled because of their overabundance of personal wealth. They were the perfect crowd to ply for donations to fund something as popularly-frivolous as reconstructing a recently novaed system, which was her latest pet whim. These partiers, though, had proved to be more greedy than bored with their fortunes, leaving the Princess' project penniless so far. She longed for the voyage to conclude, and so ordered her Guards to initiate an immediate return to the Nimbus homeworld. (This clearly predated her other memories.)

Like the crash. Uninvolved with the piloting and navigation of the cruiser, the Princess had remained ignorant of the technical necessity that had forced the ship to pause in a system on the Outer Rim of the galaxy. She had also been unacquainted with the incident that had caused the cruiser to plummet into this planet's foul atmosphere. She had not been pleased with either of these unscheduled delays.

She especially disliked being dragged physically along passages whose air was so clammy as to be gelatinous against her delicate skin. She trembled at the memory of how those beasts had stripped her naked and forced an airtube down her delicate throat. Then they dragged her down such dreadful corridors. Their scaly attributes repulsed her. (This memory was out of order, it came later, after her capture.)

It seemed to her that that capture should be the next memory in sequence…but she could not locate it in her head.

There was the terrible, smelly darkness she had endured. She assumed that part followed her abduction from the crashed cruiser. These recollections were uneventful, and although they spanned days of her life, she spared few synapses to store the details of that stage of her imprisonment.

She remembered being strapped to a table of some sort. Its surface was soft against her back. Again, the air was liquid. She breathed through a crude tube taped to her cheek. The shapes that bent to examine her wore great gills that convulsed hideously. Their eyes were lifeless and dark, their unblinking stare frightened the Princess. She remembered pain as part of this memory. First: a series of rough pokes and minor pricks. Then: a searing agony that forced her mind to retreat into unconsciousness.

There were more occasions of her being dragged down alien passages. She struggled, refusing to accompany her grotesque escorts, but her unwillingness went unnoticed by the beasts.

There were also recurrent flashes of enduring the fumbling examination of her privates by the huge fish-things. These bits were fragmentary, clouded by her acute embarrassment.

There was a particularly vivid—and unpleasant—memory of being plucked from the darkness. Dangling in the slimy fingers of huge fish-things, the Princess was extracted from her prison—a giant seashell!— and given her first view of her monstrous abductors. Their gruesome appearance started her screaming. Ignoring her manic outcries, the beasts lifted her close to study her with their unflinching fish-eyes. Their smell was the most offensive odor she had ever encountered. Their slobbering grunts were unnatural and unsettling. When they had satisfied their awful curiosity, these large beasts released her into the custody of smaller creatures, more humanoid but still drastically foreign. These fish-men dragged her away into passages filled with semi-solid air.

Her arm hurt. This told her that *this* memory was actually a current reality. She opened her eyes to regard her surroundings. Liquid air, airtube still painfully affixed to her face. No slimy hands jostled her about, she drifted free in a sac of the odious fluid. Through the murky jelly, she could see that her left arm ended at her elbow. The stump had been crudely cauterized, it looked almost as bad as it ached.

Being awake was agony, physically and mentally. Her mind recoiled from the horrors she had seen, the atrocities to which she had been subjected. She was a Royal Daughter of the Nimbus Family, she was utterly unprepared for torture and cruelty. She was a human being of regal caste, and resented being treated like an inert piece of meat. Waking up meant having to face these unbelievably agonizing realities.

But then, unconsciousness was not the escape it should have been. The Princess' slumber was plagued by dreams of a most remarkably horrific genre. She absolutely *refused* to credit them with any significance.

Professor Laramy's ghost had warned them about dreams. "The Great Cthulhu reaches out and invades the dreams of mankind. This is how he earned mortal followers, men who worshipped the Old One with such blind reverence that they betrayed their own species to the mighty hunger of the awakened Old One. You must beware your dreams, for they are easy doorways for Him to enter your mind!"

The specter's lecture reminded Pik of her recent dreams, those gloomy underwater tableaus which had haunted her nights aboard the ">%". All along, she had suspected that the dreadful presence which lurked just beyond identification had been her military past creeping up behind her to condemn her current lifestyle. But now…she feared that that unseen-but-pervasive presence belonged to a more ghastly threat. Had Laramy's monstrous devil reached across interstellar space to contaminate her dreams with foreshadowing of the fate in store for her?

The psychotic babble expounded by Elte Hortmoore just prior to his suicidal detonation came to Pik's attention. Elte' had been desperate to escape the nightmares he imagined were the handiwork of the monks he had defrauded. Pik had presumed those dreams had been products of the crimson bear's own guilt. But now… Had Elte's dreams been tainted too by the Old One's psychic corruption? How many others had felt the monster's fetid psionic contamination?

No, she reminded herself. It was no telepathic taint. Whatever it was, the process had to be of artificial origin. Which hardly diminished its cancerous effect, though.

Even if Pik believed that Laramy's Cthulhu had access to technology that could infiltrate her dreams, what could the Old One learn from her? She was totally unfamiliar with the entire planet. At best, He would only glimpse how scared she really was.

How naive she was…

The presence of herself, Etty, and Tarn on Earth implied the existence of humans beyond this world. But her dreams showed the Old One how widespread humanity was, how advanced and confident…and innocent.

Helpless under His terrible influence, Pik betrayed her kind by recalling the afternoon she met Etty in the Fulgarian Gardens.

She walked again along paths thick with splendid blossoms of the most exotic nature. The Gardens were a favorite spot for Pik during her readjustment to post-military life. The beauty of the galactic horticulture was not only a distraction, it was an emotional intoxicant, inspiring her to reject the instincts of her training. Calm and uninvolved, no longer quick to respond with overkill to every stray movement in civilian society. (Few people realized how disorienting the average city street could be to someone just exiting a regimen of military reaction-time. A hundred casual gestures or sudden, innocent moves could trigger an unwarranted defensive response.) The glorious flowers calmed Pik, aiding in the necessary sedation of her combat instincts. Waking along these public paths heightened the girl's uninvolvement as she passed among strangers who ignored her presence with equal courtesy.

It was a big and crowded galaxy. Individuals tended to be obsessively protective of their privacy, and in return paid no attention to the crowds of alien lifeforms that frequented most avenues. Such establishments as the Gardens were exemplary examples of this public blindness, catering to the needs of anonymity by immersion into crowds. This was the last place Pik expected to be approached by a stranger who smiled and asked in the most naive voice she had ever heard: "Do I know you?"

She turned and stared into the man's guileless blue eyes...and she felt an instant attraction. Her loins tingled and—

—And the dream cut off, looping to deposit Pik back in the anonymous crowd on the Garden path. She looked around, seeing but not noticing the versatility of species among the passers-by. Her subconscious mind identified each alien, briefly reviewing a capsulation of its race. She could not help noticing how long and hard (and distantly hungry) she stared at each human who strolled beside her on this dream-path through the Fulgarian Gardens.

When Etty surprised her with his bewildering-but-charming hello, she stared at him with a zestier hunger. Something made Pik think of him as a "seeder."

⁜

Etty's unconscious mind cringed from the unholy taint that seeped into his dreams. Without identifying it, he knew to avoid this malevolent cloud that crept through his dreamscape.

He ran, knowing full well how useless such flight was. He tore through a verdant forest of golden fir trees, the branches bloodied his cheeks. The darkness followed him, dogging his trail through the dense woods. Other animals fled in concert around him, all fearfully desperate to escape the nastiness that flowed at their collective heels. Behind him, Etty could hear terrible crunchings, as if the murky cloud was crushing trees in its monstrous jaws.

He almost ran headlong off the cliff. The forest ended with unnatural abruptness—and there was a narrow ledge of igneous rock that protruded over a bottomless gorge of multicolored mists. He barely halted his mad dash, teetering with one foot perched half-over the edge of the unexpected precipice. Around him, the animals—furry rabbits and graceful gazelles and colorful parrots and farting sand-narfs—all flung themselves with abject abandon from the cliff, squalling with terror and straining to quicken their plummet. For a moment, Etty believed that these escaping creatures (which clearly represented more primal portions of his intellect) might succeed in pushing him over the edge...but then he finally toppled back to scramble away from the deadly escarpment.

With his back pressed firmly against the trunks of the forest's outermost trees, Etty felt the caress of unclean thoughts as the darkness caught up with him, furiously oozing from the golden woods to envelop his cringing dreamself.

Urges filled Etty's mind, cravings that could only be sated by relentless coupling. The darkness was suddenly populated by several women, naked and willing...almost hungry. *Pik was there, and so was Princess Eden. There was even a girl he knew had been his first carnal partner; he couldn't recall her name...*

He should not have even recalled the girl, for she was among the memories that had been obliterated by the nanobot infection from his childhood.

He reached out to draw these girls closer, to share the lust that swamped his dreaming loins. Never before, he knew, had his sexual appetite been so aggressively expressed. Each intimate caress sent electric tingles racing up his spinal cord to dance in the pleasure center of his brain. The rougher the contact, the more vibrant the ecstatic stimulation. He felt the darkness prompting him to baser brutalities...

"Beware your dreams," Laramy's ghost had professed, "for they are secret doorways for the terrible Old One to enter your mind!"

Etty's carnal cruelties flourished, disgusting even his dreaming self.

✤

Pik realized that all her struggles and hopes had been pointless.

They had all been targeted by the Great Cthulhu before any of them had even entered the Earth's polluted atmosphere. At any time, the monstrous Lord could have reached out and corrupted their minds with His profane desires. *We are children*, she moaned, *lost in a Garden of Horrors.*

Professor Laramy had been right—every fanatical exclamation and portent of doom. The ghost had warned her relentlessly, but in her stupid arrogance she had dismissed his tales as the ramblings of a religious zealot. But he had been right!

The mind that had touched Pik in her dream had been impossible to believe, and just as impossible to forget. Its manifest malevolence was unmistakable evidence of abhorrent Evil. An evil that transcended mortal concepts. To this Ancient Monster, the extinction of the human race was only the most recent atrocity in a fearsome existence that stretched back before the dawn of time. Mankind was not the first species the Great Cthulhu had devoured.

The infinite scope of the Monster's being was too much for Pik's mind to digest. Several of her intuitions faded as soon as they surfaced in her inquisitive mind. The secrets glimpsed by these short-lived notions were too incredible for any mortal consciousness to grasp, much less accept. Some deep-rooted survival instinct reached out to snuff these realizations, sparing her mind the absolute devastation of their psychological hurricanes. The experience left her dazed…empty and drained.

She was left with an irrational conviction that the alien villain posing as the Great Cthulhu had won.

Pik had no idea where she was, or what had happened. Location or condition no longer mattered. Wherever she was, the girl was naked before the blasphemous might of the evil Old One. There was no escaping the long reach of His telepathic malfeasance. He controlled every centimeter of old Earth, and all its bestial inhabitants…including any visitors too. The retrieval team and the Royal Warrior were all still alive only by the grace of His monstrous caprice.

She was revolted by these realizations, horrified that she was submitting to the Old One's malicious long-distant tampering. *Grup—my religious faith crumbled like candy before the furnace of that ancient Monster's evil glow*, Pik lamented. *Am I really that weak-willed?*

"Pik?"

She started, for she was the only one inside the containment cell.

"Pik!" the whisper came again. This time, she realized that she heard it in her mind, not her ears.

"Laramy?" she gasped.

"Are you unhurt?" asked the ghost. "What happened?"

"It was a trap," Pik confessed. "I…I don't know why I leapt into it…"

"The Evil One's influence," the ghost ruefully muttered.

"It was an elevator. It sent us up the Spire."

"It took me some time to locate you," admitted Laramy. He had leaned into the cell, his pale face screwed up in sympathetic anguish. "You are nearly at the tip of the monstrous Spire…"

"Why does everything have to be 'monstrous' or 'gruesome' or hideous'?" she asked with a trace of hysterical sarcasm. "Why can't it just be a big tower?"

"Because…it is a *gruesome* and *hideous* thing," the ghost announced vehemently.

Pik sighed. The ghost's religious obsession served to clear her head, abolishing any residue of her brief certainty that Cthulhu represented a manifestation of absolute Evil. Obviously, these delusions she now shed had been implanted in her mind by the Old One's insidious psychic invasion. The effects of His telepathic apparatus had failed when confronted with her rejection of the mania exhibited by Professor Laramy's ghost.

"Did the Evil One's minions seize all of you? I cannot find your partner or the Warrior…"

"We were 'seized', sealed, and delivered gift-wrapped in ooze. There were *things*—awful abominations of translucent slime. They took us… and did horrible things to us…to me, at least. I was separated from Etty and the Warrior."

"They are seeders," the ghost remarked. "Initially, they would be segregated from you—a breeder. His blessed servants have undoubtedly been examining you, sampling your genetic structure and cellular profiles. Such things must be conducted before any mating program can commence."

His words sent chills through Pik, but these tremors failed to dispel an overall sense that Professor Laramy's ghost had *changed*. His form glowed brighter than it had previously…it was not just a trick of the eye, he was incandescent now. There seemed a more manic look to his spectral eyes, a nothing-to-lose quirk on his white lips.

"What happened to *you*?" she demanded.

"Huh?"

"You—you've changed," she accused.

"I am re-energized."

"How—?"

"The Deep Ones slain by yourself and the Warrior," the ghost revealed. "Their released ectoplasm provided me with a veritable feast."

Pik shuddered. She would never grow accustomed to Laramy's ghostly cannibalism.

"Do you think you can escape?"

She had to laugh. "Are you drunk with all that fresh stolen energy, Laramy? Do I look like I can escape this confinement cell? They took my suit and my comlink." But, she realized, *not* my *implants!* The Old One's servants had overlooked the technology buried within her body. Was there anything she could use as a weapon?

"I should continue my search to find your companion and the Warrior," the ghost remarked abstractly. Clearly, his attention had strayed from the girl's desperate plight. He vanished, going to find Etty and Tarn.

Leaving Pik alone with her terrible guilt. The sin she had not dared to reveal to the ghost: her betrayal of mankind to the evil Old One.

She sobbed, and wished she was dead.

⁘

Tarn's intensely disciplined mind remained unaware of the infiltration of the Great Cthulhu's wicked dream influence. His mind was already filled with demons and enemies, the presence of another, possibly darker monster went undetected by his untrusting dreaming self.

He stood with his toes protruding the edge of the bottomless cliff, and breathed deeply the gathering gloom. Fearless, he faced the impending darkness with a determined superiority. Indeed, the first few dark tendrils that stretched from the coalescing cloud turned to cinders in the blaze of his inner defenses.

Whatever this threat was, Tarn refused to allow it to ruin his victorious high. He stood at the edge of despair, yet adamantly resisted its enticing lure. He was the master here.

The darkness continued to methodically prod at his consciousness, finally piercing his barriers with a few insidious notions. So subtle was their invasion that the Warrior never knew he had been violated.

People were weak, every one of them. Weak and deficient of motivation, sedated by the technologies of comfort. There were even some, he had heard rumors, who no longer exerted their own muscles to promote mo-

bility, spending their entire lives, womb-to-grave, in recline, served by ma-chines that anticipated their every whim. Tarn did not like to believe in such urban legends. Despite his low opinion of other people, human and alien, the Warrior told himself that no individual could have become so absolutely victimized by the lure of luxury. There were limits, he believed, to even the most unrestrained dementia.

Tarn felt that he represented the opposite end of that spectrum. Through his psychological and physical training, he knew he was the highest example of human potential. A Royal Navy Warrior was incapable of any lesser state of being. His personal pride was that he had exceeded those definitions, be-coming better than the best. His mind was ultimately devoted to serving his Oath; even without the activation of his extensive bio-tech enhance-ments, his body was capable of exertions far beyond the tolerance of other Warriors. It frustrated him that his superiors repeatedly failed to recognize Tarn's potential.

The spying darkness took note that a single human Warrior consid-ered itself equal to an army of normal soldiers. The Great Evil was instant-ly suspicious of these biological "enhancements" that the Warrior thought of so fleetingly. Had the Great Lord's minions detected these implants and removed them?

When the Princess had been rescued from her monstrous abductors, then Tarn would be rewarded with promotion. He vowed that he would never allow his higher rank to blind him to the achievements of the soldiers under his command.

He stood firm at the cliff's edge, ready to defend his position against any arrogant foes who falsely believed themselves to be more deadly. Let them come, for they would fall before his superior might...

He awoke, momentarily uncertain what had roused him from his stupor. A second later, a facet-wall of his dark crystal cage deactivated itself. Through this opening, foul appendages dragged the Warrior, de-positing him clumsily on a surgical platform.

More physiological examinations by the Deep Ones were in store for Tarn.

Their booming grunts carried to his alert ears through the viscous liquid-air. Deep within his brain, Tarn's artificial linguistic programs had yet to decipher syntax and nuance, but he could now crudely understand the gist of the conversations of these Deep Ones. His body might have been neutralized, but his consciousness was alert and exploding with fac-ulty.

They had just been notified of the presence of technological implants in the Warrior's body. Their orders were to immediately remove these devices.

"Query necessity undamage specimen," one of the Deep Ones burped.

"(Indecipherable, presumed to be a proper noun) require(s) breeding capabilities. All other systems are unimportant," the other replied. The translations provided by Tarn's cranial implants were improving as the beasts conferred.

The monstrous surgeons were preparing to vivisect him! They entertained no desire to carefully extract his implants, their primary concern, besides maintaining the integrity of his reproductive organs, appeared to be speed. The Warrior had less than a minute before the Deep Ones began their butchery.

They leaned over him, smacking their wide lips. Their eyes betrayed no pity as the beasts positioned their grotesque scalpels over his naked flesh.

Tarn's mind raced, desperately searching for a way to avoid or halt his mutilation. His body was useless to him; as on previous occasions when he had been taken from his cage, some force neutralized his muscle control, rendering him inert for the ministrations of the Deep Ones. He could not twitch a fingertip or blink an eye. He was cut off from activating his organic body. But—what about his implants? His artificial arm was unresponsive to his commands, but he was able to access his cranial implant and a few of the sensory equipment that occupied a portion of his ribcage. So he was not entirely helpless…just unarmed.

No, wait, he realized. *My sensory transmitters use low-range X-ray emissions to discern my physical surroundings. If I can manage to step-up my output signal…*

As the dreadful creatures bent over their victim, an invisible-but-lethal burst of X-rays exploded from the Warrior's chest. The intense radiation bath fried the rudimentary neurons of the brains of the two aquatic surgeons. One slumped in death, while the other exhibited a final spasm that sent it twisting away from the surgical platform. It crashed into a squat bunch of tumorous nodes set against the wall, rupturing the organic apparatus with its agitated death throes.

As a bluish fluid leaked like a milky cloud from the tattered nodes, Tarn felt control of his body returning to him. Sitting up on the platform, he tore the airhose from his mouth (for further implants supplied him with necessary air and nutrients) and ripped free the small airtank that was taped to his side.

With his eyes and all his sensory implants, the Warrior scanned the chamber. Measuring ten meters on a side, the area resembled the interior of a pod more than any "room". Its walls supported arrays of biological technology: soft panels crowded with trigger sausages, pulsing nodules and translucent balloons, monstrous arms tipped with now-sheathed talons hung in bony cradles. The chamber's single exit was securely locked. There were no other Deep Ones present, but a second crystal cage within the room seemed to contain another human.

Without hesitation, he went swiftly to this second containment cell and shattered its shell with his metal arm. Brushing aside the drifting crystalline shards, he saw Etty through the hole. Cuffing the hole bigger, he reached in and withdrew the naked bounty hunter from the cage. Etty struggled weakly, and Tarn realized that the man was asleep, dreaming.

Professor Laramy's ghost had warned them all about the dangers of sleep. "The Great Cthulhu reaches out and invades the dreams of mankind. This is how He earned mortal followers, men who worshipped the Old One with such blind reverence that they betrayed their own species to the mighty hunger of the awakened Old One. You must beware your dreams, for they are easy doorways for Him to enter your mind!"

Remembering the hungry cloud from his own recent dreams, Tarn surmised that the bounty hunter was under similar psychic attack.

He violently shook Etty until the man's eyes fluttered open. With a dazed expression, the wiry man reached out to tenderly stroke the Warrior's muscled chest. Revolted, Tarn brushed the man's hands away. When Etty moved to replace his caressing fingers, the Warrior viciously cast him aside.

Degenerate freelancer, twitched the Warrior.

Expanding the range of his scanners now, Tarn probed the regions beyond the surgery. The strange passages and proximal chambers seemed vacant of any Deep Ones. For the moment, the Warrior's freedom was not in risk of being discovered.

Gesturing curtly, he informed Etty it was time to go. (An earlier scan had revealed that the man lacked an implant comlink—such as the one Tarn possessed. Verbal communication between them was not possible as long as they were confined to this watery environment. Simple hand gestures had to suffice.) Plucking a handful of alien surgical equipment from beside the empty platform, the Warrior passed a pair of cruel blades to his dazed companion. When Etty rejected the knives, Tarn scowled and forced him to take the weapons.

This is no time for pacifism, he growled to himself, *or a weak stomach.* He longed to be able to speak to the fool, if only to verbally abuse the obstinate moron.

But the spacer had no comlink implant, and neither did the Princess. Without his battle armor, Tarn was also deprived of any means of detecting the Princess' tracer signal. She was even more *lost* to him now than before!

Impossible odds were not a concept Tarn the Warrior accepted.

It took the Warrior only a moment to figure out how to open the chamber's doorway. He swam boldly forth, paying scarce attention whether or not Etty followed him. The corridor reminded Tarn of the inside of an animal's intestine.

After a long hesitation, tormented by the need to escape and a fear of being discovered on the loose, Etty thrashed his way to the doorway, pulling himself into the outer hallway. He marveled at the ease with which the Warrior moved gracefully through the jellied air.

By keeping his sensors active, Tarn was not surprised when a pair of small-sized Deep Ones entered the passage. He moved deliberately and with deadly precision, driving his borrowed knives deep into the side of their heads. He gouged the blades with vicious abandon, making certain that he transformed as much as possible of the creatures' brains to turgid mush before he withdrew his weapons and kicked the Dead Ones out of his way. Wedging one of these victims in the doorway which had given them access to this corridor, the Warrior dove to examine the chamber beyond.

And found himself hanging in the midst of eight more of the marine monstrosities, at least three of them belonging to the oversize variety. They marked his entrance by filling the room's liquid air with ripples born of their belched cries of surprise.

It would have been so much easier to simply X-ray blast this group of Deep Ones, as he had done with the eager surgeons, but his sensory bank needed time to recharge before its sensitive emitter could withstand another savage outburst of lethal radiation. Anyway, Tarn was looking for opportunities to vent some his repressed rage. So he settled on slaying the creatures by cruder, more personally satisfying means.

He flung one scalpel, embedding it to the hilt in the eye of one of the smaller beasts. Wielding his remaining blade, Tarn sliced the throats of two more Deep Ones on his right. Propelling himself from the rim of the doorway, he launched across the chamber, gutting a peripheral opponent on his way to collapse the forehead of one of the bigger beasts. He kicked off from the lobotomized creature, blinding another with an artful sweep of his scalpel. Midway across the crowded room, he yanked his first knife from the victim's trembling socket.

By this point, the chamber was clouding with the creatures' spilled blood, the water's translucency giving way to a murky, opaque yellow. Three Deep Ones remained active now: two large ones, and a wounded smaller one. In the time it took Tarn to dispatch the others, the two big ones had managed to pull weapons from somewhere. They swung these coral lances to bear on the naked human Warrior.

Batting aside one lance with a swift kick, Tarn wrenched the other spear from its owner. He drove this spear into his other attacker. Before the weaponless beast could realize what had happened, the Warrior twirled in the jellied air, driving his artificial arm into the creature's cranium almost to the elbow. His move had been instinctive, he had not counted on the glutinous density of the beast's head. Tarn's arm stuck firmly, imbedded in the dead Deep One's forehead.

Dammit! he swore.

Freeing himself would have to wait. The remaining, wounded small Deep One was squirming its way toward the doorway. Tarn mustn't let it escape to sound an alarm.

He plucked the unused lance from its owner's rictus grasp. The chamber was too clouded with viscera for him to depend on his unaided vision. Switching to auxiliary scans, the Warrior targeted and hurtled the spear with all his might. It caught the fleeing creature as it hung in the open portal, trying to crawl past the body Tarn had jammed there. The spear pierced its lower back, coming out of its surprised mouth. The momentum of the throw carried the victim out the doorway, to be pinned as the lance stabbed into the curvature of the passage's far wall.

A frightened Etty peered hesitantly through the doorway, surveying the terrible carnage with wide eyes.

Once Tarn had freed his arm from its grisly hole, he waved Etty to join him. Etty shook his head, refusing to enter the watery atmosphere of alien gore.

You stupid fool, fumed Tarn. *I need you to follow orders.*

He launched himself to pluck Etty roughly from the doorway. Smacking him the way one struck a rowdy child, Tarn dragged him into the cloudy mire of gore, where he vigorously applied the viscera to Etty's naked body, pulling it fresh from a wound in a Deep One's forehead. Once he had covered the struggling man with the yellow fluids, Tarn turned this grisly application on himself.

Don't you understand basic survival strategy? the Warrior raged in his head. *This blood will mask our human scent. Sooner or later, they will discover we have escaped. We must become as invisible as possible in here.*

Tarn could not fathom how Etty had managed to become a commercial bounty hunter. The man had absolutely no predatory instinct, his naked psyche was riddled with weakness and uncertainty. He was going to slow down the Warrior once the objective came into reach. Tarn knew he should really leave him behind; if he took the man with him, there were bound to be mishaps.

Dismissing the man, Tarn swam to the opposite side of the chamber, where he opened a new doorway.

The Warrior traveled down this latest passage, his scan sweep revealing things far beyond the corridor's walls. As a result of this extended vigilance, he instantly noticed the appearance of an electromagnetic pulse as it entered the region.

Whatever it was—it registered as a sharp spike on the EM graph. It had appeared from below, corresponding with no clear access route between the layers of chambers spread throughout the spike's loftiest levels. Moving easily through meat and solid calcium, the EM spike drifted in a seemingly aimless, circuitous path, moving from chamber to chamber as if looking for something specific.

More enemy defenders, his suspicious mind feared. But no—reinforcements would show up as a swarm of Deep Ones, or some other hideous monster. *That spike…it's vaguely familiar…*

The Laramy ghost! That's what it was. Tarn recognized the energy signature from before. It had deceived him this time because his implants possessed only a fraction of the rez capability of his battle suit's equipment. But yes, now he could identify the pattern. The ghost had obviously come in search of the humans.

Abruptly, the Laramy spike jerked to a halt, then raced toward Tarn. Even though he knew what to expect, the Warrior still pulled back as the ghost's pale figure exited the wall of the pulsating corridor.

"I found you!" exclaimed Laramy's voice in Tarn's mind.

The Warrior had been set to ignore the annoying specter, but when the ghost spoke, it reminded him that Laramy communicated through some telepathic frequency that did not rely on hardware receivers. This was strategically beneficial. It would allow Tarn to relay orders to Etty through the deceased Professor.

"I need you to tell this stupid spacer to follow my directions," he urgently directed the ghost.

Etty had come up behind Tarn. The Warrior noted that the man had possessed the forethought to commandeer one of the enemy's coral spears. He watched Etty tilt his head, visibly listening to Laramy repeat the Warrior's message. Then Etty scowled, and gestured with displeasure at Tarn.

"He thinks you have gone insane," the ghost told Tarn. "He claims you killed a room full of Deep Ones, and then rubbed their entrails on him. Is this some galactic ritual?"

"I was fighting the enemy," Tarn announced without hesitation. "I smeared both of us with the blood of my victims to mask our human scent from any Deep Ones that would come searching for us."

"Technically," remarked the ghost, "you were looking to mask your 'taste' from the Deep Ones. They depend on taste, not smell…"

Etty listened to Professor Laramy again, his expression of determined outrage melting into confused acquiescence.

Was it the Warrior's imagination, or was the ghost's energy profile higher than it had been before…? Tarn easily confirmed his suspicion by consulting the EM graph. Yes, Laramy was stronger now.

"He agrees with your judgment," declared the ghost.

"Not good enough. If he wants to live through this, he must follow my instructions without question," the Warrior advised. "I will not waste time arguing with him."

To illustrate his point, the Warrior pushed through Laramy's ghost, continuing down the passageway. He paid no heed to the ghost's attempts to call him back.

They can follow me, or be damned, Tarn told himself. *It doesn't matter to me.*

When he paused at a junction of corridors to survey the region with his wide scan, they caught up to him. Laramy seemed angry, but Etty acted strangely enthused.

"He believes in you," the ghost commented.

"I couldn't care less if I tried," Tarn replied.

"He wants to know if you 'really think' we have a chance of getting out of here?"

To the side, Etty drifted, nodding emphatically.

"Leaving this place is not my immediate concern," the Warrior declared. "I am here to rescue the Princess!"

"I found Pik," the ghost revealed suddenly. "She is—"

"Did you find the Princess?" the Warrior demanded coldly.

"What? No—I...I don't even know what she looks like," admitted Professor Laramy, clearly unsettled by this realization.

"What about our suits?"

"Huh? No—I...I haven't seen—"

"Then, what good are you?" Tarn sneered.

"But...Etty is concerned for Pik's safety," the ghost relayed. "He urges you to find her."

"Etty's girlfriend isn't the one I'm looking for."

⁘

Meanwhile, *Etty's girlfriend* hadn't felt better in days.

She was still ripping on the adrenaline rush of her own daring escape.

Imagine Pik: all dreary and fearful with despair, a prisoner of the monstrous Deep Ones. Naked, she floated in a jelly-filled prison...until such time (and there were many) when they wished to examine her privates again. (*The fish-things are obsessed with my crotch.*) Her existence was a tedious and often painful monotony. She had given up, blithely accepting her captors' brutal treatment. She existed only as a vessel now, awaiting whatever purpose the Old One had planned for her.

This was Pik's first taste of absolute hopelessness. She had faced many crises in her life, from a motherless upbringing to becoming a victim of the streets to enduring the physical and psychological shock of getting caught in an assassination crossfire to taking refuge from her despair by enlisting in the Space Navy to the hardening of spirit and sinew that she underwent in the military...but she had never been *broken* by any of those ordeals. Confronting the Old One within the poisoned realm of her own dreams had fractured her sanity.

Pik was almost catatonic when they dragged the girl from her cell.

Honestly, she had no idea what started her moving. Consciously, she was a null set as far as she was concerned. Then, suddenly—she was a blur of unconscious motion.

Ducking down, Pik eluded the large Deep One's grasp and slipped between its fin-like legs. Coming up behind the creature, she whirled and delivered a vicious kick to the beast. Her blow drove it face-first into the open facet of the crystal cell.

Moving as if driven by a distant guidance, Pik moved over to the controls next to the cell, and started wildly pressing buttons at random. The control board consisted of a shell that seemed to have been genetically designed to accommodate several rows of protruding sausages—the buttons. She attacked them with haste, squeezing and pulling on as many of them as she could before some other attendant recaptured her.

This wanton experimentation succeeded in affecting both crystal cells that stood before her. One snapped shut its open facet, shearing the Deep One in half. The other opened its facet—to reveal another human prisoner! A female!

Her face was twisted with inhuman torment, but Pik recognized her from holo-disk footage. The Royal Daughter of the Nimbus Family. Princess Eden! She really was still alive!

Pik's shock almost cost the girl her freedom.

She was grabbed from behind, and brusquely turned to face a furious Deep One who towered over her like a scaly mountain. Its eyes flashed dark and terrible, conveying a cruel lack of sane ethics. Its mouth opened wide to reveal a maw of jagged needle-teeth. It heaved forth a bellow of rage. Its bluntly taloned fins pawed at Pik with malevolence.

With a burst of strength she had not known she still contained, Pik wrenched the control shell from its organic mooring. Swinging it in a fierce arc, she sliced the creature's face with the shell's beveled edge. It released her, then roared and floundered back.

The rest happened on its own.

The scarred Deep One fell back, impaling itself on a scalpel held by another attendant, one who planned to sneak around and attack the escaped human from the side. The skulking Deep One was thrown back by the other's now-dying body. They collided with a wall arrangement of inflated sacs. The balloons did not burst under the impact, but instead delivered a huge voltage into the bodies of the two fish-things. The fried beasts drifted inertly to the floor of the torture chamber.

And when it was over, Pik was free!

Pik was no longer lost and broken. With her bare hands she had beaten her captors, and won herself freedom. She was no longer a prisoner of the Great Evil One. She had managed to, however briefly, free herself. She was His precious little breeder no more! Her despair melted before a blaze of newfound confidence. Her sanity poked its curious nose from a forgotten fold of her cerebellum where it had hidden itself and gave the rest of her mind a weak cheer.

Pik looked upon what the Evil One and His minions had done to her, and retched. Cruel cuts and bruises covered her torso and abdomen. Those wounds had not been professionally closed, their scabs were bright red with foul infection. One of Pik's fingers was bent at an unnatural angle; she did not recall that injury, but it could have happened during her struggle to escape.

She had *escaped!* The forces of Good had won out over the Evil One's minions.

Pik felt her own faith flowing like welcome fire in her veins, and she didn't care that it was just an adrenaline rush from her desperate exertion. She was revitalized, renewed, reborn. Facing Cthulhu's madness, she had been initially too weak to challenge the Old One Himself, but a deeper part of herself—her Warrior instincts—had been able to take advantage of an opening accidentally provided by His clumsy underlings.

Now she knew the source of that surge of independent strength. It had stemmed from her faith—not in unholy monsters of ancient design, but in the awesome well of existence that was God. Her own Lord did not need torture to inspire worship. As a result, any strength based on the God of Light was purer, more dependable than beliefs instilled by fear. Pik had "believed" in her despair, but then she had been reminded that fear and suffering were transitory aspects of life, they bore no defining power over the fate of her eternal soul. The Evil One had stripped her mind naked and poured His vile influence across her psyche, but His insidious corruption had never reached the core of her spiritual being. Pik's soul remained her own…and it was resolutely bequeathed to God.

She promised her Savior that this aberrant Evil would be eradicated. She swore that the Great Cthulhu would claim no more victims.

But—she was free! And she rejoiced in that hard-won privilege.

Princess Eden, though, offered more immediate distractions. In her glee of autonomy, Pik had forgotten that she was not the only person who had been rescued by her valiant actions.

Once she had determined that no Deep Ones waited to torment her, the Princess crept slowly from her prison. Pik was impressed by the stern poise she affected as she stepped forth. Her regal bearing blazed through her veneer of agonizing trauma, and the brutalized victim transformed into a haughty monarch before the retriever's eyes.

Pik could see what had attracted Etty's secret lust for this woman. Drifting naked in this chamber of horrors, the appeal of her curvaceous beauty was impossible to deny. Wide hips and an ample bosom provided the Royal Daughter with a classical hourglass figure. Although she was not tall, her lithe torso and slender limbs imbued her with an aristocratic stature. (Pik noticed with a shock how the girl's left arm ended at the elbow with a grisly wound. The amputation was crude, and she knew at once that it was the ghastly handiwork of the sadistic surgeons of the Deep Ones.) The Princess' face was a marvelous fusion of noble elegance and sensual innocence. Her features were angular and well-proportioned: the taut lips of a sovereign, the delicate wedge of her commanding nose, the fire of her emerald goddess eyes, the supple curves of her high cheekbones and triangular chin. Pik had seen the Princess' hair in several holo newscasts and knew it was normally a lustrous pile of bronze splendor—but now it clung like a damp golden shadow across her head and shoulders. Oh yes, her loveliness was impossible to deny.

The Princess was in the midst of demanding to know where she was and why she had been mistreated when she realized that Pik was not one of her alien jailers. Pik gestured to the second, now sealed crystal cell, hoping to make it clear that she had been a prisoner like herself. Regarding the pair of confinement cells, the Royal Daughter hesitantly nodded, conveying her understanding with her remarkably expressive eyes.

Those eyes were starting to lose their determination. Her command was crumbling under the psychic weight of her horrific experiences. If the jellied air had been any runnier, she might have collapsed in a faint.

Pik shuddered to imagine the ordeals the girl must have suffered in the clutches of the fearsome Deep Ones. Capture, mistreatment, confinement, invasive probing, even mutilation! Stranded on a forgotten planet, lost, alone, abducted by monsters, treated like an object—and all without any comprehension of the nature or scheme of her tortures. The tribulations of this poor soul's plight had been enough to wither the strongest spirit.

Giving way to sudden compulsion, Pik signaled to attract the Princess' coherent attention. Once she was certain that the traumatized girl saw her with a modicum of faculties, Pik gave her the secret salute of the Nimbus Royal Navy, exaggerating each subtle motion to insure that she caught the complete gesture. By doing so, Pik was informing the Royal Daughter that she was a Warrior. She communicated this falsehood in the hope that the Royal Daughter would assume that this was a survivor from her slaughtered personal Guard aboard the doomed Opal Cruiser. Perhaps this deception would instill the Princess with some measure of relief and confidence—she had been rescued by one of her elite Warrior Guards. The girl desperately needed some hope, for Pik feared that the Princess' mind was spiraling into a catatonic pit of no return.

After a moment, Pik saw that the girl had believed the ruse. Her face brightened briefly, displaying regal approval and gratitude…before exhaustion swamped over her with a palpable spasm. She hung limp, aware but too drained to move.

Pik could do nothing more for the Princess' state of mind, but she might be able to dress her wound. So hideous was her stump, that Pik knew it had to be causing the girl considerable pain. Leading her over to the Deep Ones' monstrous operating theater, Pik found the necessary elements to wash and bandage the terrible injury.

Princess Eden hung her head with a vacant stare as Pik tended to her wound. Not unlike her arm, her mind would need time to heal.

The retriever wondered how well she would heal on the run. For escape did not stop here. Pik still had to find Etty, and get them out this awful Spire of Condemnation, then back to the ">%" for a swift exodus from this cursed sector of space. And somewhere in all of that, she needed to destroy the Evil One.

Grup, she thought. *I'm ripped on adrenaline. That's a tremendously optimistic itinerary for a naked girl and her near-comatose companion… All that, unarmed and—*

Swollen with the confidence of sanctioned mutilators, they came through the suddenly opened doorway and froze in mid-paddle when they saw their dead associates. Before they could glimpse the freed humans, Pik armed herself with a few of the surgeon's grislier tools and leapt to attack the newcomers.

The lead beast succumbed to her initial assault, taking a knife to its hilt in the forehead. As she pushed this fish-thing's corpse back to block the doorway, the second Deep One cuffed her aside, sustaining a jagged wound in its appendage/fin for its cruel effort. The blow stunned Pik momentarily, and when her vision cleared, she found the recuperated creature diving toward her. It brandished weapons of its own now, which it had stolen from the same surgical array as she had gotten hers.

She blocked its first stab, locking scalpels in a struggle of muscles that the girl soon lost. The Deep One's massive body outweighed Pik by a factor of three; between its bulk and its marine sinews, the beast pressed her back against the wall. Its terrible wedge-of-a-grimace thrashed the jellied air before her face, snapping its barracuda-like jaws barely a centimeter from the fear-flared nostrils of her pug nose. With an impatient slap of one of the thing's blunt fins, the creature drove Pik harder against the soft wall at her back. The water before her grew pink with the blood that leaked from a tear cross her cheek. She narrowly evaded a vicious stab from the beast, gasping with frantic relief as it buried its second knife into the organic wall. As the Deep One strained to pull free its blade, contorting its versatile spine with the struggle, Pik managed to squirm from the beast's mighty grip. Its limbs were slippery with her own blood.

Somehow, in the scuffle, she had lost both of her knives. As she came up behind the beast, she grabbed the nearby operating platform for leverage and twisted to deliver a brutal kick to its thrashing torso. Before Pik could lash out, though, this enemy struck her from the side with a clenched fin, knocking her head-over-heels across the chamber. She collided with one of the slaughtered guards, then hit the opposite wall with enough force to crack one of her ribs. Her sight failed in an explosion of phosphenes, and she quickly shifted to the minimal auxiliary sensors located along her collarbones. Even this artificial view was murky with gore and distorted by minor systems malfunctions. Clutching the soft architecture with her alarmed fingers, Pik clawed her way into a corner, hoping for a brief respite to clear her head.

This Deep One was no average technician or inexperienced lackey. This beast was acquainted with battle techniques, and it possessed the size, muscle, and response-time to outclass Pik's best efforts. Outside the spike, the firepower of her suit had been sufficient to defeat such monstrous aquatic soldiers, but here, now, naked and unarmed, Pik was just a punching-bag for this beast to bat about until it grew bored with her agony.

Without a dirty trick or a fantastic run of superior luck, Pik was fish-food...

Before her perceptions cleared, the beast dragged the girl from her inadequate hiding place. Pik struggled, but the creature had her in a firm, scaly grip, held flat to its awful chest by its fins clasped across her heaving breast. She gasped now for reasons other than surprise, for the beast had dislodged the breathing tube from her mouth. It dangled away from her gulping face, sputtering its gaseous air into the atmosphere of jelly. The creature's grip held her arms trapped, Pik was unable to replace the air-tube. As its grip tightened, squeezing the remaining oxygen from the retriever's lungs, the Deep One brought her to the vacant surgical platform.

Gasping and choking, Pik flailed her limbs in a wild attempt to free herself before the beast could strap her down. Her blows were wasted on the captor. She succeeded in grasping a random surgical instrument from a tray attached to side of the operating platform, but it was not a cutting tool. Making the best of what she had grabbed, Pik scraped the stolen tool's blunt cup across the Deep One's metallic scales. Her gouging was ignored by the beast; already it had secured both of her legs to the surgical couch.

Not the deadly Warrior I thought I was... With the element of surprise on her side, Pik had proven myself victorious against her adversaries. But now—*this* beast was taking her out as if she were a clumsy child. *Where's that burst of clarifying energy when I need it?*

Finally, with a desperate lunge, she stabbed the Deep One in the eye with the blunt tool. At first, the beast seemed to give no notice of its sudden blindness, nor did it react to the pain of that injury. Then, a tremendous vibration shook the great beast; its scaly hide rippled horribly with the convulsion. The Deep One relaxed its every muscle, drifting free now and releasing Pik from its grip.

She scrambled the oxygen-tube back into her mouth, sucking air into her tortured lungs. Unshackling her legs, Pik realized that her attacker was...dead. The Deep One rolled slightly as it drifted away, and she could plainly see the large scalpel protruding from the back of the beast's head. Visible just beyond the lifeless enemy, she could see Princess Eden regarding the scene with eyes that were widened with stunned triumph.

The Princess had saved the life of her Royal Guard.

I wonder if the Royal Daughter would have been so brave if she knew this Warrior was only a commercial retriever?

Pik gathered a collection of the more lethal blades among the selection of the Deep Ones' diabolical surgical tools. There were some she recognized with traumatic shudders from half-forgotten experiences, while others seemed so horrific that she dared not touch them. She refused to speculate which of these cruel blades might have been the instrument that severed the Princess' arm with such depraved sloppiness.

Armed now, Pik escorted the Princess from this repugnant chamber. The Deep One she had pushed into the doorway had wedged there in death, keeping that portal open. The girls crawled over the beast's cold corpse, escaping to the outer passage.

The nature of that passage was grisly and disturbing by human standards. The walls were of organic construction: slabs of blue meat that trembled and pulsed with monstrous fluids. Although Pik had seen such biological materials domesticated and used in civilized construction before on other worlds, there was something unnatural and gruesome about this particular alien meat. (Perhaps she was confusing her outrage, associating the passage with the human bones the Old Ones had used to build these massive Spires. This meat was clearly not of human origin, for it was blue and its enormous veins pulsed with green fluids.) The abominable characteristics of this hideous corridor brought unwanted memories resurfacing in her agitated mind, recollections of being dragged down such dreadful passages. Only fragments of these recognitions revealed themselves with much clarity, as if the memories were intentionally blurred by her subconsciousness in an attempt to keep her sane. If moving through these aberrant passages was inspiring such unreasoning fear and loathing in her, Pik pitied the Princess for the extreme terror that must be besieging her pampered mind.

They were borne along by a current moving the viscous fluids through the ghastly corridor. This allowed Pik to keep a firm grip on the Princess, guiding her reluctant self along what must have seemed to her a journey through a nightmarish pandemonium. Alert for any sign of the Spire's unholy inhabitants, Pik ushered her down several of these repellent tunnels.

Only once did she see signs of any Deep Ones, and that time she was fortunate enough to find concealment behind a huge flap of flesh. The troop of revolting creatures swam by the hiding girls without becoming aware of their presence. Pik was grateful for that, for this group had consisted of the large, brutish Deep Ones she now knew to belong to the fish-things' soldier caste. They wore packs belted to their marine contours, and they carried spears of barbaric, lethal design. She had no desire to encounter another of these combat beasts, much less a troop of such monstrosities.

What Pik needed was to find her pressure suit. With its weapons, she could protect herself and her charge from these deadly creatures. With command of her hardware restored, Pik could fight her way out of this hellish tower.

But first—she must locate her lost suit.

And then I have to find Etty, for I'm not leaving without my beloved.

He would need his suit too, and the Princess was going to need some kind of protection. Maybe Pik's suit's grabber balloon was still intact. It was an uncomfortable and demeaning mode of transportation, but somehow she doubted that the Princess would offer much in the way of objections when it came to the stylishness of her salvation.

That was—if Pik was up to the challenge of saving anyone.

I mustn't let doubt contaminate my strategy, she reminded myself. She needed to keep a clear head, now more than ever. How tragic it would have been to waste her valiant escape by getting recaptured.

She assumed that Professor Laramy's ghost had searched the lower levels of the Spire as he trailed the team aloft. That meant that the men were incarcerated above. So she looked for routes that would take her higher up.

After two more tunnels, she came to a dead end. This produced a worried whining in the Princess; so shrill was its pitch that it carried through the jellied air, tickling Pik's ears with her panic. Pik gestured for her to calm herself, then turned to examine the alien hatch that dominated this cul-de-sac. The portal was designed to accommodate a huge Deep One; its door, a mammoth seashell, towered three times her height. The shell was a whirlpool of pastel colors, spun by madcap genetics feeding on poisoned sustenance. Its surface was pitted by age and decay, but still it retained an aspect of absolute resilience. This shell was probably centuries old, but it was clearly sturdy enough to bar forced passage. Pik suspected that even her suit's armament would be hard-pressed to violate this barricade. This portal proved to be securely locked too, no amount of fiddling with the panel of sausage-like controls opened the colossal door. There would be no continuing along *this* route.

Turning her back on the impenetrable hatch, Pik shared a surprise with a small Deep One that had just exited a side chamber a few meters away. The beast and the human stared at each other for a brief instant, their bodies and minds locked in the abrupt shock of mutual discovery. The girl acted first, and managed to become the survivor.

Kicking off from the massive seashell hatch, Pik dove on the Deep One with both her blades poised. She dispatched the creature with savage incisions across its forehead, exposing and eviscerating its foul brain.

Behind her, the Princess' meager composure had deteriorated with the sudden appearance of the fish-thing. She sank now back against the corridor's bulwark of meat, cringing and clawing at its vile tissues. Her scrabbling somehow activated a section of the wall, which split and receded like monstrous eyelids to expose a transparent lens—no, it was a window! As the Princess recoiled from the unexpected transformation, Pik kicked nearer to stare through the amazing aperture.

The view confirmed her suspicions (and, she guessed, Laramy's claims too) that they were at a point of extreme elevation within the Spire of Condemnation. They were apparently quite near its pinnacle. Outside stretched the familiar darkness of outer space. Speckled with a chaotic field of distant stars, the void was a somber backdrop for the Earth and its waterlogged moon. Below: the planet's dense stratosphere stretched away like an enormous landscape of opaque vapor, curving out of sight as it followed the Earth's hidden contour. In the fantastically far distance, backlit by the rising sun, another Spire exploded from the murky atmosphere, reaching its point into the vacuum of space. Above: the pale blue ball of the moon dominated the heavens. So close was she to it, that Pik could actually detect waves disturbing its lunar ocean.

She trembled to stare upon the imposing face of Cthulhu's stronghold in the sky. From there, the dreadful Old One reigned supreme over the ruined Earth. All creatures beneath His terrible gaze served this fearsome monster.

Pik considered the Old One: newly Awakened from his ancient imprisonment beneath the waters of the Earth's deepest ocean. She imagined His terrible desire to ascend, to reclaim the heavens that had once been the domain of his ancient, blasphemous brethren. She pictured his flight to the moon, where he established a new ocean to cloak His malicious presence. She assumed that the Spires had come later and were the actual handiwork of servile minions, generations of them dedicated to assembling and building these towers in an attempt to reunite the sacrilegious congregation with their evil deity. She shuddered, for each of these notions were unpleasantly horrific to consider…especially so in light of the fact that they probably described the doom that had come to this world with some accuracy.

The Evil One's minions had managed to bring her this close to their abhorrent Lord. It seemed so insignificant that she ran free at the moment. How real was any escape in such close proximity to the Great Cthulhu? The godlike monster could, without effort, reach out and pluck her from the tip of this calcium needle. The Old One could swallow her soul at any moment…

More defeatist ruminations, she cursed. Was the Evil One broadcasting this despondency into her already-brutalized mind? This did not seem all that unlikely now, as she stared with horror at the murky countenance of his lunar sanctuary.

Pik shook her head to clear all doubts, rational or otherwise. She refused to abandon hope. She would fight, with her entire body, mind, and soul. She would never allow the Old One victory over her faith.

We're all getting out of here, Pik swore.

With that resolution, she collected the traumatized Princess and dragged her away. The chamber that had produced the small Deep One seemed the likeliest place to start to look for another upward-bound route. Through this doorway, Pik guided her charge.

The room proved to be disagreeably familiar, containing frightening-ly well-known surgical gear—and a row of crystalline containment cells!

Have I found where the Deep Ones are storing my beloved Etty?

Pik was somewhat brusque with the poor Princess, abandoning her to float unattended by the entrance to this new jail as the retriever dove to attack the cells' grotesque control panel. Before, she had succeeded in opening the Princess' sealed cell, but her previous experience with those tubular buttons had consisted of wildly squeezing them while fending off a bestial assault. She really had no idea where to start this time. Driven by a desire to free Etty, she repeated her mad fumble, wrenching and pinch-ing the bulbous switches with feverish enthusiasm. After a few minutes of this panicky exertion, Pik was ready to give up with a frustrated wail, when the pair of cells suddenly opened, their front facets blinking out of existence (almost as if they'd been extinguished like a light).

The nearest cell proved to be empty of any occupant.

In the second cell—she found Janek!

❖

Janek blamed Professor Laramy's ghost for the relentless misfortune the retrieval team had experienced since coming to this dreadful world.

The specter's guidance had unfailingly led them into crisis after crisis, culminating with the Duuian's abduction from that cursed black beach. If Laramy had not been preaching his quasi-religious rhetoric, Janek might have detected the Deep Ones' underwater approach. But no—the ghost had blathered on, predicting doom and annihilation for everyone, dis-tracting and annoying Janek to vexation.

This belligerent dismissal of the deceased human's spirit had been Janek's last unstressed thought for some time. Shock and terror would dominate the Duuian's mind during his capture and incarceration.

The Deep Ones exploded from the surf, rushing up the beach and trampling Janek with their charge. He had small opportunity to warn Etty, but that was apparently sufficient, for the naked human swiftly scaled a rocky bluff and vanished into the treacherous hills beyond the beach. If not for the inflexible nature of his pressure suit, Janek might have been crushed by the swarm of bestial fish monsters. Afterward, the stupid creatures milled about the beach, seemingly incapable of comprehending that they had lost their human prey.

Terrorized, but not mentally paralyzed, Janek frantically activated his suit's defensive force field. This spared him more bruising by the shambling, dissatisfied beasts. At the time, he thought it also placed him beyond their reach.

But then, with a series of aggressive belches, a pair of the fish monsters assaulted Janek, or tried to. The wet blows of their spatulate arms fell uselessly on the invisible exterior of his defensive shield. This time, the Deep Ones exhibited more intelligence, certainly more than Janek would have liked. Positioning themselves behind him, the beasts proceeded to push his force bubble toward the crashing surf. He tumbled within the confines of his force field, realizing that his protection had abruptly become a dire captivity.

Once under the water, he was escorted to deeper regions by the swarm. The beasts had no difficulty keeping his air-filled force field submerged, displaying remarkable marine expertise. They swam with a hideous grace, and it was clear that the sea was their natural habitat.

Down they went, farther and farther into the dark water.

His sensors told him that this surrounding liquid was more than just "water" (H2O). Extensively polluted with toxic residue (apparently of mineral *and* organic nature), the "water" was a viscous jelly possessing translucent qualities at best. The deeper they took Janek, the more he was forced to rely on his artificial senses to observe the actions of his captors in this deviant ocean.

When the swarm halted their dive, Janek tensed, expecting the beasts to attempt another futile attack on his force bubble. But instead, the creatures positioned themselves in a circular loop around him. Hanging thus, they faced the encapsulated Duuian with their lifeless fish-eyes, and stared.

A few moments later, another Deep One approached, ascending like a huge bell from the murky depths. This newcomer sported phosphorescent, arcane symbols painted on its scaly flesh, rendering its eerie form disturbingly visible to Janek's artificial scans (since his preferred waveband of perception was not visible light). This latest beast carried artifacts of obvious primitive manufacture: a coral staff of irregular length designed to be held in the grasp of the monster's blunt fins, and an assortment of smaller, less identifiable tools strewn from a series of fibrous loops tied around the creature's immense girth. The Duuian watched this forbidding shape rise with an irrationally maturing sense of dread. Loathe though he was to admit it (even to himself), it appeared as if the wild tales told by Laramy's ghost were repeating themselves for Janek's benefit.

This newcomer could only be the swarm's leader...or shaman. According to Laramy—and later corroborated by Etty—it had been some kind of primitive wizard that had removed Etty from his suit back in the crashed cruiser. Was Janek about to be stolen from the security of his pressure suit by some incredible teleportation technology possessed by these brutish creatures?

But—I will perish! he realized. *This ocean's corrosive gelatin and the crushing pressure at these depths—I will not survive here if they isolate me from my suit!*

"No!" he cried. "Do not do this—"

In an absolute fit of panic, Janek's sub-brain asserted itself, plunging his Duuian physiology into a comprehensive hibernation. His consciousness shut off, sparing him (unbeknown to him) any blasphemous violation of his dreams.

The next thought he experienced was pain.

Agony as the Deep One surgeons examined his inhuman body in a grisly laboratory. This spurt of awareness was gratefully brief.

His next memory was one of resting in a cramped cell filled with liquid. He was dimly cognizant of air being fed into his nostril by a tube. Although he was no longer desensitized or paralyzed, Janek's movements were impaired by the snug nature of his hard prison. *They got me,* he imagined. *They teleported me right out of my pressure suit—just as the Wind-Walker's beasts did to Etty—and then they brought me here. Wherever* here *is... Deep in the toxic ocean, probably.* With a tremor of his spindly limbs, he recalled that fleeting impression of pain. Discovering a numbness in one of his six arms, he found that his captors had amputated one of his appendages. This realization was too much for the intrinsically docile Duuian, and his mind returned to the sanctuary of insensate hibernation.

There were several more brief flashes of arousal from Janek's total retreat, but each were fundamentally replays of his previous pair of unpleasant experiences. He remembered them with less than distinct affection. They blurred in his overloaded mind, and he was unsure whether they were separate tortures, or merely bleary fragments of a single torment.

Then he awoke to find himself cradled in Pik's arms.

He wanted to ask her what had happened, but vocalization was impossible in the gooey air. If he didn't keep his nostril clenched, that acidic jelly would ooze into his nose. The density of the liquid made it difficult for Janek to sense his surroundings, things were shrouded with hazy coronas as infrared frequencies diffused in the chilly muck.

Sight of the human female filled Janek with hope, for he regarded Pik with almost hero worship. She was the team's soldier. She had once been a Royal Navy Warrior, her battle skills had clearly brought her into the fortress of the enemy. She was his retrieval and his salvation. Just as she had vowed to rescue Etty from the locals, she had come after her other partner once he had been abducted.

Now he became aware of another figure in the room with them: another human…another *female* human!

He extended a slender appendage stalk in the direction of the surprise stranger, and the girl rewarded his gesture with a scream that was muffled only slightly by the liquid air. Janek tucked his arm back in. He moved instinctively away from the frightened human, intending to burrow into Pik's protective embrace, but his partner was no longer there.

She was up and kicking across the room to stifle the other's outcries. He dimly saw Pik enact a complicated salute to the now-silenced screamer. Then Pik pointed emphatically back in Janek's direction. This somehow subdued the strange girl, and Pik returned to help her alien partner to stand on his unsteady triad of legs.

Through the exchange of a series of simple gestures, the partners agreed that the best course of action now was to vacate this room before any Deep Ones discovered their escape. Pik took the Princess and led the group from the vile prison.

For *that* was who the girl was—Princess Eden! She was *not* dead! Janek was able to recognize the Royal Daughter once she came close enough for his unaided senses to pierce the thick atmosphere. How astounding! Not only had Pik rescued Janek from the enemy stronghold, she had found the missing Princess too! *This* was exactly the sort of miraculous feat that he secretly expected of Pik. She had won the golden retrieval commission for the team.

Before fleeing through the passages, there was a portal in the wall of this corridor that Pik brought to Janek's attention. He gasped to witness the celestial panorama. Not only was the view breathtaking, but it told the Duuian where they were: high up within one of the monstrous spikes that protruded from the planet's atmosphere. He nodded his mighty head, acknowledging the information presented by Pik's direction. Privately, he took notice of the dead Deep One that drifted to the side of the prison's doorway.

She herded them now along tunnels of grotesque meat. Janek had encountered organic architecture before, but these corridors filled him with unease. There was something unnatural about them. Although these walls pulsed with life, they betrayed inadequate warmth for his infrared senses.

There was little question in Janek's mind regarding Pik's immediate purpose. "Escape" lurked in their imminent future, but he knew that Pik was now devoting her energies to locating and saving Etty. That was an acceptable detour to salvation, as far as the Duuian was concerned. As one of her partners, Janek trusted Pik to defend him with intuitive fervor... but he also knew that she would fight all the harder once her life-mate was among the group she protected.

Three short corridors later, she surprised everyone (including herself) by finding their confiscated pressure suits in a chamber filled with marine weaponry. Even Janek's was among the stored suits!

The retrievers quickly donned their lost gear. Now, Janek felt even more secure. For once, he welcomed the awkward rigidity of the suit, for now that limited mobility implied solid protection. He deeply gulped in the air synthesized for him by his suit. He caressed his sensitive controls, grateful of the systems to which they linked. He relished the clarity of perception his suit's equipment afforded him.

Before, this chamber had been a hazy environment to his blurred senses. Now, with the aid of his suit's scans, his vision cleared, revealing the surrounding walls of cold blue meat and their racks of deadly coral weaponry. The swords and bludgeons all featured wedge-like handles designed for grasp by the fish monsters' flippers. The spears were conventionally slender, but sported vicious barbs along their tips.

As soon as he was sealed in, he called to Pik over their comlink, "Pik! You are a miracle worker! You've not only rescued me, you've found the Princess! Now we don't have to share the retrieval commission with that Warrior."

She nodded, distracted by some unvoiced concern. Janek followed her worried gaze...and understood the nature of her apprehension.

Janek and Pik were restored to their pressure suits, ready for battle and escape from this hellish stronghold. There was Etty's suit, and even the Warrior's battle armor. But for the Princess...there was *no suit*. There was no protection for the Royal Daughter, for she had been abducted directly from her crashed cruiser.

How are we going to rescue her without a suit? Janek fretted to himself.

A second before the doorway of the Deep Ones' armory burst open, Pik called, "Incoming!" Then she fired a salvo of pulse blasts across the ugly faces of the aquatic intruders that crowded through that aperture. She had forgotten that their oceanic habitat had toughened these beasts to the meager pressure concentrations of her suit's conventional weaponry. Fortunately, the fish-things' construction materials enjoyed no such resilient advantage.

With a guttural boom, the armory's doorframe fractured under the pulse barrage. Shell shards and torn clumps of meat zipped like bullets through the jellied air, riddling the attacking brutes. The Deep Ones' assault line saved Pik life, their bodies taking the explosive brunt and the flying deadly debris.

She had spotted the troop of monstrous soldiers creeping upon the team via a full-range scan her suit was routinely conducting. She stuck with this perception mode, for the chamber was clouding fast with the organic debris caused by the exploding doorway. With a rasping hiss, Pik recommended that Janek switch to auxiliary scans—and she ordered him to protect the naked Princess. "Get her under the Warrior's suit, its battle armor will shield her."

Then the chamber filled with angry combatants, leaving Pik little opportunity for anything other than immediate battle. They were all the large Deep Ones, seasoned soldiers prepared for brutal battle. They were not easy prey, even for the slicing beams of her refocused lasers. Once a beast had been cut by those deadly needles of light, the rest of the soldiers used its corpse as a buffer against further damage. Unfortunately for them, Pik was utilizing this tactic too.

Allowing the huge chunk of a dead Deep One to mask her presence, she edged around its glutinous contours and assaulted the creatures from their flank. Her lasers danced like a spastic lightshow in the murky gelatin, each brilliant flash slicing a grisly chunk of meat from the beasts' battle-crazed bodies. She threw a few more pulse blasts into their midst for good measure, hoping at least to agitate the stray carnage, transforming her enemies' own viscera into a cloud of gory confusion to disorient them.

After forty-five seconds of this, she dove back behind her own gory cover and moved her vantage point to the other side of the boulder of dead meat, where she resumed the assault. By repeating this maneuver several times, Pik was able to prevent any of the Deep Ones from getting past her.

Relegating this aggression to her automatic systems for a moment, she checked on the status of Janek and the unprotected Princess. Not only was a naked Royal Daughter incapable of defending herself, but Pik knew that Janek's passive nature would render her Duuian partner similarly helpless. He had succeeded, though, in moving the panicky girl to a point behind the pile of the Warrior's armor. They both cowered in this trivial safety, sheltered from most of the chamber's stray violence. As long as Pik held her position, none of the beasts were able to directly reach them.

Ironically, her advantage was spoiled by one of the monsters copying this strategy and using it against her. Even more caustic: the beast managed to use Pik's own shield to destroy her supremacy.

Suddenly, her hiding place lurched and crashed into her side. She was thrown back, but her suit's gyroscope spared her from tumbling through the viscous environment. As a result, she saw the chunk of corpse that had been her sniper-cover pitched aside to reveal a cunning and armed Deep One.

Brandishing swords of intricate and deadly coral blades, this Smart One leapt to slaughter Pik. Her escape was narrow, involving a furious scramble behind a volley of stupefying pulse blasts to the beast's face.

She ended up beside Janek. "Look out!" his voice wheezed in her ear. Pik was frantically goading her targeting software to focus her lasers on the looming Smart One—when an unexpected impossibility separated her from the impending bestial attack.

The Warrior's empty battle armor stirred and rose from its disheveled pile to stand in a defensive posture facing the charging Deep One. A flash of crimson light burst from the front of the Warrior's animated suit, and the ferocious creature charged at the empty-but-animated suit. A fin-like arm to the left, another limb on the right. Half of the beast's growling face spun over the suit's shoulder, while the rest of the creature's head cascaded by as a series of smaller bits. Diced body parts rained upon Pik as momentum carried the dead assailant's partitioned corpse past Tarn's uninhabited battle armor.

"What the—"

Then she remembered that Space Navy Warrior's possessed long-distance control of their personal armor. (Pik had always been especially jealous of this capability. Her best attempts had failed to duplicate this linkage in her current software. It was one of the perks she missed from her military days.) Tarn's suit was not haunted, it was under the telemetric guidance of the Warrior himself. He had to be nearby to affect this refined a command of the vacant battle suit.

"Keep firing!" Pik shouted, using the Warrior's private one-to-one frequency. "There's a troop of the things—and these ones are battle-trained, not like the border guards we met outside. We've got the Princess, and they want her back!" The retriever desperately hoped that Tarn was close enough for his suit to relay her advice to the absent Warrior.

"What is going on?" Janek cried. "How—"

"Quick," she urged her partner. "Get the Princess into Etty's suit. Things are about to get ugly in here, and I don't want her exposed for it." Pik gave Janek an insistent shove, then turned to join Tarn's uninhabited battle suit against the onslaught of the Evil One's grotesquely murderous minions.

There was actually very little for her to do. The ferocity of the Warrior's armament was taking a widespread toll among the monstrous creatures. She found herself battling a medium-sized soldier, and in the time it took her to defeat this adversary, Tarn's empty suit had dispatched the remainder of the assault troop.

With the last beast slain, the Warrior's suit froze like a statue. Marine gore floated like a ghastly cloud in the chamber's jellied air. Pik's instinct was to approach her battle companion, but she was uncertain whether it would recognize her as a friend or foe. Just how exact was Tarn's long-range control? Was he really guiding the suit, or was it acting in some kind of automatic defense mode?

"Tarn?" she inquired hesitantly over his private bandwidth. "Are you there?"

"I will be soon," came the Warrior's gruff voice in her ear. "Use this time to familiarize me with your situation."

She gave him an account of her escape, revealing almost every detail of her adventures since that moment. The battles with the Deep Ones. The rescue of the wounded Princess. The discovery that they were all in the tip of the Spire of Condemnation. The rescue of Janek, and the recovery of everyone's pressure suits.

For some reason, a tumorous knot of pain in Pik's heart prevented her from asking about her darling Etty.

When Tarn finally appeared in the fractured doorway, he swam directly to his waiting battle armor. He quickly resumed occupancy of the suit. Only then did he pay attention to the rest of them.

"Where is the Princess?" he demanded.

She waved him in the direction of the back of the room, where Janek had apparently convinced the Princess to don Etty's pressure suit. Pik was incapable of wrestling her attention from the doorway. Her fingertips were moist with anxiety, and she chewed her lip.

Laramy's ghost appeared next, waving to her. She ignored him. The suspense was killing her!

Then Etty drifted into view, and Pik exploded with a triumphant joy.

The Warrior moved quickly to present himself before the Princess. He cuffed the alien bounty hunter aside as if the Duuian was an inanimate obstacle.

"Princess Eden," he addressed the regal face that showed through the borrowed suit's helmet. "I am Tarn, a Warrior in the Nimbus Space Navy." He gave her the secret salute that would authenticate his words. "I was dispatched in answer to your cruiser's distress call. I am here to rescue you."

Initially, the Princess experienced some difficulty mastering the suit's comlink, but Tarn was able to instruct her with simple gestures. "But... I've already been rescued," she finally informed him.

"Excuse me?"

She pointed across the chamber, where Pik in her bulky suit was reuniting with her naked lover. "There," the Princess declared. "That Warrior. She must be one of my Guards aboard the Opal Yacht. She rescued me, Warrior Tarn. She is extremely courageous, thoroughly deserving an extravagant reward."

Tarn scowled, casting a secret glare in Pik's direction. *What game was the bounty hunter playing?* he contemplated with rancor. With Tarn's presence here and now, their claim on the Princess' retrieval commission was questionable in the first place. But it was a severe crime to impersonate a member of the Royal Space Navy, much less a Personal Guard assigned to protect Royalty. Somehow Tarn had not envisioned Pik to be so flamboyant with the truth. He suspected there were hidden agendas at work behind this impropriety.

Glancing at the Princess, noting her wistfully innocent smile and eagerly reliant gaze, the Warrior thought he understood the female retriever's deception. It was clear that the Royal Daughter was calmer than he would have expected of her in this unnatural situation. Although obviously unsettled by her predicament, she seemed generally untraumatized by her experiences; this mental stability certainly contradicted his anticipation. Something had pacified the Royal Brat...could it have been Pik's lies? Finding herself the captive of alien fiends, the Princess had developed a strong affinity with the person who had rescued her. Had Pik attempted to enhance the Princess' trust by convincing her that she had been saved by a member of her own retinue? Perhaps this deception had been warranted, in consideration of the Princess' fragile emotional state at the time. Correcting that deceit now might produce harmful reactions in the Royal Brat.

Despite his reluctance to allow Pik the shelter and profit of her falsification, Tarn was forced to admit that unmasking the bounty hunter's mendacity at this moment was unwise. The Warrior's assigned rescue of the Royal Daughter undoubtedly encompassed the preservation of her psychological stability. In the eyes of the Nimbus ruling class, the Princess' mental health was guaranteed to be as vital as her physical well-being.

"Warrior Pik mentioned you had been wounded, Your Highness...?" Tarn inquired.

"Pik..." the Princess mumbled, her attention still directed elsewhere. "Her name is Pik?"

"Yes, Your Highness. Your...wound?"

"Oh!" she started, as if suddenly reminded of some dreadful malady. "They—they cut off my arm!"

"What?!" Tarn cried. His rage was inspired by outrage—how dare these monstrous primitives mutilate a member of the Royal Family! Mixed in with this wrath was the dire realization that, regardless of the retrievers' hollow claim of rescuing the Princess, it would be *Tarn* who received the official reprimand for allowing such a physical violation of the Favorite Daughter. He was the Warrior who had been dispatched to safely recover the Princess, any damage she had suffered at the hands of her abductors was his responsibility. *I'm grupped,* he moaned.

❖

Etty melted into Pik's embrace, refusing to allow the bulky attachments that covered her suit to inconvenience his hug. How she longed to throw off her protective hardware and feel his pale arms caress her back, pressing his minimally hairy chest to her breasts. Knowing that such an action would be risky (they were still deep in enemy territory) and embarrassing (not to the lovers, but there *were* others present), Pik satisfied herself with clasping Etty with suited arms, pressing their lips until only the pane of her helmet separated their kiss.

It mildly annoyed Pik that she could not verbally communicate with her beloved. He had no comlink, and it would do little good for the girl to retract her helmet and speak directly to him, for the Deep Ones' vile, liquid atmosphere would mortally muffle their words. For now, they had to rely on the gestures that lovers share to convey basic messages…or use Professor Laramy's ghost to convey necessary instructions.

Where was the ghost? Pik had seen him enter, but her enthusiasm to be reunited with Etty had superseded keeping track of the specter.

"Professor Laramy?" she called with her mind. Glancing about, she found the ghost. Instantly, her stomach lurched with revulsion at what he was doing.

Hunched over the drifting corpse of a Deep One, the ghost had extended his incorporeal arms to pierce the cadaver's dead meat. A flow of cruel energy was snaking along his arms to cavort wildly about Laramy's hungry face. When that insubstantial arc of ectoplasmic force finally vanished, sucked into Laramy's forehead as if by some spiritual vacuum, the ghost lifted his face to reveal an expression of unholy gluttony. His hazy form glowed brighter now, riddled with flickering veins of greater vigor. There was a craziness in Laramy's eyes that reminded Pik that this "man" was no longer really "human", had not been so (by his own claims) for nearly two hundred years. He existed now as a disembodied spirit, subject to an entirely different set of physical laws (would that make them "metaphysical" laws?) than conventional "mortals". This was how the ghost replaced his precious and dwindling lifeforce, it was a necessary thing. Nevertheless, his psychic cannibalism still seemed quite objectionable.

Pik demanded that he "Stop that!"

"What…?" the ghost replied, startled by her sudden indignity.

"Just…don't do *that* around me," she barked, flinging herself away from the ghost and his feeding frenzy. Giving Laramy's ghost a shrug, Etty swam after her.

As she approached the others, Pik saw that Princess Eden stood dressed now in Etty's pressure suit. It's man-sized girth hung like a rumpled parody on her voluptuous form, giving her a hobo deportment. Her eyes peered just over the chin-lip of the suit, a pair of sad-but-regal orbs all but lost in the helmet's dark confines. While she was addressing the Warrior, Janek had drifted off to examine the crude weapons that lined the walls of the Deep Ones' armory.

"Is she okay?" Pik hovered beside Tarn. When he gave her no reply, she turned to ask the Princess, "Are you all right, Your Highness?"

The Princess nodded. Then, realizing that the suit concealed such a minimal gesture, she addressed Pik via the comlink in Etty's suit. "Yes. Your efforts to spare me any injury were successful, Warrior Pik. My arm...still hurts, but your dressing has eased the pain greatly."

She still thinks I'm a Warrior, one of her personal Guards who escaped the massacre inside her crash-landed cruiser. Pik was somewhat surprised that Tarn, the only real Warrior present, had not already denounced her to the Royal Daughter. *It was time,* she decided, *to confess my white lie before the Warrior lunged to use it against me.*

"Allow me to introduce Etty," Pik presented her beloved to the Princess. He blushed and fumbled through a clumsy curtsy hanging in the jellied air. "And this is Janek." Pik waved to indicate the Duuian who loitered nearby.

"More Warriors?"

"No, Your Highness," Tarn declared. "They are commercial bounty hunters who also answered your cruiser's distress call."

Steal my disclosure, why don't you...

"But...I thought that the alien was..." The Princess' green eyes were wide with innocent bewilderment. "You told me that the alien was a Warrior too..."

"I apologize, Your Highness," replied Pik. "To effectively rescue you, it was necessary for you to trust Janek—and myself. He is no Warrior of the Space Navy. And neither am I."

Tarn frowned, doubtless frustrated that Pik had managed to defuse his accusation by admitting her deception to the Princess.

"We're freelance retrievers—" Pik told her.

"This is not the time for confessions," the Warrior interrupted her harshly. "We must find a way out of this fortress—before an entire army of these beasts are set on us." He waved an arm to indicate the corpse-littered chamber.

You couldn't even give me the dignity of finishing...you bastard.

"The Warrior is right," Pik annoyed him by quickly agreeing. "Your safety is our primary concern right now, Your Highness."

From across the chamber, Janek concurred with her agreement, further infuriating the Warrior. The Duuian added, "These weapons all belong to a primitive culture...but applied in vast numbers, they could prove deadly to us. A hasty retreat is clearly the wisest course of action."

"Wait a minute," the Princess commanded. Everyone all paused, startled by the urgency of her tone. "What about Etty, your partner? I assume this is his suit I am wearing. What will he do for protection?"

The dilemma of Etty's unsuited state had been worrying at the edge of Pik's headful of concerns. She knew he could be encapsulated in a grab balloon, but he would be confined to it until they reached the ">%", for only a balloon (or his own pressure suit) would insulate Etty from the harmful vacuum of space once the retrievers exited this terrible Spire of Condemnation. The same could be declared about the Princess, though. Whose safety was more tantamount?

Pik knew that *her* choice would not coincide with the Warrior's assessment of the situation.

Etty interrupted the comlink conversation, leaning in and waving his hands in a manner that clearly conveyed that he wished the Princess to keep his suit. Pik had no idea how he had known the topic of the discussion, but he defused the impending crisis with a charm that she personally thought was a bit over-naive. To emphasize his acquiescence, he tapped the balloon deployment hardware that rode the side of Pik's suit's thigh.

Although she disagreed with Etty's heroic choice, Pik knew better than to oppose it. The Warrior would have argued vehemently against the Princess relinquishing the protection that Etty's pressure suit provided her. Anyway, knowing how he secretly felt toward the Princess, how could Pik deny Etty his chivalrous gesture? It was already evident in the Royal Daughter's eyes that she understood Etty's brave offer. *He's succeeded in impressing the Princess,* Pik mused.

"Your partner is the bravest of us all," the Princess announced. This declaration elicited a low moan from Tarn. He confined his displeasure to his private channel, unaware that Pik was eavesdropping on that frequency.

"Let's move out," he barked, regaining control of the situation with his baritone mandate. He assembled the group in a particular order, assigning responsibilities as if they were his own private army. With his superior military weaponry, Tarn was the obvious choice for point. He wanted Pik right behind him, their second line of defense. The Princess and Etty (the Warrior grudgingly included him in the ranks) occupied the center of the group. Janek was assigned to guard the rear. Tarn utterly ignored Laramy's ghost while outlining his plan.

The Princess, though, was unable to ignore the spectral man, whom she had just noticed hanging near the group. She gaped and pointed frantically. Misinterpreting Tarn's unwillingness to acknowledge Laramy's presence, she assumed the ghost was some new enemy sent to torment them. Janek had to calm her, explaining who and what the ghost was—or claimed to be, for it was no secret that the Duuian placed no belief in the Professor's mystical definition of his afterlife existence.

Pik thought the girl handled her acceptance of Laramy's ghostly nature rather well. The Princess was definitely not the glitter-brain the retriever had presumed she was.

"Got a problem with Laramy?" Pik inquired of the Warrior, using his private frequency.

"Useless parasite," Tarn hissed in reply.

"He means well," she remarked. "We certainly share his enemies, although our hate for them may not be as fervent as his. But then, we've only been here a few days…he's been stranded here for over two centuries."

"I do not trust him." He would say no more on this topic, switching his conversation to the communal frequencies to direct the team's progress through the passages of meat.

Something had happened between the Warrior and the ghost during the time they had been together in the Spire, before the rest of the team had been reunited. Pik had no idea what it was. Tarn would not reveal his motives for ostracizing the ghost, and the girl expected Laramy's explanation would be too steeped in his theological zealousness to mean much in the real world. (She shared the ghost's conviction now that Cthulhu was an evil of cosmic proportion, but Pik did not believe that the Great Evil One was an ancient deity with the powers of a monstrous god. The Old One was powerful, but His atrocities could all be attributed to viciously applied technologies of an undisclosed nature. There was nothing mythical or paranormal about the Evil One, although His "evil" might deceptively seem that immense.) The ghost was demonstratively insistent regarding the validity of his own personal religious outlook. Perhaps that was the root of Tarn's rejection of Laramy; maybe the Professor had finally alienated the Warrior with his obsessive delivery. Despite his anxious desire to help, the ghost did little to make himself very likable.

At one point, while moving through the vacant corridors, the group encountered another portal that looked off upon the dark void of space. Tarn took special interest in the view, muttering to himself. He seemed to take this latest bit of information as a sign that they were on the brink of their final salvation.

Pik had to question his evaluation of this point. When he ignored her inquiry, the Princess remonstrated him, "Warrior Tarn, please explain yourself to *all* of us."

He relented, but cast Pik a hateful glare first. "We are above the planet's atmosphere," he pointed out. "Therefore we should now be beyond whatever force prevented Pik from leaving the ecosphere."

Grup! I didn't think of that—he's right!

"Those same dense clouds were interfering with transmissions between myself and my flier," he continued. "At this altitude, however, I should be able to reach my ship without difficulty."

"And then—we're all out of here?" Janek whispered with anticipation.

"We're saved!" the Princess declared.

There has to be a catch… Otherwise, he would've already called for his ship.

"What's the catch?" Pik teased the Warrior.

He grumbled, revealing that these very walls seemed to be blocking his transmissions with as much interference—if not *more*—as had the planet's cloudcover. "I…need to get outside to summon my flier."

Laramy tried to explain that the Great Cthulhu's incarnate evil was blocking the Warrior's signals, but everyone ignored the ghost's babble. Except for Princess Eden, who was unfamiliar with the Professor's dubious definition of her abductors. When Laramy attempted to instruct the Princess, Janek curtailed the ghost's lecture by dismissing the veracity of the source, informing her that Professor Laramy was a religious zealot who attributed godlike qualities to what was clearly an alien despot in possession of unnatural technology. To the ghost's distress, the Princess plainly credited the Duuian's account with more believability.

Not for the first time since the Warrior had returned Etty to Pik's side, it crossed her mind that, at some point, she was going to have to declare her intention to seek out Professor Laramy's Ancient Old One. This desire to end the awful reign of the Evil One was a powerful urge in her now. It was certainly not as obsessive as the ghost's hate of the Old One, but that did not diminish its importance to Pik. The monstrous evil of this blasphemous being had to be stopped! She could not flee this star system and leave such an abomination in existence.

Besides…she carried a guilt that could not be ignored. In her dream-state, a helpless victim of the Evil One's psychic violation, Pik had revealed to the Great Lord details of the existence of galactic humanity. She had betrayed her own kind to the Monster, showing Him where to find a ready-made population of unwitting new victims for His atrocious hunger. If left alive, the Evil Cthulhu could be expected to direct His malevolent attention toward voyaging into space in search of these unenslaved humans. Against her wishes, Pik had given Him this information. Against all odds, she needed to prevent Him from using that knowledge.

There were other factors clouding her achievement of this goal now. The safety of the others could not be jeopardized by any attempt to bring down the mighty Cthulhu. The only person she was willing to put at risk was herself. Should she make this desire known, the rest of the group would undoubtedly believe she had gone mad, falling prey to the Laramy ghost's horrific babbling. Pik did not expect the rest of the team to fathom her new-born conviction. Averse to seeing her face unnecessary danger, Etty would object vehemently. Janek would not be pleased by the girl's choice either. While the Warrior would probably not care one way or the other as long as her actions did not disturb his own schemes. Pik could expect Professor Laramy to confuse the matter with his arcane praise

Another factor obfuscating her destruction of the terrible Evil One was: *how?* Pik did not delude herself to imagine that she possessed any weapon capable of exterminating such a powerful monster. She was unaware whether such a force existed. According to Laramy's own historical accounts, even the primal Elder Gods responsible for imprisoning Cthulhu had been unable to "kill" the monster, the best they had been able to do had been to place the Evil One in an eternal slumber. Even this punishment had not been resolute enough to prevent the horror from reaching out to infect humanity's dreams. As for the "eternal" part, well, the monster had found a way to rouse His dreadful consciousness from that cosmic sleep. If even the Elder Gods had failed to mete out a permanent solution to Cthulhu's perverse existence, what chance was there for the efforts of a single human being?

Perhaps the Warrior has the right idea, Pik ruminated. *Our immediate concern should be escape. Once we're all free from this insidious Spire and its terrible occupants, then I can reassess how best to end the Evil One's reign of terror. Alone, I might be ineffectual, but armed with an interstellar spacecraft…maybe I had a chance.*

"So how do you plan to 'get outside'?" she asked Tarn. This time, Pik hid her sarcasm, for she was earnestly interested in how the Warrior was going to achieve this end.

Once again, he refused to answer her, forcing the Princess to repeat the girl's question. He seemed infuriated that he had to bow to her request, violating his command position in even so tenuous a manner. "I plan to go right through this portal, Your Highness" he announced. "It seems the best choice to me, for the walls can be expected to be of more solid construction than a window."

"And what about us?" Janek inquired.

Now Tarn faced them, not only acknowledging the retrievers' presence, but commanding them as if they belonged to his precious Space Navy. "The Princess will remain here in your protection. I will go alone to summon my flier, and once I have rendezvoused with my ship, I will return to collect Your Majesty." He bowed to the Princess as he uttered the last part.

"And these brave citizens too," she declared. "We will not abandon them in this horrible place."

"They have their own ship," the Warrior told her.

"Then we will help them reclaim their vessel, Warrior Tarn." She did not raise her voice or tint her words with authority, but still she managed to convey the absolute surety of her statement.

This girl—this *woman*—was far more mature mentally than Pik had expected. The Princess blended her regal majesty with a personable common sense in a manner not evident in any news-holo. She actually *was* concerned for the well-being of those beyond her own elite bloodline. This woman might actually become a decent and fair Queen of the Nimbus Empire.

Speaking on his ethereal waveband, Professor Laramy informed them all that Etty had something to say, which the ghost wished to relay for him. "Etty wants the Princess to know that the retrieval team will stand in her defense while the Warrior goes to locate his lost spacecraft. She can depend on their protection during the Warrior's absence. We will not allow Your Majesty to fall into the clutches of the Great Evil One's profane minions."

"Please apprise Etty that I appreciate his courage, and the bravery of his team. I accept this protection with my royal gratitude." Princess Eden's smile peeked over her helmet's chin-lip, flashing with earnest geniality.

Etty nodded, executing a successful curtsy this time. His posture exhibited no embarrassment over his nudity, and Pik suspected that the Princess enjoyed the view.

Pik found herself amused by the Warrior's frustration. The exchange between Etty and the Princess had effectively undermined his orders by reinforcing them. Tarn's attempt to order them to protect the Princess had been deflected by Etty's offer to guard her…at least, as far as Princess Eden was showing. The Warrior must have been fuming. Pik was barely able to stifle a chuckle.

She stepped in to organize the Princess' removal from this particular corridor, so that the Warrior could breach the Spire's hull without endangering the Royal Daughter by exposing her to the violent decompression that would sweep the passage. While Tarn raged in the privacy of his battle armor, Pik and Janek escorted the Princess to a chamber at the far end of the corridor. After Pik confirmed that the room was vacant, she and Etty scampered into its safety. Janek followed them, giving no notice of the Warrior who hovered back beside the portal. Pik paused and waved to him. (*I knew I was being a naughty girl, teasing him so relentlessly, but I simply couldn't help myself.*)

Once the doorway was sealed, the group waited inside. Pik surveyed the room, which proved to be a cavernous chamber divided by triangular sail-like partitions. First she searched for other entry points, securing them as best she could. Then she turned to the task of examining the chamber itself. Its many sections were storage holds. Pik ripped open a few of the strange, shell-like crates, but found herself hopelessly bewildered by their confounding contents. In one section, several lockers looked as if they were large enough to hide individual people, although she suspected the width of Janek's head-crest might prove a tight fit. These would become handy if the group was discovered before the Warrior returned with his space flier. Best not to dwell on such possibilities, but it was unwise to ignore that unpleasant contingency. Pik had no desire to be so foolish, on either point.

Janek and Etty had settled the Princess in a cozy cubicle where blockish crates formed a rudimentary couch for her. She was resting, sitting back against the partition. (Upon close investigation, Pik suspected that this partition was actually a vast sheet of peeled flesh. She chose not to share this observation with the already overtaxed Princess.) Pik backed off, to join her partners in a private conference by the edge of the cubicle. Professor Laramy's ghost hovered nearby, acting as a transit for Etty's comments.

"Before we start on anything else," declared Pik, "I want to review our tactical standpoint here—just in case." She proceeded to describe the chamber from a strategic point-of-view, informing them of the entrances she had sealed, and the hiding-place lockers she had found. "As soon as she's rested, I suggest we move the Princess to that cubicle. It is a more defensible location."

Janek agreed, and Etty nodded his understanding.

Then Janek raised a question which had been prominent in his thoughts ever since the boys had reunited with the girls. In his opinion, since the Princess had technically been rescued by Pik, the team deserved the retrieval payment. They had gotten to the target before the Warrior, their claim should have legal precedence.

Pik had to admit that the situation was an awkward one. The Warrior's presence effectively outranked their freelance status.

Janek was not happy to hear this.

Laramy conveyed Etty's opinion that they should let the Princess herself decide.

Janek was quick to reject that proposal, for he harbored no faith in Royalty. In his opinion, they stood beyond the very laws they enforced.

Although Pik thought the suggestion possessed merit, she was conflicted over her acceptance of it. Throughout her life, indirect interactions with the Royal Nimbus Family had brought Pik nothing but grief. How could she possibly support placing her fate in the direct hands of a Nimbus Princess? Despite her newfound respect for the Royal Daughter, Pik was unwilling to believe that Princess Eden would pick a freelance commercial retrieval team over a Warrior of her family's own Space Navy. Inevitably, should the retrievers choose to challenge the Warrior's claim, the decision would fall to the Galactic Courts. The opinion of the Royal Daughter would count for little then.

Pik found herself remaining quiet.

Etty conveyed his faith in the judgment of the Princess.

Janek's resistance was strong. The Duuian believed that they needed to take a more assertive posture regarding the retrieval claim. Unless they declared themselves, he insisted, they would forfeit their legal right to the commission. They could not challenge the Warrior's superior might, so their only recourse lay in establishing a prior entitlement to the reward.

His vehemence bemused Pik, for it seemed to her that Janek was acting more aggressive than usual. By now, his racial passivity should have compelled him to back down and concede to Etty's obstinate argument.

But Janek was showing no intimidation in the face of Etty's insistence. Indeed, it almost seemed that the Duuian was becoming quite confrontational.

She was about to voice these observations, but their conference was cut short by the Princess' awakening.

She was thirsty. Etty instructed her how to make use of the nutritional facilities of her borrowed pressure suit. As the Princess sucked greedily on her water-tube, Pik guided the group in the direction of the cubicle which featured the hiding-place lockers.

The loathsome Deep Ones attacked before Pik and the others could reach that partition. Swarming like a malevolent maelstrom, the creatures trapped the group out in the open. Tragically, the retrievers and the one-armed Princess were easy prey for the vicious beasts.

Praylude:
Excerpts from the Diary of a Crank

There can no longer be any doubt that Marie and I have been targeted by the bloodthirsty minions of the newly freed Old Ones. Coded signals have been dispatched from Miskatonic, warning all the courageous defenders to beware. As if we needed verification of our mortal endangerment... for the countrysides of all nations are now swarming with vile creatures who slaughter with fervent glee any of Earth's natural offspring.

For centuries, occult forces have battled the unholy evils imprisoned by Elder runes. Our cause has numerous heroes, old and new, who succeeded in thwarting the Old Ones' acolytes over the years. Our most exemplary triumphs, however, have only postponed the inevitable. And now, we are not alone in our terror and dread. Now, everyone flees from the monsters that were once confined to shadows and nightmares. Now, madness has gone global.

Every human being has become prey for these savage hordes, but some are more prized victims than most. Like myself, my wife, and our valiant occult brethren who have fought unnamable depravity for so long. Those who harbor intimate knowledge of mankind's emergent nemeses are the ones sought with special vigor by these foul creatures. We are humanity's last hope, and so our prompt eradication is a priority to these prehistoric agents of corruption.

By dire necessity, our struggles have emerged from secret and are conducted in public now. Our enemy's propensity for overkill has exaggerated *our personal defeats, though, as the merciless beasts lay waste to entire cities to guarantee the deaths of single, marked individuals.*

I am certain that my past efforts to foil the Old Ones have marked me and mine for precise annihilation. Each escape I manage only serves to infuriate those evil forces, compelling them to escalate their lethal ventures. Before the Awakening, I fought psychotic cultists who aspired to league themselves with unholy creatures of darkness. In the aftermath of that terrible rising, I find myself facing demons of more strenuous capacity, things *that act in direct collusion with the liberated Old Ones.*

Last night, while fighting off a swarm of Deep Ones, I swear I caught a glimpse of abominable Dagon, trusted servant to hideous Cthulhu Himself. Armed with hardware "borrowed" from abandoned military caches, Marie and I defended a church wherein had gathered the young and helpless. The streets of Chicago ran yellow with the blood of those aquatic monstrosities…but our best efforts only delayed the inevitable. Their numbers were too great and our ammunition too meager. As my wife and I retreated before a disastrous tide of the horrendous creatures, our mental equilibrium was threatened by the sight of an enormous shape that wallowed in Lake Michigan.

I shudder to realize that my death is so important to the enemy that They would send Dagon Himself to oversee my extermination. Such a blasphemous bounty is a difficult achievement to bear, almost atrocious enough to drive even the staunchest intellect to unbridled lunacy.

I refuse to succumb to such cosmic intimidation, though. With Marie at my side, I will find a way to defeat these unleashed fiends.

❋

I am haunted by nightmares. Many of them, I suspect, are the product of my own despair rather than influenced by the monstrous Evil that has been loosed upon an unsuspecting world.

I have failed mankind. I have failed my occult brethren. And now my most grievous failure: I was unable to save my beloved wife.

This fateful night will never stop tormenting me. This terrible evening when Winslow, Arizona, suffered devastation at the hands of underwater fiends. Those beasts were after me, and the population of an entire metropolis paid the price of my blind arrogance.

No matter how vigorously I strive to forget this horrific twilight, its memory is locked in my head, emblazoned into my very cortex by the in-

tense scope of my emotional wounds. My failure will haunt me the rest of my life, perhaps even long into the afterlife.

Marie and I had fled south from the Hopi Reservation when the Amerindian medicine men had fallen before the incandescent servants of Shudde-M'ell. We barely escaped with our lives, while those brave shamans perished in the firestorm that erupted from newborn geological furnaces. The very ground opened up to release monsters that were unbothered by the terrible lava flows. These semi-molten minions rampaged across the prairie, annihilating everyone and everything in their path. This destruction was quite indiscriminate, sparing no bird or lizard or even blade of grass. It was Shudde-M'ell's dreadful desire that this territory be sterilized for His own unfathomable purpose. All evidence of mankind was scorched from the landscape.

North of Winslow, our jeep fell prey to bandits, and we were forced to continue our desperate flight on-foot. (How sad it is that in these days when our own species is under attack by depraved monsters, that unscrupulous men choose to torment their neighbors for material gain.) Although we lost our gear and the precious talismans we carried to combat the ghastly servants of the reemergent Old Ones, we escaped with our skins and wits intact. At least, that was Marie's opinion as we stumbled into the city's razed outskirts. Ever the optimist, she believed that all we needed to truly defeat the enemy was purity of heart and soul.

Ahh, how innocent and courageous she was. How sweet and beautiful and wonderful. Her stunning physical beauty hid a loving soul and an open heart that burned with passion to right all wrongs. Her fabulous auburn tresses, her delicately molded features, her soft caress...all are lost to me now. My own heart convulses with unforgiving angst over her hideous fate.

I do not want to remember my Marie's demise, but perhaps if I record the events in written words, I can defuse the awful fire that burns in my tortured chest.

We took shelter in a tall concrete tower. The occupants had long ago evacuated this building, abandoning their apartments in a mad rush to escape whatever threat had swept through uptown Winslow. We found meals unfinished on dining room tables, encrusted by mold and enveloped with putrefaction. We found beds unmade, sheets and quilts cast off in a panic as couples had run screaming from their abominable nightmares. We found stockpiles of canned goods and weapons caches, both stores forgotten in whatever abrupt exodus had emptied this condominium. We found no bodies, but somehow we both knew that no one had survived the evacuation.

While Marie prepared a modest dinner for us, I sought to contact our far-flung associates via a short-wave radio I had discovered in a teenager's dusty bedroom. Although I was unable to raise any of our secret brethren, I did hear sketchy reports of the catastrophic submergence of everything east of the Mississippi. Considering how determined the Deep Ones had been to destroy Miskatonic University in Arkham, this terrible flood came as no surprise to me. By raising the tides, the enemy had stolen mankind's best defenses against this unholy menace. I mourned the deaths of those valiant librarians who had guarded the tomes of antediluvian power, for years ago I had shared their sacred duty during my occult apprenticeship. The entire country was crumbling under the onslaught of Cthulhu's unleashed evil. With global communication crippled by Ithaqua's vicious meteorological distress, there was no word of conditions abroad. But I feared that the other continents were faring no better against this horror from beyond mortal ken. I suspected that Asia was plagued by carnivorous manifestations from the monstrous Plateau of Peng. I pitied Africa's populace as the undead denizens of the long-buried Nameless City swarmed across the desert and through the jungles. I envisioned the Mountains of Madness shattering the Antarctic ice as those blasphemous hills surged from their underground exile, and I expected that poor Australia would soon be crushed by their northward advance. I pictured Greenland scoured clean of human habitation by the Wind-Walker's foul cyclones. I shuddered to think how London's citizenry would react when herds of misanthropic beasts spilled forth from underground tunnels. I presumed that an eternal darkness was gathering over South America, blotting the sun from Latin skies. Trapped in the American midwest, I lamented my inability to stop any of these profane incursions. Humanity was dying, and all my arcane might had proven ineffectual against those deadly forces.

When I conveyed these fears to Marie, she reproached my fatalistic despair. She still believed that the vile minions of Great Cthulhu could be halted, defeated and driven back into their shadowy refuges. I longed to share her brave vision, but recent events had drained my verve and weakened my determination. Hope was no longer a factor in my mental process—only survival motivated my actions now.

She reminded me that we were only thirty kilometers east of the mouth of Canyon Diablo, where lay the arcane meteor crater that had granted me my strongest weapon against the evil Old Ones. It had been there that I had dug the sacred Mnarran star from the fused ground. That site might hold further deposits of occult armament, she declared. It was there that we should seek shelter, should make our last stand against the enemies of mankind. If only I had heeded her advice...

But destiny had other plans for my beloved wife.

That very evening, fate decreed that her *last stand would occur within that borrowed apartment.*

The attack came without warning. Burning their way through the walls, the foul minions of evil set upon us while we slept. Gruesome creatures of semi-molten consistency, these beasts were impervious to conventional weapons. My star stone warded off their hateful assault, but that protection did not extend to Marie. Before my eyes, her flesh charred into dark flakes at the approach of Shudde-M'ell's deadly servants. Her body literally melted under their hellish touch, becoming a hideous pool of organic slime on the floor. Her brutal end unbalanced my mind, sending me screaming into the night. The city of Winslow burned behind me as I fled.

When sanity returned to me, my grief was overwhelming, pitching me into an even deeper despairing dementia. I fear that this anxiety has destroyed the last iota of my courage.

I had hoped that transcribing these events might bring me some cathartic release from the guilt that plagues me, but my prayers have gone unanswered. My anguish remains unabated and unsoothed. Her death represents a failure which I cannot—will never—*accept.*

If I could not save the woman I loved, what good are my powers against the mighty evil that threatens humanity?

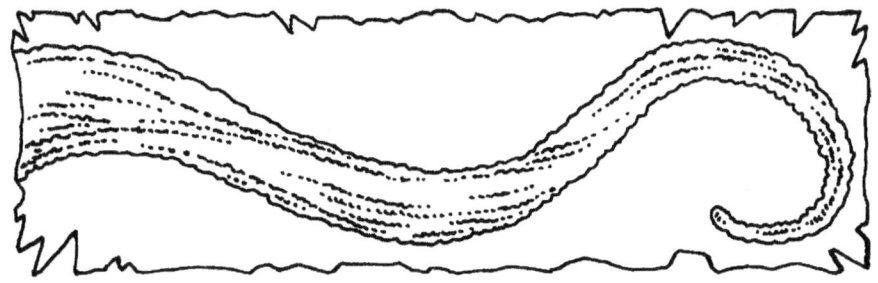

section 4:
Lunar Convergence

The unholy crystal cracked. Once fractured, the aquatic air pressure exploded the portal into a thousand shards, sprinkling the void with a haze of newborn, artificial stars.

The decompressive flow of the jellied air carried the Warrior through the ruptured window and into space. As soon as he was free of the corridor of tainted meat, Tarn activated his thrusters and soared beyond the distended crescent cloud of leaking fluid and glittering slivers of alien glass. He wanted to place some distance between himself and the monstrous spike before he summoned the needle flier he had left in orbit above the shrouded planet. As he flew, his suit's sensors swept the region, providing him with a grand portrait of the spike he left behind.

It loomed huge, blotting out a massive section of the sky. Even though the structure tapered drastically as it plunged toward the moon overhead, the spike's circumference was incredible. He had seen the base of this tower far beneath Earth's ocean, and there the surface had consisted of polished crystal. At this altitude, the crystal was wrapped in a pulsating sheath of biological architecture, its alien flesh naked to the vacuum and cosmic radiation. This gave the spike the bearing of a horrifically extended tentacle that erupted from the planet's opaque cloudcover to stretch with grotesque determination for the bloated moon. Not unlike the corridors of meat hidden beneath its skin, this flesh was a metallic blue. These outer contours were alive with flashes of liquid illumination.

What had the ghost called it...? he thought. *Right—a "Spire of Condemnation."* The terminology did not seem so inaccurately over-colorful now in such proximity to the monstrosity. As an architectural achievement, it was so impressive as to be intimidating. Once one became familiar with the horrors that lurked within that Spire, the notion of "condemnation" was not that medieval or outlandish. In a manner he could not clearly identify, Tarn felt *unclean* from his experiences inside the dreadful Spire.

The depressurized cloud of escaping jelly released with his escape from the spike hung like the ejecta of a colossal burst pimple, the debris swirling in the light breeze of the solar wind.

His battle armor alerted the Warrior that something else seemed to be following him from the Spire.

Focusing on those flickering shapes, Tarn refracted his vision until the things stood out with extreme clarity. Still their precise nature eluded his equipment. Although the comparison was inaccurate, they looked like bats with a wingspan of roughly five-to-six meters. The wings of these creatures seemed ethereal, though...formless and chaotic. It was impossible to get a good glimpse of the creatures, for not only did their frantic flapping confuse detection, but they...their very bodies seemed to flicker, as if what he saw was a rapid animation of still images presented out of sequential order. Most bewildering of all: his equipment could not analyze the creatures' physiology. Meanwhile, their energy signatures thrashed like sputtering flames in a tornado.

What manner of *things* were these...things?

That they were in pursuit of him, there could be no doubt. The beasts were lifting from supine nests hidden in the Spire's landscape of discolored meat. They fluttered after him with deadly intent. While some swooped directly after Tarn, others dove out to block his flanks. The Warrior activated his suit's protective force field.

The bellicose approach of these space-bats prompted Tarn to hesitate no longer. He broadcast the signal to summon his orbital flier.

As the lead assailant threw itself at him, Tarn rewarded the beast's audacity with a blast of pulse beams fired pointblank into the monster's hidden face. (His suit's force projector was designed to oscillate the protective shield to allow the blasts of his weapons to exit the force field.) He fully expected the creature to be flung from him, but his pulse blasts had no physical consequence on the thing. The beast came on with undeterred velocity, smashing itself in prostration on the curvature of the Warrior's force field. He batted the abomination away, and directed his full armament on the next ravager. This thing took no more notice of his firepower than had the first creature. It collided with the outer perimeter of his force field, scraping its offensive maw across the invisible surface of the energy bubble. Tarn recoiled from the frightful teeth, but he actually shuddered at what he imagined he saw within the throat of the beast—it *had* to be his imagination, for such things did not exist... Past the creature's fractal teeth, there seemed to seethe a region of absolutely soulless negation, a hungry nothingness that made the Warrior think of the unfathomable cores of black holes (not that he had any literal conception of what such a thing looked like). This dreadful maw glowed with colors that belonged to a foreign spectrum, causing his sensors extreme classification conflicts that threatened to crash his scanner system. Without questioning the irrational impression, Tarn knew that he stared at an ultimate damnation of matter and consciousness inside the beast's convulsing throat. Madness incarnate was gnawing at his force bubble!

In fact, he saw with a loud exclamation of horror, the space-bat was *literally* gnawing through the force field! Insane though that prospect was, the beast's jagged teeth were actually *tearing through the energy barrier!* The Warrior responded with frantic salvos of his reputedly mighty firepower: torturous pulse blasts, drilling laser needles, biting particle beams, lethal bursts of scorching X-rays. All types of hellishly destructive forces burst forth from his battle armor's weapons, and each barrage failed to halt or even deter the monsters as they swarmed to encompass his force bubble.

He expanded the radius of the bubble, forcing back the tide of the thrashing, tattered space-bats. Just in time too, for one of the creature's jagged wings pierced the energy bubble to tear at him. The darting claws ripped the arm of his suit, slicing through his titanium-alloy armor as if it were damp cardboard. His suit squealed as self-repair programs struggled to reseal the breach before the sudden decompression could result in severe damage. Tarn could not help but scream now; he bellowed with anger and determined perseverance, and fired his weapons with wild abandon.

He was slow to admit to the realization that these venomous creatures were thoroughly invulnerable to his array of armament, not because he believed in the supremacy of his weapons, but more out of disbelief in the monsters' incredible resilience. These creatures acted as if his firepower simply did not exist. The reality of this helplessness was not something an elite Warrior of the Nimbus Space Navy was personally willing to concede.

Further expanding the diameter of his force field, Tarn powered up his thrusters and engaged in a series of evasion maneuvers. Rocketing about the sky, the Warrior's trajectory was erratic and breakneck. If he had not confined his awareness to sensory input (with inertial dampeners), his momentum would definitely have given him a severe headache. But still the beasts hounded his unpredictable path, coating his force bubble with their stroboscopic forms and scraping their unnatural mandibles and talons across the exterior of the energy field. Even his most maniacal moves proved insufficient to shake these vampiric fiends.

Despair was unknown to the Warrior, but he was anxiously realizing that this was a losing struggle. Sooner or later, regardless of his frenetic aerial acrobatics, one of these creatures were going to burst through his force bubble, diving upon him to rend armor and flesh with its supernatural claws. He could find no way to disable or kill the beasts, and his meager success at avoiding them was a dwindling advantage. Time was ticking off the desperate last minutes of his life.

Suddenly, the space-bats flung themselves from Tarn's force field, as if its surface had abruptly become an anathema to their bloodlust. Swooping away, they retreated behind the looming girth of the Spire.

What happened? he gasped. Had one of his shots struck a vital spot on the swarm's leader? Somehow, he doubted that such a fortunate explanation was the reason for their impulsive flight of panic. His armament had quintessentially proven itself to be a futile defense against the bat-things.

Then he saw that his flier had arrived. Its approach had been hidden from him by the clustering flock of the creatures, for—he realized with a start—the beasts' opacity had closed off the reach of his scanners like a sphere of contracting darkness. *What the def were those monsters?*

Had the beasts fled from his approaching flier? If so—then what aspect of the ship had frightened them so drastically? For therein lay the only weakness that Tarn could attribute to the creatures, and he was keen to discover their vulnerability.

His flier featured a standard array of pulse cannons and narrower frequency beams. These weapons were effectively no different from the ones his suit possessed, and *those* had failed to even annoy the beasts. Could it be the ship's drive? Were the bat-things afraid of the flier's plasma drive core?

Briefly, he recalled the drive core of the Princess' crashed Opal Yacht. Had it been emptied by creatures such as this? Drained by indubitably impossible means…had that theft been done out of *fear* instead of any intent to steal the nuclear fury? This notion caught in his mind for a brief moment.

Then he gasped as the bat-things swung around the massive Spire to swarm on his interstellar flier. He saw his ship's automatic defensive system spring to life: force field crackling into existence, weapons arrays opening fire on the crowd of attacking beasts. The creatures flocked so densely that Tarn momentarily lost sight of his spacecraft in their monstrously flickering cloud. Then, with a moan of anguish, the Warrior witnessed the creatures melt through the flier's protective force bubble. A second later, the space-bats dove on his ship—and into it, passing readily through the reinforced hull.

"No!" he cried.

The creatures had not been scared off by the arrival of his flier, they had abandoned their small prey to go for the greater prize contained in the ship. The plasma drive core! The creatures did not fear the primal, nuclear energy—they lusted after it. *And I brought it here for them,* he moaned.

Tarn aimed himself for the threatened flier, opening his thrusters far beyond their recommended tolerance. Riding the insanely intense propulsion, the Warrior launched himself at his ship. His monstrous velocity crushed his feet into his boots, his body armor dug painfully into his crotch and armpits. He strained to scorn the agony and focus on the target that was zooming toward him at breakneck speed. If he could manage to board the vessel, perhaps he could still thwart the creatures. But seconds before the Warrior could make contact with the needle flier's stumpy guidance-foils, the ship lurched to the side, eluding his desperate grasp by bare centimeters. As he shot past, the ship turned to face the deadly moon in the sky. He struggled to pursue his stolen vessel, but his speed was too great and his hell-bent trajectory refused to be diverted. He had pushed his battle armor too far this time, and the maximum thrust had frozen his controls. There was no way to silence his rockets, no way to halt his infernal flight. Zooming without restraint toward the planet's inscrutable cloudcover, Tarn witnessed the moon's ghostly ocean swallow his usurped flier.

Any normal man would have despaired at that point, but the Warrior had no time for fatalistic discouragement. There were more pressing threats to overcome before he could properly lament the loss of his interstellar vessel.

His thrusters were still raging at full blast, driving him headlong toward the cursed world below. Under normal circumstances, such a drop would be a minor inconvenience for a combat suit of the Royal Space Navy...but these were far from ordinary circumstances that he faced here-and-now. His force bubble was already strained and near collapse from exhaustion, and the rest of his suit's systems were about ready to seize up from overstrain. At present capacity, he doubted that his battle armor would save him from plummeting through the planetary atmosphere to crash into the ground. Continuing *down* was not an option.

As long as his thrusters were locked at full-blast, he could not halt his movement through space. His only hope lay in diverting the trajectory of his fall. Such a change-of-course was (technically) as easy achieved as bending his knees, altering the direction of his foot-worn thrusters' propulsion. The simple act of bending his knees was a life-threatening action at this velocity, though. His acceleration was already subjecting his body to several Gs, rendering his ample muscles into weary agents of mobility. Tarn needed to meticulously swing his lower extremity only a fraction of a degree, otherwise his new trajectory would snap his spine—or worse, send him veering away from the planet, condemning him to the empty void. Any slight spasm could throw him into a tumble, the outcome of which would not be acceptable. Everything depended on the scrupulous precision of his muscular control. His legs ached; he was uncertain of his fine control of their muscles under these hellish conditions. But this uncertainty did not halt him from trying.

It was sheer anguish. The second he unlocked his knee joints from the upright position, the accumulating G-force battled to drag his upper body down upon his fractionally-bent knees. The strain was immensely painful—then even more so, as he felt one of his thighbones shatter under the stress.

Pain became a viscous shadow eclipsing his vision, swimming red to dissolve his awareness, natural and artificial. Disconnecting the pain receptors in his brain, Tarn shook off the crimson fog and strained to support his broken leg with both hands. He knew that the appropriate supercells in his bloodstream were swarming to repair the damage, but their reconstruction was going to be corrupted by the crushing Gs he fought against. He had to keep his legs bent at an exact angle (predetermined by his suit's whining systems) if he was going to avert a crash-landing or an exile to the bleak void.

It seemed to be working! His course was gradually turning away from the face of the deadly planet. It took several moments for this curve to accumulate and divert his plummet into the looming stratosphere; each minute was an exaggerated eternity of pain for Tarn. Once his trajectory was basically parallel with the opaque atmosphere, he forced his legs back into a straight position. His broken femur sent chemical objections coursing through his body, he was aware of the agony even with that portion of his cerebellum turned off. But he couldn't relax, not yet…

He was presently secure in an orbital path, but the slightest deviation of thrust could disrupt his hyperbolic equilibrium. He needed to hold his position until his jets ran out of fuel. A quick evaluation revealed that he could look forward to at least two more hours of this hell-bent velocity before his suit's thrusters emptied their propellant charges.

Two hours…enduring this oppressive G-force…suffering the strain and dreading how it would interfere with the automatic repair of his fractured thigh…

This was an ignoble test for a Royal Warrior whose talents lay in violent action, not in holding a single frozen position for hours of unnatural physical stress. To survive this horrific crisis, Tarn must abandon his frantic urge to strike back and channel that energy into remaining an unmoving statue as he tore through the vacuum of space, barely a few hundred meters above the turgid ivory surface of the planet's stratosphere.

Set to battle an entire army, Tarn knew he would emerge victorious.

Compelled to "not move" under these emotional and physical tensions…the Warrior wasn't sure if he was up to so *immobile* an ordeal.

While his conscious mind fixated on a rigid control of his physical being, his subconscious took refuge in better times, what few there were in Tarn's hard life…

There was something about the trunq trees in full bloom that brought life to Furnace 17's otherwise dull brown sky. Their oily black leaves unfurled to seek sunlight only once per season, usually early in June. After tracking the sun's scalding course across the sky for two weeks, they paled, shriveled, and flung themselves to the whimsy of the summer breezes. Their job was done. The radiant energies gathered by the trunq leaves was stored deep in the trees' resilient trunks, fueling the chemical reactions necessary to sustain life throughout the rest of the year. If a tree's hungry leaves opened to inadequate sunlight, green flowers were generated by starving trunqs, as if in celebration of their starvation. In the old days, a rainy summer would bring the forest's uppermost regions alive with the vibrant blooms of its suffering. Then humanity came to this world, and the woods grew greener still. Man's industrial necessities blackened the skies with crude pollution, starving the trunq trees to greater displays of emerald blossoming.

Little Tarn knew none of this horticultural background. As far as the child was concerned, he loved to see the woods grow verdant. It was not until he became an indifferent adult that he learned the horrific truth behind the majestic flowers. Despite that later understanding, the memory of those flowering woods was one of his most treasured recollections, one he often accessed when faced with mental distress. Invariably, though, this childhood sanctuary would turn on him, melting into the horrific doom that came to Furnace 17.

The sky changed very little from day to night under the dense pall of particulate carbon. From this darkness had descended an uglier cloud, one that spilled forth fire and death. The sky flashed yellow. The soil curdled. The air was filled with a million voices raised in terror. Then everything went forever silent.

Little Tarn was too young to comprehend what had happened or how he had survived the dreadful extermination of most of the planet's life. The ones who rescued him from the rad-pod rushed the boy and all other survivors offworld.

"The A.I.s," the adult mumbled among themselves. "Those terrible machines had sterilized another planet, rendering it useless to organic life. They'll move in now, and cover the planet with their own metal cities."

Subsequent psychotherapy stifled the refugees' traumas with holistic amnesia...but not Tarn. Somehow, the boy retained a residual memory of the massacre. Even more remarkable, the child apparently suffered no mental strife from these monstrous recollections.

It did not surprise his foster parents when Tarn chose to enlist in the Space Navy immediately after completing his required basic education. "Make a man of him," his foster father had grunted. Everyone knew that the boy was desperate for the opportunity to strike back at the soulless machines that had slaughtered his family, his friends, his planet of birth. The irony was: the Org/A.I. War had come to an unresolved end a few years ago. Neither side could claim victory, but both factions certainly felt defeated. An undeclared armistice settled upon the galaxy. There were no more sorties into "their" territory, and they stayed out of "our" space. There was no chance now of Tarn ever realizing his vengeance.

Not that soldiers of the Nimbus Space Navy went idle, for there were many minor threats to suppress among the greedier organic lifeforms. While Reconstruction dominated official agencies, pirates and small armies looking for easy conquest spread through the galaxy. Tarn saw his share of action and violence as a young Warrior. He never once realized that the hu-

man government he served was conducting its own brand of conquest in the guise of a galactic police force. When the Nimbus Royal Family was declared Rulers of the Thousand Races, Tarn simply assumed it was a result of the order mankind had restored to the galactic civilization-at-large.

In the end, he never achieved closure over the death of his family, but he proved his foster father right. The military made a man of Tarn the boy.

A sudden change in thrust wrestled Tarn's awareness from his personal reverie, plunging him into the aching reality of here-and-now. He became aggressively alert, wary for hidden menace.

But no, it was no threat this time. What had jolted him from his reminiscing had been his thrusters' guidance systems unlocking. Their fuel charges were not yet exhausted, but the force of the blast had decreased to a point that the heat no longer overloaded the control circuits. He quickly cut propulsion, and surveyed his current position.

Two hundred and thirty-nine meters above the planet's gas envelope, he apparently soared in a stable orbit. Flinging out long-range scans, he established that his trajectory was taking him far from the equatorial spikes that rose from the shrouded world. They were so far away, it was no longer possible for him to be certain which particular Spire he had escaped from.

He was safe…but moving steadfastly away from any possibility of rescuing the Royal Brat.

❖

Pik saw very little of the actual attack. The Deep Ones came out of nowhere. They struck Pik first, as if aware that the girl was the group's strongest defender. They came fast and hard, bludgeoning her with their huge, wide fins. Pik was surrounded and set upon by a crowd of the aquatic brutes. She had her force field up, so their blows did no real damage to her, but the beasts had efficiently cut her off from those who needed her protection—*Etty* and Janek and the Princess. Pik called over the comlink, but a shrill squeal was the only answer that came.

Then that squeal emerged from her ears to swim around her head and shoulders within the confines of her pressure suit. The noise pulsed with a brilliance that slowly—and entirely against her will!—sank into her skin, saturating flesh and bone and—

And then Pik was drifting naked in a familiar prison of translucent crystal.

What happened? she silently fretted. *Was I recaptured by the beasts' mysterious teleportation spell? Or,* she trembled at this suspicion, *was my entire escape nothing more than an cruel dream planted in my mind by the Evil One's insidious manipulations?* It *couldn't* have been an illusion! It had been as real as…reality. *How could I tell, though?*

Peering through the milky crystalline facets of the containment cell, Pik saw the evidence necessary to prove the reality of her post-escape experiences. There: Etty and Janek struggled with a swarm of mid-sized Deep Ones. To the side: the larger beasts were casting aside a pair of clearly unoccupied pressure suits (which she instantly recognized as her own souped-up suit and Etty's that had previously been worn by the Princess) and bustling with a pair of containment crystals (one of which restrained Pik).

We were ambushed! The enemy snatched me and the Princess from our suits with their profane technology. Now, Etty fought for his life—naked and unarmed against these monsters!

Pik shuddered as her prison was moved, and she was afforded a brief, hazy glimpse of a bilious form that caught her breath. She could not make out much detail, but the thing appeared to be a horribly deformed Deep One, its body mutated into a large and meaty jellyfish dome. The malformed head that jutted from the apex of this organic shell was grotesque, no longer retaining any fish-like qualities to give its countenance any sane description. Between the milky translucency of the lens through which she was forced to peer, and the swiftness of her glimpse of the horrific creature, she couldn't be sure, but it seemed that one of the thing's eyes was located inside its mouth.

The flesh of this deformed beast was decorated with alien calligraphy that glowed with a pulsating light. *This must be one of the Deep Ones' wizards,* she realized. This monster had cast the teleportation spell that had plucked Pik from the safety of her pressure suit!

A helpless captive of the hideous marine servants of the terrible Evil One, Pik screamed obscenities as her crystal cell was carted off, out of the large cargo chamber and into the corridors of meat. Her last view of Etty was not encouraging: she watched him jump to duck inside one of the hiding-place lockers she had discovered, only to find himself surrounded by malicious monsters.

Pik's captors moved her prison along with reckless haste. She was able to discern that the person occupying the second containment crystal was the Princess. Pik could recognize her form, but detect no emotional details from that hazy silhouette.

Then the creatures abruptly halted, to consign the crystals to a large orifice that widened at their approach. There was a period of darkness, accompanied by a gut-wrenching acceleration…they were going *up!* The Deep Ones were delivering the precious human breeders to their Evil Lord.

Doomed and damned, the two females were on their way to the moon.

❖

Etty was furious with himself. He had gone to the effort of choosing a selection of weapons from the Deep Ones' armory. He had carried those borrowed swords and spears of coral on their hideous journey through the Spire's disgusting corridors…but now that he needed them, Etty was unarmed, having set aside his weapons while conferring with his retriever partners. The beasts' attack was so sudden that he was cut off from these discarded blades and spikes.

The prospect of trying to engage these creatures without weapons or protection was sheer foolishness. Even so, Etty dove to defend the Princess from the fierce beasts. He was batted aside and ignored, as massive Deep Ones descended in force upon the Princess and Pik.

Separated from the girls, Etty dodged and squirmed his way free of the grasp of his own assailants. For once, his naked state worked to his advantage. His unfettered fingers and lithe limbs gave him nimble passage through the beasts' clumsy appendages. By sheer luck, he found himself in the corner where he had left his weapons. Grabbing a sword and a spear, Etty whirled to enter the fray.

His wrath was fantastic, instilling his wiry muscles with a ferocious strength and determination. He swung his sword, embedding the blade to the hilt in the shoulder of a Deep One. The blade refused to come loose from the grievous stab wound, though, and the boy was forced to abandon it. He jabbed his spear at a beast as it lunged at him, plunging it all the way through the thing's terrible torso. The creature thrashed wildly, tearing the spear from Etty's hands and vanishing with it. A cloud of yellow liquid clouded the gelatinous air.

And then, several beasts swam from that vile fog to herd him back. Unarmed again, he had no recourse other than to retreat before their rampaging advance. With ominous rumblings in their bulbous throats, the Deep Ones crowded him back into a partitioned cubicle.

He saw the lockers and instantly remembered Pik's description of them as viable places to take shelter. He lunged for them, but a pair of burly fish-things blocked his way. They were surrounding him—and Etty had watched enough nature holos to recognize this tactic. Any second now, the pack would pounce on him!

Suddenly, Janek burst through their hideous ranks. Snatching the human in a tangle of his spindly arms, the Duuian used his powerful triad of legs to launch himself across the cargo chamber. As they soared through the tableau, Etty caught a flash-glance of the Deep Ones hustling a pair of crystal cells out one of the side doors. More concerned now with guarding this retreat, the creatures left Etty and Janek unmolested during this procedure.

The retrievers put the respite to use with a cold logic. Janek deposited Etty atop the floppy form of a pressure suit. With a start, Etty realized that it was *his* pressure suit! Where was the Princess? His alien teammate was not willing to give him time to ponder this mystery, the Duuian was frantically gesturing the human to don the vacant suit. Etty clambered into his suit, shedding the crude breathing device he had worn.

As he clamped his helmet closed, Etty desperately switched on the suit's comlink and cried to Janek, "What happened to the Princess? Where is she?"

"They took the Princess," replied Janek. "And Pik too."

"What?!"

"With their teleportation technology..."

Etty shuddered, for he recalled the nauseating experience of displacement when Ithaqua's shaman had removed him from his own suit back in the drained drive core in the Princess' crashed cruiser. He knew that Janek shared this terrible memory, from his own abduction by a Deep One wizard. And now—Pik and Princess Eden had fallen prey to that diabolical phenomenon!

Stolen from their suits without warning, the girls must have been imprisoned in those crystal cells Etty had seen the Deep Ones remove with such haste and protection.

"We have to save them!" he wailed.

"First we must save *ourselves*," the Duuian advised testily.

Undeniably, there was more wisdom in Janek's evaluation of the situation. This did not stop Etty from leaping to attack the few remaining Deep Ones who guarded the exit taken by the retreating pair of containment cells.

With an exasperated sigh, Janek followed his reckless human team-mate into battle. As they fought the medium-sized guards with brute force, Janek confided that he was going to attempt to refine the focus of his sensory lasers, converting them into weapons.

Breathlessly, Etty agreed that it was a plausible action, confessing that his suit lacked such software to affect a similar conversion. "I hope you can do it," he gasped, "because otherwise we're about to get beaten sense-less and recaptured…"

He pummeled a Deep One with his suit's metallic fists, firing futile pulse blasts at others of the marine rear guard. He had found that although the beasts were unharmed by the concussive beams, they often spun and floundered if he hit them at just the right angle. He used this trick to send most of the guards twirling uncontrollably, buying Janek time to conduct his reprogramming.

When a host of red needles sliced through the liquid air, Etty released a passionate cheer. He ducked back to grant Janek an unobstructed aim. The Duuian's lasers swung their now-lethal beams to cut the guards to ribbons.

For a fleeting second, Etty remembered that Duuians were pacifists. He commended Janek for overcoming his inherent submissive nature at so vital a time. Without his alien partner's sudden aggression, they would surely have failed to defeat their monstrous adversaries.

As soon as the way was clear, Etty dove through the doorway, eager to track the Deep Ones with their female human cargo. He was struck down by a mammoth fish-thing, who in turn was cut in half by Janek's lasers as the Duuian entered the corridor. There were several of these big beasts in attendance in the tunnel, waiting to prevent any passage or pur-suit of the precious human prizes they had reclaimed for their Great Lord. Janek reduced them to severed slabs of fish-meat with his lasers.

"This way!" called Professor Laramy's voice in the retrievers' heads.

Etty turned to see the ghostly figure hanging at the far end of the grisly corridor. He waved his alien partner to follow as he leapt to join the ghost.

"I refuse to place any trust in Laramy's advice," objected Janek.

"We must hurry!" Etty shouted. "They're getting away with Pik! And the Princess!"

The Duuian accompanied the human, reluctantly and with wheezed forebodings. The ghost guided them through a maze of passageways… and Etty grew more and more worried.

"Where are they?" he moaned. There had been no sign of activity for several tunnel-lengths. "We should have caught up to them by now…"

The Professor's ghost answered with a hollow chuckling.

"What—"

"He's insane," Janek grumbled. "We should never be following him."

"Be quiet, Janek. He's our only hope right now."

"That is too bad," cooed the ghost. There was a distinct edge of contempt in the specter's voice. "That would make you…hopeless."

Etty wheeled on the ghost, only to discover that Laramy's hazy form had vanished. The corridor's only occupants were Etty and Janek in their pressure suits. "Laramy!" he cried. "Where'd you get to? Laramy…?"

"I warned you," the Duuian muttered. "We are on our own. I would not be surprised if the lunatic took us far from where we want to be, and now we're lost in these tunnels."

"He wouldn't…"

"Do not place any faith in Laramy's sanity, Etty," Janek advised sternly. "His help has brought us nothing but trouble."

"We've got to find Pik!"

"I concur, but I have no strategy to suggest."

"Up," Etty declared. "They'll take the girls to the moon. We need to ascend to the tip of the spike."

Janek replied with a grunt of approval. They moved off, following the passages in the direction they hoped was *up*.

❖

Pik was forced unconscious, she suspected in order to place her consciousness in the psychic clutches of their terrible Lord, the Great Cthulhu. For the Evil One had devised new mental tortures for the female retriever…

It was early evening: the bedtime for all good little children, as she well knew.

Little Pik collected her dolls and their loose attire, packing everything carefully away in a storage carton of ugly dun plastiform. Once she had cleared all evidence of her playtime from the room, she sealed the container and pressed the red button located on its side. With a shudder, the carton wheeled across the room and vanished through one of the great ballroom's many archways. Turning to leave, Pik discovered her father watching her from the shadows. His lecherous red eyes flashed eagerly in the gloom.

Her comatose mind rebelled against the unpleasant inaccuracies contained in this dream. Pik had never owned more than a single doll, for her family had been poor—too indigent to ever live in any abode that had included such a majestic ballroom. And her father... Her father had never...

She understood what would come next. Before little Pik could retire to sleeptime, there were certain duties required of her childhood self. With slumping shoulders, she shuffled to perform those unsightly duties...

No! Nothing like *this* had ever happened! Pik's father had been a wonderful man—her only parent. She had never known her mother, who had died giving birth to the child.

"You're so much better than your mother," the obscene father-thing announced, its voice booming in the empty darkness of the ballroom. "That's why she had to go away. But now I have you, my lovely young daughter..."

As Pik approached him, she shrugged off her resplendent blouse, exposing her immature chest. She trembled as the father-thing sighed in anticipation and fumbled with its pants. Before she could reach him, though, a doorbell sounded.

With a grunt of exaggerated innocent curiosity, the father-thing turned away and strode to answer the chime.

Having failed to convince Pik of this abhorrent scenario, the malignant Evil One had abandoned this line of psychic assault.

Unable to resist, little Pik trailed after the father-thing, following it to an enormous doorway of expensive gilding. The massive panels of the doorway belonged to exotic forests from long-dead other worlds. Pulling this gate open, the father-thing solemnly greeted the visitor.

It was Princess Eden! Garbed in regal finery, the Royal Daughter presented the father-thing with a Royal Decree seizing the family's land. Then the Nimbus Princess took notice of young Pik, swinging the condescending glare of her crimson eyes to survey her childhood insignificance. "What is that?" the Princess asked the father-thing.

"That is my only daughter, Your Majesty," replied the father-thing. "Her name is Pik..."

"How ugly and grotesque she is!" announced the evil Princess. "I order you to put that monstrosity to death immediately!"

"As you wish," mumbled my father. No longer misshapen or a thing, he turned and grabbed the child by her tiny neck.

Nooo!

❖

Pik was not the only victim of the Evil One's telepathic pollution. The Princess was trapped in a dream of horrific strife…

Events in the course of a lifetime had come to pass, along with her royal parents. Their unfortunate deaths elevated the Princess to her proper maturity as Queen Eden, new matriarch of the Nimbus Family that ruled the majority of the charted galaxy.

As required of her ultimate royal status, the Queen had taken a husband, to give the Empire a King. She gave her husband a casual glance, regarding Him as He sat on His slab-like throne of confusing geometry. She knew she had to be bewitched, for she felt only intense repulsion for His monstrous appearance…His awful body, bloated like a over-fed toad; His mighty talons that gripped the arms of his unearthly throne; His great bat-wings, leathery and covered with algae; His blunt and ghastly face, the chin alive with a writhing tangle of tentacles. Her husband was a hideous monster!

King Cthulhu turned to nod to her, reaching to caress her trembling cheek. She sat next to Him, ensconced on her own crystalline throne. With a start of terror, she looked down to discover her lap and legs were encased in the block of green crystal. She gasped to find that her forearms and hands were similarly immersed in her throne.

Her husband returned His attention to address the throng of dignitaries that were gathered to hear the latest regal proclamation. He welcomed the masses into His splendid presence, promising them all a ghastly damnation for the privilege. In a booming voice that was heard throughout galactic civilization, He recited His many atrocities, providing details that made the Queen retch. Then He announced that the Queen had a statement to make.

All eyes (human, alien, and monster) turned on her, and Queen Eden found herself praising the cruel wisdom of her husband, King Cthulhu. She waxed prosaic, revealing intimate secrets of the horrors He had subjected her to in the privacy of their boudoir. The words she spoke turned her stomach and made her dizzy with revulsion. It was her voice coming from her own mouth, but another's mind guided this unholy recitation. Her husband chuckled proudly throughout her sermon, ruffling His tentacles with repugnant satisfaction. He could taste her mortal shame, ripe and feverish on the psychic ether, and He relished its despair like a glorious delicacy. His blasphemous, crimson eyes drank in her fearful despondency.

And she continued to glorify the deviant sexual behavior of the ruler of the known universe. "Many children have I borne my monstrous husband," she declared. "And without fail He has eaten every one of them." She gagged, bile rising in her spasming throat as she choking on her own claims. "Soon, I will undergo surgery to enlarge my womb, so that I may breed vast litters from my Lord's unholy seed."

At that point, her disgust grew so intense that the dreaming Princess passed out, effectively awakening to the reality of her ghastly captivity.

❖

Meanwhile, Pik remained unconscious, facing the Evil One's tortures.

She was strolling through a concourse outside her high school, oblivious to her surroundings and lost in cherished memories of the debaucheries her young lover had subjected her to that very morning. Pik's crotch would sting for days from his cruel manipulations.

Before her unconscious mind could disavow this painful coupling, laser beams sliced through the crowd of pedestrians—and Pik knew where she was! This was the site of an assassination attempt between rival Nimbus cousins. Pik was fifteen and caught in the deadly crossfire. She could not fail to recognize this horrific scenario from her young life.

But things were different this time. Her aching privates restricted the girl from full mobility. Her lunge to the safety of the ground was too slow, and she caught a lethal beam across her forehead. Her head fell into two pieces, and Pik died before her body hit the grassy knoll.

Detached from this lifeless body, her spirit rose above the grisly courtyard. The crowds had suffered far worse this time, and only a few students flailed on the green. Everyone else had been shredded like Pik. Their own ghosts were rising now, following her into the bright white light that burned just for them in the afternoon sky.

She was dead...and was going now to her ultimate judgment. Pik's posthumous fate would depend on God's assessment of her life. She was not afraid, for Pik knew that she had lived a good life. The girl's faith had guided her along ethical paths during her fifteen years. Now she would soon stare full upon the mighty and benevolent face of God.

Imagine her surprise when it turned out that God wore Princess Eden's face!

"Pik Gundermergen," God bellowed. "You come before Me with an untainted soul."

"Thank y—" young Pik started to reply.

With eyes flashing red, the Princess God roared, "You leave Me no re-course but to condemn your arrogant soul to the eternal tortures of Hell!"

Huh—?

"How dare you imagine yourself so important that you would pit your fledgling intellect against the natural order! You have violated My basic laws of existence with your feigned 'goodness'. You have failed to function as a vital cog in the food chain. You have never brought pain and suffering to your neighbors. You have loved and tasted love in return. You have been faithful to Me in all the wrong ways!"

"But..." was all Pik's spirit could mumble. This simply could not be so. God was Good, not Evil. God was supposed to be benevolent, forgiving, kind... According to what source? Faith! Could her faith have...erred? Had Pik chosen the wrong path in life? Had she mistaken God's wishes? If God was Evil, then Pik had flagrantly violated His Great Plan with her every waking moment. She was a sinner extraordinaire.

"Now you will suffer forever, tasting the agonies you were too egocentric to share with your brethren!"

Panicked and confused, Pik found herself drawn toward the Princess God's disapproving crimson glare. With dread, then fear, Pik fell into those blood-red eyes. Inside that gaze, her spirit twisted in pain and anguish.

Forever...

By the time they reached the tip of the monstrous Spire of Condemnation, Etty's temperament was as confused as his notion of up and down.

At first, the gradual change of gravity had disoriented both retrievers. Then Janek had deduced that they must have climbed high enough to be beyond the planet's gravitational attraction. They were now near enough to be touched by the pull of the lunar gravity. As a result of this turnaround, their final *ascent* was conducted by climbing *down* the narrowing tunnels of meat.

"This means that we are almost there," Janek declared. He was growing annoyed at having to repeatedly remind Etty of their purpose. His human partner's erratic memory was experiencing fuzziness again. Janek knew that these mental lapses were not Etty's fault, but that did not abate the Duuian's rising tension.

"Where are we?"

"We're almost there, I think."

"On the moon?"

"That's where you wanted to go, right?" The Duuian was puzzled. Now that they were faced with the imminence of their terrible destination, the human seemed reluctant. "Are you...afraid to continue?"

Etty gasped, denouncing Janek for even thinking that he would leave Pik to the awful whims of this monstrous Cthulhu. "She's my girl!" he yelled. "We're going to rescue her!"

Well, Janek noticed, *there's one detail he doesn't have trouble remembering.*

"And the Princess too," the Duuian reminded him. "We have gone through too much to lose her retrieval commission."

"Grup the commission," Etty snorted. "I'm going to rescue Princess Eden because I'm her hero."

"Yes, and you'll be Pik's hero too," mumbled Janek. He leaned over and stared at the floor of the Spire's final corridor. "Well, how do we proceed from here?"

Etty could only shrug. If he even understood that there was a dilemma, he remained unstymied by it.

"Then step back," Janek directed with an exasperated huff. "And I will cut our way through with my lasers." He bent to aim his souped-up sensory beams, and the meat of the passage sizzled and discolored, finally splitting wide like an eager mouth. Without preamble, Etty crawled into the incision and disappeared from sight.

The human is blinded by his eagerness, Janek fretted. *He's driven by a duality of mating urges, one for his lifemate, the other for a celebrity he secretly lusts after. He's not taking the time to devise any plan of attack, he's just barging ahead—empty-headed and for all intensive purposes unarmed. He's going to get us killed...*

Janek was still unused to his own newfound courage, this defiant predilection for violent solutions. His natural docility seemed so remote now, like a dream experienced years ago and remembered only with hazy disapproval. Recent events had changed the Duuian, submerging his passive upbringing and granting him the ability to equate aggressive conduct with survival. There was nothing wrong with pacifism—as long as that was the universally practiced philosophy. But, in the face of the gruesome atrocities Janek had suffered at the fins of the Deep Ones, remaining neutral was quantifiably suicidal behavior.

As long as Etty remained mired in a psychological fog, *someone* had to adopt the mantle of protector and defender, especially when everyone and everything around them constituted a viable threat to their safety and sanity.

At this point, greed was not the only compulsion that motivated Janek. Survival had become of utmost importance.

He followed Etty through the organic crevice, pausing only to widen the aperture enough to accommodate the span of his headcrest.

At least they had been spared the unhelpful company of Laramy's ghost. The specter had not returned to torment them. Janek had always instinctively distrusted the ghost, but he wondered what had prompted Laramy to finally drop the deceptive guise of their companion. Something had changed in the deceased religious fanatic, driving him even further insane. *Maybe he ate too many contaminated souls...*

Beyond the floor that was in truth the tip of the Spire, Janek found himself hanging in water. From the pings that came back to his suit, he knew the liquid to be rather deep. This must be the lunar ocean. The pointed end of this Spire of Condemnation was dragging its way through the ocean as the moon revolved around the planet. The realization of the entire, incredibly outlandish construction was breathtaking. As the moon orbited the Earth, the planet turned on its axis. Orchestrating this intersection was a phenomenal achievement...even if it did belong to merciless creatures that served a psychotic master.

Releasing his grip on the Spire, Janek tumbled in the wake of the traveling tip. Adjusting his position, he rendezvoused with Etty who floated alone and muttering in the dark waters.

That part puzzled the Duuian: these depths bore little resemblance to the seas of the parent planet. Where the earthbound ocean had been a thick jelly with its burden of toxic pollutants, these lunar waters were pure H_2O. Did the reigning Lord demand purity for himself, consigning his worshipers to the filthy seas of the poisoned Earth? It certainly seemed that way.

In the far distance, a marine mirage of awesome proportions flickered with profane iridescence. Was it a huge underwater city? Or perhaps a monstrous temple for evil incarnate?

Where had that *come from?* he pondered. He held no belief in the Lord Cthulhu as an Ancient Evil; that was just part of Laramy's lunatic babble. Janek knew Earth's Supreme Lord was only a malevolent alien. Armed with superior technologies, the creature had terrorized this world, embellishing its terrible reputation with myths of ancient horrors rising to devour the unbelievers. These local beasts might be taken in by such pompous legends, but Janek was not afraid for his soul, just his life. Trespassing here, on this mad Lord's private moon…he and Etty were risking their lives simply being here! And they planned to go against this Supreme Lord, challenging the monster's claim to hold their partner and the Royal Daughter. Whatever terrors the Old One had in store for its captives, Janek and Etty were here to spoil those plans. *What a farce,* he moaned. *We're going to get ourselves killed…*

Janek knew there was no other way, though. The retrieval team had been separated from their ship, then, one by one, captured by this world's primitive beasts and taken from the planet's surface into one of the monstrous spikes that reared beyond the atmosphere. Now they were on the Earth's moon, deep in the Great Lord's lunar ocean. If only they could simply flee these deadly waters and return to their spacecraft; then they could escape this brutal mistreatment. But no…first they must rescue one of their own: Pik, who the reigning monarch had apparently claimed for his own harem along with the lost Princess. (Grup only knew what that creature intended to do with—or to—the human women, for there were no male humans left alive on this planet to mate with the girls.)

Since Janek and Etty had not fled, but stayed to steal back their abducted partner, the Duuian saw no fault in extending that rescue to include the missing Princess. At least the retrieval reward for her might compensate the team for all their suffering, all the abuse they had endured at the hands of this world's lunatic creatures. A small part of Janek desired some form of vengeance against the beasts that had amputated one of his arms. And the Duuian understood he was not the only one to lose a limb to the Deep Ones' cruel surgeons; the Princess had been similarly mutilated. There must be *some* form of retribution for these disfiguring injuries.

This need for revenge was a new emotion to Janek, it was a sentiment not practiced by his Duuian kind. He wondered if he had caught this emotion (like some psychic infection) from close habitation with his human partners. Six years (five by human standards) traveling together aboard the ">%" had effectively fused some humanity into his Duuian consciousness, just as his presence had refined the humans' appreciation of greed. Janek was grateful that none of mankind's violent nature had transferred itself into his pacifist psyche; those feelings would have fractured the very foundations of his Duuian heritage.

He did not perceive that his aggressive actions against the Deep Ones in any way violated the innate peaceful nature of his species. The beasts had been intent on inflicting grievous bodily harm, his pacifism allowed for the need of self-preservation. However, the toll of his savage behavior was beginning to eat at the edges of his racial confidence. How many more of these awful beasts could he slay before he relinquished his integral Duuianhood?

He struggled to avoid this topic in his thoughts, for the prospects were simply too dreadful to contemplate. The horrors of this cursed planet paled before the possibility that Janek was losing his Duuian spirit.

He was having enough trouble with his agoraphobia. These waters were so vast and empty…

Not to mention a burning need to feed his input addiction. For much too long he had been deprived of plugging new data disks into his neural net. The absence of fresh hardwired data (for daily experiences did not fulfill Janek's insatiable need) was becoming a turbulent psychological storm waiting to erupt from the Duuian's normally placid personality.

He interrupted Etty's chaotic mumble to point out the distant submerged city/tomb/temple. "That would seem the likeliest destination for any valuable captives." When Etty only peered in mute surveillance, Janek continued, "We should approach it with extreme caution."

Resuming his barely audible gibberish, Etty followed Janek into the watery depths.

⟨⊹⟩

When Pik was finally able to escape her dreadful nightmares, she awoke to discover herself no longer imprisoned in a crystal cell.

She lunged to assume a defensive pose, but her body refused to heed those heroic instructions. Pik remained supine and inert.

Above her, she detected a vast area of transparent liquid, as if she reclined at the bottom of a lucid lake. Circular tiers ringed her peripheral vision, their basaltic rows rising to exaggerated heights. These bleachers pulsed with the presence of a thousand creatures who were too distant and small for her to discern the horrific details of their individual nature. There was an expectancy in the water. From the region beyond her paralyzed feet, a mammoth pillar glimmered in the clear waters. It was squat and tall, dark and slimed with patterns of luminous green jelly that dripped from its swollen apex. Far above, a murky shape was circling the coliseum.

Pik could feel the probing of a new tube being inserted into her mouth, bringing precious air to her starved lungs…but she was unable to open wide her own mouth in eager desire of that air. Some unseen attendant needed to manipulate her jaw and lips, forcing the tube down her throat with incautious finesse.

Then a blubbery tentacle passed before her face; it gyrated as if conducting a mystic gesture. And then—Pik could move her head!

Still mostly paralyzed, she turned to peer at her surroundings. She lay on a stone slab that was stained from frequent bloodletting. To her side, Princess Eden was supported by a companion altar. With wide-eyed terror, she turned her head to gasp at the sight of the bound and immobile retriever.

Pik could see their attendants now, and wished she had been spared this spectacle. Deep Ones they were, but hardly recognizable for the profusion of their ghastly deformities. Their number of limbs varied, as did their subjective symmetry. Bulging eyes and great flabby lips were scattered without reason across their hideous torsos. Even in this liquid environment, some of these monsters experienced difficulty moving about. Their ugliness was unbelievable! And they persisted in releasing a constant barking mutter that betrayed bestial qualities.

Beyond these immediate surroundings, Pik saw the coliseum—which turned out to have been converted from a huge lunar crater. The ranks of "seats" were absurdly tall, hinting at the audience's monstrous scale. The abominations she glimpsed in that crowd were too awful to describe.

Even more soul-shattering was to finally look upon the Great Evil Lord Himself: Cthulhu!

A large section of the crater wall was reserved for the mighty Lord. He was…immense! His Deep One servants had towered over humans like herself, but the Evil One was the size of a mountain! He was so huge that only His chest and awful head protruded from His mammoth subterranean private seating box. His torso was obese and exhibited the skin texture of flayed whale meat. Flaps of flesh hung from His terrible flanks in lumps bigger than boulders. His face appeared to be mostly a tangle of tentacles, writhing like softly pliant sausages the size of tree-trunks. Almost human eyes burned luminous crimson beneath brows furrowed with cosmic disdain. A pair of shriveled batwings rose behind that gruesome head. Looming over everything, the Evil One sat in unholy attendance for whatever ceremony was about to be conducted.

A ceremony that Pik feared featured herself and the poor Princess as its likeliest victims.

She noticed that the Princess' head had slumped and her regal eyes were closed. The Royal Daughter had looked upon the visage of the Great

Evil One and fainted with shock. She might possibly have been the lucky one for that.

"This is your fate," a voice spoke in Pik's mind.

"Laramy!" She spun her head in a frantic attempt to spot the ghost. "Where are you?"

Then she saw his hazy figure, pearly white against the sterile waters. He stood beside her altar with his shoulders unnaturally hunched, and he was smirking. His eyes were engorged and beginning to bulge from their sockets.

"You've got to do something," she pleaded with him.

"I would *never* interfere with the Great One's divine scheme," the ghost replied innocently.

What the—

"You have been chosen!" Laramy declared, displaying his religious fanaticism. Then he spoke in a breathy rasp, "You are so fortunate..."

"Where's Etty?" cried Pik.

"I'm afraid your companions will not be coming to your rescue." He grinned, and the girl shuddered to see how wide and fish-like his lips had become. "I seem to have led them astray."

"What—?"

With webbed fingers, Laramy's ghost held his star-stone-shaped amulet gingerly by the string that had once encircled his neck. He dangled it in the water, holding it as far from himself as he could. "I have a gift for you. You need it more than I now." He cackled madly and draped the ghostly necklace around Pik's neck. "Not that even *it* can save you now."

"What the grup has happened to you?" she gasped.

"I've seen the error of my foolish ways."

"You—you've become contaminated by the souls of the Deep Ones you cannibalized!" Just as Pik had feared—nothing good had come of the ghost's disgusting dietary habits. His spirit had consumed tainted ectoplasm, and that sustenance had warped the Professor's personality, replacing his own fervent beliefs with more revolting motives...and the deceased human served the Evil One now!

"I have...attained clarity."

"There's got to be a part of you that's still human, Professor Laramy. You mustn't let the Evil One do this thing!" she begged him.

"You are about to blessed beyond imagination."

"No, I'm not! You've got to help me, Laramy. You don't understand...I can't be impregnated." Fear was making Pik's mouth wild, blurting secrets that she had never even confessed to Etty. "I'm *sterile!*"

"Foolish woman, do you think Great Cthulhu would be using you if you were not perfect for his plan?" the ghost chastised her. "I'm sure you've been modified and repaired and prepared for this sacred event—just as He, in His unholy wisdom, has restored your Princess' detached arm."

"What—no—huh?—" She stole a glance at the unconscious figure, and saw that the ghost spoken true. Princess Eden's arm was no longer half-gone!

"You're going to change things…"

"You've got to stop this, Laramy!" Pik screamed. "If they hurt the Princess, they're risking calling down the vengeance of an entire galactic empire! She's Royalty! You mustn't let them use her for common breeding purposes!"

"Do you still think that's why you're here?" Laramy's ghost chuckled maliciously. "That's what I thought too, but I've learned *different!*" His bulging eyes blinked with spastic glee.

A great shadow dropped across the altars. Descending from above, the serpentine shape swam closer and took on odious detail. Long and eel-like, its tubular blackish-brown body was frilled with bilious frippery. These fleshy ruffles undulated with fearsome strength. As it advanced, a pair of man-like arms reached from the forest of ruffled flukes to unfurl unboned fingers. The thing had no face: a huge, single, unblinking eye peered from the end of the beast. It's mud-brown iris was flagrant, leaving hardly any pale cornea visible. Its pupil gaped like an enormous maw.

"See? Mighty Dagon approaches even now!" called Laramy's ghost, flinging open his pale arms as if to welcome this descending horror.

"Who the grup is 'Dagon'?"

"The Fish-God. He who serves the Great Cthulhu, acting as an interface between Old One and followers," the Professor told her with a petulant tone. "You were not paying attention, were you? When my foolish earlier self tried to familiarize you with the dogma of the ancient Old Ones. You were ignoring me, weren't you? Well, soon enough, you'll wish you'd been listening…"

"What's going on, Laramy? What did you mean when you claimed the Old One has changed our fate?"

"The Great One is interested in a much bigger prize than the irrelevant perpetuation of any single victim race. Not unlike His infinite might, Cthulhu's depravity can be an awe-inspiring thing to behold!"

The Dagon thing had reached a point barely twenty meters above the submerged altars. It continued to swim in a wide circle as its unearthly telepathic voice echoed in every mind present at this profane gathering.

"Worship the superior malevolence of His terrible Lord Cthulhu," chanted the slavering utterance, *"and rejoice in this fateful congress, for the word of Cthulhu is Law and will be commanded in all expressions physical and mental. The Old One welcomes His Ancient Cousins of blasphemous lineage, and acknowledges the eternal fealty of their endless offspring. Praise Cthulhu."*

A cacophony of psychic voices recited the phrase, and the coliseum's ether rang with the fear-inspired taint of sacrilegious subjugation.

"In accordance with the Great Lord's decree, You have all been summoned from Your far-flung lairs and pits of iniquity to witness an event of unprecedented significance. Through the cosmic efforts of His Greatness, specimens of pureblood humans have been donated to fuel His mighty scheme..."

Oh, Pik moaned, *I really don't like the sound of* that.

⁘

As the mismatched pair of retrievers approached the unspeakable underwater city, Etty's mumbling petered out and with a rheumy gaze he focused on the realm's disturbing architecture.

According to the fantastic lore which Professor Laramy had expounded earlier in their journey, this unorthodox metropolis was the blasphemous residence of fearsome Cthulhu, the monstrous despot who had conquered mankind's homeworld.

The city consisted of mammoth ebony slabs arranged in a perplexing jumble. The positions—indeed the very structural lines of the towering edifices were difficult to make out. Etty assumed that this mirage-like quality was caused by the wavering waters that covered the lunar surface, for he had never heard of matter that was capable of defying stable viewing. Even in the scans of his suit's artificial perception, the shapes refused to make sense. These towers seemed possessed of a non-Euclidean geometry that no human mind could hope to comprehend.

It didn't look like much of a "palace" to Etty, but then, his judgment probably differed from the opinions of the reigning Lord of Earth's moon. To Etty, it seemed to be a chaotic vivisection of blunt rectangular blocks. The surface of these deranged towers were unbroken, smooth and gleaming with an unnatural dark light. There were no doorways, portals, or windows. There was, in fact, absolutely no sign of life or habitation at all.

Now that he thought of it, Etty could not recall seeing *any* marine life—fauna or flora. This lunar ocean was apparently sterile, shunned by all lifeforms.

The compulsive reflex to be *gone* from this unholy place tugged at the edges of his subconscious. There was an aura to this oceanic moon that goaded him to flee this aquatic landscape in abject insanity. To avoid falling prey to this ethereal urge, Etty had to remind himself why he was here.

"Pik!" he declared. "My Pik needs rescue!"

"Yes, Etty," grumbled Janek. "I am still aware of this fact."

"We must save her!"

"How do we get in?"

"In?" Etty stared around, confused by the angular panorama.

"In," affirmed the Duuian. "We need to get inside to find Pik and the Princess."

"We could try forcing our way in," Etty suggested. "Our pulse blasts can blow holes in these walls."

"If they are walls…"

"Huh? Of course they're walls. Every building has walls—on the outside—like these walls here…" Yet, the structures resisted substantial definition under the regard of his suit's technological sensors. No matter how hard he stared at the oily black towers, their shapes eluded him. Not unlike his lost memories, the ghastly architecture refused to focus in Etty's critical examination. He knew they existed, but no clarity or comprehension came with that assumption. Perhaps Janek was accurate in his suspicion that these walls were no normal barriers.

"I propose that we reconnoiter first," the alien suggested. "It would be unwise to risk set off any external alarms or automatic defenses."

"Okay, uhmm, that makes sense." Although he concurred with Janek, Etty had the vague sense that he was missing a crucial observation regarding the strange city. He knew that he was periodically prone to memory gaps, especially in situations of excessive stress. Now was definitely not the time to experience such a lapse. He resolved to focus his concentration and fight any amnesiac tendencies that lingered in his brain from his old A.I. infection. If Etty didn't remain sharp and alert, how was he going to rescue Pik and save the Princess?

The retrievers rose through the clear water, following the towers as they swam to higher depths. To reduce the chance of being noticed, they kept close to the starkly ominous walls. These barriers were frustratingly impenetrable to their deepscan capacities. It was as if the towering slabs were uninhabitably solid.

Reaching the uppermost precipice, Etty peered out across the top of the Evil One's underwater lunar city. The topography of the cityscape was less chaotic than the outer walls, but the angles and planes still shunned linear logic, oscillating convulsively between concave and convex curves. The distorted cacophony sprawled before the retrievers like a perspective from some insanely-cubist nightmare. A soft filter of daylight streamed through the water, illuminating the baffling rooftops with lattices of glowing swirls. In this light, something caught Etty's eye. It was severely out of place, its sleek metallic form contrasting violently with the dreadful slabs of inky black and ruddy scarlet. It…was a *spacecraft of human design!*

Etty waved, bringing the ship to Janek's attention. They both grunted wordlessly in the sanctity of their pressure suits.

The craft was parked atop the peak of an angular steeple; it drifted in the water without obvious restraint or attendants. Although Etty was no authority on spacecraft design, he thought this one looked particularly streamlined and…lethal. There was a distinct *military* air to the ship. Could this be the Warrior's Space Navy flier?

Janek concurred when Etty confided his suspicions to his alien partner.

"But—what's Tarn doing here on the moon?" Etty mumbled. "He was supposed to come back to get us at the Spire…"

"Apparently, the Warrior is no more trustworthy than the ghost," Janek remarked. "Everything about this cursed world reeks of treachery." His raspy voice trembled with rancorous resentment.

"I can't believe he'd abandon the Princess. He was determined to rescue her."

"And he still might," the Duuian snorted. "But she is no longer with us, is she? For all we know, the Warrior followed the re-abducted Princess. Remember—he was homing in on her via a tracer implant. He would know his target had been moved from the Spire."

"But then…he left *us* stranded back in the spike…"

"*We* are of no importance to the Warrior, Etty. As you stated, his only concern is the safe rescue of Princess Eden."

"So he abandoned us and came here… The bastard!"

"Without a doubt, Tarn is unfriendly. Unfortunately…he is also our only chance of getting off this moon alive."

Etty gagged, refusing to believe Janek's advice.

"What choice do we have, Etty? We are far outclassed by the enemy we face. Unaided, we will never succeed in freeing Pik."

"We must save her!"

"But—*only* with the Warrior's assistance."

Etty was resistant, for his passion was consumed with the need to rescue Pik, but Janek's arguments were forcefully convincing. The Duuian was (once again) right. Neither he nor Janek were properly armed or trained to conduct an assault against the Evil One in His own horrible stronghold. Etty had been blindly rushing in, without a plan, without a chance. His furious desire to save Pik had overwhelmed him, driving logic to the far winds (or "waters" as the case might be). And what would happen when they stumbled on the Old One's precious captives? How long would Etty or Janek last against the Great Cthulhu's palace guards? The Warrior's protection was a necessary ingredient for success…and survival.

Aware that his memory had gotten spotty, Etty wondered if this was the first time he was noticing how aggressive Janek had become. The Duuian was relentless about the necessity for them to seek out the treacherous Warrior.

The human finally relented, and the pair of desperate retrievers swam furtively across the brown vista of strangely contoured attics. They moved from facade to tower, approaching the Warrior's parked spacecraft with paranoid caution. Etty flung a sensitive scan over the area, wary of any hidden or bestial sentinels. Nothing showed to the curious instruments of his suit, only the ship itself and the barren rooftop over which it hovered. With only twenty-or-so meters left to go, Etty spotted the ship's unsecured access hatch.

Why would Tarn leave that open? he pondered. The open hatch was a bad sign.

Janek, however, saw the open hatch as a fortuitous discovery, for it afforded them easy entrance into the Warrior's ship.

Creeping through the airlock, they found the craft possessed only a pair of parallel corridors, and they were quite empty. Narrow and undecorated by style or design, the two corridors connected the forward control chamber with a midship supply depot and the vessel's aft drive unit. According to Janek's estimation, the latter seemed drastically compact to propel any craft, much less one of military deployment. They shrugged, accepting that they were in the presence of advanced technologies not yet released for commercial use.

As far as Etty could tell, the ship's command chamber was Tarn's only living space aboard the craft. Awake or in stasis, the Warrior reclined in the cabin's single couch, around which clustered an array of control consoles. There was little else to the cramped cockpit.

"What accommodations does Tarn plan to offer the Princess once he's rescued her?" Etty wondered, but his Duuian partner was distracted, consulting the ship's controls, and did not respond. Etty peered back down the spartan hallway, frowning. *Does the Warrior's ship hold hidden quarters?*

A grunt from Janek brought Etty's attention back to the ship's controls. "I do not think the Warrior knows his ship is here," the Duuian commented.

"Huh? But—"

"The drive core is empty," announced Janek. "Drained dry, exactly like the plasma core on the Princess' crashed cruiser." His sensory tendrils twisted to regard Etty, interwoven in a manner the human knew was the alien's expression of disbelief.

"That's—but that's impossible…"

"I concur: it is equally as impossible the second time as it was the first."

"Why would Tarn do that?"

"It is not probable that the Warrior is responsible for this, Etty." Janek leaned back from the console on the stalks of his arms. "He may have landed his ship here, but while he was away searching for the Princess, the enemy drained his ship's drive core."

"Why would they just leave it out here?"

"They did not salvage the Princess' cruiser either, Etty. In both instances, they took what they wanted…and left the rest."

Etty shuddered. "Let's get out of here…before they come back and find us here."

"I am unable to broach the Warrior's security protocols. We will need to find him to pilot this ship to safety." The Duuian reluctantly stood back from the control consoles. He was clearly not happy with his inability to hijack the Warrior's craft.

"And what is Tarn going to do when he gets back? This ship isn't going anywhere, not with a dead drive core," declared Etty. "Anyway, we can't wait around for Tarn to return. We have to find Pik before something terrible happens to her."

"Yes," Janek started down the hallway to the airlock. "Pik and the Princess will be together. That is where we will find the Warrior."

Outside the Warrior's crippled flier, Etty and Janek hung above the abstract sculpture of the abnormal cityscape, pausing to decide on their next move.

"Look!" Etty pointed to a dark hole in the rooftop beneath them. "Was that there before?"

"I...didn't notice. We were concentrating on the ship."

Janek waved a dismissive claw at the solemnly open doorway. "I do not trust it. It is a trap."

"This could be our only way in, though," Etty muttered. "We've seen no other means of entering the city. If we don't take advantage of this, we may never find a way in."

"I feel much safer out here, where there's open space to facilitate a speedy retreat, should one be necessary," asserted Janek.

Etty paused to digest the outlandishness of his partner's statement. He knew that Janek—indeed, all Duuians—suffered severe agoraphobia. Under normal circumstances Janek was unwilling to leave the safe confines of the ">%" or wander far outside before his ancestral psychosis drove him back to the ship. Etty had been surprised to find that the Duuian had accompanied Pik down to Earth in search of him. Janek's outdoor exile had lasted for a few days now, broken only by brief respites from the oppressive emptiness when he had been imprisoned and tortured...certainly not the most pleasant relief. By now, Janek should be a drooling catatonic.

Apparently, the Duuian's mistreatment by the Deep Ones had deeply warped his psyche, assigning reckless priorities to previously abhorrent concepts. Lately, the alien had been displaying decidedly aggressive tendencies, in direct conflict with what Etty knew about the inherent pacifism of the denizens of Duu. And now, Janek was arguing to remain outside, basking in what was normally a frightful emptiness. What was next? Charitable generosity?

Ordinarily, this would have worried Etty. But so far, these changes in his partner's alien psychology had been reasonably helpful in the task of rescuing Pik. Etty knew that his own ferocity would not be enough; everyone's survival depended on Janek's ability to act contrary to his racial meekness. To question the Duuian's inordinate assertive behavior might lead Janek to unconsciously revert to his original pacifism. The last thing Etty needed now was an unviolent partner.

Janek's sudden love of open areas was another matter entirely, and not one that coincided with Etty's goals. In order to perform their job and rescue Pik (and Princess Eden too), the retrievers needed to get into the Evil Lord's dreadful city.

"We'll never find Pik unless we go inside, Janek. They aren't going to keep their precious captives imprisoned *outside* their stronghold." He decided to act, forcing Janek to join him or be left alone in the alien waters. Etty swam down to the questionable entrance.

Questionable, but necessary, he reminded himself. There was no point in lurking *outside* when Pik was a prisoner somewhere *within* this monstrous citadel. The search for Etty's lost mate had been delayed too much already. For all he knew, lovely Pik was even now going under the scalpel again in furtherance of the Evil Lord's insidious breeding program to restart a new human race of victims for his vicious vices. Every second counted…for she could be anywhere in this huge metropolis of terrible slabs. *The search starts here!*

Down into the triangular doorway he went. His lights showed him a jagged interior: the walls consisted of cones of varying size clustered together in a manner to transform the chamber into a giant maw lined by teeth. His first instinct was to retreat from the room and flee before these walls closed to grind him into a ghastly pulp. His artificial senses gave him a more accurate impression of the enclosure: those pointed teeth were actually cones of porous foam. They were soft and incapable of injuring him. The chamber only *appeared* inhospitable. It was, in fact, unthreatening and uninhabited. The chamber also appeared to actually be a passageway, for it extended off beyond both sides of the doorway. He instinctively chose the right passage and launched himself into the thin liquid that filled the corridors. This way soon became a dead end, leading to a large hatch. He had seen the like of this huge conch back inside the horrible Spire of Condemnation, during their escape from captivity. Even the Warrior had been unable to coerce such portals to open. Etty doubted that he would fare much better with this barrier.

Janek's sudden presence at his elbow made Etty jump inside his pressure suit.

"I accompany you under protest," the Duuian remarked. "We are ill-equipped to invade this monstrous complex."

"It doesn't look as if we're going to get very far this way," Etty muttered.

"It's an airlock," the alien declared. "Beyond it, the room is filled with air…my sensors read it as a fair approximation of the planet's partially breathable atmosphere."

"Doesn't do us much good to know what's beyond the door if we can't open it." For a fleeting second, he wondered how the Duuian's sensors could penetrate the city's enigmatic walls. Etty's own gear was still befuddled by the abnormalities displayed by the dark slabs. Was this deficiency authentic? Or a byproduct of his own confusion?

The Duuian brushed him aside and bent to examine the hatch. His nimble claws danced along the seam where the huge seashell met the coarse granite of the wall. He took particular note of a thin slot which had escaped Etty's notice (and apparently the Warrior's too, back in the Spire). While Janek probed the minor anomaly, Etty threw a few scans at it, but learned nothing of any use. The slot was only a few centimeters deep, designed for the insertion of a flat key. Since there was no mechanism to turn the key, the apparatus must read some code from the key's chip-like wedge. There were hints of circuitry and wires hiding inside the wall, but they were too foggy to analyze with any depth.

Fishing something from one of his suit's pouches, Janek tentatively reached out to boldly insert a standard data disk into the alien slot. When nothing happened, Janek withdrew the disk. Instead of replacing it to his pouch, though, he peered at it for a contemplative moment, then popped it into one of his suit's unused inputs.

"Hey!" Etty piped. "Now isn't the time for that—"

Janek waved him away with one of his arms. Then he stiffened, as if suddenly mentally hypnotized by another world.

Oh Janek, Etty moaned silently. *You hopeless data junkie… What have you done now?*

Finally, for Janek's fugue lasted for several minutes, the Duuian spoke, "It is not a keyhole. It is a node for the distribution of data. It…the *city* has downloaded a massive amount of information onto my disk…I am examining it now…parts of it, at least. It's…there's too much for me to assimilate at once…"

"You shouldn't be 'assimilating' any of it, Janek!" Etty told him sternly. "Who knows what head games that alien data could do to your mind?"

His partner waved a petulant arm, silencing Etty's objections.

"This place…is huge! But only a few hundred creatures reside here. The rest…the bulk of this city is…machinery…technology…massive arrays of incredible power generators… The moon itself is riddled with gigantic batteries to store all the awesome fury generated by these cosmic engines…"

Machinery? So—Laramy's ghost had been wrong all along. The dead Professor's monstrous Old Ones were indeed impostors, using hidden technologies to create their impossible deeds and unspeakable atrocities. Laramy's ultimate nemesis, this "Great Cthulhu", was no gruesome deity, he was not the embodiment of evil—he was simply a cunning technician, an alien poser hiding behind the advantage of a superior technology.

"...so few inhabitants," Janek continued to ramble, "and yet...they all require different environmental conditions. I'm picking up entire sections designed for methane breathers...and nitrogen suckers...even helium-based physiologies..."

"Can you pick out where they might be keeping Pik?" Etty whined. "A prison, maybe...or detention lab...?"

"...yes...but there are so many...I detect entire levels devoted to containment cells not unlike the ones we were in back in the spike... Why are there so many...? Ah, I see...to house the serviles. Each Lord maintains a retinue of loyal followers to worship the Great One for them..."

"That's not going to help. What about the girls themselves? Are you picking up anything about them?"

"...no...nothing about any 'special prisoners'... But...so much else!"

"Grup the rest," Etty decried. "We need to find where they're holding Pik!" He kicked the seashell hatch and cursed it for barring their way.

"I know how to open this doorway now," Janek admitted. He reached to slide a claw across a seemingly innocuous section of the shell—and the mighty hatch opened, swinging up to hang above their startled heads like a menacing awning.

"Okay!" Etty cheered. "This is a start—"

They entered the small chamber that lay beyond this yielded hatch. As the outer shell clamped shut, a rumble shook the floor, and the water drained away. Once the chamber was dry, a hiss announced the introduction of a gaseous atmosphere. This was followed by the inner hatch gaping wide to finally admit them to one of the city's rare avenues.

This passageway was mammoth and ominously vacant. There was no trace of habitation, recent or ancient. The chamber was abnormally angular, its wall were lined with drastic crevasses along each wall. The floor was not flat, but consisted of a spiraling swirl pattern that Etty could see was repeated like tilework across the ground. The pattern itself was rather large, featuring a sloping peak that stood higher than a man. A luminescent cumulous vapor hung near the steepled ceiling, refusing to mingle with the air in the curious corridor.

"According to the enemy database I've downloaded," Janek claimed, "this passage belongs to an oxygen-breathing species native to the planet Earth..."

"This corridor was designed for humans?" Etty was steadfastly unconvinced of that possibility. "Are you certain you're looking at the right map in your head?"

"Of course!" the Duuian snapped with a rising temper. "Each data distribution point has a specific Ident code, establishing a referential map based on its location."

Etty intended to say "Okay," but his face froze on the first syllable as he gawked at the monstrous spectacle that suddenly thundered by.

The creature was immense, standing over fifty meters tall. It possessed a simple body: slender and conical, with three stumpy legs and no visible arms. Its skin, a mottling of green and brown, exuded a pale grease that lent the beast a softly wet veneer. There were no signs of any face or features, the creature's body was a bulging landscape of mighty sinews. Feathery tufts protruded from its pointy top, the strands dancing gaily in the phosphorescent mist as the beast capered past Etty and Janek. It moved with a fantastic twirling stride, landing each columnesque leg in a pumping motion that propelled the great creature spinning down the passageway. The interaction between the thing's huge feet and the strange spiraling floor-tiles was not lost on Etty or Janek.

They stood like insignificant microbes while this monstrous creature spun its hideous way down the avenue. Fortunately, the retrievers remained unnoticed by the beast as it rushed along.

"Can we find a side tunnel that isn't so dangerous?" Etty whispered.

"In this place? Probably not. I will see what is available, though…" Janek paused, his mighty head hanging loosely as the Duuian reviewed the unholy map he carried now in his brain.

I've got to keep a watch on Janek now, Etty told himself. *As long as he's got that enemy database in his head, there's a chance it could usurp control of him—turn him against me.*

Throwing off his data fugue, Janek danced away across the passageway's uneven floor. Etty stumbled in his partner's wake, finding his two human legs were significantly challenged by this footing.

Stroking a plain wall, Janek called forth a doorway scaled more to their own size. Leaving the huge passage, they scuttled down what Janek revealed was "a service duct restricted to repair modules." The alien paused once to insert another data disk in a wall slot that had eluded Etty's detection. After a second, Janek withdrew the disk and greedily slid into one of his suit's inputs. He resumed running along the cramped tunnel, apparently accessing his new datapack without fugue this time.

As they traveled along this service duct, Etty thought of the tremendous acres of alien machinery that must exist all around them right now. They were effectively tunneling into a city-sized nest of apparatus designed to maintain the illusionary godhood of the Evil Lord to his awful followers. Etty trembled to imagine the megatons of power that were being generated and harnessed for evil by this undersea island of hardware. *No wonder this moon was impervious to our scans from the ">%", he realized. The energy signature of this city would drown out all the other details.*

"With all this energy already at His disposal," he commented, "why does the Evil One need to steal power from the Princess' cruiser and the Warrior's flier?"

Janek's grunt told him that the Duuian's newfound information did not explain that contradiction.

"It doesn't make any sense. What would an alien deity want with plasma cores?" Etty mused.

"Perhaps this local despot intends to power his own interstellar armada…and invade the rest of the galaxy."

As if we didn't already have enough things to worry about…

Janek slowed down his speedy dash, finally stopping to indicate a hatch in the side of the corridor. "There," he wheezed.

Once they were through this exit, Janek again busied himself with procuring another data dump from a nearby distribution node. "Each one," he confided to his human partner, "contains different data blocks."

You're just being a junkie, Etty ruminated. But he refrained from voicing any objections, for he also knew that the Duuian was gaining fresh data about their surroundings. Sooner or later, Etty hoped that one of these purloined datapacks would contain a mention of the Evil Lord's recent captives.

The two retrievers were in a passage now that was quite different from the last one. Here: the walls were cylindrical and flowed like turgid mercury, flooding the chamber with a harsh, silver glare. Here: the scale was half the size of the cone-creature's runway, but still designed for something bigger than a man. Here: the air was a dense orange gas. Here: traveling beasts swam in the center of the passageway, undulating their way along in discordant orchestration. These creatures appeared to be chromium centipedes five meters long. Their many spiny legs were webbed for use as airfoils to glide through the orange vapors. There seemed to be hundreds of the things.

"I thought you found that there were only a few hundred occupants in this city," Etty muttered. "What about those?"

"Serviles," the Duuian asserted. "These…these belong to Musse-Ulu, a lesser Old One…or maybe one of that Lord's priests. For every bit I can tell you about this dreadful city, there are a thousand aspects I am unable to comprehend. 'Priest' is a hazy approximation. I get the feeling that although these Old Ones consider themselves to all possess godlike powers, they seem to attribute Cthulhu with some kind of *more-supreme* power. They've pretended to be ancient deities for so long, they're beginning to believe their own propaganda."

"Just as long as you can find some clue that'll lead us to Pik."

"Aha! Hold on—" Janek grunted with ill-concealed excitement. "I think I have something!"

"What? Where is she?"

The Duuian hurried them across the cylinder of molded mercury. Although the metal flowed like a liquid, it provided a stable, hard surface for their feet. Breathlessly, Janek explained as they ran. "I have accessed a daily itinerary. And there is only one event scheduled for today. Attendance by all the Old Ones and ranking clerics is mandatory. The Great Lord will be unveiling some secret—it can only involve Pik and the Princess. There is no mention of 'captives' or 'breeding' schemes, but what else would cause Cthulhu to assemble His ghastly hierarchy of fellow evil gods?"

"You're starting to weird me out," Etty commented. "You're talking like you worship this 'Great Lord'…"

"No…"

"You just called them a group of 'evil gods'…"

"It's the database," Janek mumbled. "These Old Ones actually consider themselves to all be gods—monstrous deities from the Dawn of Time…"

"Don't get sucked into it, Janek. They're just aliens who have all this monstrous technology at their disposal." He waved his arms to indicate their surroundings. Was his alien partner already starting to show signs of contamination from the enemy's datapacks?

Pausing by another secret doorway, Janek stole some more data from the city before he opened this hatch and guided them into another service duct. He took them swiftly through this passage, bringing them to a panel that was uncharacteristically obvious and unconcealed. While the Duuian dismantled this access grid, he told Etty that the High Summit was being held in the Great Lord's coliseum, which was located at the far end of the city. "This duct," he nodded his wide head at the dark region he had exposed, "leads into a network of tubes which run directly to that coliseum. We will be able to get there without risk of being discovered by any of the Lord's minions or the Old Ones' servile beasts that roam the city."

Etty lunged for the transit tube, but Janek held him back. "Let me go first," advised the Duuian. "The map is in *my* head." With visible frustration, the human acquiesced. Janek crawled into the dark hole, then Etty followed him.

The instant they were inside this transit tube, the retrievers were propelled along by a surge of chunky liquid. Safe in their pressure suits, they tumbled and bounced between sticky lumps, some of which possibly equaled their own size. Beyond the faceplate of his helmet, Etty beheld a miasma of darkness, viscous and fetid with barely perceived debris. He told himself that he was grateful for his ignorance concerning the nature of the liquid that rapidly coursed with them through this tube. Then a mass flung itself to press lifelessly against his faceplate, and he screamed with terror and disgust. Terrible and horrific—at first he thought it was the half-dissolved corpse of some deviant creature. But no—it was something unborn! A creature of absolutely grotesque nature—in a half-formed state! It was a monstrous *fetus*! His empty stomach wrenched, but could fling nothing more than foul bile from into his throat. The monstrosity slid across his faceplate, its incomplete face fixing him with a ghastly grin, and then it was gone, torn away by the tremendous current to embark on another trajectory through the terrible ichor.

A fetus! In the fury of his vivid anguish, Etty was unaware whether he shrieked aloud with his mouth or vented privately in his stunned mind. *That thing was an unborn freak of nature!* Then it hit him—if that had been a creature unborn, then that would make these tubes some kind of linear womb! They were riding through a hellish incubator, swept on their way by placental fluids. What monstrous purpose could such a circulatory system serve in this submarine lunar citadel? Were these grisly embryos future minions of the Old Ones? Or did their destinies involve far more horrendous functions?

Desperately craving no answers to these obscene puzzles, he closed himself off from the incoming images and analyses of his artificial senses. He maintained a tenuous thread of contact with Janek's form, though, as the alien was his guide through this revolting waterworks; if he lost track of his partner, then Etty was doomed to ride this flue of depravity to its unthinkable termination.

No sane creature was intended to witness abominations like this. Such hideous atrocities should not even exist in the first place. This entire planet and its attendant moon had become ecologies dedicated to the celebration of terrible crimes against nature. The Earth and humanity had been subjected to atrocities beyond mortal imagination, the Old Ones had left no microbe or innocuous concept undamned by their momentous appetites. Etty's already-impaired mind was incapable of retaining these memories and their horrific implications. The details of these dreadful recollections gradually slid from his consciousness, bleeding away from synaptic storage as if the neural cells of his brain refused to accommodate such horrors.

If Janek was aware of the gruesome nature of the things that flowed alongside the retrievers, the Duuian remained silent. Or maybe his silence was caused by his own inability to cope with such appalling realities. By the time Janek grabbed his human partner and drew him to a side vent, Etty was nearly catatonic with fear, his mind riddled with gaping holes. Without comment on this leg of their loathsome journey, the retrievers made their escape from the city's obnoxious wombways.

After a short exit tunnel, they came to find themselves once again in a watery environment. Peering through a ventilation grill, they stared down upon a massive coliseum which was open to the outdoor ocean. Wavering sunlight drifted through the aquatic depths to illuminate the horrible assemblage. From their vantage on the coliseum's upper rim, Etty and Janek could see that the tiered bleachers were filled with creatures of baffling and revolting guise. The amphitheater itself appeared to have been built into a huge lunar crater, perhaps to accommodate the immense scale of some of the beasts who were gathered in attendance.

None of these spectators, though, were as monstrous or disquieting as the mountainous shoulders and head which rose from a submerged forum across the stadium from the retrievers' concealment. This creature's head alone was over a hundred meters tall. A chin of tentacles writhed impatiently across the beast's broad and masculine chest. Eyes of brightest scarlet blazed under the hillock of its gray-green forehead. Huge batwings hung behind its wide shoulders, disturbing the sea currents with their twitching.

How could the retrievers' crude weaponry hope to have any effect on a monster of such intimidating size?

"Look," hissed Janek's voice in Etty's comlink.

"What?" The Duuian had broken his concentration, and once again Etty lost access to the string of his recent thoughts.

"There," Janek pointed a wiry limb. "Apply magnification to your scanners."

Following the direction of the alien arm, Etty regarded the center of the colossal stadium. There, a black tower rose to considerable height, its surface contaminated by impure reflections. At the base of this sullen pillar was a stone dais of unnatural contours that supported a pair of small slabs. Above this tableau, a great aquatic snake unfurled its mighty coils as it circled the arena. Descending, this festooned eel curled around the centerpiece altars, as if taunting the poor captives who were spread there for sacrifice.

With a desperate cry, Etty zoomed his optics and recognized Pik as one of the victims on display.

And then a psychic articulation of resounding proportion blared in his mind, drowning out all human thought with its sacrilegious praise. Etty reeled under the cosmic force of the mental declaration. Beside him, Janek spasmed with discomfort from the same telepathic maelstrom.

"*Worship the superior malevolence of His terrible Lord Cthulhu,*" the unclean voice was chanting, "*and rejoice in this fateful congress, for the word of Cthulhu is Law and will be commanded in all expressions physical and mental. The Old One welcomes His Ancient Cousins of blasphemous lineage, and acknowledges the eternal fealty of their endless offspring. Praise Cthulhu.*"

Across the stadium, the tentacle-faced monster shifted in its forum, expanding its enormous chest as if swelling with profane pride.

The Evil One—Great Cthulhu! Etty gasped.

This was the Lord of this terrible domain, the fiend who had caused so much suffering and torment, the genocidal extinction of every lifeform naturally spawned by the Earth, the ongoing madness and bestial torture of the surviving monstrosities. This brute commanded the fealty and fear and shame of every micro-organism with its sphere of unholy influence. There had never been a being that deserved more aversion or inspired more fear. It was evil incarnate, and Etty had foolishly violated its lunar stronghold.

A psychic mutter rose from the stands, affording only a brief respite before the frightful voice continued:

"*In accordance with the Great Lord's decree, You have all been summoned from Your far-flung lairs and pits of iniquity to witness an event of unprecedented significance. Through the cosmic efforts of His Greatness, specimens of pureblood humans have been donated to fuel His mighty scheme...*"

With an anxious certainty, Etty knew that his beloved Pik was one of these "pureblood humans."

"Many of You have heard rumors of these specimens and how they arrived recently from beyond this solar system," the giant eel continued. *"Called to Earth by the Great One's psychic lure, they came to offer themselves as the necessary catalyst for the Miracle We are about to witness. Heed the words of Dagon now, for I tell You that the universe will soon tremble before the unleashed fury of the One who is mightier than all of Us combined!"*

An uneasy whisper spread through the spectators.

Etty could endure no more. Whatever ghastly fate the horrifying Evil One had planned for Pik—it was about to happen! But—what could Etty do? He was a lone and insignificant mortal facing beasts that commanded the powers of this incredible lunar citadel of terrible machinery. His measly pulse cannons could not hope to overcome the furious monsters contained by this terrible underwater coliseum.

"Not only have these outsiders come to offer their pureblood to Our needs, they have brought gifts of incalculable measure," the monstrous eel's unclean telepathic broadcast resounded. *"Witness: primal residue! The naked souls of two cosmic furnaces have been collected to facilitate this ambitious atrocity!"*

The arena trembled, its sediment dancing into filmy clouds in the abnormally clear water. Then a pair of new columns rose from the gray silt to flank the central pillar of black immorality. When they stood their full height, these attendant towers were barely half as tall as the great pillar, and only a few meters in diameter. Their ebony surface glowed with an inner wrath of incredible force.

"Combined with the spilled lifeblood of these specimens, these stellar demons will—"

It was happening *now*! His lover was barely seconds away from hideous damnation. If he intended to save her, Etty had to act now!

Bursting from concealment, Etty plunged down into the horrible stadium. Screaming aloud with his voice and every available waveband, lights flashing, pulse cannons blaring, arms waving with frantic frustration, he plunged from the aberrant rooftops of this marine necropolis to rush the coliseum. He had to save her!

He did not care whether his Duuian partner joined him in this suicidal attack, the only thing that mattered was trying to save Pik. Etty would understand if Janek chose to remain safely hidden from the Evil Lord's naked gaze. But—he was surprised to discover the Duuian charging at his side, his own weapons blasting in conjunction with Etty's.

They descended on the stone dais that supported the centerpiece altars like insects attacking an angry stormcloud. The massive serpentine bulk of the Dagon creature contorted as it twisted to block their approach. The combined potency of the retrievers' pulse blasts drove back this mammoth sea-snake, clearing a route for them to the immobile victims.

As Etty swept upon Pik's body, he was startled to find the Laramy ghost hunched over his girlfriend.

"Go away!" the specter wailed. "You'll ruin everything!" Laramy struck at Etty with his useless and immaterial fists.

Ignoring the traitorous ghost, Etty severed Pik's bonds and scooped the paralyzed girl up into his arms, cradling her limp body to the breastplate of his pressure suit. He had her! He had rescued her from the monsters—right out from under their dreadful noses (or "tentacles" as the case might be). He moved to carry Pik away, but was struck from behind by a savage blow as one of the eel's coils slammed viciously into the human. He fell across the horribly stained altar, spilling Pik from his grasp. Laramy's insults rang in his mind, only to be drowned by a deafening psychic blast emanated from the monstrous sea-snake.

"*You dare to violate this most sacred moment with your puny attempts to steal away Our human specimens! The Great Cthulhu will not tolerate your infernal meddling!*"

But, Etty observed, the Great Cthulhu didn't seem to be particularly outraged by what was transpiring in the coliseum. The huge brute continued to stare with mild reproach gleaming in his terrible eyes, but little else. It was as if what was happening, this little drama to save Pik's life, was utterly inconsequential and beneath the Old One's notice. His massive shoulders had not twitched; but for the writhing of the nest of tentacles on his face, the Great One was wholly immobile.

Etty scrambled across the altar-stone, eager to reclaim Pik's discarded body.

Above him, the huge mass of the sea-snake was writhing and thrashing in conflict with Janek. The Duuian was pumping volley after lethal volley of pulse blasts into the creature's body, but this barrage only served to keep the monster temporarily at bay. Even Janek's lasers were having scarce effect on the constricting behemoth.

"*I am Dagon, who is voice for the Great Lord's commands,*" the beast roared across the ephemeral ether, "*and you will not disgrace Me before His Unholy Eminence!*"

Casting a brief, final glance at the towering, still-impassive bulk of that Unholy Eminence, Etty grabbed for Pik—only to discover that she was no longer inanimate. Once her body had been removed from the altar, she had apparently reclaimed use of her muscles. She was floundering slightly, waving at something behind Etty.

He turned and a mutant Deep One attendant slammed into him. The impact sent air flooding from Etty's lungs. Awareness momentarily rushed from the retriever's mind.

⁜

Pik had not seen the beast that struck Etty. Her warning involved a familiar shape that dove toward the stadium through the lunar ocean. Headed their way like the cavalry in some fairie tale was their ship, the ">%"!

Having caught a few glimpses of Janek as she was thrown from the terrible altar, Pik was only dimly aware of her alien partner's battle with the sea-serpent above the dais. More pressing matters required her immediate attention, such as the crowd of deformed Deep Ones that were swarming up the corkscrew base of the platform. They were large, armed with ample and cruel blades of refined coral; they were furious, outraged by the retriever team's desecration of their ceremony.

Dodging the first beast, she power-kicked its cohort from the summit of the dais. As it fell, the brute dislodged several more that were floundering up the spiral ramp. This gave the girl a chance to get to Etty's side.

He was just coming around, the Deep One's bodyslam had stunned him. Pik shook him, and once he was roused enough to notice her, she pointed vigorously at the Princess who still lay paralyzed on her own sacrificial altar. Etty understood instantly.

As he dashed to the Princess' rescue, Pik snatched a wire antenna from the shoulder of his pressure suit as he moved away.

Whirling, she executed a somersault over an onrushing bestial priest. Her momentum was sluggish in the watery environment, but she was still nimbler than any of these lumbering, malformed fish-things. As she came down behind her confused attacker, Pik sent the creature from the platform with a two-handed shove. She swung her antenna-saber in a sharp arc, splitting the slavering faces of three other beasts as they came bounding up the ramp.

She stole a quick glance over her shoulder to assess the rest of the battlefield…

Etty was pulling the Princess from her altar. Away from the slab, she would regain movement and stand on her own. Whatever firepower Etty had would be devoted to the safety of the Princess now.

Janek was still hidden from Pik's view by the massive coils of the Dagon thing, but she could tell from the beast's convulsive writhing that the Duuian was still pounding away with his pulse beams.

The ">%" had swooped down to hover above the coliseum. As Pik stole a glance, the ship's pulse cannons flashed, distributing mayhem and alien bloodshed throughout the stands. (*It has to be the Warrior,* she thought. *No one else could have gotten past my onboard security.*) The crowds of the ghastly devout were fleeing the stadium in a panicky uproar. The ship turned with steady grace, firing upon the dreadful assemblage. As its rotated aim fell upon the Great Lord Himself, the ">%'s" contraband plasma cannons roared to life, venting their hellish beams on the alien monster.

The Lord Cthulhu remained immobile, unperturbed by the attack. The Evil One seemed unbothered by the sudden ruination of His grand scheme…almost as if He really didn't care… This absolute arrogance and contemptuous superiority infuriated Pik, driving her to act on that fervent revulsion.

Leaping from the platform, Pik swam through the sluggish fluids, heading for the Evil One Himself.

✢

The Princess instantly recognized the one who had come to her rescue. His name was Etty, and earlier (hours, days—she really had no way of telling for certain) he had donated his pressure suit to protect her from the terrible creatures that had sought to recapture her. This time, he had come wearing that suit and he was here to save her. As the handsome savior hoisted her from the horrendous altar, sensation returned to her limbs.

In her fanciful life, Princess Eden had wanted and had many men. These liaisons had been initiated by her, for she was far too cunning to fall prey to the sweet-lipped lies of the hordes of self-important nobles who came to court the Royal Heir. Initiated by whim, her choices had exhibited a baser criteria, catering to her need for instant gratification. Sometimes she kept these lovers around for a while, so that she could enjoy a familiar toy for a few weeks, but inevitably these individuals were transient fixtures in her extravagant lifestyle.

For an instant, she recalled a recent nightmare, and the recollection of a Royal Husband made her tremble with nausea.

This "Etty" was different. He had not come to woo her, he had fought his way across half a planet, facing monstrous dangers to rescue her from the vile clutches of her dreadful abductors. He was no suitor, he was a savior. And such a handsome one too…

This Etty was the first person outside her bloodline who had ever shown earnest concern for the Princess. He had proven his devotion with blood and suffering—and still brave Etty had refused to abandon her to the cruel fates. He had battled creatures of unbelievable repugnance. He had *rescued* her!

Maybe this was the one…if they survived this present, horrific ordeal.

The Princess brought the descending spacecraft to the attention of her savior. She was unable to identify it as the retrievers' ship, but she knew, whatever this ship was, it was clearly of human design. And as it fired upon the gathered ranks of her monstrous kidnapers, she knew that this vessel had come to liberate, not torment her.

Etty pulled her to him in a traditional heroic posture, then he launched them both from the edge of the dais. On gurgling thrusters, he flew/swam to the side, evading the clutching fins of the swarming Deep Ones. Once he was away from the altars, Etty angled his flight upward. By a margin of several meters, he flew beyond the outermost coils of the Dagon creature and headed toward the hovering spacecraft. She could tell by the absence of any drag in the surrounding water that her rescuer had triggered his force field, protecting them both from any hostile intervention.

She traveled the last hundred meters of her escape from the stadium of horror in complete safety.

❖

Although there was no opposing current, Pik swam with all her naked vigor, yet she made scarce headway through the clear water. Some force was repelling her, not unlike the intangible barrier she had encountered in the planet's upper atmosphere. She was even more helpless here, for her thrashing arms and legs were not equal to her lost suit's thrusters—and that equipment had failed to best the stratospheric barricade. What hope did Pik have now?

She prayed for strength. She prayed for a failure to afflict the monster's protective barrier. She prayed for unseen, sacred forces to aid her in the destruction of this terrible abomination.

And when her prayers went unanswered, Pik prayed all the harder.

Slowly, the Evil One's repellent presence forced her back in the direction of the raised altars.

❖

Hours ago:

The Warrior orbited the Earth, unsure what his next move would be.

He lacked the necessary thruster propellant to safely reach the planet's surface or even the moon. Maybe, if he carefully calculated trajectories, he could bring himself swinging by one the planetary spikes. If he could get to one of them, he might be able to resume his rescue of the Nimbus Family's Favorite Daughter.

That is, he mused, *if I can make it past those space-bats that guard each spike's tip.* Tarn considered himself fortunate that none of the creatures had discovered him in his planetary loop. They had pierced his shields while his resources were at their prime; now, the beasts would make short work of him once they penetrated his weakened defenses.

His primary concern was, of course, returning to where he had left Princess Eden in the guardianship of the bounty hunters. The Princess would not be truly safe until she was in his presence, under Tarn's protection.

He had left the Spire of Condemnation to summon his Navy flier—only to have it stolen from him by space-bats that served this world's cruel despot. Now, he had no means to transport the Princess to safety. Now, he lacked the means to even return to her!

Tarn thought of the galactic adage that a naked Royal Warrior could conquer an entire planet in two days, and he laughed aloud. Admittedly, it *had* happened, but Tarn doubted that those lauded Warriors had faced worlds where every lifeform was dedicated to the instant destruction of any intruder, much less lifeforms possessed of such unbridled brutality and virulent technologies. Those Warriors had faced standard defense armies, not hordes of monsters that defied the Navy's best armament. Those Warriors had known the desperate nature of their missions before going in, they had not swaggered in expecting to be a lowly taxi-driver for a spoiled Royal Brat.

I've done pretty decent, all things considered, he told himself. *So far, I'm still alive...and so is the Princess... Right?* He quickly consulted his suit's trace on her telltale implant, confirming her survival. It would switch to a secondary signal should her life signs cease. Yes, the Brat was still alive. But...

Her telltale placed her location in a different quadrant of the sky. What had happened? But he knew what had happened... Those worthless bounty hunters had screwed up, and the enemy had recaptured the Princess! *Now I have to rescue her again...*

He cross-referenced the tracer signal with a wide-range scan of the sky, and found that the Royal Brat had made it all the way to the moon this time.

Def, it's only a couple of hundred-thousand kilometers between me and the moon. There must be a way...

Tarn's mind refused to accept the impossibility of his situation. *I've got to get my orbital trajectory to work for me,* he reminded himself. *Get to a spike, and climb it to the moon. See? Simple...*

Except that, after several orbits, he had been unsuccessful in plotting a modification that would set him on an intersection path with one of the massive needles that protruded from the planet's atmosphere.

On his fifth pass over the polar cap, the Warrior detected something sharing space with him. It went by too fast, and he had been unable to focus his sensors...but it had looked like a *spacecraft* to him. What the... Then he realized that he must have found the bounty hunters' ship! Now, *there* was a solid means of regaining an advantage in reclaiming the abducted Princess. He used his sixth arctic pass to pinpoint the freebooters' vessel, then crunched some numbers to get him there. The prospects were dangerous, for to deviate from his current orbit and intersect with the ship would require the majority of his suit's remaining thruster fuel. Leaving him almost no opportunity for a second approach.

He did not hesitate, though, to trigger his fuel cells at the precise instant and the necessary angle on his seventh orbit. As the Warrior shot off toward the bounty hunters' abandoned ship, he studied it with a refined sweep of his scanners.

It was a standard commercial vessel, actually a rather old model used to mine less-crowded asteroid belts. It's hull was festooned with numerous additions, several of which brought impressed grunts to Tarn's reluctant lips. Whoever had rigged this ship, had done a serious job, supplementing sensory arrays and grafting (Were they?—they *were!*) cannons onto the node that contained the ship's drive unit. Pik—for it had to have been the ex-Warrior—Pik had armed her craft with illegal weapons! And Tarn couldn't have been happier!

You're a bad little girl, he told his mental image of Pik. *And I love you for it.*

The ship was coming up fast. *Too fast?* he wondered. After consulting his suit's assessment of his velocity (relative to the abandoned spacecraft's orbit), he wasted the rest of his fuel on a controlled and gradual deceleration that brought him expertly tapping the ship's hull beside the airlock hatch.

Besting the exterior lock was child's-play. Outwitting the interior lock proved more challenging. His opinion of Pik went up another notch when he found the ship's controls guarded by admirable firewalls. The Warrior was forced to do a selective purge of the ship's database in order to remove her impenetrable security and replace it with a download of his own Space Navy protocols.

Now I'm ready, he warned the fates.

As he piloted the ship toward the moon, targeting in on the Princess' remote tracer signal, Tarn examined his new attack vessel's firepower. His suspicions had been correct, Pik had connected those rear cannons to the ship's plasma drive unit, contrary to all civilian restrictions. (Tarn was not as outraged by this infraction as one might have expected. In truth, such weapons violations were fairly common among ships that frequented the frontier rim. Rarely were citations or arrests made in such matters. Even a battle-hardened Warrior knew to turn a blind eye on such illegal armament.) There were also the standard pulse cannons mounted on the stern, along with what appeared to be a comprehensive array of particle beam emitters. An outrageous collection of weapons for a commercial ship—but then, retrievers were known to spend the majority of their time in frontier space, tracking down fugitives who fled Galactic Law. Tarn praised Pik's scofflaw tendencies, for her many violations would be put to righteous use when the Warrior assaulted the enemy to reclaim the Royal Brat.

The ship's shields had surprised him too, for they had masked much of the vessel's hidden strength. Once inside and in command of the craft, though, Tarn became conversant with the inordinately mighty drive core and the strenuous armor that lurked beneath the ship's deceptively rusted and falsely pitted bulwarks. He marveled at how Pik had transformed an antique mining vessel into a deadly battleship, hiding its extensive and impressive teeth behind a junkyard facade.

As the moon filled his forward scan, the Warrior emptied his mind and assumed a battle attitude. He gripped the controls and primed all weapons...then sent the blunt ship diving into the lunar ocean. Down he went, into depths that revealed a landscape of soggy craters—and a fantastic fortress of chaotic towering slabs. Nestled in the midst of these massive structures was an open stadium. It was *there* that the Princess' tracer signal was leading the Warrior.

He was momentarily startled by the huge creature that seemed to lord over this coliseum, and it took him a minute to guess that this must be the Evil One himself: the local dictator who had tormented the Princess, ordering her abduction and subsequent mutilation. This was the creature to blame for all sorts of horrors, many of which the Warrior did not believe in. But there were more than enough documentable atrocities that Tarn could blame on this cruel and mad despot. The time had come to show the Lord Cthulhu the measure of a determined Royal Warrior of the Nimbus Space Navy.

Using deep scans, Tarn located the Princess at the center of the stadium's arena, atop what looked suspiciously like a sacrificial altar. These scans also revealed the presence of the three bounty hunters engaged in battling the Evil One's monstrous minions. So—they *had* survived.

Tarn was privately glad that Pik was not dead, for he held her in quite a different light now. Before, he had branded her as someone who had violated her Warrior Oath when she left the Navy. Now, he thought she was a spunky criminal whose grievous weapons violations were about to save the day. He admired her nonconformism, for without it, they would all probably have died this day. He thought it only proper that Pik should benefit from a rescue achieved with her own illegal firepower.

He brought the ship out of its descent to hover above the arena's occupants. On the seabottom, a naked Pik and a suited Etty were struggling to defend the Princess from a horde of loathsome Deep Ones. Suspended between the altars and the spacecraft, a suited Janek battled with a monstrous sea-snake.

Immediately, Tarn commenced firing the pulse cannons into the stands, crushing the Lord's devout who were foolish enough not to flee. Hanging above the center of the coliseum, the ship rotated slowly, panning its punishing weaponry through the stadium. The Warrior waited until the ship faced the Great One before unleashing Pik's illegal plasma cannons, though. Their hellfire struck at the mammoth creature...and had no visible effect!

With desperate attention to detail, Tarn surveyed the ship's scans of the mighty beast. Were his beams going right through the behemoth? Perhaps it was just a grotesque enormous hologram! But no—the beams *were* striking the Evil One…but they were simply not bothering the creature. It soaked up the plasma beams with a greedy hunger. The ship's sensors showed how the beast routed those excessive energies to subterranean storage. Not only was Tarn failing to injure the Great Lord, his blasts were revitalizing the monster! He instantly deadened the ship's plasma cannons.

Beneath him, the combat between the sea-snake and the Duuian bounty hunter raged on. The beast's contortions churned the water into a froth of abnormal bubbles as it sought to crush the brazen invader with its great flexing loops. Janek struggled valiantly to bludgeon his way free of the creature's strangling enclosure. The bounty hunter was hidden from visual sight by the serpent's fiendish thrashing, but Janek's top-heavy form and his vicious pulse blasts showed vividly on the scanner imbedded in Tarn's cornea.

Determined to sustain his assault on the Evil One, the Warrior strained the ship's conventional weapons to their limits, sending salvo after salvo into the immense monster's tentacled face. The ship's particle beams repeatedly stabbed with searing force at the beast, but they brought no damage to the mountain of abhorrent alien meat. Nothing seemed monumental enough to rouse the Great Cthulhu from his contemptuous lethargy.

Swooping from below the conflict of snake and Duuian, a muffled figure flew through the water, carrying with it the Princess' tracer signal. As Tarn pounded away with useless fury at the massive facade of the Great Lord, he tweaked his sensors to provide more clarity concerning the Princess. She was with Etty, and was being borne up to the rescue ship by the bounty hunter. The Warrior poised a finger over a switch that would open one of the ship's exterior hatches, awaiting the precise moment to coincide with their arrival. Etty and the Brat surged nearer, swinging out to avoid the writhing coils of the sea-snake. They were barely three meters from the ship's hull before the Warrior threw open the hatch to swallow the end of their flight.

She's in! he rejoiced. *I've got her!*

⁜

Naked and armed with a length of antenna, Pik realized that she was being irresponsible. She could not even get close to her loathsome prey, but if she did—what then? How much damage was she going to do to this monstrous creature? Any wounds Pik might inflict with her wire-saber would be less than feeble scratches to a beast of this immense scale.

The point had come for the girl to repress her pious fury and save her own skin. The Evil One's downfall would have to wait for another day, preferably one that saw Pik better dressed and wielding weapons of cataclysmic destruction.

Twisting around, she set her strokes to carry her away from the un-approachable Lord. She headed up, where the ">%" still hung over the arena like a vengeful angel.

With a grimace, she noticed that the Warrior (for that was who Pik believed piloted the ship) had found the proscribed plasma cannons she had secretly installed on the retrieval vessel. *Well,* she mused, *at least somebody is using my armament against the enemy.*

Her heart sank when Pik saw that those plasma blasts were having no effect on the Evil One's mountainous facade. What kind of being was this monster?

What if there was *no way* to kill Cthulhu…?

There were few courageous heroes among Janek's species, for no Duuians ever dared to such reckless bravado. They were passive creatures, more fascinated by wealth than physical intimidation. Battles were un-known between Duuians, unless the combatants were mental deviants. As a result of this, Janek found himself deprived of any comparison for his bravery or aggressive behavior. For him, the experience was wholly original: unprecedented, even unthinkable among his kind. Violence and hate were things he had heard about, but never had he imagined that he would experience the flavor of these excessive emotions.

He fought the Dagon beast with an aggressive fervor, and he loathed the monster with a passionate bloodthirst. While Janek's tortures had warped his personality, they had also released in him a devout need to strike back, to revisit his mistreatment onto his enemies. A violent vic-tory over this behemoth would be a deeply cathartic experience for the tormented Duuian.

I am the first of my kind to spill blood in anger, he realized. *These villains have turned me into a monster!*

His eagerness heated up Janek's infrared perceptions, his own wrath briefly blinding him. He struck out with impetuous blasts to mask his sudden weakness.

"The Blind Idiot God must be freed!" declared Dagon's psychic scream. *"This* will *happen, even if it is* your *foreign blood that motivates the spell—"*

When Janek's infrared vision cleared, he found himself trapped inside an enormous scaly silo. The Dagon snake surrounded him like a huge prison of meat, the great length of its body encircling the immediate region with multiple coils. The lunar waters were fouled now with stadium debris and the ruptured viscera of slain beasts. Beneath Janek, the altars were vacant of any victims. At his back, the monstrous pillar loomed closer as the serpent's body constricted, forcing him into its deadly refuge. Above him, hovered the ">%", venting blasts of malevolent force in all directions.

How did the ">%" get here? he puzzled.

"Janek," growled a voice on the Duuian's comlink. *"I have the Princess and Etty already aboard. Come straight up the second I start my next barrage..".*

He immediately knew that voice—the Nimbus Warrior!

His surprise was compounded when he was seized from below. The Warrior's sudden call had distracted Janek from his sensory grid, allowing a Deep One to surge from the depths and grab one of his startled legs.

His new aggression took control. Janek triggered his boot thrusters, and the jet stream melted the beast's flesh from its fin bones. The propulsion flung the Duuian wildly up, where he collided with—the naked body of Pik!

The two retrievers floundered for a moment, tumbling in the stained water. Before Janek could recover his composure, though, Pik had launched her still-spinning self to engage another Deep One rising in attack.

"Pik!" he cried. But she could not hear him, she had no comlink.

The Warrior *could* hear him, however. *"Is Pik there?"* demanded Tarn's voice. *"There's too much debris down there, even for this ship's souped-up scanners. If she's there, grab her and get up here. Now!"*

Janek lunged to pull Pik back from the battle, but the horrific bulk of another Deep One rose in his way. Before he could fire his jury-rigged lasers, though, another beast hit him from behind, crushing his laser array with a club-like appendage of massive size.

As the Duuian sank like a stunned rock, Pik flitted from beast to beast, dispatching each Deep One with lethal efficiency. She held a slender blade that shredded their flesh with lightning slashes. Janek grabbed for her, but she easily eluded the grasp of his spindly arms. Waving him off and urging him to head for the ship, Pik dove to battle another bestial attacker.

But her Duuian partner refused to leave her. His new aggression was sacrilegious if he used it only in his own defense. Janek leapt to aid her, warding off approaching Deep Ones with his pulse blasts.

"Come on, Janek!" hissed the Warrior over the comlink. *"That snake is moving in on you. And there's an ominous power-surge building down there..."*

On both counts, Janek could see what Tarn meant. The Dagon thing was tightening its coils, forcing them all into proximity of the monstrous pillar. Janek also saw that the twin, auxiliary columns were growing translucent now, as if their inner glow strained to burn free of their basaltic casing.

"Grab her and get up here!" the Warrior ordered.

With that, a rain of dazzling beams stabbed through the bloodied waters. Even the miasma of irreverent flotsam failed to conceal the vivid needles of lensed light that struck from above. These beams burned with fiery resolution on Janek's artificial scan of the region. And as instantly as the Duuian recognized them for what they were, he observed the terrible destruction they wreaked. The lethally-enhanced lasers of the ">%" sliced the great sea-snake's irate body into grisly sections.

The creature's psychic voice exploded with a wail of delirious rage and unparalleled agony, blotting out all reason or mortal understanding.

Great lengths of the beast's severed coils tumbled away to create a writhing heap around the base of the dark sacrificial pillar. Dagon's stumpy head section swung into view; the beast had suffered a decapitation just at the crest of its long neck. Its massive unblinking eye was clouded with pain and hate. The serpent's arms snatched at phantoms with its disturbingly human hands. The behemoth conducted a spasmodic death dance, pouring forth more profane blood to stain the ocean.

"Okay, that takes care of that beast," Tarn's voice insisted over Janek's comlink. *"Now get up here fast! That power-surge just increased!"*

Janek scanned the filthy water for Pik, and found—to his horror—that she was swooping to assault the Dagon thing's truncated head. Staring on, he watched her slam into the beast's enormous eye. She swung her antenna-whip, lacerating the huge orb with her puny weapon.

"There is no stopping it now!" screamed the serpent's telepathic wail.

There was no time to puzzle over the creature's elation, for something of cosmic impossibility was happening. The sea-snake—the beast's amputated head! It was growing a new body! Already Dagon's new tail was long enough to bend around and snare the tiny human who tormented it with such vehemence.

"It's regenerating!" cried Janek. "You did not kill it!"

"I will this *time..."* the Warrior announced.

"No!"

But it was too late.

The ">%" tipped to aim its rear armament at the recovering creature, and four incandescent plasma beams descended to vaporize the Dagon behemoth. Water turned to furious steam, and the altars collapsed like molten butter. The glare blinded every one of Janek's suit's sensors.

"Pik!" moaned the Duuian.

✤

If Pik was denied the destruction of the Great Evil Lord, then she was going to vent her vengeance on the Old One's self-professed sycophant.

She dove for the great serpent, kicking off from the drifting corpse of one of the Fish-God's minions. The Warrior's tremendous salvo of particle beams had diced the beast, leaving Dagon's decapitated head to telepathically fume, polluting the psychic ether with its rage. Swimming close, Pik struck at the beast's monumental eye with her antenna-saber. Again and again, she eviscerated the monster's wall-sized cornea.

Dagon's hate boiled across her like a physical current in the blood-murkied water. The incredible power of the beast's consciousness seethed with vile and loathsome intent. Its awful mind swept over Pik like a scalding waterfall.

She returned the gesture, flooding the monster with the full potency of her own outrage and disgust. Thinking of all the atrocities attributed to the Great Cthulhu and His dreadful followers, Pik focused her moral condemnation on the serpent-head. (Not graced with any psionic abilities, she had no idea how effective this psychic outlash would be against the monster's enormous essence. Her mental fury was a purely instinctual expression.)

Then she remembered how Professor Laramy had praised the power of his five-cornered star-stone amulet, claiming it was capable of repelling, even harming the Old Ones themselves. She conjured a blazing image in her mind of this sacred symbol and projected it at the unholy monster.

"There is no stopping it now!" screamed the serpent's telepathic wail.

No, she snarled in reply, *there* is *no stopping me now.* While Dagon (hopefully) squirmed under her mental barrage, Pik lashed away at the beast, blinding it and digging deep with her naked fingers for the monster's blasphemous brain.

Then suddenly, something foul and slimy circled her waist, and she was pulled away from her vicious mutilation. She hung in these clutches, gaping to discover that the beast had regrown itself. Dagon had plucked her from its punctured eye with its own newborn tail!

Her hardened muscles and augmented skeleton lasted about two seconds in Dagon's physical grasp. His tail, roughly three-times as thick as the girl's torso, crushed her chest with effortless ease. Pain hurricaned through Pik's defiant mind. Casually repositioning its tail's grip, the beast shattered her legs and—

Janek was dazed by Pik's abrupt vaporization. His voice shrieked a nonverbal wheeze of despair.

"Get moving!" a voice commanded. *"It looks as if the entire moon is getting ready to blow!"*

The Duuian wanted to save himself. He also longed to save Pik…but that was no longer possible. She was dead, gone; there was no human girl to rescue now, there weren't even any remains to collect.

And it was Tarn's fault! The Warrior had fired the plasma beams that had dissolved Pik!

All that Janek could do now was save himself.

Below, he could see the pillar's twin attending towers. They were aglow with a cosmic fire. Their brilliant blaze was being drawn in sinuous tendrils to caress the dark pillar. That squat column was inflating now, swelling up into a monstrous egg. The furious energy was feeding the egg…and Janek knew what it was!

The collected mega-ergs of the Great Evil One—channeled up from the deep subterranean storage batteries to be discharged from these two electrodes! For some purpose too hideous to even guess!

Grup, he realized. *This* was what had happened to the stolen drive cores! They had been collected and added to the Evil Lord's already incredible energy stores. To Janek and the humans, the naked manipulation of such enormous power was unthinkable—but to these New Lords of Earth, two plasma cores were thoroughly petty. Petty, but coveted nonetheless. The Evil One had drained the drive cores of the Princess' yacht and the Warrior's battle flier, adding those furious forces to His mammoth stockpile.

A stockpile that Cthulhu was hoarding no longer!

Activating his thrusters, the Duuian plummeted through the sea of gore. Up, and into the ">%'s" waiting open hatch he went.

Seconds later, the ship flung itself away from the polluted basin of the Evil One's coliseum, leaving behind an aloof and indifferent Lord surveying his violated domain. The ">%" shot from the troubled surface of the lunar ocean and entered the vacuum of space at accelerating velocity. Instead of fleeing into the open void, the Warrior guided the ship down to surf above the stratosphere, still building speed. Across the gaseous landscape it sped, finally disappearing behind the planetary horizon.

The ">%" was safely hidden behind the Earth's mass when the moon became a small star on the far side of the planet.

—and folded her head into a grisly paste. Pik died.

There was nothing noble or courageous or righteous about it. There was an awful lot of pain for the stalwart retriever, but death put a stop to that agony. It put a stop to *everything,* as if someone had switched off her consciousness like a light. There was no warning, no nanosecond of regret or lifetime review. It was all over.

A second later, the ">%'s" plasma beams vaporized the regenerated serpent, along with the crumpled ruin of the girl's mortal body. Sizzling meat became liquid protein became gaseous remains became loose molecules. Dagon was gone. And so was Pik.

(Later, she would be grateful that her body had been atomized, thereby excluding her blood from the travesty that was about to unfold.)

At first, the afterlife was a blinding light, but Pik soon realized that that was only the fury of the plasma strike. Once the beams snapped off, her surroundings reverted to their familiar, however ghastly, nature. She was still adrift in the lunar sea, down amid the torn bodies of the Great One's followers in that Lord's own temple. The waters ran viscous with basaltic debris and pulped monsters. The stadium was rubble, its tiers battered by pulse bursts. The sacrificial altars and their corkscrew dais were melted by plasma discharges. The gigantic pillar stood unharmed and dreadful. Its pair of flanking columns glowed with vibrant determination, casting an eerie yellow-white light through the multicolored hemoglobin of monsters. Of Dagon, there was no sign—unless you counted the pile of severed coils that girdled the base of the dark pillar like logs of meat in preparation for some deviant submarine bonfire.

Pik glanced down at herself and found her naked flesh paler than normal. She was positively…ghostly. And to some degree, translucent. To test her substantiality, she waved a hand to brush aside a chunk of bestial meat that floated too near her face. Her colorless hand passed right through the fleshy lump, disturbing its underwater path not in the least. Although she had no tactile effect on the dead meat, that chunk had an effect on her. Ghostly contact delivered an electric charge through her awareness. Despite its pleasantness (or perhaps because of how good it felt), Pik recoiled from the sensation.

She was dead…but still here. *Why?* she pleaded the silent unknown. *How? I'm—a ghost, just like Laramy!*

With a start, she found the Professor's star-stone necklace around her spectral neck. *That's right,* she realized, *he put it there to taunt me, back before Etty freed me from the altar's paralyzing effect. Had it—was it the reason I was a ghost?*

Things were happening all around Pik.

The terrible pillar was acting quite unnatural. It was bulging, swelling like an expanding black balloon. It was feeding on the glow from the two towers!

She saw Janek flee the madness, soaring to higher waters and (hopefully) the safety of the ">%".

"Run!" she urged her alien partner. *(Ex-partner? Or, since I had been the one who had died, was I the "ex-partner"?)* "You can make it, Janek…"

There was no escape necessary for Pik, though. She was dead, beyond the reach of any corporeal forces. Or so she thought.

"Look what you've done!" a voice wailed in the back of her mind.

Laramy!

Pik whirled to find the Professor's insane ghost lunging at her through the contaminated waters. Reflexively, she adopted a defensive posture, her Warrior training kicking in before her mind could motivate her spiritual muscles. Death may have separated the girl from her physicality, but it had done nothing to impair the alacrity of her instincts.

When he hit her, Pik rolled Laramy's clumsy assault over her spectral hip. This sent his ghost careening to the sagging altars below, where he wallowed half-immersed in their molten forms. Unharmed but shamed, he scrambled to hover and rush the ghostly retriever again.

All the while, his hollow voice rang with condemnation, "You've ruined *everything!* You've spoiled the Unspeakable One's Raising! You assassinated *Me!* Now, there will be no Awakening! Puny, sterile breeder—you've destroyed schemes that took centuries to prepare!"

He was completely *turned* now. His lunacy showed in his manic words, in his persistent attack, even in his grotesque countenance. For Laramy's face had undergone a ghastly transformation. Gone were his gaunt, human features, replaced now with the bulging eyes and wide flapping lips of a Deep One. His pale shoulders humped with their monstrous crouch. Why—even his spectral fingers were webbed now! His corruption was complete. The taint of evil in the minion souls he had consumed had infected his mind, erasing his original personality and rewriting his ghostly synapses. Professor Laramy was no longer an enemy of the Evil Cthulhu; now he was one of the Great Lord's devout followers: malevolent and insane.

"You killed me!" he bellowed. "You forced me to take refuge in this spiritual body—this atrocious parody of ectoplasm!"

His insanity was blossoming.

Pik sideswam his assault, and his next pass too. For someone who had been a ghost for over two hundred years, Laramy was acting awfully awkward, almost as if he had forgotten how to coordinate his spiritual limbs.

"Dagon will not be degraded like this!" he raged.

He thought he was the beast that had just died. Pik almost laughed. Then…she sobered with a pang of deep fear. Somehow the monstrous possibility did not seem that fantastic. She had been killed, but now she was a ghost. The Dagon serpent had been killed too…what if the Old Ones possessed an afterlife technology of their own? Had Dagon continued on in a ghostly manner? Could the beast's mind have infiltrated Laramy's ghost?

"Laramy…?" Pik croaked. "Are you…still in there?"

"I will swallow your soul!"

It wasn't Laramy, not any longer. It was a fiendish thing, an ancient primal force that had spent an infinity of lifetimes in corporeal form, being worshipped by sailors since Earth's dim infancy. It had worn many bodies over the millennia, each defined by the beliefs of its followers. Its familiarity with the spiritual realm had atrophied eons ago. Confined now to Laramy's hazy materialization, the Fish-God was tormented by the compression forced on its mammoth, corrupt essence by the insignificance of its new vessel. Dagon's malignancy and hateful wrath blazed like an erupting red star behind Laramy's protruding eyes.

In life, Pik had doubted the deification which Laramy's tales had attributed to these Old Ones. In death, face-to-face with one of these ancient forces, Pik knew at last that these were not just clever aliens wielding supernatural technologies. There was no mistaking that Dagon's spirit was monstrous and fertile with profane power. This was no pompous alien despot—this was a being of godlike capacity dedicated to ghastly oppression.

If Dagon, a lowly monster in Professor Laramy's pantheon of demons, was *this* powerful...what must the Great Cthulhu's strength be like...? Pik's spirit shuddered as her imagination answered that desperate inquiry.

So far, the devil had been unable to coordinate Laramy's simple ghost to successfully attack the girl. That ineptitude could not last for long. She had to take action now, before Dagon's undead spirit gained a mastery of its new manifestation and eradicated her in one of the thousands of ways available to its monstrous power.

Her time ran out. The Laramy Thing expanded, growing far beyond its normal size. Its legs fused into a single, sinuous trunk. Laramy's long hair flowed to become more like rippling fringe. This inflated monster scooped Pik from the polluted water, raising her to its gloating fiery eyes. Those scarlet orbs were as big as her spectral head. The creature's own head was wider than her arms-span. Evil satisfaction gleamed in the Thing's eyes as it held her puny ghost close to its ecstatic grimace.

"You are unique," the Thing told her. "Your heresies against the Lord Cthulhu are more grievous than any mortal enemy before you. Your crimes have earned you a punishment of unspeakable proportion."

Without thinking, Pik plunged her ghostly forearms into the Thing's broad forehead...just as she had witnessed Laramy do to newly slain Deep Ones. She felt her invasive hands pierce the Fish-God's spirit, and its essence burned her phantom. Without her military training, Pik would have immediately withdrawn her scalded limbs from the profane incandescence of the beast's darkness. Instead, Dagon's intensity goaded her to delve deeper, raking her crooked spectral fingers through his unearthly consciousness. Super-ego bled into id, raging determination was tainted by wary hesitation. The beast's mind was already in chaotic disorganization, which only went to further conceal the depth of Pik's reach from the mighty Fish-God.

If the creature had realized what she was doing, it would have atomized her spirit with its cosmic indignity. Blinded by its own arrogance, the beast cackled with lunatic intimidation.

If *Pik* had realized what she was doing…

Fortunately, they both remained ignorant of the magnitude of her brazen invasion until it was too late.

Pik felt a tingle on her shoulderblade, marking where the star-stone amulet lay against her back. Agitated during her brusque elevation, the amulet had swung loosely around her neck, finally coming to rest near her spine. There, it had remained hidden from the gigantic beast.

Yanking her arms from the beast's spectral head, Pik's grasp came free, all clammy and hot with a double-handful of Dagon's raging essence. The frothing ectoplasm was nearly impossible to hold, it squirmed and burned to escape her grasp with an electric frenzy. Its presence in her clutches was a complete surprise to Pik. How could a child pluck the essential nucleus from a devil's monstrous mind? She had no idea what to do with it.

So…she peeked inside…

And she learned the *truth!* So many dreadful truths…

Pik peered into the unholy memories of the Fish-God, and she witnessed horrors beyond telling, miracles beyond believing, mendacities beyond deception.

—Ancient times, before there had been worshipers. In those times, there had been no need of forms, and Dagon had coexisted with the other Old Ones in the homogenous chaos that was the Blind Idiot King. It had been Nyarlathotep who had first ventured beyond this zone, to discover regions where order reigned and evil was unknown. But it had been the Great Cthulhu who had led the Old Ones to this virgin universe. There, these incarnate evils had thrilled to introduce horror and mayhem to this plane of stability. In time, though, They had been punished for Their joy.

—Ages, eras, eons spent in the company of brutish submariners, swimming endlessly through forests of algae-adorned columns decorated with the inaccurate portrait of the Great Sleeping One. The primitive creatures that had carved these horrific bas-reliefs had possessed bestial intellects that were incapable of remembering the Evil One's awesome likeness once they were freed from their nightmares. As a result, the Deep Ones and their human sympathizers worshipped false idols that only vaguely resembled the countenance of the Great Cthulhu. This troubled Dagon, but it was not His place to question the incoherent wisdom of the Great Lord. Once, a courier from Shudde-M'ell had hinted at rumors that the Burrower suspected the Great Lord intentionally tolerated this false icon, for it kept His True Self safely concealed from the profane brethren who coveted Cthulhu's power.

—Barely two hundred passes-around-the-sun ago, the culmination of preparations that had taken many centuries to coordinate. Incredible patience had gone into the slow and subtle tainting of mankind. Miscegenation had produced hordes of devout followers, but there was more value in corrupting the human purebloods, for those troops followed out of faith born not of bloodlines. These human worshipers would betray their own species to the imprisoned Old Ones. There was joy to be had in such pollution of common sense. Finally, after millennia of covert manipulation, enough believers had infiltrated positions of power to generate a manifest hostility between territorial factions of mankind, resulting in an overwhelming mood of suspicion and unreason among the human populace. By relentlessly fanning these flames of distrust, the Old Ones had brought mankind's mass psyche to a boiling point of outraged tempers amidst a mania of arrogant entitlement. Triggering a global conflict had been easy; redirecting the sophisticated weaponry of these human nations had taken a more refined hand. But it had been done—all to Awaken the Great Sleeping Lord, loosening His blasphemous presence upon the naive universe again.

—Atrocities of staggering proportion…too many to face and remain sane—

Up to that point, the undead Laramy/Dagon Thing had regarded Pik's ghost with visible contempt. Now, the beast became frantic. With a spastic twitch, Dagon flung her from its ghostly new body—then clutched to recapture the girl, suddenly realizing the danger of letting Pik take a part of It with her. Again, the Fish-God's unfamiliarity with the ectoplasmic realm was its undoing.

Tumbling in the direction of the fractured tiers of alien seats, Pik's own sense of revulsion pinnacled. She was certainly not about to consume the hellish ectoplasm she clasped in her spectral hands—look what had happened to the Professor, and he had only cannibalized some Deep Ones. Its blasphemous cold and murderous blaze became a psychic anathema, and she could no longer bear to touch it! With a desperate heave, Pik cast the monster's stolen essence from her. She wanted no part of it.

By now, the dark pillar had swollen to become a massive egg, fueled by the raw energy that was pouring forth from the smaller, supplemental columns. A section of the engorged pillar was churning, coalescing into a nebulous hole in space. The cosmic puncture was gradually gaping to reveal a chaos that defied description. At the bloated pillar and into this insane abyss Pik threw Dagon's horrific memories.

The Fish-God lunged to retrieve its lost spark.

"You primitive savage!" bellowed the beast. "The Gate needs a *human* soul to make it permanent! Not *mine!*"

Pik fled, her flight propelled by the vast madness she had glimpsed…a perception of reality that that threatened to turn her mind into a soap bubble thrown into a hurricane.

Behind her, the Gate swallowed the monster piecemeal.

The Raising had been terminally interrupted. In failing, the abhorrent scheme transformed the moon into a small star.

Praylude:
Excerpts from the Diary of a Crank

I have often pondered why the Elder Gods abandoned mankind, leaving the Old Ones incarcerated in tenuous prisons that restrained Their ghastly physical forms, but were incapable of blocking Their monstrous psyches from bleeding through those cosmic barriers to contaminate the rest of the universe.

Why were the cosmic tombs of the Old Ones so badly constructed?

Had it been the contention of the Elder Gods that Cthulhu and His vile brethren needed access to the minds of men? Was the taint of the Old Ones a necessary component in humanity's overall temperament?

These questions have no sane answer, and the doubt they seed in my intellect serves only to increase my despair and confusion. Is this universe forsaken by the powers of order? Is disorder the proper state of our existence? This cannot be...

I pray for the return of the Elder Gods, for only the incomprehensible might of those primordial deities can halt the horrific expansion currently practiced by the New Lords of Earth.

Please...send your agents to end our suffering...

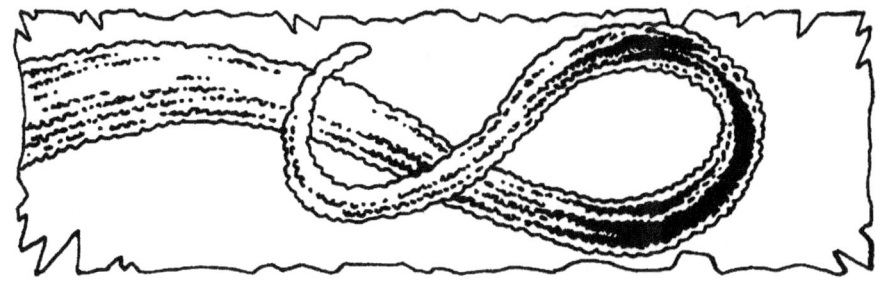

section 5:
In Necessary Shadow

"**D**ead...?"

Janek scratched two of his claws against the under-ridges of his massive headcrest, his method of expressing unwillingness-to-tell-a-friend-about-the-death-of-a-loved-one. He hesitated a long time before confirming the bad news.

Etty did not take the news of Pik's demise elegantly. In fact, he did not give his alien partner's claim much credence. Ignoring Janek's evasive guilt, he stormed off in search of the Warrior.

Tarn had not left the ">%'s" command deck since they had come aboard. During the mad escape from the cursed moon, the rescued passengers had suffered the riotous ride out of necessity. Now, though, having shed their pressure suits (and seen the Princess attired in some of Pik's clothes), they were all disturbed by the Warrior's continued absence. They milled uneasily in a lounge before Etty stormed off down the depreciated passages.

"Where the grup is he?" Etty snarled. "He has to go back for her!"

"Etty, no..." Janek moaned, shuffling after him.

The Princess followed them into the corridor. Pik's clothing was baggy on the buxom Royal Daughter. "Surely you must be mistaken, Janek," she mumbled. "Pik was a courageous soldier. She can't be dead..."

"How could you let the bastard run off and *leave Pik* back there?" Etty turned to scream at the Duuian.

"We did not leave her, Etty. She was already…dead." Janek hung his wide head in personal shame. "I…I saw it happen."

"No!" Etty declared. Whirling, he vented his anger by banging on the closed door to the ship's command deck. "You're wrong! You only *thought* you saw her die."

Janek sadly shook his head, his sensory tendrils strangling each other with emotional distress.

"Open up in there!" Etty yelled, kicking the sealed door repeatedly.

"What do you want?" came Tarn's voice over the ship's intercom.

"Remember us? The ones whose ship you've hijacked! Unlock this grupping door!"

"I am busy," replied the Warrior. *"Leave me alone."*

"You left Pik behind, didn't you?" Etty shouted. "You left her to die!"

The door snapped open, and the Warrior stood there: stern and tall in his imposing yet scorched battle armor. He glared at Etty, conveying defiance like a blinding beacon.

"I don't have time for this, boy," Tarn growled. His face lost its stern design to express brief shock as he peered past the retrievers at the Princess. "Your Highness," he nodded. "I see your amputated arm has been replaced."

The Royal Daughter protectively hugged her repaired arm across her chest, then nodded in mute agreement.

"Make time!" announced Etty as he tried to sidle by the Warrior. "This is *our* ship, not *yours*."

"That is not an accurate statement at this point," Tarn grumbled.

"Piracy?" Janek bristled.

"Royal conscription," clarified the Warrior.

"Get out of my way," Etty grated. "We've got to go back for her—"

Tarn let the boy force past him, but remained resolute. "There's no way this ship is going back to where the moon used to be."

"—Used to be—?" wheezed Janek.

"For the moment, we're unharmed. But I cannot predict how long our safety will last." As he spoke, the Warrior stepped back to admit the Princess and Janek to the command room.

"—Used to be—?" Janek insisted. "What the grup happened to the moon?"

"These brave souls rescued me from my monstrous captors, Warrior," the Princess remarked. "You really must go back for Pik." Although her voice started out meek, with each word she reclaimed more command.

"I'm sorry, Your Highness," replied Tarn, "but that's one order I am unable to obey."

Sitting at the controls, Etty found they no longer responded to his touch. "You bastard," he fumed, unhappily returning to his feet. "You've programmed new control codes into our ship!"

This was a last straw for Etty. He had suffered the Warrior's insults, been abandoned in the Spire of Condemnation by Tarn, and now the man was actually stealing the team's ship from them! And by doing so, the Warrior was also denying Etty the chance of going back to save Pik. The bastard had left her on the moon—he had actually stranded her there among the monsters!

Rage devoured Etty's restraint, and he jumped the Warrior. His attack was shrugged off as if he were a paper tiger.

"It's for your own good, Your Highness. Your safety is my primary concern."

"Is that why you stranded Pik back on the moon?" Etty wailed. He pummeled uselessly against the Warrior's armor with his needy fists.

Tarn ignored the boy's futile violence. Locking eyes with the Princess, he pointed her attention to the scanner screens on the main control console. Darkness was the predominant feature of these views, broken only by an excruciatingly brilliant corona that blazed at the curves of the horizon. It was as if a monstrous fire burned on the far side of the planet.

The Princess approached the viewscreens, entranced by the impressive display. "How beautiful," she cooed softly.

"But deadly," the Warrior announced. "The full fury of a sun unleashed."

"The star went nova?!" the Duuian gasped.

"No, it isn't this system's resident sun—it's a new star," confided Tarn. "Right on the other side of the planet...where the moon *used to be*."

"That's absurd!" scoffed Janek.

"Believe whatever you want," Tarn grunted. "It will not make this newborn sun go away." Etty continued to beat on the Warrior's armor, and Tarn continued to not acknowledge his attack.

"Grup—that *is* a star!" wheezed the Duuian once he had peered close at the analysis graphs next to the scanner screens. "How the— Where did—"

"Right now, I'm busy keeping the entire ship from being vaporized by that infant sun." Tarn strode over to the controls to adjust the ">%'s" position relative to the looming shadow of the eclipsed planet. A second later, the eerie corona centered itself in the viewscreen pictures. "I do not have time for your partner's inability to accept the death of his lover."

"How can you be so uncaring?" complained the Princess.

"I'm trying to keep all of us from following Pik into the Great Beyond." Soberly, he faced Etty and declared, "She was a brave Warrior who proved herself in battle. I mourn her passing. Having seen and piloted this ship—the handiwork, I suspect, of her tinkering, yes?—I have considerable admiration for her spunk."

Again, Etty threw himself against the Warrior. "Stop talking about her as if she's dead!"

"He's the reason she's not here," Janek cursed. "Tell him, Tarn. Tell him how you murdered Pik!"

"What—?" Etty stepped back, stunned.

"That can't be true," gasped Princess Eden. "He's a Royal Warrior! He would never—"

"She…can't be dead," Etty sobbed. *She couldn't be dead…*

"I saw it," the Duuian asserted. He poised tall on his three legs, rocking his huge headcrest intimidatingly from side-to-side.

Was this the real reason behind Tarn's refusal to return for Pik? wondered Etty. If the Warrior had been responsible for her death—but no, Etty refused to accept her death. There had to be a mistake. Janek couldn't have seen Tarn kill Pik. She was still alive, back on the… No, that was not possible either. The moon had become a newborn star, anyone still there was now burned up…gone… *No!* No matter which way Etty examined the facts, Pik was dead. And *that* was the most unthinkable of options.

Etty exploded. Pulling loose a pry-bar from behind a console seat, he swung it on the Warrior, screaming in rage. The plastiform rod caught Tarn across the temple, dazing him. Both Etty and Janek moved in like hungry dogs, pushing the Warrior from his feet before he could recover. Once they had him down, the enraged retrievers attacked him with full fervor, kicking his armor and hammering away at him with the pry-bar.

"Murderer!" Janek hissed.

"Stop!" the Princess cried. "You can't—"

"Did you kill my Pik?" Etty shrieked as he struck the Warrior repeatedly across the face with the pry-bar. "Or did you just leave her behind? So she'd die in the exploding star?"

"What are you doing?" demanded Pik's voice. "Stop that!"

Etty froze. Clutching his bludgeon to his chest, he darted his eyes about the control room, searching for his dead lover. She was *alive*, he had been wise to doubt the lies of his companions. "Pik?" he whispered. "Where are you?"

With the cessation of the skirmish, a quietude descended on the scene; even the Princess' cries of objection fizzled into a breathless stupefaction.

"I'm right here," the ghostly voice came again.

Then Etty saw her—framed in the doorway. Flinging away his weapon, he whooped her name and leapt to hug his lover.

"Pik?" gasped Janek. He turned to direct his sensory tendrils toward the door. "But—"

"She's alive!" exclaimed Princess Eden. "See? There was no reason to attack Warrior Tarn."

Joy erupted in Etty's desperate heart. A moment ago, he had feared never seeing Pik again, and now, here she was! Alive and safe. That clever girl! She had managed to find a way onto the ">%" before the ship's lunatic departure from the moon. Pik wasn't dead. Tarn hadn't killed her. Janek was mistaken. And Etty was ecstatic.

His feet pounding on the ship's weary deck, he crossed the room and flung himself at his girl. He rushed right through Pik's hazy silhouette, spilling into the corridor with a startled squeak.

"What's gotten into you guys?" she commented.

"You—you're—" Janek choked out.

Pik's ghost shrugged, stepping into the room. "Yeah, well…I had an accident."

"You're a ghost—like Laramy!" Etty gasped.

"I told you the Warrior killed her!" Janek growled. He trounced Tarn with a pointy foot.

"The Warrior didn't kill me," Pik declared. "That Dagon thing caught me and crushed my body to a pulp."

"I was there," professed Janek. "I saw you die when the Warrior fired a plasma barrage that vaporized that snake creature."

Pik coughed politely and reminded him, "I was there too, Janek. And I know how I died. Crushed by the sea-monster."

"But—"

"That's why I fired, you morons," Tarn grunted. He slowly rose from the floor, scowling at them all. "I could see her on my monitors. I saw the beast crush her. *That's* why I blasted it."

"As it turns out, it was most fortuitous that you vaporized my body," Pik told the Warrior.

"What?" wailed Etty. This unreal situation was getting even more fantastic.

⁜

Pik told them about the mind-boggling atrocity that had been averted back on the moon in the Evil Lord's necrotic coliseum. That terrible scheme to unleash an ultimate destruction on the entire universe.

It had been a doom far more desperate than the notion of breeding a new human race for Cthulhu to victimize. *That* scheme had existed only in the delusions of Professor Laramy's ghost—and in the false evidence that Etty's dreaming mind had picked up among Ithaqua's jealous psychic rantings. Although those "breeding" rumors were circulated to obfuscate the Evil One's followers, the Great Lord had privately desired the capture of these newly-appeared pureblood humans for *other,* far more abominable purposes. Ithaqua had not been aware of the Evil Lord's secret intentions. No one had known, for if any of those monsters had realized the incredible scope of the "real" plan, even the most devout brethren might have rebelled, refusing to allow the Raising to occur. It was *that* horrific.

The Warrior interrupted Pik's tale, questioning whether this "horrific danger" still threatened them—he waved a tense arm to indicate the group: himself, Etty, Janek, and the disheveled Princess. (*Are those my clothes on her?* Pik noticed. *Yes, I suppose they'd have to be.*)

She assured Tarn that the Evil Lord's scheme had failed—at least, theoretically. For it had.

To understand how blasphemous this scheme had been, Pik revealed, one had to accept the hierarchy of these Ancient Ones who became the New Lords of Earth. She was unwilling to declare the Old Ones as ancient deities (which she unfortunately knew them to be), for the ghostly retriever knew it would undermine the rest of her explanation. The group would dismiss her claims with the same suspicion they had all shown Laramy when he had attributed theological definitions to the enemy. Ultimately, perhaps it was for the best…for Pik doubted that humanity was really ready to believe in the existence of such monstrous things as Cthulhu or Ithaqua or Dagon or Azathoth… So, for the group, Pik expressed the unholy truth in terms and concepts that complimented reality instead of violating it.

The truth: The Ancient Ones were *indeed* deities, possessing immortality and infinite power. Imprisoned by the Elder Gods in the universe's infancy, the Ancient Ones had plotted their escape for epochs, lusting after the vengeance they would wreak on their jailers. Cthulhu, Ithaqua, Shudde-M'ell, Dagon and other lesser devils were imprisoned on Earth. Hastur (the blasphemous rival of Cthulhu) lay trapped by the black waters of Hali in the Hyades. Nyarlathotep (the Great Messenger) was exiled to the immaterial void. After eons of confinement, the Earth-bound devils had risen to conquer this world and exterminate all its native lifeforms.

What Pik told the group: "The Ancient Ones are long-lived alien criminals, possessing incredible hidden technologies. When they conquered the Earth, they exterminated all the natural lifeforms."

The truth: Among the pantheon of these Ancient Monsters, the most horrific was Azathoth. This Blind Idiot God had been so uncontrollable that the Elder Gods had banished Him to another dimension of total emptiness. There, He could rage forever but never destroy anything. (The curious part about Azathoth was that, although the Ancient One's viewed the Blind Idiot God as Their—indeed, everyone's—superior, the hazy description Pik got from Dagon's consciousness was remarkably close to pure nuclear fission, a constant and ongoing particle decay. This posed the question of how many more of Cthulhu's monstrous kin corresponded to basic aspects of quantum physics.) The latest atrocity of the Ancient Ones involved an attempt to open a portal to this other dimension, freeing the Blind Idiot God and loosening His all-encompassing wrath upon the universe-at-large. These ancient deities wanted to release Their own lost god, and restore Him to His rightful place as the universe's annihilator.

What Pik told the group: "Their latest atrocity involved an attempt to tear a hole in Space/Time, and gain access to a dimension of raw, furious energy."

The awful truth: According to Dagon's scheme (for this plan had been the product of the Fish-God's psychotic intellect), by feeding every mega-erg of hoarded energy into a single point, the fabric of Space/Time could be breached—but only for the briefest instant. To establish stability to this dimensional Gate, the unpolluted blood of ancestral victims was required. When the Princess had crash-landed on Earth, the Evil One had sensed her human blood from His underwater throne on the moon. The arrival of subsequent rescuers (the retrieval team and the Warrior) had only increased the potentiality of Dagon's terrible plan. The blood of any one of these galactic citizens would have served (with perhaps the exception of Janek, but then—who could predict the effects of his Duuian blood to the paranormal physics of the Raising), but for some warped reason, the Great Lord had obsessed on spilling *female* human blood. These monsters were not only profane and insane, they were fetishists, harboring obscene desires to mate with females of any inferior species. So it was that, although the Deep Ones gained male and female prisoners, the female humans had been the truly important prizes all along.

This time, what Pik told the group was basically the truth. "According to the religion practiced by these Ancient Ones, the blood of female aliens was necessary to the ceremony. It was not entirely ritualistic either, for a chemical contained in human hemoglobin aided the mysterious technology employed. Without the application of this human enzyme, the interdimensional hole could only last a second, and the Ancient Ones would be unable to harvest the limitless power they were after."

The truth: Without the application of this human enzyme, the Ancient Ones' interdimensional Gate could only last a second, and They would fail to unleash Azathoth into the universe.

"So, you see," she told them, "Tarn actually helped to avert disaster when he vaporized my corpse. I was already dead, my body meant nothing to me anymore. But I'm glad the enemy was unable to make use of it. They could have used my corpse to stabilize their Gate. With access to this dimension of raw energy, they would have become invincible."

The audience seemed to accept her filtered version of the truth.

"So—how did you learn these secrets?" the Warrior inquired cagily. Apparently, he still harbored some reservations with the ghost's story.

"I can partially corroborate what she has told us," Janek commented. He related how he had found a way to download data packets from the Great Lord's database in the lunar fortress. "Some of what she says is confirmed by referents in this stolen data."

"Some?" Tarn scowled.

"There is a tremendous amount of information in the files I stole, much of which is heavily encrypted." As he spoke, her Duuian partner swung his sensory tendrils briefly in Pik's direction, hinting at shared secrets. She wondered what "truths" Janek had uncovered that he was unwilling to share. Were any of them the same as hers?

"How did you become a ghost?" the Warrior demanded of Pik.

"I don't know," she confessed truthfully. "I glimpsed fragments of Dagon's mind when he died, that's how I learned about his secret Gate scheme. The fish—" *Oops*, she caught herself. *I almost called Him the Fish-God.* "—the fish-thing knew nothing about any afterlife."

"You have Professor Laramy's amulet," the Princess observed.

"Apparently, yes," Pik admitted. "It was there once I found myself as a ghost. Perhaps it is responsible for my posthumous existence. I really do not know for certain." This was a mystery for which she really had no viable answers. Why Pik was a ghost, she did not know. How it had happened was an unsolved puzzle. How Laramy's amulet necklace had gotten around her spectral neck was another "fact" she was unwilling to share with her ex-partners or the Warrior. Explaining Laramy and the vile contamination that led to his unpleasant fate would only confuse the "truth" Pik was attempting to relate.

The existence of an afterlife was an accepted dogma among the unified galactic religion. Despite the species, the concepts of reward and punishment were universal. All believers (such as Pik) knew that death was only a doorway to another level of existence. Her own posthumous existence did not contradict this theological certainty.

But being a "ghost" did. If interaction between the living and the dead was possible, this phenomena would have been observed long ago. Death was meant to be an impervious dividing line between life and the hereafter. But…if this was irrefutable, then how could Pik explain her ghosthood?

What incredible element had made her death different? Laramy had claimed that his amulet had made possible the continuation of his spirit… but how plausible was that? Once Laramy's ghost had become tainted by Deep One ectoplasm, he had discarded the charm…but he had remained a ghost. Was it something deeper than the star-stone amulet? Was it "faith"? Was Pik's faith *that* strong?

"More strange alien technology," mumbled Janek, as if this explained everything.

Pik could only shrug.

Tarn found it difficult to accept the bounty hunter's ghostly survival. Death was an absolute to the Warrior, it was the goal in battle, it defined triumph. How could there be any victory if one's opponents didn't stay dead?

Unconsciously, though, he was glad to find that Pik had escaped death. He had developed a respect for her determination and cunning. In the end, she had lived up to the Warrior Oath that he had accused her of violating. She had given her life in defense of the Nimbus Galactic

Empire…and she had survived to talk about it. That alone marked Pik as an exceptional individual. Her ghostliness troubled him for its abnormality, but he rejoiced that this impossibility had happened to her.

Although he bore neither of them any actual animosity, had Etty or Janek gotten killed during the mission, their deaths would not have bothered the Warrior. Etty was too emotional, a trait that Tarn found "unprofessional". Nor did the Warrior like the way the Princess was taking to the boy, for he was certainly unworthy of such royal attention. Meanwhile, Janek had been increasingly argumentative throughout the mission, a trait Tarn thought was unfound among Duuians. Furthermore, he had accused Tarn of intentionally murdering Pik.

Indeed, Pik's death had tormented the Warrior when he had witnessed what had happened in that fateful submarine stadium. Energy scans had revealed the cessation of her life functions thirty-five seconds before the Warrior's plasma blasts had vaporized the huge sea-snake and Pik's corpse. Twenty of those seconds had been spent in examining the scans to ascertain and then confirm Pik's abrupt demise. Ten seconds had been wasted in anger. It had taken Tarn three seconds to blame it all on the Dagon thing, and two seconds to aim and activate the plasma cannons. The beams of unbridled fusion had atomized the beast a second later. Although he knew she had not died by his hand, the Warrior felt responsible for her fate. Never once did Tarn privately reproach Janek for the Duuian's inability to retrieve the girl. They had all been soldiers under Tarn's command, however informal and unauthorized that collaboration had been, and, according to the Oath, a Warrior always assumed responsibility for every accident and injury that befell those under his command. Pik's death had been specially deplorable because Tarn had learned to respect her. He almost considered her his equal: a Royal Warrior of exquisite talent.

To find Pik still alive (if that was not a misnomer) was truly a miracle.

His astonishment over her ghostly reappearance did not blind the Warrior, though, to the changes that were occurring in the other members of this Royal Rescue.

Janek was clearly harboring some secret. There was something the Duuian had found in the alien data that he was unwilling to share with anyone. Considering the archetypal greed of his kind, it was probably something profitable. In all likelihood, Janek's uncharacteristic aggressive nature would belligerently resist any of Tarn's attempts to expose this "secret."

Etty was undergoing an adverse reaction to his lover's life after death. His initial joy had soured, darkened by the realization that she was really *dead*. Gradually, his surprise had become revulsion, sending him to the room's furthermost point from Pik's ghost. He stared now at his ex-lover with an expression of abject fear. Facing the undead nature of his ex-lover had been too much for the boy's average psyche. He had no capacity to differentiate between death and undeath. As far as he was concerned now Pik had become an abomination—a contradiction of nature laws that inspired a deep-rooted revulsion in his mind.

Meanwhile, Princess Eden was fawning over the desolate Etty, comforting him in his "moment of crisis." Known for the revolving door on her boudoir, the Royal Brat was unfurling her emotional hooks, baited with her tender sympathy. No doubt she had fixated on the boy because of his role in rescuing her from the lunar stadium. Her idle fascination would quench itself briefly with carnal trysts, and six seconds after she discarded him, she would not remember Etty's name. Although he had no great like of the boy, Tarn believed that Etty did not deserve this emotional scar. Keeping him out of her clutches would annoy Her Highness, but Tarn was convinced that her Royal Parents would condone keeping their Favorite Daughter from sharing fluids with a commoner—a criminal, even. The Princess' parents would be the ones granting the Warrior his reward, not the spoiled and vindictive Brat.

As to the matter of what to do about these quasi-legal bounty hunters, Tarn was again torn between conflicting judgments. On one hand, they *had* assisted the Warrior in rescuing the Royal Daughter from the evil Lords who had conquered Earth. On the other hand, he had discovered considerable galactic infractions in their ship's armament. Granted, these violations were minor, and had eve been integral in the triumphant outcome of this rescue. If it were up to Tarn, he would casually have overlooked the freebooters' transgressions, but he could not guess how his own superiors would view all this. How many of the occult details concerning this mission were the admirals of the Nimbus Space Navy going to believe in the first place?

All of which were moot contentions unless they got safely out of this predicament. The Warrior wished he was more confident about that assumption.

While Pik's ghost had been telling them about the Great Lord's evil scheme, Tarn had detected no further growth in the newborn sun that hung on the opposite side of the planet. The ship's sensors showed that the stellar anomaly had apparently stabilized.

The threat it posed to them aboard the spacecraft was not reduced by this sudden stability, though. As far as the Warrior was concerned, even the Earth's planetary mass was inadequate protection from the blazing star's violent emissions. Pik's private customization had equipped the bounty hunters' ship with excellent shields, but that augmentation was hardly capable of repelling such malignant radiation at this proximity. They were simply too close to the monstrous thing. Escape along the planet's cone of shadow was the group's only hope of survival.

He had initiated that course moments ago. Unknown to the rest of them, the ship was already moving away from the dark face of old Earth, building velocity for a mad-dash escape from the tip of that shadowy cone. Tarn could only hope that the ship's shields would provide ample protection for the occupants once the vessel was exposed.

In preparation for that escape run, the Warrior had investigated the ship's schematics, determining that the forward cargo hangar (usually reserved for the crew's food supplies) possessed the strongest shielding. He had originally opened the doorway of the ship's command deck in order to herd the Princess and the two surviving bounty hunters in that direction. Etty's impotent assault had forestalled the Warrior's intended evacuation, which had been further delayed by the unexpected appearance of Pik's ghost.

Interrupting Pik's feeble explanation of her ghosthood (another secret that needed to be unveiled), Tarn outlined his plan for escape in curt sentences. In conclusion, he announced: "The Princess must be moved to the safety of the forward cargo hangar immediately. If the rest of you wish to survive this journey, I suggest you join Her Highness there."

"What about you?" Pik's ghost inquired.

"My battle armor should be sufficient to protect me from the dangerous radiation."

"The Warrior has hijacked our ship," Janek announced nastily. "He has programmed new control codes, locking us out."

"That was presumptuous..." muttered the ghost.

"But necessary," the Warrior told her. "As is *haste* right now." He started toward the Princess, frowning, "Allow me to escort you to safety, Your Highness..."

"Why should she go with *you*?" grunted Etty.

"Because her safety is my primary concern."

When the Warrior attempted to guide the Princess to the doorway, she pulled away, hugging Etty with possessive determination. "No," she moaned. "I will not go without Etty."

"The bounty hunters are free to follow and share the protection I have prepared for you, Your Highness." He reached for her again, but she hid behind the boy.

"What if we do not trust you?" Janek sneered.

"That is your prerogative," Tarn declared. "The Princess does not have that luxury. I cannot allow the heir to the Nimbus Empire to risk her life."

While they had been exchanging threats and doubts, Pik had wandered over to examine the ship's sensory consoles. When she spoke, her comments brought their confrontation to a pause. "You should do as the Warrior suggests. The exterior radiation level is quite lethal. Even the auxiliary shields I installed might not adequately protect you from the new star's virulent output."

"You trust this soldier?" Janek countered.

"He will give his life to protect the Princess," remarked Pik. "If you share the refuge Tarn has readied for her, you will share her survival."

"Please, Your Highness," the Warrior urged, offering her his hand. "Time is running out..."

Holding tight to Etty, she still resisted his salvation.

"Etty!" Pik spoke sharply, gaining his startled attention. "Escort the Princess to cargo hangar 2, then remain there until you hear from Tarn. Please—you're all in danger unless you follow the Warrior's directions."

Tarn watched the ghost's ex-lover struggle with his imagined conflicts regarding Pik's unnatural presence. Finally, the boy nodded and led the Princess from the command deck. Etty advised his Duuian partner to join them. Janek cast a doubtfully-knotted tendril nest in Pik's direction. The ghost nodded, waving him to follow Etty.

As they left, Tarn wearily reoccupied the control seat. Despite the support of his battle armor, his broken thighbone had complained bitterly as he stood his ground against the rest of the group. His suit had protected the Warrior from the bounty hunters' crude assault, but *standing* had been painful. He had deactivated the pain receptors in his brain, but the throb and unnatural set of his leg were tactile sensations he could not ignore. Once he was seated, though, his physiological distress abated, at least to a point that could be consciously disregarded.

Hunched over the controls, Tarn began adjusting the ship's systems for the imminent speed run.

"I heard what you told Etty," the ghost commented, "about how you 'admire my spunk.'"

"You should join your companions in the hangar."

"Why? The radiation can't harm me. Not now." She chuckled lightly, but the sound still drove a shiver down Tarn's spine.

"Where did this new star come from?" the Warrior asked as he continued to prepare the ship for sudden acceleration.

"Basically, a bit of raw energy leaked through from that other dimension before Dagon's Gate snapped shut."

"And that energy transformed the moon into a star…"

"Yes…but, technically, it isn't a star," her ghost told him. "Cthulhu had a huge energy storage buried beneath the lunar fortress, including the pair of plasma cores that were stolen from the Princess' cruiser and your battle flier. Everything combined, and the reaction converted the moon into a low-level fusion mass."

"So…that's what happened when those space-bats seized my flier."

"The Hounds of Tinaldos…" she mumbled.

"Excuse me?"

"Nothing." But Pik's tone was noticeably furtive.

"You're hiding something," he accused her ghost.

"As are you," she declared.

Tarn grunted, "Two Warriors with secrets… How dramatically poignant." He glanced over his shoulder—to discover that she was gone. Her spirit had left the command deck.

He had no chance to ponder her whereabouts or the nature of her hidden secret. The moment of truth was near, and the Warrior needed to concentrate on piloting the ship through the outer edges of the new star's radiation.

Their survival depended on him mastering this deadly challenge.

⚜

He's too cunning, Pik mused. *Too observant, and too curious.*

The Warrior did not trust her, and she could easily imagine why. They had once shared the same outlook: rigidly empirical and suspicious by necessity. Warriors needed to remain invariably wary, perpetually alert for hidden or unexpected danger. If Pik had been presented with the ghost of a previous competitor, she too would not have trusted the specter's claims. Ghosts should not exist—he knew this as resolutely as she did. Alas, there were no explanations to satisfy his or her doubts.

Tarn also seemed unconvinced by Pik's attempt to account for the birth of the new star. He was not alone, for the dead girl knew how little she really comprehended of the entire affair. Granted, a portion of Azathoth had seeped through the Gate before it closed. Granted, that furiously directionless and insane force had collided with the Great Lord's hoarded energy stores. All of this probably defined the moon's abrupt conversion from an aquatic satellite into a primal stellar explosion. But Pik had also thrown Dagon's captured essence into that collision of epic intensities. Who knew what effect the addition of the Fish-God's evil energies had caused to that catalyst?

At this moment in time, Pik realized that a distracted Tarn could get everyone killed. He needed his undivided concentration to pilot the ">%" to safety. So, she withdrew, leaving him to the heroic task ahead.

She wanted to check on Etty. There had been a distinctly unwelcome edge to his response when he had discovered that she was dead-but-still-alive-as-a-ghost. This troubled her, for never before had Etty doubted or rejected her. Death was a decidedly traumatic separation, but…she was a ghost, she wasn't *gone*. Was her beloved incapable of accepting her spectral existence?

She wanted to confront him, to challenge this new aversion. This distrust threatened their relationship, literally more so than Pik's mortal demise.

When she entered cargo hangar 2, though, Pik discovered that Etty did not recognize her in the least.

"Who is this?" he asked, cradling the Princess in arms that had once held Pik just as close.

"It's just Pik, Etty," declared Janek. "What are you playing at?"

"Pik…? Am I supposed to know her?"

"She used to be your partner," the Princess told him. "Before she *died*."

"But," Etty frowned, "we don't have a third partner. Right, Janek?"

The Duuian snorted, but before he could denounce Etty's assertion, Pik cautioned him to silence.

"Don't worry yourself, Etty," she told him. Her heart ached with this tragic turn. "I'm here to help. I'm…with the Warrior."

"The Warrior's going to save us," Princess Eden announced.

"Yes," Pik agreed. "He's very brave and capable." She drifted aside, signaling Janek to join her for a private conference on the far side of the hangar.

Concealed from the others by a large cache of still shrink-wrapped nutrition crates, she confided to Janek that she suspected Etty had undergone a synaptic loss, probably caused by his dormant nanobot infection.

The stress of his Earth adventure had brought about another memory lapse in her beloved. "This has happened before…"

"Yes," he recalled. During their partnership, there had been several instances when Etty's unreliable memory had endangered the retrieval of an escaped galactic fugitive. Janek had always accepted this flaw, knowing that Pik would be there to cover Etty's gaps. "But…you are no longer *here* to fulfill that need. What should I do now?"

The Duuian had a valid point. As a ghost, much less a person whom Etty no longer remembered, Pik was in no position to help him readjust or cope. Even if she could, he had been repulsed by her ghostly self back in the command room. If he finally recognized Pik, would he once again be revolted by her undead status?

She peeked around the stacked crates, and caught Etty and the Princess in an ardently carnal grapple. She withdrew, shaking her spectral head. All of this was burning a hole in her soul, but…it appeared to possibly be for the best. Etty was lost to Pik now; death had separated them with a distance that not even her own afterlife could bridge. But it seemed that he was not alone, for Princess Eden had taken a fancy to Pik's beloved. His dream of impressing her with a courageous rescue had apparently worked, attracting her amorous gratitude. (Pik wondered if Etty had also forgotten his secret fascination for the royal celebrity. That would have been a pity, leaving him unaware of the true scope of his secret success.) Princess Eden would take care of him now, undoubtedly better than Pik or Janek ever could. It looked as if Etty was destined to be the next courtesan of the Royal Daughter. It was a fate Pik knew he would enjoy.

None of this rationalization alleviated the anguish she felt, though. Her Etty was lost to her. While his happiness was important to Pik, it was still a *loss* from her point-of-view. A loss that hurt.

"The Princess will take care of Etty," she told Janek.

"And the partnership?"

"I'm dead, and Etty will be…otherwise occupied. I suspect you've inherited the '>%'."

"So," he waggled his wide head at her ghost. "You will not be accompanying us…"

"I think that's the…best course of action," she admitted. "Yes."

"I will miss you Pik," the Duuian told her. He braided his sensory tendrils to express sadness-over-the-absence-of-a-trusted-companion. "What will you do? Where will you go?"

"I'm not sure…"

"You are welcome to remain partners with me. A ghost would make a valuable retriever."

Pik smiled, sincerely honored by his offer. But she knew there was no place in galactic civilization for a ghost. Pik was not even certain whether her afterlife extended very far beyond old Earth. Nor could she guess how long her spirit would retain its integrity. Professor Laramy had required supplementary ectoplasm to perpetuate his spectral life. Pik knew that she was incapable of resorting to such psychic cannibalism. *Her* future was dubious.

Maybe someday, if she survived, Pik would track Janek down. Finding him would not be difficult for a retriever of her experience.

Before she left, Pik wanted to question Janek concerning the secrets he had learned from the Great Lord's database. Especially the arcane information that he was keeping unvoiced.

"You found secrets too," he replied. "In the mind of the Dagon monster…"

She nodded her spectral head, remaining mute.

"Things you will not speak of…"

They stared at each other, neither of them willing to discuss these things.

✢

"There are some things not meant to be known," declared Pik's ghost.

Janek concurred, but kept his own counsel.

Indeed, there were horrors beyond belief contained in the data Janek had stolen from the lunar fortress. He shuddered to imagine what further atrocities lurked in the files he had yet to decrypt. The Duuian absolutely refused to discuss these matters.

Cthulhu and the other New Lords of Earth were alien despots sworn to destruction and oppression. They commanded incredible technologies that indeed made the users appear godlike. (Those technologies lived in Janek's head now, lurking in the stolen data files. How he longed to purge all recollection of those horrible files, for *no creature* was sane enough to possess such absolute power. If anyone ever suspected that the Duuian carried such awesome secrets, Janek knew he would be hunted down and psychically dissected for that monstrous information.) Besides their sterilization of this world, their dreadful appetites had wreaked unspeakable crimes against nature—the details of which were graphically chronicled in the stolen data files. These evil Lords were long-lived, and blindly malevolent. They had striven to open a dimensional wormhole to gain access to unlimited energy. They would have used that infinite powerbase to conquer and destroy the galaxy. "Annihilation" was literally a laudable goal in their malignant opinion.

Janek hoped that the moon-to-star conversion had brought these barbarous creatures all the *annihilation* they deserved. He took solace in the existence of this newborn sun. Its birth had vaporized the wicked Cthulhu. As the moon-star orbited the planet, its deadly radiation would scorch the Earth clean of Cthulhu's worshipers and minions. The other Lords, Ithaqua and Shudde-M'ell, would undoubtedly burn too.

All this destruction and the death of millions of cruel creatures sated Janek's bloodlust, his desire to seek vengeance against his prior captors. This was another thing he was unwilling to share with Pik's ghost—or anyone, for that matter. The children of Duu were supposedly incapable of the violent thoughts that swam now in Janek's mind. By the definitions of his own species, Janek had become a monster. If news of his unique aggression ever got out, it was likely that other Duuians would track him down and exterminate him for his thought-crime.

There were many detestable secrets spinning in Janek's consciousness.

⁜

Leaving Janek in the cargo hangar was comparable with leaving Pik's old life behind. She was abandoning her beloved Etty, her trusted partner, their relationships and history and lives. She was turning her back on a galaxy that had given her birth, then subjected her to a motherless childhood and a heritage of poverty. Except for Etty and Janek, Pik wasn't leaving behind a life worth caring about. She was dead now, and there was no place for her out there. *(Had there ever been?)*

She wandered the ">%", visiting rooms and things that meant something to her...*had* meant something to her.

The quarters that Pik and Etty had shared, with its clutter of discarded clothing and their mutual toiletries. She stared long and hard at the bed, straining to recall their last bout of lovemaking, but the memories were fuzzy, clouded by the tension of these last few days. Perhaps those synapses had even been muted by her untimely demise. Fingering the amulet that hung around her ghostly neck, Pik regretted losing those recollections. It was as if she was falling prey to Etty's faulty memory, losing a quarter of her lifespan. She fought to retain certain incidents that she considered precious, but the memories eluded her, slipping beyond her concentration like air through a hull-breach. Her grief became too much to bear, and she moved on (through a bulkhead) to the next stop on her sentimental tour.

Her exercise room, with its impressive collection of bodybuilding equipment and biofeedback devices. Here, Pik had maintained her physical prowess, following the strict regimen she had learned during her military training. She had retired from the Space Navy because of emotional incompatibility with authority figures, but she had never abandoned the lifestyle and devotion to health and agility. Her years as a freelance retriever had benefited from this dedication to fitness, professionally and privately. Her own peace-of-mind owed its stability to the hours she had spent in this gym. Here, losing herself in physical exertion, Pik had turned her focus inward to soothe her troubled mind. This room had been witness to many healing epiphanies for her…but now, no flash of insight rose to placate her tension. She was going to have to face her afterlife and accept the losses that came with that change. Thoughts of her beloved's tender caresses drove Pik from her old gym.

To her workroom, with its ranks of technical apparatus and boxes of chips and bay-frames and resistors and superchargers and the rest of the mismatched hardware she had collected over the years. There, still out on the worktable, were the pieces of a pressure valve she had been upgrading before the ">%" reached old Earth. This job would never be finished now, which was a pity, since Etty had complained bitterly about their shower's inability to efficiently deliver hot water… Etty again.

Pik wandered from her workroom, searching for something to distract her grieving mind. She found such a distraction by watching Tarn pilot the ">%" through its perilous final escape.

❖

As the Earth rotated, the monstrous Spires of Condemnation swung around one by one to be vaporized by the new star. Their tips went first, liquefied before they could reach the moon's blazing incandescence. A percentage of the point of each Spire was reduced to loose molecules, blowing off into the vacuum, while the rest of the meat-shrouded calcium melted down the length of the spike, tenderizing the structure for the destruction to come. As the planetary/moon dance continued, the succession of Spires came beneath the full vehemence of the new star. Groaning and warping, they finally toppled into themselves like hollow candles under a blowtorch. Their bulk came sagging down, molten matter congealing with the furious broth of the already-boiling atmosphere. These gargantuan collapses momentarily emptied new basins at the bases of the Spires, blasting ocean, land, and air across the wasteland. By the time each Spire had passed beyond lunar alignment, their remains consisted of droopy equatorial mountains of de-ionized grit, fused into a previously unknown compound of decay.

The moon-star's radiant fury bathed the Earth from its orbital position, evaporating the global gas envelope, scorching the tortured continents, boiling the seas into a brief replacement atmosphere, which was soon freed from the planet's gravity to escape into the thinly hydrogenated void.

Life? The fiendish denizens of the Earth were history long before the moon-star's wrath denuded the planet's atmosphere. Deep Ones boiled alive in the oceans. Ithaqua's brutish minions baked on their feet in the newly-tropical polar wastelands. The servants of the Burrower Beneath cowered in deep tunnels that failed to protect them from the cell-rupturing bath of deadly gamma radiation. Other, less notable monsters all lost their devout armies to the hideous sunrise and hellish afternoon. Within a single rotation, the Earth had been sterilized of its malignant fauna.

Although old and riddled with tectonic fractures, the planet refused to come apart. With the resiliency of an obstinate stone, the Earth turned under the furious glare of its satellite sun. It was charred, dehydrated, and decontaminated, but remained stubbornly whole and unbroken. It was as if some ancestral spirit held the planet together, determined to outlive the monsters that had polluted its ecology.

Tarn the Royal Warrior, Princess Eden, Etty, and Janek huddled inside their tiny metal shell and prayed for deliverance. The human spacecraft raced at incredible velocity, moving along the planet's cone of shadow. Pik's enhanced shields strained to ward off the moon-star's lethal emissions, as the ship's crew dared to attempt to survive the celestial atrocity that strove to consume the Earth.

Pik watched the Warrior pilot the ship that was the result of years of her laborious tinkering, and her own silent prayers went with the ">%'s" passengers. She hid her ghostly self within a wall, so that her presence would not disturb his concentration. She was suitably impressed by Tarn's helmsman expertise; the Warrior handled the vessel as if he had flown it for years. With him navigating the ship, they all stood a good chance of getting away—safe and still breathing.

The ">%" was responding eloquently to its new pilot's subtle directions. Its plasma drive raged at full capacity, sending enormous amounts of thermalized matter gouting from the ship's propulsion nozzles. Tarn had even tapered the configuration of the ship's protective force field to give the mass less drag in the thickening void.

The moon-star had transformed the region of the Earth into a soup of loose and newly charged particles. The star's own radiation saturated the area. The Earth's atmosphere and polluted seas had been blown off into space. It was hardly a clean vacuum through which the ">%" raced.

As for the newborn sun itself, it was not of immense size, measuring barely a thousand kilometers in diameter. Its raging core was dense, though; comprised of hellish forces natural and profane, it burned with abnormal turbulence. Within this freakish nucleus, matter underwent grotesque transformations. Crude elements fused into implausible isotopes that were atrociously unstable. The aberrational core of the moon-star seethed to expand, to contort, to violate—all in vain. The fabric of the continuum zealously complained under the tension of these forces that contradicted the basic laws of physics, but the structural integrity of the continuum remained undefiled, as if Space/Time itself refused to cooperate with such a blasphemous phenomenon.

Not unlike most lifeforms possessed of rudimentary sanity, even inanimate matter and raw energy wanted no part of the monstrous Old Ones, their vulgar handiwork or their impure aspirations.

❖

Pik watched Tarn pilot the ">%". Her silent prayers wished him strength and courageous fortitude. The range of his mastery did not escape the dead girl. She began to suspect that he had done much more than simply reprogram the ">%'s" systems with new access codes. Some of the commands he issued to the ship's instruments were unfamiliar to her—punching those key sequences should have resulted in terminal conflicts within the ">%'s" databanks, yet the vessel responded in concordance with the Warrior's unconventional instructions.

For a moment Pik was angry, resenting this outsider for his mastery over systems she had designed and codified. It was as if Tarn had found her teenage diary and memorized every neurotic entry. She felt…violated.

Then she felt a little embarrassed. Pik realized that without his reprogramming of the ">%", the Warrior would have been unable to readily navigate this ship to the terrible coliseum beneath the moon's ocean to rescue everyone (well, almost everyone), or even pilot the ship now. His expertise was not with the ship, it was with his own command software. She smiled, wondering if he had been forced to overwrite the ">%'s" database in order to sidestep her own security protocols. It was nice to know that her handiwork was capable of confounding a Warrior of the Royal Navy.

Anyway, this was no longer *her* ship. For the moment, it was under the command of Tarn, but once the Warrior had successfully escaped this abysmal sector of space and restored Princess Eden to her Royal Parents, Pik expected the ">%" would become Janek's property. Would the Duuian seek new partners to share his retrieval vessel? It would be his choice now…

The moment of truth was drawing near for the Warrior. The ">%" was swiftly approaching the outer edge of the protective shadow thrown by the Earth. The dividing line was invisible to the naked eye, but it stood out with dire importance on the scan readouts displayed for the ship's pilot. Faster than Pik thought was prudent, the ship's white marker rushed through the dark cone, headed with hell-bent speed for a region whose orange display bespoke menace. Her gaze was held transfixed by that screen, watching the marker race along.

And then the ">%" was out—into the noxious territory of the moonstar's malevolent radiation. From Pik's spectral point-of-view, there was no horrific instant of transition. Nor did the Warrior take much note of the sudden change from safe shadow to savage space. He was intent on goading the ">%'s" drive to give two-hundred-percent of itself.

According to the sensors, the shields were strained…but holding.

If anything was overtaxed, it appeared to be the plasma drive's thrust nozzles. While retooling them, it had never seemed important to Pik to fortify their construction to withstand prolonged exposure to the drive's full potential. Even now, she could imagine few instances that would require a need for such sub-C speed, and all of those situations were as unlikely as the current predicament. She prayed for the thrusters…but these petitions went ignored.

With a lurch that shook the entire ship, the three rear drive thrusters buckled and liquefied themselves in the now-unfocused blast of plasma energy. As luck would have it, all three of the thrust nozzles vaporized together, avoiding any inequality of momentum. The ">%" stayed on-course. The noticeable result of this accident was a slight decrease in the ship's velocity, for wide-beams produced less propulsion than the previous, narrowly directed jets.

Tarn's solution exhilarated the ghost.

He shut off the ship's thrusters—and rerouted the tremendous output of the laboring drive core to vent itself through the illegal plasma cannons! He swiveled the array of cannons to face the rear. Their terrible beams now supplied the spacecraft's thrust. On six beams of vicious force, the ">%" escaped the contaminated zone.

On-screen: the white marker plunged into "normal" space beyond the orange region of deadly radiation.

Pik wanted to cheer and slap Tarn across the shoulders and give him a congratulatory kiss—a deep, wet one. Instead, she told him softly, "Nice piloting."

"Nice illegal weapon conversion," he replied, seemingly unshaken by her unexpected presence. (Or had he been aware of her lurking observation all along? Peering at a sidereal screen, Pik saw a familiar energy spike: the same type of signal she had detected to mark the presence of Professor Laramy's ghost. Yes—the Warrior had known Pik was near, probably from the instant she abandoned her sentimental tour to spy on him.)

She shrugged, smiling pleasantly. "You going to arrest me?"

"I'll let you take that felony to your grave."

"Looks as if I beat you to that one, Warrior," she chuckled.

He did not express any mirth.

"I...uh...won't be coming with you," Pik told him.

"By choice? Or by limitation of your posthumous extension?"

"I'm not really sure. There's nothing left for me to go back to...out there." She tossed an idle hand in an unspecific direction.

"What about your lover? And your other partner?"

"It's...all very complicated," Pik mumbled. "Suffice it to say that there's no place for a ghost in galactic society."

"So, you're staying here?"

"Yeah."

"Are you going to tell me the real reason?" he squinted at her, his leathery skin conveying mild suspicion.

"I...don't think so."

"It has to do with something you learned from your contact with that Dagon thing, doesn't it?"

Grup, she thought. *He's so damned intuitive...*

When she gave no response, Tarn folded his arms across the bulk of his suit's chest. "Will you tell me this much? Is the rest of the galaxy at risk?"

"I...don't know..."

"Any lack of an affirmative answer to that inquiry can be considered confirmation of a continued threat," he declared. "You force me to press you for details, Pik."

"You won't believe me, so why bother?"

"Are you sure? Or have you just adopted Laramy's paranoia by becoming a ghost like him?"

"Laramy was right," Pik revealed. *There—I told him. Let's see how he takes that. He'll probably think I've caught Laramy obsessive delusions too... which, in effect, I* have.

The Warrior allowed a long moment to stretch out without comment. Finally, he asked "About what?"

She told him: "The Old Ones really are ancient deities, monstrous creatures who cannot die, cannot be destroyed. Everything the Professor's ghost claimed is based in abominable truth."

"You're saying that this Cthulhu creature did not perish when the moon became a newborn star..."

"If the Evil One had really been there, no—He would not have been exterminated by the star-birth." she sighed. There was something cathartic about sharing this unpleasant secret. Even Professor Laramy's ghost had not realized the awful truth, even at the end when his monstrous diet had affiliated his loyalties with the Old Ones.

"Cthulhu escaped?"

"Cthulhu was never there."

Tarn shook his head. "But—we all saw—"

"An illusion. A very elaborate hoax. It had to be painstakingly accurate, for it has fooled everyone (mortal and monster) for two centuries."

"More details are necessary for me to understand what you're trying to tell me."

And so Pik told him the ultimate secret she had glimpsed in Dagon's profane consciousness: The Great Cthulhu had never thrown off His cosmic shackles. He had never Awakened. He had never Risen. He had never conquered Earth and ordered the extinction of all terrestrial life. The masterfully orchestrated nuclear barrage on His submerged city of R'lyeh had failed to rouse the Old One from His ancient slumber.

Dagon had been desperate. The full force of the Old Ones' hidden armies had publicly exposed themselves to mankind. There could be no return to secrecy. The humans knew, and if left alone, they would devise means to hunt down and exterminate the Old Ones' minions. The conquest of the Earth needed to continue to its dire fruition. But—Dagon feared that without the Great Cthulhu leading the attack, the other monsters would squabble among themselves for domination of the attacking forces, destroying themselves from within. Or worse—they would lose faith and abandon the war altogether.

So it was that Dagon the Fish-God, a lower devil in the Old Ones' pantheon of monsters, had decided to fake Cthulhu's awakening. Claiming the Great Lord would see or speak to no one besides the Fish-God, Dagon became the Evil One's divine Voice.

"I failed to discern exactly how Dagon pulled this off," Pik confessed. "Whatever illusion he created, though, it must have been superlative. It had to fool Ithaqua and Shudde-M'ell and the other Old Ones, for these creatures share a telepathic affinity."

"He moved his nonexistent Lord to the moon to distance the hoax from the rest of the followers," the Warrior remarked.

"Yes..."

"An obvious strategy, considering the situation."

"So, you believe me."

He shrugged. "What difference does my belief make?"

"I..."

"You believe it enough to stay here. Why? What chance do you think a single human spirit would have against a monster as powerful as you describe?"

"He's still asleep," Pik mumbled. "I...want to keep Him that way."

"You're still an insect taking on a behemoth."

Tarn was right, but Pik could not swayed from this destiny she had chosen for her ghostly existence. There were extenuating circumstances, facts she was unwilling to confess to the Warrior or anyone. She still harbored a sincere guilt over unwittingly betraying galactic mankind to the Evil Lord's attention. Even asleep, the monster had aided Dagon's hoax, spreading aberrant contamination through nightmarish dreams. Cthulhu had supplied the Fish-God with the guidance necessary to perpetrate the series of cosmic atrocities. The moon-star had effectively halted those schemes, but the Old Ones were not defeated. They remained, sleeping or stranded on the Earth's charred husk. They would rise again, and when

They did, Their targets would be humanity-at-large. Pik's honor compelled her to stay here, for someone needed to guard the universe from this profane menace.

"It has to be me. I'm the only one who knows that Cthulhu still slumbers in His tomb in R'lyeh"

"Now that you've told me, I know it too."

"Okay—I'm the only one who *believes* that Cthulhu still slumbers in His tomb in R'lyeh."

"Point taken."

"You could say I'm acting on *faith*," she told him. "So…what are your plans?"

"Returning the Princess to her Royal Family is my priority right now."

"And later…?"

"I do not know," the Warrior admitted.

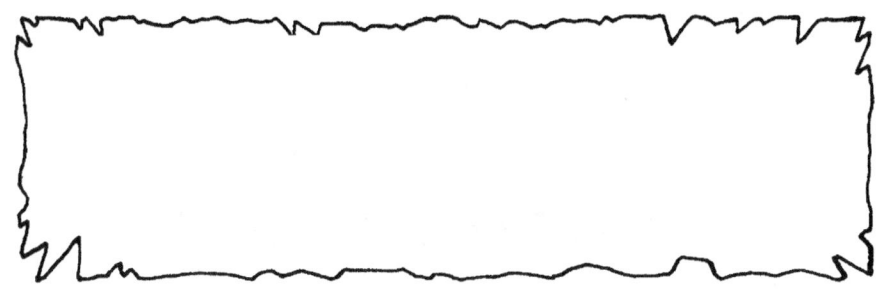

exit log

A few hours later:
Janek negotiated a shrewd deal with the Warrior to pool their claims on the Eden retrieval. Tarn would get his promotion, and the bounty hunter team would collect the retrieval commission. Each party would support the other's claims, citing invaluable assistance by the other party in their own account of the rescue.

Janek considered it "profit through unification."

Tarn viewed it as a way of honoring Pik's spunk.

How long Princess Eden's fascination with Etty would last was a mystery to all involved.

Although she wondered about these things, Pik knew nothing of these compromises. Her ghost returned to the sterilized Earth to await her fate. Either she would stand guard over the planet's dreadful monsters, or she would fade and cease to exist. Whatever happened, she had faith that it would be for the best.

end file

Also by Matt Howarth
from Merry Blaksmith Press

by MATT HOWARTH

USING A CONVERTED SPACE HOTEL as their base, Peri Fairchild and the other freelancers dive into the clouds of Baltuss to mine gases. Their activities are challenged by the extreme capitalists of Harvest Corporation who view them as pirates. With the illegal radio station Red Sky Radio providing free entertainment, follow Peri, her boyfriend Taz and the other miners as the final showdown with Harvest Corporation leads to irrevocable changes, both for the miners and Harvest.

The Merry Blacksmith Press

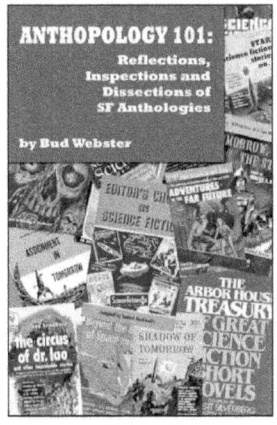

Locus 2010 Reommended
Reading List – Nonfiction

The print edition of the
latest Marla Mason novel

Revised & expanded. First
time in print in 50 years!

**Free US shipping on all
orders over $50.**

**Special dealer
rates available!**

info@merryblacksmith.com

www.merryblacksmith.com

www.ingramcontent.com/pod-product-compliance
Lightning Source LLC
Chambersburg PA
CBHW070329260626
47160CB00003B/992